"I want to live inside this wonderful book! Every single page is sweet, quirky, charming, and one hundred percent delightful! I absolutely loved it!"

—Sarah Beth Durst,
New York Times bestselling author of *The Spellshop*

"This book is pure magic. Warm, cozy, and gentle; fiery, passionate, and angry; joyful, insightful, and hilarious. It's full of love and heart and emotion, and I adored every moment of it. I so wish I could check in to Sera's inn to hang out with her and Luke and Jasmine and that delightful undead rooster."

—Jasmine Guillory,
New York Times bestselling author of *Flirting Lessons*

"Magical in every sense, not just the spell-casting kind! Sangu Mandanna uses her signature whimsical writing to tell a story filled with love, heart, and hope, where every character is unapologetically themselves and good always triumphs. Without shying away from the tougher realities of life, Mandanna somehow captures the essence of *everyday* magic—the magic we find in the love of our friends and family."

—Rebecca Thorne,
USA Today bestselling author of *You Can't Spell Treason Without Tea*

"Funny, cozy, heart-wrenching, romantic, and Just Right in every way, this is a story to treasure."

—Stephanie Burgis, author of *Wooing the Witch Queen*

A

WITCH'S GUIDE
to
MAGICAL
INNKEEPING

SANGU MANDANNA

BERKLEY
NEW YORK

BERKLEY
An imprint of Penguin Random House LLC
1745 Broadway, New York, NY 10019
penguinrandomhouse.com

Book design by Marlyn Veenstra
Interior art: Fox © Alenka Karabanova / Shutterstock; Rooster illustrated by Lisa Perrin

Library of Congress Cataloging-in-Publication Data

Names: Mandanna, Sangu, author.
Title: A witch's guide to magical innkeeping / Sangu Mandanna.
Description: First edition. | New York : Berkley, 2025. |
Identifiers: LCCN 2024060144 (print) | LCCN 2024060145 (ebook) |
ISBN 9780593439371 (trade paperback) | ISBN 9780593439388 (ebook)
Subjects: LCGFT: Fantasy fiction. | Witch fiction. | Novels.
Classification: LCC PR6113.A487 W58 2025 (print) | LCC PR6113.A487
(ebook) | DDC 823/.92—dc23/eng/20241223
LC record available at https://lccn.loc.gov/2024060144
LC ebook record available at https://lccn.loc.gov/2024060145

First Edition: July 2025

Printed in the United States of America
3rd Printing

The authorized representative in the EU for product safety and compliance is
Penguin Random House Ireland, Morrison Chambers,
32 Nassau Street, Dublin D02 YH68, Ireland, https://eu-contact.penguin.ie.

This one is for Past Me,
for all those times she kept going.
Future Me finally gets it.

A
WITCH'S GUIDE
to
MAGICAL
INNKEEPING

CHAPTER ONE

*I*t was hardly ideal weather for the resurrection of one's great-aunt, but Sera Swan's magical power, while impressive, hadn't the slightest influence over the obnoxiously blue skies. Autumn had only just arrived in the northwest of England, bringing with it an unseasonably merry sky, leaves of toasted gold and burnt orange, and, most distressingly, the corpse in the back garden.

"You could do with a cup of tea first," Clemmie remarked. "You're a mess. You can't go resurrecting people when you're all blotchy and snotty."

Sera chose to ignore the insult, as well as its dubious logic. "Are you sure this will work?"

"Would I lie to you?"

"You lied to me an hour ago when you told me the Tooth Fairy ate the last of the peanut butter. The Tooth Fairy! How old do you think I am?"

"Yes, yes, all right," Clemmie cut in hastily. "I may have been known to fib in the past, but new leaves have been turned."

Sera was quite sure a barren wasteland stood a greater chance of turning new leaves than Clemmie did but decided not to say so.

With a swish of her bushy red tail, Clemmie turned and trotted back to the house. "Well? Are you coming? Jasmine's dead and I haven't got opposable thumbs. That tea won't make itself, you know."

It was just as well the inn was empty this weekend and there were no bystanders to observe this scene, for as scenes went, it was decidedly peculiar. It was like the beginning of a bad joke. *A corpse, a witch, and a fox walked into a bar . . .*

(Actually, it was more like a corpse and *two* witches, and one of those witches happened to be trapped in the form of a small, chubby red fox. Sera wasn't sure if that would improve the joke or not.)

Sera, who was fifteen years old and frankly out of her depth, hesitated beside her great-aunt's body. Was she really going to cast a spell with nothing but Clemmie's word to go on? Clemmie, who had turned up out of the blue a few weeks ago and had yet to offer any real answers about who she really was or how she'd ended up trapped in fox form? She was the very *opposite* of trustworthy, but Sera was going to have to trust her today or she would lose Great-Auntie Jasmine for good.

The upshot was that Sera had plenty of power and not enough knowledge, while Clemmie had plenty of knowledge and not enough power. That was all that mattered right now. And anyway, if Clemmie *was* lying to her, what difference would it make? Jasmine was dead. A failed resurrection spell couldn't exactly make her any deader.

The azure skies wheeled above, still objectionably cheerful. Sera couldn't believe that it had only been a few minutes since

Clemmie had found her in the kitchen, said "There's a situation you have to deal with outside, but just so you know, I hate tears and hysterics," and led her out to where Jasmine had dropped dead in the garden. Sera remembered little of what had happened after that, though her raw eyes informed her that there had indeed been plenty of tears and probably one or two hysterics.

Sera *did* remember that she'd stood up to go find a phone. The sensible thing to do, she'd reasoned, was to dial 999 and let a grown-up take charge.

Then Clemmie had tutted, stopping her in her tracks. "How tiresome. I expected Jasmine to have more sense and better manners than to die in the garden. On a warm day like this, she'll get icky very quickly. We'll have to work fast."

"What are you talking about?"

Whereupon Clemmie had revealed she knew how to resurrect the dead. As a collector of rare, powerful spells of dubious legality and even more questionable morality, Clemmie knew all sorts of spells that other people didn't. Sera already knew this because Clemmie could not resist telling her at every available opportunity. She had never had the power to *cast* most of said spells, she'd admitted somewhat petulantly, but that had not dampened her fondness for knowing more than everybody else.

Sera hadn't known that *this* particular spell was in Clemmie's hoard, however, because the legality of a resurrection spell wasn't dubious at all. It was, in fact, *very* illegal.

"It's a law from back when witches actually had the magic necessary to cast a spell of this size," Clemmie had explained. "None of us have had that much power in yonks." Then she'd cocked her fox head, eyeing Sera with a bright, speculative gaze.

"*You* might, though. You're the most gifted witch the Guild has seen since Albert Grey. You might actually be able to bring Jasmine back."

"Tell me what to do," Sera had said at once.

"Don't you want to think about it first?"

"No." *Thinking* was exactly what Sera wanted to avoid. If she started thinking, her heart would crumple at the thought of losing the woman who had been more of a parent to her than her own parents had ever been. No, *thinking* was out of the question.

"A spell like this will require a great deal of your magic," Clemmie had warned.

"I have plenty to spare."

"And what about the Guild? What happens if they find out?"

Choosing her love for Jasmine over her loyalty to the British Guild of Sorcery wasn't exactly difficult for Sera. The Guild was strict, stuffy, and entirely too fond of looking down their noses at almost everybody. Their snobbery (and the inevitable generations of inbreeding that came with it) meant that of all the witches born in the country each year, the vast majority were born into the fifteen or so families who could trace their magical history all the way back to the founding of the Guild in the 1600s. As soon as these precious darlings took their first steps, off they toddled to be educated in the ways of magic and their own intrinsic superiority at the Guild's opulent estate in Northumberland.

And while it was true that even young witches born outside these lofty circles were invited to share in the same education, it was worth mentioning that the ones who accepted were certainly not given the same treatment once they got there. (Luckily, most sane outsiders, upon ascertaining that magic was a real thing and, moreover, that they could do it, were understandably of the view that mysterious, hitherto unheard-of guilds were not to be trusted, and chose instead to remain in their homes and study the textbooks the Guild sent them there.)

Sera's Icelandic mother didn't have so much as a magical hair follicle. Also, she was Icelandic, ergo *foreign*. Sera's witch father, meanwhile, had limited power and had been the first known witch in the history of his Indian family. Also, he was Indian, ergo *extra* foreign. Sera's lack of Guild-approved pedigree was the reason, therefore, that no one from that prestigious society had bothered to pursue the matter when Great-Auntie Jasmine, left to care for tiny, mischievous, terrible-twoing Sera after her parents had ambled off on one of their many adventures, had declined their token offer to educate her at the estate.

Eight years had passed, during which time Sera had practically memorised every book that the Guild had sent her, before Albert Grey, who was by far the most powerful witch in the country, had noticed that one of her monthly progress letters mentioned the successful casting of a spell that was *well* beyond the talents of most fully grown witches, never mind those of a ten-year-old. He had descended upon the inn with the Chancellor of the Guild in tow, whereupon they'd ridden roughshod over Jasmine's objections and insisted that Sera be sent to their country estate at once to be appropriately educated as Albert's apprentice.

That had been five years ago. More than enough time to discover exactly what the Guild was and what it wasn't.

All of which was to say that Sera knew the Guild hadn't given her a second thought until she'd proven herself too gifted to ignore, so as far as she was concerned, Jasmine, who had loved her without question since the day they had met, came first.

Now Sera wiped the last tears off her face, turned away from the corpse at her feet, and followed Clemmie back into the house.

As she crossed the kitchen to turn the kettle on, Sera could smell sugar, the soda bread she and Jasmine had baked that morning, and the familiar scent of Jasmine's Nivea cream. A lump settled into her throat and made itself thoroughly at home. What if the spell didn't work?

It was horribly unfair. Jasmine was only fifty-six. She had a clubfoot and used a cane, but Sera couldn't remember the last time she'd even had a cold! Why hadn't she been allowed to have another thirty years?

An excessively sweetened cup of tea soothed her nerves a little and, thanks to Clemmie's impatient tsking, almost burned her tongue right off as she drank it too hot and too fast.

"Done?" Clemmie demanded. "Ready? Let's go. We've done quite enough dillydallying. What if someone turns up looking for a room? We could do without a witness."

Her phone rang and Sera jumped.

"Ignore it," said Clemmie.

Sera ignored her instead. The only people who ever called Sera on her own phone were her parents (infrequently) and her best friend, Francesca (at least twice a day). Knowing full well that whichever of them it was, they would keep calling until she answered, and that that was hardly going to help her concentrate on the most difficult spell she'd ever cast in her life, she sought out the phone and answered it.

"Hi." Sera's voice was a little raw from the tears and the nerves, but she felt sure she sounded mostly normal.

"I have the *most* exciting news!" Francesca squealed on the other end of the line, her usually crisp vowels and faultless enunciation lost in what was obviously very great excitement indeed. "You'll never guess!"

"Francesca, I can't—"

"Father wants you to come skiing with us this Christmas!"

It took Sera a moment to make sense of these words. With her thoughts full of death and illegal spellwork, *skiing*, of all things, felt like a concept from another universe altogether.

"Um, that's very kind of him," she said politely, and winced as she heard the lack of enthusiasm in her voice.

Sera had a complicated relationship with Albert Grey, who, in addition to being her instructor, also happened to be Francesca's father. When he'd first accepted her as his apprentice and introduced her to the strict but dizzyingly magical world of the Guild, she'd had a childish, naïve hope that he'd become something of a father figure to her. They were the two most powerful witches in the country by a mile, after all, which was an immense privilege but a lonely one too. There was no one else like them.

To anybody looking in from the outside, Albert probably *did* seem fond and parental, but Sera had never been able to shake the feeling that he was faking it. That, in truth, he resented her intrusion into a space he'd enjoyed ruling alone.

Fortunately, Francesca was too excited to notice Sera's tone. "Please say you'll come, Sera! I know you won't want to leave Great-Auntie Jasmine alone at Christmas, so I persuaded Father to invite her too. You'll both come, won't you?"

Sera was touched by this gesture, but with Clemmie pacing in front of her and jabbing a paw pointedly at the clock, it was difficult to give it the response it deserved. Guiltily, she tried to rush her friend off the phone. "I'm so sorry, can we talk about this later?"

"What's the matter?"

"I feel a bit sick. I'll call you this evening, okay?"

"I notice they didn't invite *me* to go skiing," Clemmie remarked as soon as Sera had ended the call.

"They don't know you exist," Sera pointed out. "Which was what you wanted, I might add, or have you forgotten the eighteen times you've warned me not to tell anyone outside this house about you?"

Clemmie made a disgruntled sound. "Come on. We've wasted enough time."

The garden, green and summery and overgrown, sloped quite dramatically downhill and was drenched in sunshine and the pinks, yellows, and whites of wildflowers. At the bottom, past a tiny orchard of fruit trees, the beehive, and the little mound of grass beneath which they'd buried Jasmine's beloved pet rooster, a low stone wall and latticed arch gave way to a narrow lane and rolling green hills.

As Clemmie circled Great-Auntie Jasmine's silent corpse, muttering under her breath about compass points and grave-witchery, Sera knelt on the grass in the shade of the citrus trees and squeezed her great-aunt's cold hand.

"It's going to be okay," she whispered. "I promise."

Clemmie came to a halt beside Sera and sat back on her hind legs. "Ready? Repeat after me."

Magic was a funny thing. You were either born with it or you weren't, but how much you had and how it made itself felt was as unique to the witch wielding it as a fingerprint. For Sera, it was a wild, joyous updraft that set her soaring into a night sky lit by thousands of tiny twinkling stars, each shining as brightly as suns. (For Clemmie, before she'd lost the ability to use it, it had been teeth and claws, which was rather fitting considering she now quite literally had both.)

The act of spellcasting wasn't quite as chameleonlike as magic itself, but spells could still be wrought in a dozen different ways. Some, for instance, were cast with just a thought, while others were cast with a wiggle of one's fingers, with the meticulous tying of tidy knots, or with a set list of ingredients. And then there were the rare spells, the enchantments that only a handful of witches had the power to conjure: these spells had to be spoken aloud, *had* to be shaped and contained by the eerie, musical dialect of sorcery, or else they might go wildly wrong.

Sera had cast such spells before, but the stakes had never felt so high. Her throat felt too tight and her heart thumped so fast it almost made her dizzy, but she said the words without faltering.

The moment Sera finished speaking the incantation, her magic rose to answer her. Whole galaxies of stars exploded behind her closed eyelids, and she felt better at once: her heart took wing, her grief lost its sharp edge, and her fingertips tingled with joy.

This. *This.* This was why she loved magic so much.

She opened her eyes.

Her hands were wreathed in threads of warm, soft light, each as delicate as if it were made out of the easily dissolved substance of dreams. The spell had taken shape and was ready to cast.

Sera gathered the threads, placed her hands over Jasmine's heart, and *pushed*. The shining strands spun through her fingers like she was Rumpelstiltskin at a loom.

Light flooded from Sera's fingers to Jasmine's heart, suffusing cold skin with warmth and magic.

Beat, Sera silently ordered the silent heart beneath her hands. *Beat.*

The glorious, dizzying joy gave way to needles of pain. It was so unfamiliar and disconcerting that Sera felt a moment's doubt. The spell was pulling more power from her than she'd ever had to give before.

It wasn't too late to undo it, to break the connection and pull the magic back, but she couldn't do that. She had to do this for Jasmine.

The world tilted. She pressed one hand into the grass to keep herself upright, not noticing as she did so that a little bit of the spell burrowed into the earth.

Then, miraculously, Jasmine's stiff limbs softened. Her greying skin flushed with new colour, a healthy, rosy shade of pink setting into the warm brown of her cheeks. Her heart gave a vigorous thump.

Her eyes opened and settled at once on Sera. She offered the gentlest of reproofs. "But, my love, how *could* you let me fall asleep out here? The sun is the *worst* possible thing for the skin!"

Sera's shoulders dropped in exhaustion. A happy, overwhelmed sob caught in her throat, but she choked it back, scrubbed a hand across her wet eyes, and offered a wobbly smile.

"You weren't asleep," she confessed, reaching for Jasmine's fallen cane. "You were dead, so Clemmie and I brought you back."

Jasmine, who never liked to make a fuss and held good sense in great regard, accepted this revelation calmly. "That was very clever of you, dearest," she said. "You're much too young to fend for yourself, and your parents are dreadful cooks."

"Dreadful parents too," Sera pointed out. Jasmine tsked.

With her cane in one hand and Sera's arm in the other, Jasmine clambered slowly back to her feet. She was a delicate, bony woman who looked like a strong breeze would knock her over (and indeed, the strong breezes of Lancashire had been known to do so), but even after her untimely demise, she was impeccably put together. Her hair, luxuriantly black through the religious application of henna, was still in its neat bun; her berry lipstick had not budged; her long, prim, lace-edged nightdress remained miraculously unwrinkled; and neither of her specially made boots had slipped off her feet in all the hubbub.

Sera put her arms around her great-aunt, hugging her fiercely. "Don't ever do that to me again."

"Oh, pet," Jasmine said tenderly.

At that precise moment, there was a small commotion from the bottom of the garden. The bees in the hive, who were usually placid and gentle, were abuzz, enormously offended by something.

That something turned out to be the disturbed lump of grass near the hive, from whence there came a shrill and cheerful disembodied crowing that made Clemmie rear back in outrage. The crowing was followed swiftly by the appearance of an energetic jumble of bones that clattered straight over to Jasmine.

"Bok," said the skeleton, which, on second glance, bore a striking resemblance to a chicken.

Sera's mouth fell open. Jasmine let out a cry of unalloyed joy. "Roo-Roo!"

"Marvellous work," Clemmie said to Sera. "I was *just* thinking this morning that what we really needed in our lives was not a new fireplace or a nice car but, in fact, a resurrected fucking rooster."

CHAPTER TWO

*I*t ought to have been a wholly happy ending, but that, alas, was not in the cards. Scarcely two days had passed before Sera, still reeling from the toll Jasmine's death and subsequent resurrection had taken on her, made a most troubling discovery.

"Clemmie," Sera whispered, so Jasmine wouldn't hear. "Clemmie, the stars are almost all gone."

Clemmie was across the room, suspiciously eyeing the rooster Sera had inadvertently resurrected, but her fox ears pricked up at this and she padded over to where Sera was on the sofa hugging a cushion to her chest. "What do you mean, the stars are almost all gone?"

"The ones inside me." Sera swallowed hard, trying not to panic. No matter what, the one thing she'd always been able to count on was the stars. "The ones I used to see every time I closed my eyes. There used to be whole galaxies there, but I only see a few constellations now."

Clemmie stared at Sera in consternation. "Bollocks, bollocks, and more bollocks! I was *so* sure this wouldn't happen!"

That was not the response Sera had hoped for. "You were sure *what* wouldn't happen?"

"You pushed yourself too far," Clemmie said in a tone that suggested *she* was the one most inconvenienced by this development. "Magic's like anything else. It gets depleted when you use it, and then time, rest, and a nice cup of tea top it up again."

"Does that mean I just have to wait a little longer?" Sera asked hopefully. "Because the resurrection spell was so big?"

"I certainly bloody hope so," Clemmie replied. "I'm not optimistic, though. You should have stopped when it started to hurt. I think you pushed yourself so hard that you didn't just deplete the stars. I think you fractured the *sky*. It can't hold all the stars you used to have. Those constellations you see are all you've got left."

Sera's fingernails dug into the soft fabric of the cushion. She wanted to reject everything Clemmie was saying, but she could feel that there was truth in it. She could feel a heaviness in her limbs that had never been there before. She could feel that where that infinite sky had cradled her magic before, keeping it safe, it was now full of exit wounds that were quietly, relentlessly bleeding stardust.

"Maybe I just need more time," she said desperately. "My magic will come back. It has to."

"It had better," Clemmie muttered. "Without it, I'll be stuck like this forever."

Sera blinked, momentarily distracted. "You were hoping I'd break the curse that turned you into a fox? *That's* why you came to the inn? Why didn't you ask me before?"

"I was getting to it!" Clemmie said indignantly. "You've only known me a few weeks. If I'd pushed too soon, you might have said no! Believe me, I wish I *had* just come out with it and asked!"

"My magic," Sera repeated, furious, "will come back."

Pretending to be struck down with the flu, Sera put off returning to the Guild estate, hoping her magic just needed a few more days. Hoping the galaxies would return to their skies.

It wasn't to be. The vast dark spaces behind her eyelids remained unchanged, interrupted only by a handful of stubborn, surviving stars. Everyday spells that had come as easily to her as breathing, like the vanishing of the pain in Jasmine's clubfoot or the transformation of gooey batter into delicious cake in four seconds flat, were now impossible. Her magic did not come back.

Panic gave way to dismay, and dismay to heartbreak. Shutting herself in her room, Sera sobbed long and hard. The magic she'd loved so dearly, and taken so thoroughly for granted, had left her. She didn't know who she was without it.

If there was one thing the last five years with the Guild had taught her, it was that her power was everything. From the moment she'd arrived at their towering, gargoyle-bedecked castle in Northumberland, her instructors, Albert Grey among them, had given her test after test to find out just how much power she possessed. Surrounded by glittering workshops and endless libraries and magic everywhere she looked, she'd mended broken bones. Alchemised scrap metal into gold. Enchanted bolts of silk so not even a bullet could pierce it.

"You're the future of magic, Sera Swan," old, doddery Chancellor Bennet would say, oblivious to the way Albert's eyes would harden. "Don't you think so, Albert? Why, she's the next you!"

Sera's future, everyone had agreed, would be extraordinary. And now that future was gone.

Days passed, muddling together in a tempest of grief, until, inevitably, fear found its way in too. Sera felt nowhere near ready to face a future without magic, but she had no choice. There was only so long she could delay returning to the Guild.

"I have to go back," she said to Clemmie.

"Of course you do. If there's some way for you to get your magic back, you're not going to find it here. You need the Guild's library."

"And this?" Sera gestured at her almost magicless self. "How am I supposed to explain this?"

"Lie to their faces, of course," Clemmie said at once. "Tell them you woke up one morning and your magic was just gone. They absolutely must *not* find out you cast an extremely forbidden resurrection spell, not least because they'll realise *I* was the one who taught it to you."

Before Sera could ask her why they'd come to such a conclusion and, moreover, exactly *why* Clemmie was afraid of attracting the Guild's attention, Jasmine popped her head around the door of the kitchen. "My love, could you show Mrs. Cooper and her little girl to their room?"

Sera obliged. Jasmine's clubfoot caused her a lot of pain if she navigated the inn's many stairs too often, so when she'd first reopened the inn, she'd hired a taciturn woman from the village to come in for an hour each morning to keep the four guest rooms in order. Bryony's ability to make sinks gleam and bed linen crisp was nothing short of enviable, but she took great pains to avoid everyone except Jasmine and was, therefore, not the best person to ask to make a guest feel welcome.

"I'm really glad you had a room," Mrs. Cooper said to Sera in a soft, tired voice as they made their way up the stairs of the guest wing. "I'd been driving so long I didn't think I could stay awake another minute, and then I turned down the lane and there you were. It was like magic."

"Magic isn't real, Mummy," her young daughter said with a giggle, and Sera smiled for the first time in days.

The inn was more magical than any of its guests knew. The actual house was almost two hundred years old and had been in the possession of a feckless viscount before an enthusiastic innkeeper had acquired it and named it Batty Hole for reasons that would forever escape Sera. It had changed hands a few times since then, becoming a boardinghouse for unwed mothers, a hospital during the First World War, and an inn once again, before ending up an unwelcome and run-down part of someone's inheritance.

Enter Sera's parents. Enchanted by the name, the history, and the leaky, crumbly mess before them, they'd bought it. Restoring it to its former glory, they'd decided, would be their next great adventure.

Between Sera's father's magic and Sera's mother's money, they'd turned the old house into something approaching liveable. They'd also refused to change the name, which was why Sera's postal address all her life had been the intolerably precious *Sera Swan, Batty Hole Inn, Briercliffe, Lancashire.*

As was their way, her parents had soon grown bored of the house, and of parenting too. So, when Sera was two, they had invited Jasmine, her father's favourite aunt, to move all the way from the south of India to this lovely but secluded pocket of northwest England. Jasmine's bags had scarcely been unpacked before Sera's parents were gone, destined to visit only a few times a year for the rest of her childhood.

In hindsight, it was the best possible thing they could have done for everyone. They got their adventures, Jasmine got Sera, and Sera got Jasmine.

Sensibly realising that the money Sera's parents sent back for their upkeep covered little more than the mortgage, and possessed of a deeply welcoming nature, Jasmine had decided the best course of action was to resurrect the old inn. Sera, brimming with too much magic to contain, had eagerly helped her with clever bits of spellwork.

Then, shortly after Sera's tenth birthday, they'd had a trying few months. They'd had an epidemic of difficult guests, the sort of people who turned up expecting pillowcases of mulberry silk and threw a fit upon discovering that a bed-and-breakfast didn't actually involve being served breakfast *in* bed. When a particularly shouty twosome had driven Jasmine to tears, Sera, vibrating with fury, had cast a spell.

What that spell was, she couldn't say. That was what was so extraordinary about it. It was heartfelt, it was huge, and it was inexplicable.

The difficult guests had stopped coming. The guests who did come were usually sweet in temperament, often buffeted by tempestuous weather or circumstances, and always relieved. The inn, it seemed, had become a port in a storm. Whether they were the exhausted parent who needed just one night away from it all, Mrs. Cooper with the bruised cheek she'd been trying to hide since she'd arrived, or the boy who'd left home for the first time and had had his wallet stolen outside Preston, they all came for *something* that the inn could give them.

The best way Sera could describe her spell was this: if you didn't *need* the inn, you'd drive on. (And if you were a dick, you'd definitely drive on.)

This was the spell that had first brought the Guild to her door. Some weeks after casting it, she'd described what the spell had wrought in one of her progress letters and had piqued Albert Grey's interest. When he and Chancellor Bennet had come to see her, they'd cast the spell that revealed the presence of other spells, and Sera would never forget the look on their faces when they discovered that the entire inn shone warm, bright, and dazzling, like a single lit window on a dark night.

"You're wasted here, Sera," Chancellor Bennet had said, and she had believed him.

What was she supposed to do now?

The inn's doorbell pealed, rescuing Sera from her increasingly bleak thoughts. She ran quickly downstairs, the worn steps creaking beneath her feet, calling "I'll get it!" to Jasmine as she went.

She opened the door.

And froze.

"Francesca?" Sera's heart gave a violent lurch. This was very, *very* bad.

"What's going on?" Francesca demanded, throwing her hands in the air with an exaggerated air of drama. "You won't answer your phone, you haven't come back to the estate, you— WHAT THE HELL IS THAT?"

Sera squeezed her eyes shut in despair. She had known, of course, that the Guild would find out she'd lost her magic sooner or later, but losing one's magic wasn't a crime. Resurrecting a person from the dead, on the other hand, *was*, and that part she probably *could* have kept a secret.

If only it hadn't been for the rooster.

Jasmine had been dead only minutes when she'd been brought back, but Roo-Roo had been dead a full year. He had, to put it delicately, *decomposed*. He was simply not alive in the way Jasmine was alive. He was, in fact, decidedly zombified.

He clattered up to Sera's feet now, pecking at her in order to convey his desire to be picked up. Sera did pick him up, but only to prevent him from scuttling out the open door.

There was nothing to be done but tell the truth.

"*Shhhh*," Sera said fiercely. "We have guests upstairs! I'll explain everything, but you have to promise not to tell anybody what I'm about to tell you. Especially not your father."

"I promise," Francesca said at once, her wide eyes watching Roo-Roo like she couldn't tear them away.

"Jasmine died two weeks ago. I brought her back."

Francesca's eyes snapped up to Sera's face. "What do you mean, you brought her back? Like, with CPR?"

"No, she was *dead* dead, not whatever kind of dead CPR works on. I cast a resurrection spell. It brought her back, but it took away most of my magic."

There was a long, incredulous silence. Sera watched Francesca anxiously. Then Francesca said, "Okay, first things first. Can I use your loo?"

Sera let her breath out in a relieved whoosh. Maybe she'd lost most of her magic, but at least she hadn't lost her friend. She'd go back to the Guild and she'd study every book they had until she found a way, *any* way, to get her magic back.

Everything, she was certain, would be okay.

Three hours later, Albert Grey was storming into the inn,

and Sera had no choice but to accept that everything would most decidedly *not* be okay.

Confined to the inn's living room while Albert went outside to examine the skeletal rooster, Sera, furious and feeling utterly betrayed, couldn't bear to look at Francesca. It was almost a relief when Albert marched back into the room.

"A resurrection spell," Albert said coldly, spelling the door shut so that Jasmine could not follow him in and intervene on Sera's behalf. "All that power, and you throw it away. After everything we've done for you."

Sera had expected those words, or something like them, and yet she couldn't help feeling like Albert's tone was all wrong.

The truth struck her almost at once. *It's because he's only pretending to be angry.* Every time she'd ever doubted Albert's sincerity as her mentor, every time she'd caught the hard look in his eyes when someone else praised her, she'd glimpsed the *real* Albert Grey. Whatever he thought of her casting a resurrection spell, it was outweighed by far by his pleasure that her magic was now a sliver of what it had been. He was, once again, without rival. His throne, once again, was wholly his own.

That Albert was capable of pride and petty jealousy didn't exactly come as a surprise to her, but it still hurt. She'd been his apprentice for five years. Didn't he care about her at all?

"Sera." Albert's voice grew softer and coaxing, which was never a good sign. "Where did you learn the spell?"

Sera fidgeted with the ragged end of one fingernail. "It was in one of my library books."

His eyes narrowed. "Don't lie to me. For one thing, you're not very good at it. For another, Francesca has already told me about the fox she spotted slinking up the stairs shortly after she arrived. Curious behaviour for a fox, don't you think?" Gripping her chin between his thumb and forefinger, Albert tilted Sera's face up so she had nowhere to look but at him. "Clementine has been here, hasn't she? Did she teach you the incantation?"

Sera jerked out of his grip, teeth clenched, and stayed quiet.

Albert, who was accustomed to getting his way, looked both surprised and irritated. Sera was suddenly reminded of the time she'd asked him if his magic was a night sky, like hers, and he'd said no, his was lightning. She hadn't understood what that meant then, but she did now. His was an angry, pitiless magic, quick to lash out and indiscriminate in its destruction.

"You've forgotten who you're talking to, Sera," Albert said sharply. "I am still a Grey, born from a long, unbroken line of witches, and I still have every bit as much power as I did a week ago. You, on the other hand, do not. You are just a swan who has clipped her own wings. So when I ask you a question, you *will* answer."

Unfortunately for Albert, this speech just made Sera angrier. Albert, it seemed, had forgotten that *his* history might be a legacy of power, but *hers* was a legacy of resistance. Not to get too dramatic about it, but Sera's ancestors had not defied tyrants and broken free of empires for her to now give this man a single inch.

"I told you," she said, "I found the spell in a book."

To her surprise, rather than losing his temper, Albert tilted his head at her with sudden interest. "You've grown fond of her, haven't you? Good God, Sera, I'd credited you with more intelligence than that." Whatever he saw in her expression made him bark a laugh. "She hasn't told you what she did, has she?"

Later, Clemmie would tell Sera the whole story. In short, she had once been a witch of moderate talent and great ambition, and, bitterly resentful of Albert, who'd been insufferable throughout the years they'd known each other, she'd decided (in her words) to strike a blow for underdogs everywhere by cursing him.

As in, with a literal magical curse.

(That *anybody* would do something as seismically senseless as attempt to curse the most powerful witch born in generations was, frankly, ludicrous, and yet Sera found it remarkably easy to believe that Clemmie would do just that.)

The curse, a rare spell that turned its unfortunate target into an animal, was supposed to be temporary, but as was always the way with Clemmie, she hadn't thought it through. She hadn't considered that she might not have the power to break the curse after casting it. She hadn't even considered that she might not have the power to *cast* the curse in the first place.

Plot twist: she *hadn't* had enough power to cast such a curse. Not properly, anyway. Her spell had backfired, trapping *her* in the form of a fox.

The undoing of a curse was no easy matter, and the few witches who possessed the power were unwilling to risk Albert's wrath by doing so. At that point, the Guild had felt that being stuck in the body of a fox was adequate punishment, but that had by no means been adequate for Albert. He'd wanted Clemmie under lock and key in the Guild's castle.

Declining to be imprisoned, Clemmie had flexed her claws, bitten Albert around the ankles, and bolted.

On that afternoon in the inn, however, all Albert said about it was, "She tried to curse me, but ended up cursing herself instead. She's been in hiding for years, but I should have realised she'd come to you as soon as word of your existence made its way to her. I have no doubt she thought she could hoodwink a young, powerful, and unutterably naïve witch into breaking her curse."

Sera maintained a stony silence, refusing to give him the satisfaction of a reaction.

"Fortunately for you, Sera," Albert went on, "I'm minded to be lenient. You've lost your power, possibly for good, but you needn't lose your place among us. A resurrection spell is no small thing, and the Guild does not make it a habit to overlook such egregious lawbreaking, but if you help us capture Clementine, I'm sure I can persuade the Chancellor to forgive this transgression."

Sera knew that she was being offered a lifeline, and she wanted very, very badly to take it. The only way she'd ever get her magic back, if such a thing was even possible, was with the Guild's help. Without them, without their resources and their libraries and their scholars, she'd have no chance at all.

All she had to do was betray Clemmie first.

All she had to do was give an inch.

She couldn't. Clemmie had kept secrets from her, including deliberately neglecting to tell her that *she'd* been the one to cast the curse that had turned her into a fox, but without Clemmie, Sera wouldn't have been able to save Jasmine.

So Sera looked her former mentor in the eye and said, "I can't help you. I found the spell in one of my books."

As soon as she said it, she realised she'd made a mistake. This was what Albert had *wanted* her to do. He didn't care about capturing Clemmie. He probably hadn't even spared Clemmie a thought in years. But the moment he had clocked that Sera cared about her, Clemmie had become a convenient way to use Sera's loyalty against her. The only thing Albert cared about was his own pride, and now that Sera's magic was no longer a threat to his, the *last* thing he wanted was for her to come back to the Guild and get a second chance.

"Then, on behalf of Chancellor Bennet and the Guild," said Albert, not bothering to hide his satisfaction, "I leave you to the consequences of your choices. You are exiled from the Guild from this day forth. For the safety of all witches, you will still be beholden to the Guild's laws, but you will not receive any further education or assistance from us. You will not be permitted on Guild property. You will have no access to library books or spellcasting materials. Not a single witch in the country will extend a friendly hand to you now."

Well, there was really nothing left for Sera to do but lean into the drama, point a warning finger like a sorceress of old, and say, "You will rue this day, Albert Grey."

And, most magnificently, it even rhymed.

CHAPTER THREE

*T*hat rooster," Sera declared, fifteen years later, "is a menace. Why can't he crow at a reasonable time? Why does he insist on cock-a-doodling at three, four, five, six, *and* seven in the morning?"

"Now, Sera," Jasmine said with a mixture of sympathy and reproach, cuddling the aforementioned rooster in her arms and covering his ears like Sera's criticisms might otherwise hurt his feelings, "you know Roo-Roo can't tell the time. He gets discombobulated, on account of being"—and here Jasmine lowered her voice to a whisper—"*undead*. Which was *your* doing, my love."

"Resurrecting him was an accident! I agreed to a lot of things when I cast that spell, but a lifetime with a zombie chicken was definitely not one of them!"

Jasmine's dark brown eyes, so like Sera's, were dewy as she gazed upon the skeletal abomination in her arms. "But he's so fond of you," she cooed. "Look at the way he's trying to nibble your sleeve. If that's not love, I don't know what is."

Sera retrieved the sleeve of her oversized sweater from the

bony beak clamped around it and stomped across the kitchen to fortify herself with the booziest coffee that had ever boozed. Was it only half past ten in the morning and, strictly speaking, too early to be consuming anything with more of a kick than a triple espresso? Yes, but the prospect of a glug of Baileys in her coffee was the only thing keeping her from returning to her bed immediately and just letting everyone fend for themselves.

Everyone, these days, meant Jasmine (briefly deceased great-aunt), Clemmie (overly opinionated witch doomed to live out her days as a fox), Sera's young cousin Theo (also a witch, but thankfully not one doomed to a lifetime as a woodland creature), Matilda (geriatric oddball and aspiring hobbit), and newest arrival Nicholas (a knight).

It sounded madder than a box of frogs, and yet it was, somehow, the reality of Sera's life. She had achieved a remarkable feat. Not many people went from where she'd been (the most powerful witch born in a generation, the Guild's golden child, and glittering with promise) to where she was now (thirty years old, almost magicless, and running an inn filled with more than its fair share of people who were not, it had to be said, overburdened with normalness), but she'd done it.

Sera had never *planned* to run the inn. It creaked, it leaked, and worst of all, it had people in it. Still, with Jasmine getting older and Sera all too aware that it was *her* spell that had made the inn a beacon in the dark for the lost and adrift, she had found herself doing more and more.

Setting Roo-Roo back on the floor, Jasmine stacked the breakfast bowls into a tidy pile and said, "At the risk of adding another straw to your back, dearest—"

"Are you calling me a camel?" Sera asked.

"—I feel you ought to know that Matilda saw daisies burst forth from one of the teacups this morning."

The universe was enjoying itself just a little too much at Sera's expense. "What did she say?"

"She pretended she didn't see it, but I know she did."

"When I get my magic back," Sera said emphatically, "the first thing I'm going to do is put an end to the magical mischief running amok in this house."

When was doing a lot of heavy lifting there, considering she was well and truly stuck, but *if* would feel too much like admitting defeat.

In truth, Sera had a pretty good idea of how to get her magic back, and that idea was a book called *The Ninth Compendium of Uncommon Spells*. The problem was getting her hands on it.

As she helped Jasmine load the dishwasher, she put her mind to this conundrum, an oft-repeated exercise in futility that involved brilliant notions like "Just beg the Guild for a favour, pride be damned" and "What if I planned an ingenious heist instead . . ."

It was maddening. After years of exhausting the few magical texts still in her possession, chasing ideas dredged from Clemmie's memory, and some dubious and desperate Googling, the injustice of finally having a real answer and for that answer to be *just* out of reach was almost too much to bear.

The Guild had twelve compendiums of unusual spells in the estate's enormous library, all collected and compiled by different witches over the centuries. They sat in the restricted section, gathering dust. Sera could picture them in her mind's eye. She'd walked past them a hundred times as a child.

The Ninth Compendium was there. If she weren't in exile, she could walk in and simply borrow it.

The fact that she even knew this much was down to her little cousin Theo, who was living with her at the moment. As he was technically under the aegis of the Wise Women of Reykjavík, the Icelandic equivalent of the British Guild of Sorcery, he'd never been to the Northumberland estate. Nevertheless, he *did* live in Britain, at least for the time being, so the Guild let him use their online library and borrow magical texts to study at home. (*Not* texts from the restricted section, alas, which could only be studied in person with special permission.)

Within weeks of receiving access to the library, Theo had pointed out that *Sera* could use his account too. How would the Guild ever know the difference?

It had been the first chance Sera had had to study new texts and spellbooks since her exile. With Clemmie peering over her shoulder, she'd scoured the extensive index of spells, and there, under the Rs, the word *restoration* had caught her eye. A single click later, she knew where to find the spell. *The Ninth Compendium of Uncommon Spells.*

She just couldn't get to it.

"You could ask someone to get it for you," Clemmie had suggested. Having extracted a promise from Sera that she would break Clemmie's curse if she ever got her magic back, Clemmie was every bit as invested as Sera was.

Sera had laughed bitterly. "Ask who, exactly?"

Albert Grey's cold voice had echoed in her head. *Not a single witch in the country will extend a friendly hand to you now.*

"You've gone away again, my love," Jasmine said gently, trying to shut the dishwasher door.

Blinking out of her reverie, Sera stepped out of the way. She lifted the bubbling kettle off its cradle and looked for her favourite mug, which was, of course, missing. It was the most ordinary of drinking receptacles, ochre with tiny blue flowers on it, and yet it was never around when Sera wanted it because, for absolutely no reason Sera could fathom, every other person in the house insisted on using it.

She made do with a subpar mug. There was a clatter of armour behind her, and she turned to see Nicholas trip into the kitchen. He stopped in the process of pulling on his gauntleted glove, black hair flopping into his earnest green eyes, and snapped to attention.

"Lady Sera!" One loose gauntlet flapped from his hand as he smacked that hand over his heart. Slashes of mortified pink appeared on his white cheeks. "I didn't know you were here! Forgive me for presenting myself to you in such a state of unreadiness!"

Sera sighed. "You look ready to me, Nicholas." Then, encountering his hopeful puppy eyes, she corrected herself: "*Sir* Nicholas. In fact, you look splendid."

Nicholas, who was twenty-three years old and declared at least twice a week that he was willing to fall upon his very real and very literal sword for Sera, lit up at this compliment. "You honour me!"

Sera glanced at the clock. "Shouldn't you have been at the Medieval Fair an hour ago?"

"I could not depart without polishing my armour first," Nicholas replied gravely.

He gave Jasmine a courtly bow, patted Roo-Roo on the head, and snatched up the sheathed sword propped against the door on his way out. A moment later, the sound of his Jeep sputtered up the lane.

Nicholas had arrived four months ago, on a stormy evening with rain lashing against the windows and every fireplace ablaze. Sera had answered the polite ring of the doorbell and found him on the doorstep, soaking wet and shivering.

He had also been dressed in medieval armour from neck to toe. And there had been a sword at his side.

"Sir Nicholas of Mayfair, at your service," this apparition had said, attempting a very wet bow, his teeth chattering and his sword clanking against the various layers of steel on him. "There seems to be a mistake with the flat I rented in the next town over. I was driving past and I saw your lights . . ."

"Come in," Sera had said. "Tea?"

Sera hadn't expected Nicholas to stay longer than the night. She'd assumed all he needed was a toasty fireplace on a stormy night and would be gone when the skies cleared.

But when Nicholas had not gone, when he had abandoned the perfectly nice flat he'd rented and settled down at a rickety old inn instead, becoming more lodger than guest, she had realised that the thing he'd needed hadn't been a toasty fireplace at all.

He'd needed someone to see him, armour and sword and all. To hear his ridiculous introduction and accept his courtly bow. And still say *Come in*.

"He's been with us some time," Jasmine mused now, leaning heavily on her cane. "Do you think he still believes the story we tell the guests about Roo-Roo?"

"That the skeletal rooster is one of Theo's toys and runs on batteries?" Sera winced, wishing for the thousandth time that she had the ability to cast a decent glamour over Roo-Roo. "I have no idea, and I don't plan to ask."

Jasmine acknowledged that this was a can of worms best left unopened. Roo-Roo scuttled out of the kitchen to go bother the actual, *living* chickens by the coop, and for a few moments, there was peace in the house. Jasmine wiped down the old breakfast table while Sera sought out a speedy slice of toast.

"Have you seen Theo today?" Sera asked Jasmine, smothering her toast in lavender jam. "He wasn't in his room when I came downstairs."

"I think he was up before any of us," Jasmine replied.

"On a weekend? That's not like him."

"I suspect he decided to set off on an adventure," said Jasmine. "His coat and bicycle are missing."

This struck Sera as suspicious. Theo, who tended to stay up late reading and normally stumbled yawning into the kitchen after everyone else had already finished breakfast, was not the sort of child who decided to embark on adventures at dawn.

"I'll text him," Sera said, mouth full of jammy toast. "He never goes anywhere without his phone."

A moment later, the merry trill of an alert echoed from Theo's bedroom above them and proved that this was not in fact the case. Where could he possibly have gone, and why wouldn't he have taken his phone with him?

"Where's Clemmie?" Sera demanded suddenly.

"If I had to guess, asleep," said Jasmine, always prepared to believe the best of everyone.

Sera, who was not by any means prepared to believe the best of anyone, let out an unladylike snort. Before she could put her mind to the mystery of where Theo and Clemmie might be, however, a piercing, plaintive cry pealed across the garden.

"SERAAAAA!"

Sera had no one to blame for this but herself. She could have abandoned the inn years ago. She could, at this very moment, be living on one of those tiny islands off the coast of Norway with only a polar bear for company. *She'd* decided to stay. *She'd* decided to take on more and more of the running of the inn. And *she'd* cast the spell that had brought people like Matilda and Nicholas to her door.

Sera had made her bed.

If only she could go lie in it.

"Could you call Alex for me?" she said to Jasmine, shoving her socked feet into the pair of red wellies by the back door. Alex was Theo's best friend, so it stood to reason that their house was the most likely place he'd be.

"SEHHH-RAAAA!"

Sera clomped out into the cold and sun, making her way down the garden to the spot where, fifteen years ago, Jasmine had died.

The garden hadn't changed a whole lot since then. The stone patio right outside the kitchen had new raised beds for herbs and edible flowers, there was now a chicken coop near the beehive, and Matilda had dug herself a vegetable patch. Other than that, time had more or less stood still. The orchard of fruit trees was still there. The grass was still too long and the wildflowers too wild.

Sera came to a halt beside the vegetable patch, which was near to bursting with the colours of its harvest. There was a wheelbarrow beside it, as well as a trowel, a bright red watering can, and a wooden stool topped with a teapot and cup.

It was an idyllic picture, so long as you ignored the two people glowering at each other right in the middle of it.

The first of the two was Matilda, a smallish and oldish Black lady who had arrived almost two years ago, pronounced the inn perfect, and had never left. She was the first of Sera's guests who had seamlessly segued into becoming a lodger. Clad in brown dungarees, she had a straw hat wedged over her cloud of grey corkscrew curls and was pointing an accusing finger at her archnemesis. "Sera, make him go away!"

"Malik," Sera said, exasperated, "I love seeing you every Saturday, I do, but you know what would make me love the experience even more? If you gave me the week's delivery *without* making Matilda's voice go all high and screechy first!"

Malik, the extremely fetching archnemesis in question, pointed to the vegetable patch. "I'm a farmer!" Unlike the rest of them, with their mix of accents, his voice was all Lancashire. "There's a time and a place for minding your own business, but the sight of cabbages and peppers planted side by side isn't it!"

"Now you listen to me, my boy," Matilda cut in, before Sera could reply. "If I wanted your advice, I'd ask for it! I am in the twilight of my life! I have earned the right to grow my vegetables, hunt for mushrooms, eat eight meals a day, and sing rousing drinking songs without interruption!"

"Rousing—" Malik cut a look at Sera, obviously trying to decide whether to be annoyed, incredulous, or simply delighted that he was thirty-eight and had been referred to as a boy.

Feeling that his sensibilities, so offended by the cabbages and peppers, might go either way, Sera intervened. "Quit it, both of you," she said. "This week, it's the cabbages. Last week, it was the sunflowers. I don't care how many crimes against gardening Matilda commits, Malik! You're just going to have to learn to not look! And as for you," she went on, spinning round to Matilda, "Malik has a job to do and other places to go to. If you don't want him examining your handiwork, don't waylay him every time he walks through the gate!"

"I waylay him because a farmer should appreciate excellent produce when he sees it!" Matilda insisted. "Look at those pumpkins! Look at my precious babies! They're perfect! But did he mention the pumpkins? No! He couldn't get past the cabbages!"

"*And* the peppers," Malik reminded her. He clutched the old key hanging around his neck as if it were a talisman that might protect him from the horrors before him. "And are those artichokes?"

"I like the artichokes," said Sera.

"Jesus, it's a miracle any of this has grown."

Sera, who snuck out in the dead of night twice a week to cast reviving spells on Matilda's beloved plants with the minuscule amount of magic she had left, said nothing.

"You don't deserve to have such beautiful cheekbones," Matilda informed him, snatching the teapot off the stool. "Now if you'll excuse me, I'm going to top up my tea and forage for mushrooms."

Malik, who seemed both surprised and pleased by the tribute to his cheekbones, loped off in the direction of the van parked outside the gate. "You want to give me a hand with the crates? El sent you a massive pot of fahsa too."

Sera bought all the inn's fruit and veggies from Malik and

his husband Elliot's farm, which was quite a lot even when they didn't have any extra guests. It took the two of them two trips to move a handful of wooden crates and a tureen of Yemeni stew from Malik's van to the kitchen. After they were done, Sera pressed homemade honey into Malik's arms and walked him out.

"Until next week, love." Malik climbed into the driver's seat. "As always, ta for supporting the efforts of your local farmers. El may be the better cook, but I take comfort in knowing I have the best cheekbones."

Sera laughed. "Dinner on Wednesday?"

"We wouldn't miss it."

She watched him drive off, shielding her eyes against the sharp, angled sun. The last twenty minutes had left her with a throbbing pain precisely behind her left eyebrow. She shut her eyes, pressed the heel of her hand to the spot, and summoned the little magic she had left.

Most witches possessed a respectable amount of magic, enough to glamour an undead rooster or fix a broken chimney. Some had more than that. Some had less.

Sera, these days, had even less than less.

Years ago, when she had closed her eyes and reached for her magic, it had answered her instantly. Now it took a moment or two. Now it was like standing in the dark, calling for help and hoping to see the glow of a rescuer's lantern. She was always afraid that this time would be the time she'd call, and call, and get no answer.

But there was still a little magic in her, and it answered. Just a few stubborn, twinkling constellations of stars. Not enough to glamour an undead rooster or fix a broken chimney. A headache, though? *That*, it could fix.

Sometimes Sera wondered what she'd have done if she had known what the resurrection spell would cost her before she'd cast it. She liked to think she'd have cast it anyway, that she'd have chosen Jasmine over her magic, but every now and then, in the guilty quiet of the night, she wondered.

"Bok!"

Apparently, Roo-Roo had lost interest in annoying the chickens. Sera nudged him away from the open gate with the toe of one wellie. The inn was at the bottom of a narrow, winding country lane that hardly anyone except delivery drivers and the occasional guest ever found themselves on. Sheep-dotted farmland, wild woods, and green hills stretched out for miles around. It was a half mile up the lane to the nearest pub and another mile beyond that to the nearest Tesco. A zombie chicken, therefore, *could* probably slip through the open gate and meander around the nearby countryside for a bit without being noticed, but it was best not to take any chances. Sera could do without breaking any more of the Guild's laws.

She turned back to the house. It was a three-storey, 1840s hodgepodge of cream stone and brown brick, with multiple chimneys and sharply slanted red roofs long faded by the sun, and looked like it ought to belong to a Victorian dowager. The ivy climbing the walls was so overgrown that very little of the original brick was visible. The house was surrounded by low, weathered stone walls on all sides, and a shallow brook babbled its way past one corner. The front of the inn faced the same winding lane as the back, just farther uphill, and above the front door swung an ancient sign that read BATTY HOLE INN.

Sera was lucky fairy tales weren't real, because a wolf could huff and puff and *absolutely* blow the whole thing down.

Moreover, the house needed lit fires and Sera's heat spells for ten out of twelve months of the year, most of the furniture was old and worn, the hot water was a bit sputtery, the Wi-Fi was temperamental, and Clemmie left claw marks in the wood whenever she fancied a tantrum.

And then there was the magic. Whenever Sera checked, she could see that the inn still glowed bright with the spell she'd cast over it as a child. Spells were supposed to be finite, so there was no reason it ought to still be going strong, but somehow, it was. Unfortunately, it had also evolved. Over time, the spell had developed a most inconvenient propensity for whimsy and mischief. Wildflowers bloomed spontaneously in empty teacups at unexpected moments. The sunlit rooms teased her with echoes of her past selves. Doors opened and closed on a whim. One of the guest bedrooms rained apple blossom tea for exactly one hour every Sunday, after which said tea vanished like it had never been there. And it was anyone's guess what might come next.

The most exasperating thing was the knowledge that if she could just get her magic back, the house's inconveniences would be moot. The boiler wouldn't need to be replaced if it was enchanted. Her heat spells would last weeks, not hours. With a wave of her hand, she'd be able to fix a crumbling chimney, seal a leaking pipe, mend a cracked window frame. With just a thought, she'd be able to paint walls, clean smoky fireplaces, and polish the wood until it gleamed. These spells had seen them through her childhood, had been *easy* back then, and it was utterly galling that they were now beyond her.

The house was an albatross around her neck, but it was, nevertheless, *her* albatross. Just weeks after she'd turned eighteen, her parents had decided she could now stand on her own two feet. They'd signed over the deed and the mortgage, kissed and congratulated her as if they hadn't just plonked a crumbling colossus in her lap, and tootled off on their next adventure.

Jasmine had kept the inn going, but she wasn't young, and as the years had gone by, Sera had taken on more and more of the work.

And lo, here she was. Exiled witch and cranky innkeeper.

Theo was fond of wholesome video games in which his character ran farms, tea shops, and inns with little more than a rusty axe and a winning smile. Sera, glancing over his shoulder every now and then, was more than a little bitter that real life wasn't quite so easy.

Then again, she had neither a rusty axe nor a winning smile, so maybe that was the problem.

The ping of her phone started Sera out of her thoughts. Jasmine, who was not the sort of woman who bellowed across the garden (or, indeed, at all), had sent her a text.

Alex says they haven't seen Theo since school yesterday.

Which brought Sera rather neatly to: how the *fuck* had she misplaced an entire eleven-year-old boy?

She stormed back inside. Jasmine was at her worktable in the large living room and, amazingly, remained unfrazzled. "Now, pet," she said soothingly, "I'm sure there's a very good explanation for this. Theo wouldn't do anything untoward."

"Wouldn't he?" Sera replied. "Not even if Clemmie asked him really, really nicely? Untoward is her middle name!"

"I think she once told me it's Mary, but I take your point. I do feel, though, that whatever Clemmie may or may not be capable of, Theo wouldn't let himself be led astray. He's an angel."

"So was Lucifer," said Sera darkly.

"And I'm sure that was a very upsetting situation for all involved, my love, but it seems unlikely to be repeated. Oh! Theo!"

Sera whirled. There, in the doorway, his coat still on and his cheeks all pinked like he'd been outside for hours, stood her young cousin. He gave her a look of complete (even—dare she say it?—angelic) innocence.

Clemmie, on the other hand, looked enormously satisfied as she sashayed into the room. "Good morning, Sera," she said cheerfully, an emotion so removed from her usual self that Sera was instantly suspicious. "How are you?"

Sera scowled. "Where have you both been?"

"Nowhere." Clemmie sat on her hind legs and examined one of her front paws. "That is to say, *I* haven't been anywhere. I couldn't tell you where Theo's been."

Sera raised her eyebrows at Theo.

He was a lanky, lively young boy, with short, untidy brown hair, a firm jaw, and bright, eager blue eyes. He shook his head at her, though he couldn't quite meet her eyes and kept glancing sideways at Clemmie. "I've just been out on my bike."

"Theodór," Sera said sharply, switching to Icelandic so Clemmie couldn't interfere, "you're a terrible liar. I don't care if you've promised Clemmie you won't say a word. You tell me where you've been right this minute."

The doorbell rang.

Theo's face went pale.

"I'll answer it," Jasmine said, retrieving her cane and leaving the room with all haste.

Clemmie bounded up to the windowsill and craned her neck to catch a glimpse of the front stoop. "Drat. I thought we'd have more time."

Dread seized Sera. "What have you done?"

Jasmine reappeared in the open doorway before either Theo or Clemmie could answer, a most peculiar expression on her face. "Sera," she said, a great deal shriller than normal. "You have a visitor."

She stepped aside to reveal Francesca Grey, Sera's former friend and the new Chancellor of the British Guild of Sorcery.

CHAPTER FOUR

*I*t had been fifteen years since Sera had seen Francesca (unless you counted the moody greyscale photograph in the announcement the Guild had sent out when Francesca had been elected Chancellor, which Sera didn't), and she scarcely recognised her.

Teenage Francesca had had a rebellious sense of mischief, an almost manic energy, and a loud, easy laugh. *This* Francesca, on the other hand, was cool and collected and looked like she wouldn't know laughter if it smacked her in the head. Her mouth was pressed into a straight line, her hair was arranged in a complicated updo designed to make her look older, and she wore a slim black pantsuit that had been pressed to within an inch of its life.

"Chancellor Grey." Sera was immediately her spikiest self. "I'd say it was nice to see you, but it isn't."

"I see your library of talents is still missing the book on diplomacy," Francesca replied. "May I have a word?"

Sera gestured vaguely at a chair, using the opportunity to glance around. Theo edged closer to her, but Clemmie, as she'd suspected, was nowhere to be seen. How she'd vanished so quickly and thoroughly was anyone's guess, but Sera knew from experience that Clemmie's speedy, sneaky fox form had its advantages.

Francesca stepped into the room. Her eyes flickered to Theo, who was practically pressed up against Sera's side by now. The top of his head reached her chin, and she could feel how shallow his breathing was.

"I'll make tea," Jasmine said too brightly, which was also code for *I want to get as far away from this room as I possibly can, and keep the rest of our nosey household at bay while I'm at it*. She shut the parlour door as she left.

"You must be Theodór," Francesca said. Her eyes flicked briefly to Sera's. "I gather from his records that he reads a great deal of advanced texts."

"How are your children?" Sera asked, ignoring the implication that Francesca had guessed who was really reading most of those advanced texts. At Francesca's furrowed brow, she explained, "They were mentioned in the Guild's newsletter about the election."

"Oh. Of course. The twins are well, thank you. They're three years old now."

"And learning from the best and brightest already, I imagine."

"No. They're not magical."

Had Sera been crueller, she might have laughed at the thought of Albert Grey's reaction when he realised his grandchildren, the future of his illustrious family tree, had not a speck of magic between them. Instead, she found herself feeling sorry for the young twins, who would no doubt have discovered already that their grandfather had no interest in them now that he had no use for them.

Her voice softened slightly. "Three's very young. Their magic could still show itself."

"They've been rigorously tested. Father insisted."

And because Sera was Sera, she couldn't help pointing out the obvious. "So was it before or after you had the twins that you noticed how much of a fuckwit your father is?"

Theo had a sudden, conveniently timed coughing fit. Francesca's cheek twitched with what may have been the third cousin twice removed of a smile, but she only said, "Father and I have a complicated relationship."

"Do you?" Sera asked, a distinct bite in her voice. "I don't remember you feeling so ambivalent fifteen years ago."

"You broke our laws, Sera. You brought someone back from the dead! Did you really think there wouldn't be any consequences?"

"Consequences?" Sera laughed without any real humour. "I expected consequences, Francesca. I risked those consequences because I couldn't stand the thought of losing my only real family. What I *didn't* expect was for you to look me in the eye, swear to keep my secret, and immediately turn around and throw me under the fucking bus!"

Francesca dropped her gaze to the floor. "I shouldn't have done that. I couldn't lie to Father, but you were my friend. I should have at least talked to you before I told him what you'd done. I'm sorry."

Sera, who had never imagined for a moment that Francesca would acknowledge she'd done anything wrong, was so taken aback that her anger popped like a balloon. In its place, she found pity. Francesca had been a child too. She'd been a product of the Guild's centuries of snobbery, the only daughter of a proud, immensely powerful man, and the haste with which she'd told her father what Sera had done might have had as much to do with fear as with loyalty.

"Having said that," Francesca went on, "what I did fifteen years ago doesn't excuse your idiocy last night."

Sera could make no sense of this. "And which of my illicit activities are you referring to on this particular occasion?"

Francesca raised elegant eyebrows. "*The Ninth Compendium of Uncommon Spells*, obviously."

Sera stared. Theo went very still beside her, which told her just about everything she needed to know. She set her jaw. "I have no idea what you're talking about."

"Oh, for God's sake." Francesca's poise finally cracked completely. "We have CCTV at the estate these days, Sera. How could you have been so stupid?"

Sera was so irked that she almost set Francesca straight and informed her that, believe it or not, Sera *had* assumed that there was CCTV at the estate these days and therefore would certainly *not* have done the thing Francesca was obviously implying she had done.

She bit back this reply and said, struggling to keep her voice even, "Are you saying you have footage of me at the estate? Breaking my exile?"

"Of course not," Francesca said impatiently. "We have footage of *Theo* at the estate. He broke into the restricted archives last night. In the company of a red fox, no less."

Sera looked at Theo. Theo looked back at Sera. His eyes were wide, apologetic, and terrified.

Then, with rare good timing, there was a sharp tap on the outside of the window. "Sera!" Matilda called from the other side of the pane of glass, a basket of mushrooms hanging off one arm and a cup of tea in the other hand. "The fishmonger wants you, duckling!"

"I'll be back in a minute," Sera said to Francesca, seizing the opportunity to get some proper answers out of Theo.

Francesca's mouth pressed into a frustrated line, but she didn't argue. Taking Theo firmly by the arm, Sera whisked him out of the room with her. She marched him down the hallway, past the old study they'd converted into Jasmine's bedroom, and planted him firmly in the kitchen with a stern "Don't move an inch."

Then she stomped back down to the bottom of the garden, where she collected the week's fish delivery from the gruff fishmonger. Returning to the kitchen, Sera found Jasmine encouraging Theo to eat a waffle smothered in chocolate. Sera, who felt that if anyone deserved sweet treats right now, it was *her*, gave this scene a cranky look, put the fish away in the freezer, and set about getting some answers.

"Hurry up and eat that waffle before I steal it," Sera said to Theo. "If it were up to me, you'd have to subsist on broccoli and broth for the next seven years, but alas, Great-Auntie Jasmine seems to think even juvenile criminals must be allowed more than their fair share of sugar." Theo gave her a sheepish grin. Sera refused to allow it to melt her heart. "Clemmie, I know you're tucked away in some hidey-hole listening in, so get out of there and start talking."

"I'm almost twice your age, you know," Clemmie said with a

sniff, emerging from an upper cabinet. "A more respectful tone wouldn't go amiss."

Sera looked up at the chubby red fox on top of the cabinets. "I hate to break it to you, Clemmie, but your advanced years have no meaning when you failed so utterly in your quest to become the Wicked Witch of the Northeast that you trapped yourself in a form that attracts fleas."

Clemmie let out a wail. "Not the fleas, Sera! You promised you would never tease me about the fleas!"

"And you promised you would never involve Theo in your nonsensical schemes!"

"I *wanted* to help, Sera!" Theo insisted earnestly, his mouth full of waffle. "Clemmie hasn't got opposable thumbs! She needed someone to carry the spellbook!"

Jasmine gave Sera an aghast look. Sera wondered if any jury in the country would convict her if she drowned Clemmie in a well.

"Please tell me the two of you didn't *actually* steal the spellbook!"

"What other choice did we have?" Clemmie demanded. "*You* wouldn't do it!"

"And do you know why I wouldn't do it?" Sera snapped back. "Do you know why I only ever daydreamed about stealing that book? Because I knew we'd never get away with it! And would you look at that, I was right! Now tell me exactly what happened!"

Theo and Clemmie, it turned out, had left on Theo's bicycle the night before, after pretending to go to bed (Jasmine looked so faint at the thought of Theo biking around the dark Lancashire countryside that Sera feared for a moment that a second resurrection spell would be called for), and had ridden all the way to the nearest train station in Burnley. There, with Clemmie hiding in Theo's backpack, they'd taken the eleven o'clock train to Haydon Bridge in Northumberland and had biked the eight miles from *that* station to the Guild's estate, where Theo had snuck into the restricted section of the Guild's library and nicked *The Ninth Compendium*. (At this point, Jasmine had to sit down and soothe herself with the tea she'd made for Francesca.) With the spellbook safely in their possession, Theo and Clemmie had returned in time to catch the six o'clock train back to Lancashire.

"We didn't know about the CCTV," Theo said, hanging his head.

Clemmie thumped her tail irately. "The estate didn't have any of that technological nonsense when I lived there."

Sera struggled to find the words to adequately express her feelings. "You're a *child*, Theo. You just went halfway across the country and back in the middle of the night! Anything could have happened to you!"

"That's not fair," said Clemmie, sounding genuinely wounded. "I would never have let anything happen to him."

"*You're* what happened to him!" Sera reminded her.

There was a pause. Then Clemmie said, more quietly, "I can't live like this for the rest of my life, Sera. Look at me!"

With a sense of impending doom, Sera saw exactly how this would go and did her very best to stop it. *You have a heart of stone, Sera Swan,* she told herself sternly. *You are not going to feel sorry for the fox curled up on top of your kitchen cabinets.*

"So you did it for you," she said. "I promised I'd break your curse if I ever got my magic back, and you got tired of waiting."

"I did it for both of us."

"You got Theo involved," Sera repeated. "I *told* you I didn't want him involved. You did it anyway."

"Did you not hear the part where I lack opposable thumbs?"

"And I'm already involved," Theo insisted. "This matters to me too. I know how much you miss your magic, Sera. I wanted to help you get it back."

Sera's heart ached. She kissed the top of Theo's head. "Thank you." He wasn't really the one she was angry with. "Where's the book?"

"Hidden," said Clemmie.

"Unhide it," said Sera. "If we return it to Francesca now, we might be able to get out of this without the entire might of the Guild coming down on us."

Clemmie's tail twitched. "We can't do that! Not after all the trouble we went to!"

"I don't want to hear it. Give. It. To. Me."

Clemmie growled low in her throat. "Under that chair."

Sera reached under the old armchair tucked into the corner of the kitchen, beneath the draped blanket hiding the space from view, and retrieved a large, heavy tome wrapped in one of Theo's jumpers. Checking under the fabric, she saw the embossed gold letters of the title and felt a sharp needle of regret. God, she was so close.

"Stay put," Sera said, and walked out of the kitchen. Spellbook or no spellbook, the first thing she had to do was keep Theo out of trouble.

CHAPTER FIVE

*T*heo lived with Sera because his parents were afraid of his magic. He'd been seven years old when his magic had made itself known and a few days shy of his ninth birthday when Sera's aunt Lilja, who had found out about Sera's own magic when Theo's had first appeared, had called her in tears to say she couldn't do it anymore.

She couldn't sleep for fear that Theo would burn the house down or make the hymnbooks dance in church, she'd said, and nothing Sera had said could convince her that witches didn't actually do things like that in real life. So Sera had flown to Reykjavík, taken one look at Theo standing anxiously at the edge of the room like he was trying not to frighten his parents by saying or doing the wrong thing, and said, "You can come stay with me if you like."

It was a splendid idea, in theory. Theo spoke fluent English already, a phone call to the village school had assured them that he'd have a place there as soon as he wanted it, and Jasmine had been thrilled at the prospect of having someone new to fuss over.

How Theo would get to Batty Hole Inn, however, was another matter. A new witch could not come to live in the country without the Guild's permission, and Sera could not conceive of a universe in which they were likely to grant her any favours.

Fortunately, the Wise Women of Reykjavík had pulled some strings, and within a week, Sera and Theo were on a flight home.

Two years on, Theo was still here. He had never asked to go back, his parents had never suggested he go back, and Sera didn't want him to go back unless he had a safe and welcoming place to be. He FaceTimed with his parents every week, had made friends, was thriving at school, and, as far as Sera could tell, seemed happy.

So Sera would be *immensely* displeased if, after all that, Theo were to be locked up in a dungeon.

She returned to the living room. Francesca had taken a seat in an armchair by the log burner, but Sera's eyes skated past her and landed in the corner of the room where, out of Francesca's line of sight, the house had shaken loose a translucent memory of Sera's much younger self. Thirteen or fourteen years old, in her Guild school uniform, at the peak of her friendship with the old Francesca, bouncing excitedly on her toes like she was trying to get *this* Francesca's attention.

Sera, too accustomed to the house's tricks, didn't react. A blink later, the ghost was gone and Francesca looked up as Sera entered the room. "Well?"

"Here," Sera said, handing the jumper-covered spellbook over and collapsing wearily into the opposite armchair.

Francesca unwrapped the book, folding Theo's jumper neatly and placing it on the arm of her chair. "Out of curiosity, why didn't they just take a photograph of the spell you wanted? Wouldn't that have been easier than absconding with the entire book?"

"Much easier, but Theo left his phone here. I'm assuming his reasoning was that if Jasmine or I happened to glance at his location on *our* phones, we'd see him safely at home."

"So he didn't want you to know where he was?" Francesca raised her eyebrows. "You really *didn't* know about this, did you?"

Realising she'd said too much, Sera backtracked. "No, I knew. I must have misspoken about the phone thing. It was all my idea." Technically, that last part was true. Sera had once said to Clemmie, *sarcastically*, that stealing the spellbook would be easier than convincing the Guild to let her look at it. And look where that had got her. "Do whatever you need to, but leave Theo out of it."

Almost as if he had not stayed put as he'd been told to, and had in fact been listening in from just outside the door, Theo burst into the room. "No! They can't blame you for something *I* did!"

Sera glared him into silence. Francesca looked between them. "What about Clementine?"

"What about her?"

"She was obviously involved."

You're welcome to have her, Sera wanted to say, but didn't. She'd regret it later. Clemmie had gone too far, as she so often did, but she'd been a part of Sera's life for too long for her to abandon her now.

"You have evidence there was a fox with Theo," Sera said.

"You can't prove the fox is Clemmie. Like I said, this was my idea."

There was a long pause. Theo was practically quivering with outrage, his jaw set so mutinously that Sera just knew he was getting ready to insist all over again that if anyone ought to be punished for his youthful wrongdoings, it should be him. Really, this was all Nicholas's fault for putting ideas about knightly honour and noble sacrifice into Theo's impressionable young head.

To her surprise, however, Francesca smiled. "Still loyal to the bitter end, I see."

Sera said nothing.

"As soon as I saw which book had been taken," Francesca went on, "I knew it was the restoration spell you wanted. This is about getting your magic back, isn't it?"

There was no point denying it, so Sera nodded.

Francesca held *The Ninth Compendium* out. "I'm afraid it's not quite as easy as that. Take a look."

Wary of a trap she couldn't yet see, Sera took the spellbook. The edges of the book were uneven, the pages not all the same size, the parchment varying from yellowed whites to faded browns. Fascinated, Sera touched the edges of the paper with a careful finger, thinking of all the possible places these spells might have been found, imagining the rustle of a scroll in the Library of Alexandria or the puff of an old man blowing dust off his late great-grandmother's trunk and finding a spell tucked between her gloves.

(Of course, none of these spells could have *actually* come from the Library of Alexandria, not just because any such spells would rightfully belong to Egypt or Greece but also because the oldest spell in all twelve compendiums was only about four hundred years old. The old man and his glove-wearing, trunk-owning great-granny, though, could have been real.)

The witch who had compiled the volume had created a table of contents in neat, beautiful handwriting, the ink bleeding very slightly. About halfway down the list were the words *A Spell of Restoration.* Sera turned to the right page, fingers trembling slightly.

Her heart sank a bit. "Oh."

Theo, looking eagerly over her shoulder, was confused. "What is that?"

There were words on the page, in dark, slightly smudged ink, but they were not written in any script Sera could read.

"It's a spellcasting language that predates the one we use now," Francesca explained.

"I know." Sera had come across it a few times as a child. Every time she'd expressed an interest in learning it, Albert had reminded her how lucky she was to be apprenticed to him and had made it clear that he had no intention of wasting his time teaching her outdated, unnecessary things. It had not escaped Sera's notice that *he* had clearly deemed those outdated, unnecessary things worth learning, but it was only much later that she'd really appreciated how much of the five years she'd spent with the Guild had been dominated by Albert trying to keep as much knowledge from her as possible.

"Look," Francesca said quietly, "I'd rather pretend this never happened. I don't want to punish either of you for, shall we say, *borrowing* the book. I have to take it back with me today, but if you wanted to take photographs of the spell before I go, I wouldn't stop you."

Sera was quite certain she had to be misunderstanding this, because surely, *surely*, Francesca wasn't actually *helping* her?

Theo ran out of the room, excitedly yelling, "Clemmie! We're not in trouble! And Sera gets to take photos!"

"Theo, I am on the *lam*." Clemmie's outraged voice could be heard in reply. "You can't just announce my presence to the blooming Chancellor of the Guild!"

"I'll pretend I didn't hear that," Francesca said to Sera.

Sera was still at a loss. "Why are you doing this?"

Francesca shrugged, one hand toying restlessly with a single loose thread on the cuff of her jacket. "Why not?"

"When we were kids, you used to fidget with your clothes when you were hiding something," Sera commented.

Francesca yanked her hand away from her cuff. "Can we not overthink it? Don't you have better things to worry about? Like, say, how you're going to translate the spell?"

"I have no idea how I'm going to translate the spell! How many people still alive today have studied this language? A handful? And I can't imagine any of them helping me!"

Francesca opened her mouth and then shut it again.

Sera frowned. "What?"

"Nothing."

"No, it was definitely something. What were you going to say?"

Looking rather annoyed with herself, Francesca said, "Do you remember Verity Walter?"

"Professor Walter? Yes, of course. She was one of the few people who spent more time in the library than I did. Your father would try to put me off reading books that were, quote unquote, *too advanced*, but Professor Walter would put them in my hands, wink, and walk away."

"She would have helped you. She *can't*, which is why I didn't say it, but she would have. Under different circumstances."

Sera narrowed her eyes at her. "What are you talking about?"

"I can't really tell you the—"

"Well, you're going to," Sera shot back. "Why can't she help me? And why are you so sure she'd even want to?" A sudden, horrible thought struck her. "Has she tried before? When? What happened?"

"Ugh," Francesca huffed, her carefully cultivated poise abandoning her altogether. "Father told Professor Walter that if she helped you, he'd make sure she's never allowed into the Guild's libraries again."

"When?" Sera asked again. "Last month? Last year? How long after I lost my magic?"

Reddening, Francesca said, "Straight after."

"Straight after," Sera repeated, her voice tight with rage. "Straight. After."

"I don't know if you ever read the newsletter that went out at the time, but Father made sure everyone in the Guild knew about the resurrection spell, the fact that you'd lost your magic, and that you'd been exiled," Francesca explained, still pink. "He said it was important that everybody knew that meddling with dangerous spells had real consequences, but you know what he's like."

"He mostly just wanted to make sure everybody knew he no longer had an equal," Sera guessed, unsurprised and unmoved. "Yes, that's very him. Where does Professor Walter fit in?"

"She demanded a meeting with Chancellor Bennet and the Cabinet as soon as she saw the newsletter. She brought *The Ninth Compendium* with her and showed them the spell. She said it would be a disgrace if the Guild let a gift like yours disappear when they had the power to restore it. She acknowledged you had been reckless with your magic, but you were also just a child and she said you deserved a more appropriate punishment than exile."

Sera swallowed, touched by the unexpected kindness of a woman she'd only known in passing. "But?"

"Chancellor Bennet agreed with her," Francesca said. That didn't surprise Sera. The ancient and perpetually confuddled former Chancellor had certainly enjoyed basking in the glory of her extraordinary magical gift, but for all that, he'd also been something of a softy. "But ending a person's exile has to be put to the entire Cabinet for a vote." The streaks of red on Francesca's cheeks were now crimson. "Ten of the twelve Ministers voted to let you come back, but, well, one of the two who didn't happened to, um, have the veto."

"I'm sorry, how does that make any fucking sense?" Sera demanded. "Albert gets to just veto everyone else whenever he wants to?"

Francesca shrugged. "It's in his contract. His, um, magically binding contract."

"Magically binding contracts only work when people are stupid enough to sign them!"

"My father can be very persuasive."

"Then how come *he* isn't the Chancellor of the Guild?"

With a short, mirthless laugh, Francesca said, "Getting eleven Cabinet Ministers to sign a document is easy enough when you've known their families for years and the ones who don't fawn over you are terrified of you. Persuading a few thousand ordinary witches of the Guild to vote for you to be in charge, on the other hand . . ." Another shrug. "Father is feared, admired, and maybe even respected, but he'll never be *liked*. He's spent too long flexing his power, sneering at the riffraff, and ignoring the plebs."

"Well, *you're* the Chancellor of the British Guild of Sorcery now," Sera said sharply. "*You* got enough people to vote for you. If you want to do better by the *riffraff* and the *plebs*, if you want to be different from your father, then do it. *Be* different."

"I'm the puppet dancing at the end of his strings, Sera. I always have been. I don't know how to be different."

Sera shook her head. "If that were really true, you wouldn't be here right now."

There wasn't a whole lot else to say, so Sera took several photographs of the restoration spell and then filmed a short video of the page from every possible angle to make sure she didn't miss a single bit of ink. Theo came back in, immediately dismissed Sera's assurance that she'd taken plenty of footage already, and took a few videos of his own. ("You're too old to properly understand how technology works," he said wisely, to which Sera replied that he was lucky he was cute because he might otherwise have found himself unceremoniously ejected out the window.)

When Theo was at last satisfied, Francesca placed *The Ninth Compendium* into a protective case and stood up. Her hand on the doorknob, she paused and said, simply, "Father mustn't find out about this, Sera. He'll find a way to stop you."

Sera nodded. "I know."

Almost as soon as the front door clicked shut, Matilda came in to show off the mushrooms she'd collected, which put an end to any talk of magical compendiums and untranslated spells.

Sera sent Theo, who had obviously been running on little but adrenaline for the last twelve hours, off to bed, and promptly relieved Matilda of every poisonous mushroom in her basket. (This wasn't for Matilda's sake, because Matilda knew which ones were deadly and knew better than to go about eating wild things willy-nilly. Nicholas, on the other hand, had the courage of a lion, the lovability of a puppy, and the common sense of a goldfish.)

By the time Sera had dispensed with the mushrooms, run a hoover around all the rooms, collected fresh basil and rosemary from the garden, recast her heat charms, and almost tripped over the undead rooster eighteen different times, she was exhausted.

Exhausted, but more hopeful than she'd been in a long time.

It was just after four o'clock and the inn was quiet at last. Theo was still asleep, Jasmine and Matilda typically retired for a nap in the afternoons, Nicholas wouldn't get home from work before six, and they had no other guests with them at the moment. The big kitchen captured the last of the day's golden light, and with a fresh pat of homemade butter sitting in the fridge and a loaf of bread baking in the oven, Sera curled up in an old and immensely comfortable armchair in the corner of the room and watched the sun tilt over the hill.

"So?" she said into the silence, toying with the thin gold chain of her swan necklace. "What's the rest of the story?"

Clemmie's red ears poked around the edge of the open back door, followed shortly by the rest of her. She padded into the kitchen, tail swishing. "I see your feathers are still ruffled."

"You can't possibly be surprised I'm still angry."

"Why? We got what we wanted."

"We got lucky. *Theo* got lucky." Even as she said it, she knew there was no point. Clemmie was incapable of hearing anything that might inconvenience her. She was not outright villainous (that would require a certain level of competence, and Clemmie had, after all, cursed *herself*), but she certainly seemed to *aspire* to villainy and, therefore, thought of little but herself.

"Well, be that as it may, Theo and I already told you everything," Clemmie insisted.

"Nice try, but you left something out, something I'm guessing Theo doesn't know either. I know what the restricted archives are like, remember? You can't just stroll in, and as Theo doesn't know the right unlocking spell and you can't use your magic, I'm at a loss as to how, exactly, you got in."

"I hate it when you do that," Clemmie complained.

"Do what?"

"Work things out," said Clemmie sulkily. "If you must know, everything went perfectly until, as you suspected, Theo couldn't unlock the door. We stood there for fifteen minutes, getting ourselves worked up into a right tizzy and probably arguing louder than we should have been, and then, all of a sudden, the door just *opened*."

"Oh, it did, did it? Just like that?"

"Obviously not," Clemmie retorted in annoyance. "Someone must have been working late in the library, overheard us, and decided to unlock the door for us. Knowing we'd been spotted would have just frightened Theo, though, so I told him *his* spell must have worked."

Sera stared at her. "To be clear, you're saying an unknown individual decided for equally unknown reasons to help a child and a talking fox get into the restricted archives of the Guild's library?"

"Exactly!"

Acutely pained, Sera said, "And that strikes you as a normal thing to do? It didn't cross your mind that this unknown individual might actually have been setting a trap to catch you in the act of stealing from the Guild?"

"So what if they were? We got the book, didn't we? *And* Chancellor Grey let us get away with borrowing it. Happy days! Now I, for one, would like to talk about what we're going to do about that spell."

Sera gave up. "Fine. Do *you* know the language it's written in?"

Clemmie made a grumbly, growly noise in her throat. "No. We'll have to get someone else to translate it for us."

"There *isn't* anybody, Clemmie! We're exiles! Who would *you* trust not to run straight to Albert?"

"An irksome but fair point," Clemmie acknowledged grudgingly. "Then the only other option is to speedily acquire books about this dratted language and translate the spell ourselves."

"You want *us* to learn an obscure spellcasting dialect? Without help, supervision, or timely intervention if and when we make a mistake?"

"You don't sound very open to this," Clemmie observed.

"I am not," Sera assured her.

"And I suppose you think it's silly and irresponsible to cast a spell that may or may not have been translated properly."

"You suppose correctly."

Clemmie plonked herself on her tail and crossed her front

paws over her chest, which made her look like a petulant and unusually furry toddler. "Then I'm not budging from this spot until you come up with a better idea."

This dire reality, thankfully, did not last long. Moments later, Matilda trotted into the room, oblivious to the bushy tail whisking itself out of sight above the kitchen cabinets, and peered at Sera with interest. "Are you talking to yourself again, dear heart?"

"Usually," said Sera.

"Such a good habit," Matilda said approvingly.

Jasmine joined them as dusk turned to deep dark, whereupon she noticed the fox but somehow failed to notice the gooey, adoring way that Matilda looked at her, and then Nicholas clanked in without noticing anything at all. By the time a rumpled, yawning Theo came downstairs for dinner, completing the household, the concept of peace and quiet was but a fond memory.

That said, maybe there was something to be said for mayhem. With Matilda chopping carrots and singing a sea shanty, Jasmine dancing to said sea shanty, and Nicholas and Theo engaged in a noisy, vigorous duel with wooden sticks one careless elbow away from the lamb stew reheating on the hob, there simply wasn't room for Sera to think about the restoration spell, the vote that could have changed the entire course of her life, and the fifteen years Albert had taken from her.

Halfway through the fourth sea shanty, Jasmine limped up to Sera's spot by the stew and said, in an undertone, "You don't happen to know where Roo-Roo is, do you?"

Sera did a double take at Jasmine's empty arms. She was so used to seeing Roo-Roo there that she hadn't even noticed he wasn't.

She cut a look out of the window, down the length of the dark, starlit back garden, and saw the very thing she'd hoped she wouldn't see: the white gate, open, swinging gaily in the breeze.

"Take over the stew, would you?" Sera said, and exited the kitchen with all haste.

She wasn't far from the gate, having almost broken her neck tripping over uneven knots in the ground in the dark, when the beams of headlights flashed past the hedge and she heard the unmistakable sound of a car screeching to a halt.

Sera rushed through the gate, where she found a skeletal chicken in the middle of the lane, a car about ten feet away from the aforementioned chicken with its headlights pointed straight at it, and a man standing beside the driver's door.

She ran into the lane, snatched Roo-Roo up, and swiftly sidestepped the beams of the headlights. Trying (and failing) to think of an explanation while also trying (and failing) to stuff a jumble of animated bones into her armpit and out of sight, she was about to give up and flee without a word when the driver of the car did the most peculiar thing.

He sighed.

"Of course it's you," said the stranger, and far be it from Sera to quibble at a time like this, but she couldn't help noticing he didn't sound especially pleased. "Hello, Sera."

CHAPTER SIX

*A*bout seven hours earlier, in the Guild's towering castle in Northumberland, Luke Larsen, highly respected scholar of magical history and considerably less respected caretaker of one very determined witch, had been having a fiasco of a day. Week. Month, even.

Over the last few weeks, between endless battles over funding, tortuous bureaucracy, and far too little of the work he actually liked, Luke had had to, in short: retrieve his sister from the roof of the Guild's greenhouse, track her down in the gigantic hedge maze, rescue the three *other* children she'd stranded halfway up a wall of ivy after inadvertently including them in her levitation spell, and explain to his employer that the reason her ornamental ginkgo tree was bare was because Posy had appropriated its leaves.

And those, it had to be said, were just the highlights.

While it was tempting to lay the blame at Posy's door for her obsession with leaves, or even at Mother Nature's for having the temerity to *invent* leaves, Luke was only too aware that *he* was the one who had brought his small, impulsive, autistic sister to stay at the Guild's estate, a place of rules, decorum, and one too many disapproving gargoyles roaming its hallowed halls.

Which brought Luke to today, and the entirely unwelcome presence of one of the gargoyles in question.

"This," said Bradford Bertram-Mogg, materialising beside Luke with the air of a horseman of the apocalypse and scowling up at Posy, who was nimbly pirouetting on the very edge of a balcony in her quest to reach a particular leaf on a vine, "is what comes of allowing foreigners into the Guild."

"Not that it should make any difference, but we're Scottish," Luke said coldly.

"Exactly," said Bertram-Mogg.

Of the Guild's predominantly ancient and intolerable ruling Cabinet, Bradford Bertram-Mogg was by far the most ancient and very nearly the most intolerable, an anachronistic and malevolent old man who looked like he had one foot in the grave already.

Luke, for one, couldn't wait for the rest of him to catch up.

"Posy, get down here," Luke said for the third time, trying to ignore the harbinger of doom beside him.

She replied with a definitive shake of her head.

"*Yes*," Luke insisted.

Another, crosser shake of the head. She even stamped one foot to make doubly sure he'd noticed her displeasure.

Luke wasn't actually afraid she'd tumble off the balcony because Posy, at just nine years old, had the agility of an Olympic gymnast, the evasive talents of Houdini, and, if all else failed, a brother whose magic could keep her from falling. *This* time. But what about next time? He wasn't with her every second of every day. He needed her to understand that heights and small children, even small witch children, were not a happy combination.

Of course, therein lay the rub. Posy didn't, or *couldn't*, understand. She could figure out the best way in and out of a hedge maze in seconds, but she could not fathom the concept of an obstacle like personal safety. For her, it was a simple matter of "there is a thing I want, so I will go get that thing," and it was incomprehensible to her that there might be a reason not to.

This, however, was incomprehensible to other people. No matter how many times Luke explained that Posy wasn't *trying* to be difficult or defiant, nobody else seemed to see it that way. Not even their own parents, whose oft-used argument was "but you had some peculiar habits as a young child too, and *you* grew out of them."

"Stop calling them peculiar habits," Luke would reply. "She's autistic."

"You coddle her."

And repeat.

"What do you intend to do about this?" Bertram-Mogg inquired now, waving a hand in Posy's direction. "And I am not referring to this precise situation, young man, but rather to the veritable cornucopia of discord that awaits us if we continue down this brambly path."

As the Scottish son of an English father and a Danish mother, both of whom were professors of classical studies at Edinburgh University, Luke had been fluent in six languages before he was a teenager. Insufferable Toff, alas, was not one of them.

"If you have something to say, just say it. In small words, ideally, seeing as I come from a strange, foreign land a whole fifty miles away."

The old gargoyle harrumphed. "The crux of the matter is that that child has no idea how to behave! How old is she? Eight? Nine? Does she even know how to read?"

"I don't know. Nobody does. She hasn't done anything to suggest she can, but I'm not going to assume—"

"She just put a *leaf* in her mouth!"

"She has sensory—"

"In my day, we knew how to deal with things like that," Bertram-Mogg informed him.

Luke's temper kicked at the iron battlements that kept it tightly confined, but as ever, the battlements won. Posy might wear her heart on her sleeve, but Luke did not, so his voice remained cold and expressionless. "Then it's just as well your day is over."

"Well, I never—!"

Luke ignored him. "*Now*, Posy."

Recognising that that particular tone meant she had lost the battle, Posy jumped off the balcony, blithely confident he would find a way to catch her. (He did, but that wasn't the point.) There was a collection of leaves clutched in one of her fists, and she tucked her free hand into his and said, "Car."

"No. We're not leaving yet."

"*Car*," Posy repeated.

"Not yet. Sorry."

Rounding the side of the tower, they entered a round, cobbled courtyard with a stone fountain in the middle. There were a handful of visitors' cars parked in the courtyard, and the fountain, which was dry as bone, was topped with an old, cracked stone statue of three witches: Meg of Meldon, Michael Scot, and Mother Shipton.

The castle towered over the courtyard, complete with flying buttresses, mullioned windows, and spires. Luke strode up the front steps, Posy in tow. Inside, people were crisscrossing the huge entrance hall, ascending flights of stairs or passing through the tall archway ahead on their way somewhere else. As always, all conversation was pitched politely, decorously low. ("Like a museum," Bradford Bertram-Mogg had once said, to which Luke's employer, Professor Walter, had replied, "Yes, specifically those museums where they store the corpses of the deceased. I believe they're called tombs.")

Luke had been eighteen years old the first time he'd come here, and all things considered, thank fucking Christ he'd been as old as that. As a child with absolutely no magical history in the family and an unremarkable amount of magical power, he wouldn't have stood a chance.

Levitating in one's sleep was almost always the way a witch's magic first manifested itself. Luke had been just shy of his seventh birthday when the startled cries of his parents had woken him from what he'd thought was a perfectly normal night's sleep. He'd crashed into his bed, realising only then that he must have been *above* it in order to crash *into* it, and all three of them had stared at each other in disbelief.

When it had happened a second time, and then a third, Luke's parents had taken him to the family GP. Hushed conversations, psychiatric referrals, and home visits from two nurses had led to a final, decidedly clandestine visit from a woman who had introduced herself as a witch from the British Guild of Sorcery. Later, Luke had learned that there were people working in the NHS, schools, and government whose job was to spot these signs in children, notify the Guild, and smooth things over with everyone who was not in the know.

The Guild witch had been polite but aloof, as if she wasn't thrilled about having to be there, and everything she'd said had seemed to actively discourage Luke from inflicting his unpedigreed presence on the precious darlings already taking lessons at the estate. Upon discovering that an alternative to going to the Guild's grand estate in Northumberland was studying magic on his own time at home, with access to as many books as he needed from the Guild's library, and the only requirements of him being that he had to keep secrets, send in progress letters once a month, and never use his power in public, Luke had immediately said, "Yes, that. That's what I want to do."

He'd never expected to grow up and spend so much time within these walls, but navigating the Guild as an adult was far less intimidating than doing it as a child, and he wouldn't have brought Posy here if he'd been able to think of literally anywhere better.

Five minutes and two spiral staircases later, Luke and Posy crossed the third storey of the library to the nook Professor Walter had claimed as her own, where the lady herself stood beside a table strewn with old maps, documents, and books, gazing into the distance with a furrowed brow.

"There you are, old chap!" a voice boomed from the other side of the nook. "Good God, you look absolutely knackered! It's just as well I popped by with a nice pot of tea!"

Howard Hawtrey, Cabinet Minister and scion of an old magical family. He was in his early forties, rotund, and always inexplicably jolly, like a very posh Santa. Against all odds, he was one of very few people in the upper echelons of the Guild that Luke actually liked.

Luke settled Posy in an armchair with her tablet, her fluffy headphones, and a biscuit off Howard's tray. Howard poured tea into three cups and said, "You take yours black, don't you?"

"As my heart," said Luke.

Howard slapped his knee and laughed way more than the joke deserved. "I was just asking Professor Walter if she's planning to attend Bradford Bertram-Mogg's winter masquerade this year."

"There's no easy way to break this to you, Howard, but she would sooner die. She would welcome death with open arms if the alternative was to go to Bradford Bertram-Mogg's winter masquerade."

"That seems a tad pigheaded," Howard pointed out, not unreasonably. "It can't possibly be true, can it, Professor?"

"Why doesn't he ever stop talking?" Professor Walter asked Luke in a beleaguered tone of voice.

"Tea?" Howard said at once, delighted to have her attention at last.

"Only if it's been steeped in the thrice-blessed waters of Elysium."

"What she meant to say was yes, and thank you," Luke said to Howard. Over the last sixteen years, he had ascended from a rare, coveted spot as one of Professor Walter's apprentices to very nearly her scholarly equal and was, therefore, the only person alive who dared remind her of pedestrian concerns like manners.

Verity Walter was a brilliant historian, an exacting instructor, and, in her own words, a walking, talking funhouse mirror the Guild didn't particularly enjoy catching a glimpse of themselves in. She was fiftyish, had short grey hair and a deep voice, only ever wore tweed and riding boots in spite of having never been within ten feet of a horse, chomped on the end of a pipe that she never actually smoked, enunciated her syllables with more cutting precision than any monarch of England, and was so committed to the act that even Luke had never seen her out of character (though every now and then, he thought he heard a bit of Suffolk creep back into her voice when she spoke to her sister on the phone). Her family had just enough magic in it to be considered reputable but not so much that they were considered important, which meant the respect (and terror) she inspired in everybody who knew her had very little to do with pedigree and a whole lot more to do with her talent, work ethic, and disinclination to accept any nonsense.

"Isn't Posy supposed to be in school when you're working?" she asked now, observing that there was a child curled up in one of the armchairs with enormous fluffy headphones over her ears. "Is this why you look like you haven't slept since the heyday of the Ottoman Empire?"

"You have such a marvellous way of putting things," Howard swooned.

Verity ignored him. "By the way, if you saw a fox in the library on your way out last night, you didn't."

"I didn't," Luke agreed.

"Very good, Luke. That's very convincing."

"No, I really didn't. Should I have?"

"No," said Verity at once.

Luke looked at Howard, who was contentedly sipping his tea. "Really? You have no questions at all?"

"Too exhausting, old bean," said Howard cheerfully.

"While we're sharing things," said Luke, turning back to his redoubtable employer, "I hope you aren't counting on Bradford Bertram-Mogg's vote for any funding at the moment, because I'm pretty sure I poked the old gargoyle in the eye."

"In a literal sense?" Verity asked, looking happier than Luke had ever seen her.

"No," said Luke.

"I suppose this means *you're* not coming to the winter masquerade either," said Howard gloomily. "And don't say you were never planning to in the first place."

"I was never planning to."

"Damn it, Luke! I just said don't say it!"

"Even if I *had* been about to apply for additional funding, I would never have counted on that walking cadaver's vote," Verity reminded Luke. "He doesn't so much as scratch his nose without Albert Grey's permission, and we all know how *he* feels about me. He didn't even want me to have you! I had to get a private grant to pay your wage!"

"Well, you're always saying you don't want us to be beholden to them." Luke shrugged.

But Verity was on a roll. Having polished her tea off in a single, efficient gulp, she seized her pipe and clamped it between her teeth. "The Guild has never been perfect, but Albert Grey has all but ruined it. The sooner we can throw him and that entire spineless Cabinet in the bin, the better."

"*I'm* in that Cabinet," Howard protested.

Verity gave him a puzzled look, like she either had no idea who he was or had no idea why it ought to matter whether or not she threw him in the bin. As most of her interactions with

Howard involved the words "my friends call me Verity. You may call me Professor Walter," Luke thought it was probably both.

"I have yet to decide how I feel about the new Chancellor," Verity went on. "The ghastly, nepotistic antiques surrounding her, however, are another matter."

"Nepotistic!" Howard cried, apparently deciding *that* was the descriptor he objected to most. "The Cabinet is democratically elected!"

"Does he actually believe that?" Verity asked Luke, but didn't wait for an answer before moving on. "So if you didn't actually take out his eye, what *did* you do to Bertram-Mogg?"

"I told him it's a good thing his day is over."

"Is that all? I say far worse things to him at least twice a week."

"*How* did you say it?" Howard wanted to know. "Did you, er, raise your voice?"

"Of course not. I was completely, unshakeably calm."

"Ah," said Howard, wincing.

"I see," said Verity.

Luke sighed. "What?"

"Er," Howard floundered, flustered. "The thing is, um, well, sometimes what you think is you being calm can sometimes, er, come across as, er . . ."

"Arctic," said Verity succinctly. "*Ant*arctic, even."

"I wouldn't go that far," Howard objected loyally, but Luke only shrugged, unbothered.

Verity gave her pipe an emphatic chomp. "It's a compliment. You know how I feel about drama." She glanced down at a translation she'd been working on, scratched out a word and scribbled something else, and looked back up. "You still haven't told me why Posy's not with one of the governesses. And yes, if you're curious, I am indeed cringing at the fact that I have just had to unironically use the word *governesses*."

"She absconded again," Luke said. "I'm not even sure I blame her because, as we've established, *governesses*. I think it's time I took her home."

"Whose home?" Howard asked.

"Hers, obviously."

"Your parents' house? At the university?"

"My flat is the size of a shoebox, so yes, our parents' house."

"You brought her here because she *couldn't* stay there, old chap," Howard reminded him somewhat unnecessarily. "You said she'd started using her magic in front of other people because she doesn't understand she has to hide it."

"And I hoped this would be the one place that wouldn't matter," Luke agreed, looking over to make sure Posy still had her headphones on. (She did, and seemed to be absorbed in a game involving tucking farm animals into bed.) "As the last month has proven, though, all I've done is swap one set of rules Posy can't follow for another."

Apparently at a loss, Howard resorted to appealing to Verity. "Don't you think Luke ought to stay?"

Verity had once again been gazing into the distance with a furrowed brow, but she turned abruptly back to them and said, "No, I don't. He should go."

"Well, fuck you too," said Luke mildly.

This was too much for poor Howard, who let out a piteous, scandalised whimper.

Verity chuckled. "Much as I like having you at my beck and

call seven days a week, may I refer you back to the part about you looking like you haven't slept since the siege of Carthage?"

"I thought you said it was the Ottoman . . ." Quailing at the look she gave him, Howard wisely abandoned the rest of his sentence.

"Setting aside my opinion that you are Posy's *brother*, her well-being is not your responsibility, and your parents are a disgrace," Verity said to Luke, pulling, as ever, not one single punch, "I think the best course of action is a break."

"A break," Luke echoed.

"Yes. Take your sister to a quiet spot by the sea and do nothing for a few days."

With absolutely perfect timing, Posy took off her headphones, put her tablet down, and came over to squeeze herself into the tiny gap between Luke's arm and his torso. It was her usual way of letting him know she just wanted a warm, quiet moment, but this time, she also pointed at the nearest window and said, again, "Car."

"I rest my case," Verity said with great satisfaction.

"And I suppose you have an opinion on where we ought to go too."

"Er," said Verity. "Er, yes. I do. You should go to my weekend cottage in, er, Lytham St. Annes."

Luke gave her a long, sharp look. "You hate people who have weekend cottages."

"I've never said that."

"You absolutely have," said a very bewildered Howard. "It was just last month that you told Eustace Cholmondeley that anyone who acquires more property than they need to live in is a twa—"

"Good God, you're a nuisance," Verity snapped. She stomped to her computer, seized the mouse, and clicked aggressively until she reached the page she was looking for. She turned the screen around to face Luke and jabbed a finger at it. "There. A cottage by the sea. Go forth."

"Verity, there isn't a universe in which I believe that's your cottage."

"Fine, it's my cousin's," she said in great irritation. "Just go, would you?"

Howard examined the little red pin on the map. "Isn't that in Lancashire? Is there something else in Lancashire? Why does Lancashire ring a bell?"

"Get out of my library," said Verity.

"It's not your—"

"OUT!"

CHAPTER SEVEN

*T*he thing a great many witches never understood about magic was its heart. It grew in the bones of witches, just as it had once grown in long-lost creatures like wyverns and six-tusked elephants, but what so many of those witches did not realise was that what it wanted was to be loved. It could be tender in one witch's hands and violent in another's, it could be vast or it could be small, it could be a night sky or teeth or lightning, but the one thing that never changed was that what it sought and what it repaid, above all else, was love.

There had been a young girl, once, who had loved magic with every bit of *her* heart, and so, when she had needed it, magic had repaid her with a spell. A spell that had transformed an inn into a flame in the dark, an outstretched hand to the ones falling over the edge and a warning to the ones pushing them.

No one could make sense of the spell. It wasn't how spells were supposed to work.

And yet.

Albert Grey had spent years trying to understand Sera's spell, or, rather, seething at its existence and trying to conjure something just as vast and unending for himself. He had never been able to because Albert Grey ruled with a boot on the neck of anything and anyone he was ruling, including his own formidable magic, and what he had never realised was that his magic, recognising that it was not and had never been loved by the man who wielded it, had simply decided not to play along. It did as it was told because it did, after all, have a boot on its neck, but it did not do one bit more.

Meanwhile, across the country, a certain innkeeper was about to discover that when you hold tight to the little magic you find, when years go by and the world loses much of its colour and still you refuse to forget the magic, magic will go out of its way to show you that it remembers you too.

When Luke got in his car, with Posy buckled into her booster seat in the back, and drove into the wild, hilly wilderness of Northumberland, he had the address of Verity's cousin's cottage in the car's satnav and the most efficient route plotted out ahead of him. ("You will arrive at your destination in three hours and six minutes," said the satnav helpfully.)

The drive went just about how he'd expected it to, complete with two bathroom breaks and a stop for Chinese takeaway. In hindsight, given the way things had gone over the last few weeks, such a suspiciously smooth journey ought to have been a dead giveaway that everything was about to go tits up.

When they pulled up outside the cottage, all of the lights were on. That was Luke's first sign that all was not as it should be.

The second sign was the literal sign outside the cottage that proudly announced that there was a dentist's office within.

The final nail in the coffin was the dentist's receptionist, who assured him that yes, he did have the right address, but also yes, this was indeed a dentist's office, and no, she was not aware of any Verity Walter or any of said Verity Walter's family members.

Naturally, Luke called Verity, who didn't answer.

"I'm getting the impression she lied through her teeth," Luke said to Posy. "What I haven't yet worked out, though, is why."

As she had more pressing matters at hand, specifically watching a YouTube video of someone going up and down a set of escalators in Sweden, Posy paid him no attention.

With no alternative but to accept the inevitable, Luke shook off his exhaustion, got back in the car, and started driving again. He hadn't yet decided whether to go back to the Guild or back to his parents' house in Edinburgh, but as both were in the same general direction, he drove back along the route he'd used to get here and hoped he'd find the choice easier in a couple of hours.

Then, about ten minutes into this second trip, somewhere near a hamlet called Bay Horse, something very odd happened.

First, the satnav switched itself off and simply wouldn't come back on. Moments later, when Luke felt around for his phone, it was unexpectedly and inconveniently out of reach in the passenger footwell.

"I guess we're navigating the old-fashioned way, Posy."

Signposts, however, weren't easy to come by. It was only just after five o'clock, but the clocks had just changed, and the nights had started sweeping in early, especially once you left behind the streetlights and lit windows of cities. The rural roads were black as pitch. Luke aimed north, or tried to, but found that every time he reached a crossroads or came to a fork in a winding lane, there was always one particular direction that beckoned, that simply felt *right*.

Into a valley, around a bend, up a twisting lane, and then—

The headlights caught the movement of something small and white up ahead. Since he expected to see a cat or rabbit (or, indeed, literally any other *normal* small animal), it took Luke a few extra seconds to clock that the creature standing in the middle of the road and inquisitively watching his car approach was, impossibly, *bones*.

"What the—"

Luke hit the brakes, and the car squealed to a halt very, very close to the bone creature. It gave a single, excited flap of its skeletal arms.

No, not arms. Wings.

Wait. Bones. Lancashire. Weird technical glitches. The way he'd driven this way just *because*. If he added all that to Verity's inexplicable behaviour . . .

"Posy, stay put," Luke said, unclipping his seat belt without taking his eyes off the bizarre bone creature.

"Stay put," Posy agreed.

He'd barely taken a step away from the car when the sound of footsteps thudded from somewhere beyond the low stone wall nearby. A woman burst through a gap in the wall, ran right into the beams of his headlights, and scooped the bone bird into her arms.

In the few seconds before she dodged out of the beams of the lights again, Luke saw a jumble of pieces that didn't quite resolve themselves into a whole. An oversized, burnt-orange jumper falling off one shoulder. Bronze skin. Long, dark waves of hair haloed in gold by light coming from somewhere behind her. Black leggings and boots. Ragged, bitten fingernails on the hands clutching the bundle of bones to her chest. Wide brown eyes that reminded him of a deer on the verge of bolting.

Then the disjointed pieces snapped into place and Luke arrived at the unwelcome realisation that the face he was looking into, while older than he remembered it, was unmistakable.

"Of course it's you," he said, resigned. "Hello, Sera."

CHAPTER EIGHT

*E*r, pardon? Sera was instantly suspicious. Nothing good could possibly come of anybody who not only knew her name but also, apparently, saw fit to react to undead farmyard animals with a *sigh*.

"Jesus, you really *did* reanimate a dead chicken," said the unknown man, managing to sound fascinated and disapproving all at once.

Fear clutched Sera by the throat. This wasn't someone she'd once met at the pub or talked to on a train. He knew about magic. He knew what she'd done fifteen years ago.

Swallowing, she drew herself up to her full height and instantly transformed into the prickliest version of herself. "How do you know about that?"

"Who *doesn't* know about that? I know it's been a decade or so, but you can't really have forgotten that everyone once knew everything about you."

"So you're from the Guild, then." Sera bit the words out. "Albert couldn't be bothered to come himself?"

"Albert?" His eyebrows twitched together. "Albert Grey?"

"Didn't he send you?"

"As I try to have as little to do with the Great and Powerful Wizard as possible," the stranger replied in a clipped, icy voice, apparently unimpressed with both her tone and her question, "I can't imagine why he'd send me anywhere."

"The Wizard?" Sera was momentarily distracted. ". . . of Oz?"

"Who else?"

Sera collapsed into helpless laughter.

The stranger stared at her for a bemused moment before turning away to check on something in the car. "I'm still here," Sera heard him say, at which point she realised that between the darkness and the whole Roo-Roo debacle, she hadn't noticed that there was a young girl in the back of the car.

From the little Sera could see of her through the glass of the closed window, the girl seemed to be contentedly watching a tablet, one hand twirling a lock of her blond hair while the other held what looked like an assortment of leaves.

"So Albert *didn't* send you?" Sera was beginning to feel like the emotional hullabaloo of the day had taken a greater toll on her than she'd thought and she had, perhaps, overreacted a smidge. "You're not here because of him?"

"I'm an academic, not an errand boy."

"You could be both."

The man gave her a look.

"Oh, quit looking so fed up," Sera said. "You'd want to be absolutely sure, too, if you were me."

He sighed again. "What have you done this time?"

Sera was by no means planning to tell this stranger anything, no matter what he'd said about wanting as little to do with

Albert as possible, but even if she *had* been so inclined, she was otherwise preoccupied with an unexpected and overwhelming sense of déjà vu.

It was that sigh, and the Scottish-ish accent, and those exact words said in that exact tone of resignation—

Reluctantly, she pulled on that thread. Visiting her past wasn't exactly a pleasant stroll down memory lane. It was a lane of teeth, crooked and sharp, and the pleasant stroll was more of a panicked scramble to find what she needed without slicing herself open on the sharpest edges. It was inevitable, then, that some things, normal things, things that were perfectly *fine*, were overlooked, and it was there, between the sound of Albert's impatient voice and the smell of spellbooks, that Sera found him.

Luke Larsen.

She must have said it out loud because he looked surprised. "You remember my name."

Before Sera could reply, the bright, slightly translucent figure of a teenage girl ran past her, skidded to a halt at a desk that materialised out of thin air, ducked past the legs of the slightly translucent boy standing beside the desk, and concealed herself under the desk.

The boy, who'd had his head bent over a hefty book in his hands, snapped the book shut and sighed. "What have you done this time?"

"*Someone* drank half a bottle of Chancellor Bennet's favourite brandy," the girl whispered, smothering a giggle. "Well, *two* someones, really, but only one of those someones confessed."

As abruptly as they'd appeared, the girl, boy, and desk faded away. Sera scowled at the spot where they'd been.

"What was that?" Luke demanded.

Sera scowled some more. "The house does that sometimes. It's a side effect of my old magic. It throws up echoes. Memories. Ghosts. Whatever you want to call them."

He looked past her at the crooked, starlit inn, reassessing it. She searched his face for the young, quiet apprentice she'd just seen and was somewhat annoyed to discover that Luke in his thirties was even nicer to look at than his younger self. And, considering the exact words she'd used to describe him to Francesca at the time were "gah, he's *so* hot," that was saying something.

He'd grown into himself. He was less lanky than he'd been, his shoulders broader than she remembered and his forearms lightly muscled. His jaw, which had once had the softness of youth, had settled into sharp lines. His blond hair was shorter, too, and a lot less boyish, ruthlessly pushed back from his brow.

His eyes, on the other hand, were just as she remembered: glacier blue and maddeningly difficult to read.

"Do you still work at the castle?" Sera asked.

"When I'm not working from home." He was still studying the inn. "Eighty percent of my job is reading old books and documents, so it goes a lot faster when the entirety of the Guild's library is right around me. On the other hand, there are fewer distractions at home." He shrugged. "The professor I work for isn't fussy about where I am as long as the job gets done."

Sera couldn't quite resist fifteen years of curiosity. "What's the castle like these days?"

Luke seemed to think he'd already said more than he'd planned to because his jaw tightened and he ignored the question. He nodded in the direction of the house instead. "I didn't know you still lived here. It used to be an inn, didn't it? Your great-aunt used to run it? The one you—"

"Brought back to life with a forbidden spell that cost me pretty much all my magic? Yep, that's the one. It's still an inn. We both run it now." Rearranging Roo-Roo in her arms, she gave him a wary look. "Why were you surprised that I remembered your name? I know you were a few years older and we weren't exactly friends or anything, but we both spent so much time in the library that—"

He gave her a politely puzzled look. "We weren't exactly friends, as you put it, because I was working, you were doing whatever the Wizard of Oz wanted on that particular day, and it was generally understood that you were too important to be bothered by anyone whose name wasn't Grey."

"I would never have said that!"

"You didn't have to." Luke shrugged like he didn't care either way. "Besides, you were gone about six months after I started working in the library. I only remember you because you were *you*."

It didn't sound like a compliment. "Because I was me," she echoed. "Right. Of course."

She wasn't sure why she'd expected anything else. *She* might remember Luke as the apprentice she'd had a big schoolgirl crush on, the one she'd looked for excuses to talk to, but all *Luke* remembered was the mythology the Guild had spun around her from the moment she'd crossed their threshold.

Pulling herself together, she said, "If the Guild didn't send you, what are you doing here?"

The silence lasted only an instant, but it was unbearably loud.

Oh. *Oh.* She'd been so prepared for the worst that she hadn't even considered the most obvious answer. "The spell brought you here."

"I always thought the stories were exaggerated." He shook his head. "I couldn't believe any spell could call to somebody, beckon them from miles away, but yours did."

She softened just the tiniest bit. "Well, you're in luck. We have exactly two empty rooms."

He shoved his hands into the pockets of his jeans. "It's fine. It's not that long a drive back to Edinburgh." He looked over his shoulder at the girl in the car and reconsidered. "I'll find a hotel."

"Good idea," said Sera agreeably. "If only there was something of a hotel-esque persuasion close by."

"I don't need—"

"Maybe the spell didn't bring you here because you need something," she replied. "Maybe it brought you here because *she* does."

A muscle twitched in his jaw. They both looked at the child in the car, who now had her head propped against the window like she was getting tired.

Sera shifted the undead rooster to her shoulder, freeing her hands, and decided to proceed like the matter was settled. (As far as she was concerned, it was.)

"We're doing dinner at the moment," she said, nodding back at the house. "There's plenty, but if you're not up for some extremely eccentric company right now, I'll bring something upstairs for you. There *are* two rooms going, but one of them has twin beds if you'd rather stay with your daughter."

"She's my sister. Posy." He hesitated. "She's like us."

"Magical?"

He nodded.

Sera had a lot of questions, but now wasn't the time to ask them. "If you follow the lane a bit farther uphill, you'll see the front of the inn. I'll meet you there."

"Wait." The muscle in his jaw twitched again. "You should know Posy doesn't understand she has to hide her magic. She could give all of us away."

"How old is she?"

"Nine. And no, before you ask, I can't just *tell* her to hide her magic or *tell* her it's really, really not safe if other people find out what we can do. I have told her. Every witch she's ever met has told her. I don't really know how to explain it except to say she knows it, but she doesn't *get* it."

He sounded tired, like it wasn't the first, second, or even hundredth time he'd had to explain his sister. *Justify* her. Sera's wrath kindled and she was suddenly, utterly furious for both of them. "Just to be clear," she said gently, "I don't care. And I mean that in the kindest possible way. If Posy gives us away, well, we'll cross that bridge if we ever get to it."

"That's it?"

"That's it."

But Luke wasn't done. "I don't think you understand. It's a when, not an if. We *will* have to cross that bridge."

Sera was cold and cranky and had a very bony pair of wings squashed against her neck, but she took a second to look at him, *really* look at him, and where she'd expected to find fear or anxiety or even anger, she found only resignation.

"You're expecting me to come to the conclusion that this is too much trouble," she realised out loud.

"That's usually how it goes, yes," Luke said icily.

"Not here it doesn't," said Sera. "This spell I cast? I cast it to keep us safe. It's never been wrong about anybody, not once. Believe me, I've had my doubts about Clemmie, yet here she remains."

"Who?"

"The *point*," Sera pressed, "is that if my spell invited you in, you get to stay. See you round the front."

She promptly walked away to avoid any further back-and-forth (and any encroaching frostbite), leaving the choice up to him.

She genuinely had no idea which way he'd go. It wasn't often that someone at their doorstep turned away again, but on the other hand, it also wasn't often that that someone at their doorstep already knew her. If she absolutely *had* to bet on it, she'd have bet that Luke would leave.

And yet, when she reached the front of the inn, there he was.

Luke switched the engine off, got out of the car again, and said, like *he* was doing *her* a favour, "Just for tonight."

Sera gave him a look that would have annihilated an individual made of weaker stuff. "I'm sure I'll cry myself to sleep as soon as you're gone."

His mouth twitched in a brief, speedily suppressed smile. "Are you always like this?"

"Like what?"

"Tetchy."

"Yes," said Sera succinctly.

"You never used to be."

Well, it was *high* time this conversation came to an end. "I'm a lot of things I never used to be. Are you planning to leave your sister in the car all night?"

He gave her a long, thoughtful look before turning away to unlock the back door. Posy hopped nimbly out of her booster seat and regarded the house with curiosity. Sera couldn't help noticing she'd left the tablet behind but kept hold of the leaves.

"We're staying here tonight," Luke explained to her. "It's an inn." This seemed to mean nothing to Posy, so he added, "This is Sera's house."

"Sera's house," Posy echoed cheerfully.

"And this is Sera," Luke went on.

Sera smiled. "Hello, Posy."

Posy smiled back, took Luke's hand, and then, still refusing to relinquish the leaves in her other hand, used a finger from the hand holding his to point decisively at the front door of the house.

"You don't waste any time, I see," Sera said appreciatively. "Come on in, Posy. Are you hungry?"

"Chockit cake?" Posy asked.

"Chocolate cake," Luke translated automatically, then shook his head. "That was pretty obvious, wasn't it? Sorry. Habit. She doesn't speak much, so sometimes it's hard to work out what she's saying if you don't know her. She's autistic. She doesn't seem to have any problem understanding what you say to her, though, and she finds her own ways to make herself understood."

"You really don't have to explain," Sera assured him. "And yes, there's always cake."

Posy beamed at her.

Luke examined the old, rustic wooden sign creaking over the front door. "Batty Hole?"

"Yes, it's ridiculous." Sera sighed. "And also, as you'll soon discover for yourself, it really couldn't be more apt."

As soon as she opened the front door, the sounds of clinking tableware and overlapping, animated voices drifted to them from the kitchen, but thankfully, none of those sounds involved the giveaway creak of the floorboards in the hallway. Sera was very, very certain that the last thing Luke and Posy needed right now was an encounter with an overly earnest (and overly armed) knight.

The house's entryway was an open, comforting space covered in rugs and cluttered with shoes of many sizes. A tall, crooked table, made out of lovely knotty wood and painted with flowers, stood beside the shoes, and Posy, observing the proximity of the shoes to the empty shelves built under the painted tabletop, put the shoes away at once.

"Oh, you don't have to do that," Sera said, but Posy, humming contentedly to herself, kept going.

"She likes things to be in their proper places," Luke said in a voice that suggested he was very much in sympathy with his sister on that score. "She doesn't, admittedly, always *agree* with other people's opinions on what the proper places for things are . . ."

"This time, she's absolutely right," said Sera, watching Posy take her own shoes off and put them away as well. "Thank you, Posy. If only Theo and Matilda were even *half* as inclined to put things where they belong."

On the wall opposite the front door were shelves crammed

with books, places for everybody's post, hooks for coats (Theo's coat, Sera noted, was on the floor), and the old, overstuffed journal where Jasmine still insisted on writing by hand the names and details of every guest (cheerfully ignoring the fact that Sera had started using a spreadsheet five years ago). On either side of the shelves, the entryway branched off into two long, airy hallways, one of which led to the living room, Jasmine's bedroom, and the kitchen, while the other led to the stairs, the downstairs loo (built *under* the stairs, so good luck not hitting your head on the ceiling if you happened to be taller than a garden gnome), and the bedrooms above.

Sera led Luke and Posy upstairs. The first landing was a snug, in-between space that had decidedly not been designed for people to linger for a chat (and yet it was, inevitably, the place where people lingered for a chat), with a single window on the tiny wall and two more hallways leading to a jumble of rooms on either side. Matilda and Nicholas had the bedrooms on one end, while Sera's mostly tidy study and a significantly less tidy box room sat on the other. Then it was up the next and last flight of stairs to the top of the house.

"Theo and I are down there," Sera said, pointing to the right before pivoting left. "And these are the two empty rooms. This one here's got the twin beds." She fished the key out of her pocket and handed it to Luke. "Dinner?"

"No, we're okay, thanks. Posy ate her weight in spring rolls about an hour ago."

"I think Posy and I are going to get on very well." Sera smiled at her. "I'll just go get you towels, tea, and that chocolate cake, and then I'll leave you both to it."

Luke caught her elbow before she could walk away. "I . . ."

He glanced down at Posy, looked back at her, and cleared his throat. "Thank you."

"You're welcome. Now I really *do* have to go. I've left the others alone too long already."

Luke gave her a look she recognised from fifteen years ago, the one that said he thought she was being unnecessarily dramatic. (She usually was, but still.) "What exactly do you think they might have done in the last twenty minutes?"

"I don't think you appreciate the sort of nonsense the inhabitants of this house are capable of when left unsupervised," Sera said with feeling. "I may just go downstairs and find out Matilda has adopted a goat, or Nicholas has heroically stabbed a burglar, or Clemmie has convinced Theo to kidnap someone. And don't get me started on the zombie chicken."

Amusement sparked in his eyes. "You're not really selling this, you know."

"You're only here for one night, remember? I don't need to sell it." She smiled angelically. "Also, I hope you have an umbrella. It rains apple blossom tea in this room every Sunday."

CHAPTER NINE

S era returned to the kitchen to find that, happily, no stabbings, kidnappings, or livestock adoptions had taken place in her absence. This unexpected stroke of good fortune seemed too good to be true, or at the very least unlikely to last, so Sera was not surprised when, the very next morning, a frazzled tavern wench from the Medieval Fair called to tell her that Nicholas had been knocked off his horse during the jousting.

"Can you come pick him up?" said the harried girl on the line. "He keeps saying he'd rather die than face the dishonour of retreat, but he hit his head when he fell and the doctor says he isn't allowed back on a horse for two days. He's not supposed to drive himself home either."

Sera *had* hoped to spend the morning putting her mind to the problem of translating the spell from *The Ninth Compendium*, but Jasmine couldn't drive and Matilda was splashing ankle-deep in the brook, so off she went.

Without the benefit of being able to cut across fields, and with the sharp hills and narrow lanes making it necessary to drive slowly, it was a good fifteen minutes before she drew up at the entrance to the Fair. There, she collected a dejected Nicholas, who was still in his knight's armour (though his oversized jousting helmet, thankfully, remained inside somewhere), scabbard at his waist. He clanked his way into the passenger seat of Sera's car.

"I must ask that you not look at me," Nicholas said miserably. "I have failed you. I have failed everyone."

Sera, quite unable to decide whether to feel sympathetic or amused, started the engine. "Don't be a ninny. Knights get knocked off their horses all the time. Isn't that the whole point of jousting? You must have been knocked off before."

"Of course, but I always got up and went again! I've never pulled out of a tourney before! Knights must always get back on their horses or die trying."

There was no use reminding Nicholas that the tourney was about as real as Clemmie's conscience, so Sera only said, "You got a clonk on the head. I know employee safety might seem like a distressingly modern concept to you, but they had no choice but to send you home. In fact," she added, patting him on the shoulder plate, "you did your duty. They told you to go home. You obeyed. *That* sounds like something a good knight would do."

"I suppose that's true." Nicholas perked up. He turned from the window to look at her, distracted from his own woe. "Jasmine told me our new guest is an old friend of yours."

Those were definitely not the words Sera had used when she'd told Jasmine about their new arrivals the previous night. "I wouldn't exactly call him a friend."

Instantly, Nicholas's hackles rose. "Why not? What did he do? Shall I take up my sword against him?"

"And do what after that?" Sera asked with interest. "Throw him in our invisible dungeon? You'd probably like him if you met him, actually. When I knew him, he was, er, really into history."

Well, it wasn't like she could say *He was studying magical history at the only library for witches in the country,* could she?

"If you wish it, I'll guard him with my life," Nicholas vowed. Apparently, with Nicholas, there was no middle ground between a duel and undying devotion.

"He was only planning to stay the one night. He might not even be there when we get back."

Nicholas grinned at her. "I remember when *I* was only planning to stay the one night."

"Trust me, Nicholas, Luke's not like you."

"He doesn't have to be. You have a way about you. It makes us want to stay."

"The inn tends to do that," Sera said without thinking.

"No," Nicholas said earnestly. "Not the inn. *You.*"

She couldn't correct him again, not without saying a great deal more about magic than she ought to, but luckily their timely return to the inn spared her having to reply. She pulled into her usual parking spot, next to Matilda's comically tiny electric two-seater, and noticed at once that Luke's car was still there.

"He's still here!" Nicholas almost tumbled out of Sera's car, armour clanking, and, on the off chance that she had lost her powers of observation in the last thirty seconds, added, "Sera, look! He's still here!"

The front door of the inn was standing open, as if someone was just inside, and sure enough, Luke materialised in the doorway a moment later.

"My lord!" Nicholas's earnest cry was dented only slightly by the fact that he was swaying due to a possible concussion. "Consider me your loyal subject!"

If Luke was surprised at being accosted by a youthful knight swearing lifelong fealty, he recovered quickly. "Thank you. I'm Luke."

"Sir Nicholas of Mayfair, at your service." Nicholas paused, and reconsidered. "Actually, my family's from Mayfair. I'm a knight of Batty Hole now."

Nobody but Luke, Sera suspected, could have kept a straight face at that, but he didn't even blink.

Jasmine limped out of the inn, positively aglow with happiness. "Look, Sera," she called, as if she, too, was fearful that Sera might not have noticed the full six feet of human man standing right there.

"Are you on your way out?" Sera asked him.

Luke shook his head and said, in a perfectly even voice, "Something's come up. Jasmine said Posy and I could stay a few more days, but if you'd rather we didn't—"

"I told you!" Nicholas cried triumphantly.

"Don't mind him, he just fell off a horse," Sera said to Luke. "Of course you and Posy can stay. Come on, I'll show you the lay of the land."

Sera paused to take Nicholas's sword away from him before leaving him to Jasmine's tender care. Leading the way into the house, she glanced back at Luke and said, "So that was Nicholas. Have you met the others?"

"Just Jasmine. What's with the armour?"

"Nicholas's armour? He works at the Medieval Fair near Winewall."

Luke was unconvinced. "That was not medieval armour."

"I don't think the Fair's overly concerned with historical accuracy."

Sera had never seen anyone look more appalled than Luke did in that moment. "Not. Concerned. With. Historical. Accuracy?"

She tried and failed to suppress a giggle. "I gather you won't be visiting, then?"

He didn't dignify that with a response.

They ran into Matilda on their way to the kitchen. She had a sticky cinnamon bun in one hand and the front pocket of her dungarees was bursting with autumn wildflowers. "Sera, we need to revisit the question of the baby goat."

"I am not getting a baby goat," said Sera.

"What about *two* baby goats?"

"No."

"*Half* a goat?"

"In a stew?" Sera asked hopefully.

"I walked into that one, didn't I?" Matilda said regretfully to Luke, and then, like she'd only just taken proper notice of him, did a comical double take. "Well. *Well*. Did it hurt? When you fell out of whichever Norse myth you came from?"

And with that, she was gone, trotting up the stairs and vanishing out of sight. Luke gave Sera a look that suggested he thought she had not adequately prepared him for the trifecta of Nicholas, Matilda, *and* an undead rooster, but really, who could?

In the kitchen, they found Posy wearing a pair of fluffy headphones, arranging the pieces of a jigsaw puzzle in a line along the surface of the dining table, and eating what looked like her third cinnamon bun. Sera also observed that, predictably, the mug Posy had been drinking out of was Sera's beloved, chipped, and perpetually purloined favourite.

"So are you going to tell me why you changed your mind about leaving?" Sera asked Luke, putting the kettle on.

"No."

Having had better luck getting blood from a stone, she gave up. "Well, if you're going to be here a bit longer, you'd better get acquainted with the corkboard." She pointed to the wall. "That's where everything important goes. Shopping lists, reminders, the shared calendar, the key to the first-aid box, emergency phone numbers, et cetera, et cetera."

"*Inn Rules*," Luke read out loud, starting, unsurprisingly, with the sheet of yellow paper pinned to the very middle of the corkboard. "One. *No goats.*"

"Zero goats," Sera confirmed.

"Two. *Do not under any circumstances eat any mushrooms without checking with Jasmine, Matilda, or Sera first.*"

"I find it best to leave no room for ambiguity where Nicholas is concerned," said Sera.

"Three. *Do not wake Sera from her slumber.*" There was a pause, and then a suspicious tremor in Luke's voice as he added, "Except someone's crossed out *Sera* and replaced it with *the dragon.*"

"Potayto potahto," said Sera.

"And four. *Don't be alarmed by the fox. She's harmless.*"

"Would that I lived in a universe where that were true," said Sera wistfully.

Posy, who had completed a perfectly straight line of jigsaw pieces and had moved on to drawing on the inside of the box with her crayons, took her headphones off, put her empty plate and mug neatly beside the sink, and trotted into the garden to acquaint herself with her new surroundings.

Luke set two empty cups beside the kettle. "Do you still drink your sugar with a splash of tea?"

Sera was startled into laughter. "How do you even remember that?"

"How do I remember having to pour excessively sweet tea down your throat to rapidly sober you up after you and our new Chancellor stole our former Chancellor's brandy?"

"Well, when you put it like *that*, I can see how that might be, um, memorable."

"Just a bit, aye."

Sera was about to reply when, out of the corner of her eye, she saw her again, that younger Sera, fourteen and silly and blindingly magical, brimming with endless, infinite possibility.

Just a ghost now, sitting quietly at the table, watching her.

A blink, and the ghost was gone. By the time Luke followed her eyes across the room, there was nothing to see.

She snapped her gaze back to him. "Sorry. Four sugars, please."

"Where did you just go?"

"Oh, you know. Away."

Luke's eyes dropped to her throat, to where her hand, without permission, had started fidgeting with her necklace. She let go immediately, dropping the pendant beneath the neckline of her jumper, but he'd already seen it. "Was that a swan?"

It wasn't the first time Sera had wanted to throw her necklace in the bin. It also wasn't the first time she knew she wouldn't. "It *is* my name."

"Why are you wearing your name around your neck? Are you thirteen?"

"I'll answer that when you tell me why you're still here."

Silence.

"I didn't think so," said Sera.

She took her tea outside and found a perch on the edge of one of the raised herb beds, setting her steaming cup down beside her. Cross-legged, chin propped on her fists, she breathed in the lavender, rosemary, and hollyhocks and absently watched Posy assess the shape and quality of one of Matilda's cabbages.

She became aware that Luke had followed her out. He stood at the opposite end of the herb bed, his eyes on his sister, the rigid, unbending lines of his shoulders positively screaming at her to keep her distance.

And then, unexpectedly, he said, "My mother didn't think it was a good idea to take Posy home."

"Is something wrong?"

"With our parents? As in, are they both gravely ill and concerned they won't be able to care for their own child at this exact moment? No. They're fine."

"How long has it been since Posy was home?"

"About a month."

"I see." Sera's mind flashed to Theo standing at the edge of the room in his parents' home, trying to make himself as small and unthreatening as possible. She clenched her jaw. "What happened?"

"Posy doesn't hide her magic. If she wants to use it, she does." Luke's voice was perfectly, painstakingly level. "There'd been awkward questions from the staff at her school, so I took her to the Guild. It wasn't right for her. They were fine with the magic part, but . . ."

Sera could guess. "They were fine with the magic part, but not the rest of her?"

"More or less."

"What would have happened if you *had* gone back to Edinburgh last night?"

"Nothing. It's not like our parents would have kicked us out. I could take Posy back right now if I really wanted, but after that, as our mother took great pains to explain on the phone an hour ago, they'd have no choice but to pull her out of school and keep her away from other people until she learns to hide her magic. One of our parents would have to quit work and stay home with her." Luke's voice was a sea in outer space, miles and miles of frozen, unforgiving desolation. "It would be the easiest way to keep her safe, but they'd hate it. *She'd* hate it. So she's staying with me for now. Our mother assures me we're more than welcome to visit, though."

"Big of her," said Sera.

Luke cracked a smile. "Your turn."

With an enormously martyred air, Sera tugged her necklace out from under her jumper. The pendant was a small crystal swan, each clear facet refracting a rainbow of light, its wings outstretched in flight. "After the resurrection spell," she said, "when Albert exiled me, he gave me this big speech about how *he* was still the powerful descendant of an old and distinguished magical family, whereas *I* was nothing but a swan who had clipped her own wings."

Luke looked at her for the first time. "Sounds exactly like him."

"To my great and enduring irritation, it got to me," Sera went on, with a fearsome glower. "Then, a few weeks later, I was in this dusty, poky charity shop and I found this."

She extended the chain away from her neck, as far as it would go, so he could see the pendant properly. It was hard to tell unless you looked very closely, but there was a hairline fracture down one wing where someone had broken the swan and mended it again.

"It's silly, but it was the thing I needed at exactly the moment I needed it. When I put it on, it felt like I was saying *fuck you, I can still fly.*"

Luke looked at the pendant for a long time before saying, "No. It's not silly."

"Well, silly or not, I don't know how true it was. I'm not the girl I was. I'll never be her again."

And that, Sera felt, was *quite* enough truth-telling for one day.

Before Luke could say anything, she asked, abruptly, "What are you going to do if taking Posy home is out of the question for now?"

"I don't know yet." He looked away. "Don't worry, we won't stay long. My flat in Edinburgh's tiny, so Posy can't live there with me, but as soon as I find somewhere bigger—"

"You can stay as long as you need to."

"You don't have to—"

"I'm not saying it again," Sera said, immediately ruffling the pointy, spiky ends of her feathers. "You need time to find somewhere new. Make a plan. Whatever. I'm giving you that time. So stay. For fuck's sake."

The corner of Luke's mouth twitched. No, that was an understatement. It *quivered.*

Sera scowled. "Yes, yes, I'm an intolerable grump. A belligerent harpy. A cantankerous shrew. Well, too bad. If you wanted someone warm and welcoming and snuggly, you should really have had this conversation with Jasmine instead."

Luke's first laugh was a rusty, startled sound. Then he kept laughing.

Sera was furious. She had (mostly) been able to avoid noticing how (very, very) attractive Luke was, but now he was laughing (at her! The nerve!), and as if that weren't enough, the sun had decided *this* was the very moment to sally forth from behind the clouds and halo him in gold like he was a fucking archangel or something. It was unacceptable.

He was still laughing.

Sera drank her tea in wrathful silence.

CHAPTER TEN

Rescue came in the form of Posy, who ran over to get Luke's attention. "Chickens!" she said excitedly, pointing, and insisted on dragging him over to the coop to show him the chickens in question.

Sera checked her phone. She had an email updating her about an online order, a slew of new photos of Malik's baby, Evie, and a new text from Theo. Still at Alex's.

Sera was not a parent and hadn't had the faintest idea what to do with a child who had crossed the breadth of the country in the dead of night without so much as a courtesy text, however noble his motives. So, after much discussion with Jasmine, she'd gone with what had seemed to her to be the most straightforward option and had told Theo that until she could trust him to make sensible decisions, the only places he was allowed to go without supervision were school and Alex's house. And she expected regular status updates too. Hence the text.

She texted him back. Lunch?

Alex's grandma says I can eat here, is that ok?

Yep. Remember your manners.

On cue, Theo sent her the emoji of the smiling haloed face. Sera grinned.

She looked up to see that Luke was returning from the bottom of the garden. He jerked his head in the direction of Matilda's vegetable patch. "There's a spell keeping those pumpkins and cabbages alive, isn't there? Is this the right season for cabbages? Is this even the right *climate* for artichokes?"

She shrugged. "If you ever see the way Matilda's face crumples when one of those stupid plants dies, you'll understand why I do my best to keep them alive."

He gave her a long, curious look. "I also noticed there are heat spells in all the rooms."

"You sound surprised."

"From the way people talked about it, I always assumed the resurrection spell left you with no magic at all."

"No, not quite."

"If there's something there, why hasn't the rest of it come back? Magic is supposed to replenish itself."

"I think it tries."

"So why doesn't it work?"

"Exit wounds," said Sera, thinking of the holes she'd punched through the night sky, those wounds that still bled stardust. "I went too far."

Luke's brows twitched together in confusion, but something in her face made him let it go. He nodded at the kitchen door. "What's the spell clinging to all the doorways?"

"That's for hygge," Sera explained.

"Excuse me?"

"Hygge. Cosiness and contentment."

"My mother's Danish, Sera, I know what hygge is. What I don't know is what a spell has to do with it."

Delighted to discover she possessed some magical knowledge that Luke didn't, Sera very nearly clapped her hands with glee. "Why, Luke, you disappoint me. With all the reading you do for a living, you're telling me *Eighty Spells for a Suitably Toasty Winter* hasn't yet made the cut?"

He didn't rise to the bait. "How have *you* read it? It was out of print until six years ago."

"Theo. Thanks to the agreement the Wise Women of Reykjavík made with the Guild when I brought him here, Theo can request books from the Guild's library. I read them too."

Luke looked amused. "I bet you do."

She looked up at the doorway, her eyes tracing the lines and knots of the invisible spell that clung to the corners. "It's supposed to provoke a feeling of warmth and well-being."

"Does it work?"

"It had better," said Sera. "God knows I could do with it."

A familiar sadness swept over her. It was the sort of sadness that made her want to double over laughing until tears rolled down her face because, really, when you thought about it, it was absolutely ludicrous that hygge and a bit of warmth and cabbages, fucking *cabbages*, were the sum total of her magical power. She was Sera Swan, and those ridiculously ordinary, outrageously unexciting *cabbages*, remarkable only because they were still there, were all she was capable of.

And if she couldn't find a way to translate that spell, it was just about all she would *ever* be capable of.

Before she could succumb to a full, vigorous emotional breakdown, there was a rustle of grass nearby, and Clemmie slinked around the side of the house.

"Sera, your rooster has spent the last hour following me around," she announced, completely unconcerned with Luke's presence. "I tolerated that with saintly patience. Then he tried to demand a cuddle from me, so I decapitated him. You'll have to reassemble him. He's over there, running around like a headless chicken. Actually," she added reflectively, "I suppose he *is* a headless chicken."

"Stop decapitating the resurrected rooster," Sera said crossly. "It's impolite."

"Well, you made me promise not to eat the other chickens anymore, so this seems like a happy compromise."

Sera went around the side of the house, where Roo-Roo's headless skeleton was dashing this way and that, bumping into the oak tree every so often. His head lay close by, squawking with such merriment that Sera suspected he was enjoying himself enormously.

She reattached his head, but before she could set him down again, he curled up decisively into a bundle of bones in her arms. Resigned, she took him back with her.

If Clemmie had hoped the arrival of a talking fox would terrify the living daylights out of Luke, she had picked the wrong target.

Luke, entirely unsurprisingly, just sighed. "A fox. *That's* what she meant."

"Who? What does that mean?" Clemmie demanded.

Sera interrupted. "Aren't you supposed to be in hiding? Weren't you insisting just yesterday that we shouldn't be—"

"The way I see it, if the Chancellor of the Guild is willing to overlook my presence, everyone else can stuff it," said Clemmie smugly. "Including What's-his-name over here, who is very obviously a Guild spy on a mission to ferret all our secrets out."

Sera picked up her tea and tried in vain to seek comfort from it. "He's not a spy. I don't think."

"Forgive me if I'm not reassured," Clemmie growled.

Luke had turned away to check on Posy, but now he met Clemmie's glower with a narrow, assessing stare of his own. "You know, Howard Hawtrey once told me a ridiculous story about a witch, a curse, and Albert Grey. I thought he was fucking with me. I couldn't bring myself to believe anybody would do something so daft. And yet . . ."

Clemmie's fur bristled so hard, she looked like a very angry basketball. "I may be a fugitive and a laughingstock now, but you mark my words, when I recover my human form and become Chancellor of the Guild, everyone will be sorry they—"

"When you become what?" Luke demanded. He looked at Sera. "Is she joking?"

"We should be so lucky," said Sera.

"Under what circumstances, exactly, do you imagine any of the Cabinet Ministers will vote for you?" Luke asked Clemmie.

"I haven't thought that far ahead," said Clemmie haughtily. "Now that you mention it, though, I think my tragic curse would be a good place to start. Sympathy votes and all."

"Sympathy?" Luke's voice got more Scottish in his disbelief. "Weren't *you* the one doing the cursing?"

Taking great comfort from the fact that a shoe would be more likely to be elected Chancellor than Clemmie, Sera left her to her happy daydreams and said to Luke, "Look, I know she's obnoxious, but she *is* on the lam, as she likes to put it, so if you could maybe not mention to anyone that you've seen her . . . ?"

"I can't begin to express how uninterested I am in mentioning anything to anyone," said Luke.

"A spy would say that," said Clemmie.

"They probably would," Luke agreed.

Clemmie glowered at him. "Fine. Let's say, *hypothetically*, that you're not a spy. What are you?"

"A historian," said Luke.

"What sort of historian?" Clemmie persisted. "Magical relics? Arcane languages? Document recovery? Botanical study? History of magical peoples?"

"All of the above," said Luke. "I work for a professor of magical history who doesn't believe in narrowing down her field of study."

"What about—" Clemmie started.

Sera shushed her. "Which professor of magical history?"

"Verity Walter."

Sera's cup slipped out of her hands. It hit the grass, spilling the dregs of her tea.

Even Clemmie faltered. "Did he just say Verity Walter? He works for Verity Walter?"

Luke gave her a wry look. "So you *do* know her."

"What does *that* mean?" Clemmie demanded.

Luke sighed. Again. "Before I left the castle, Verity mentioned a fox."

"She did?" Excitement had Sera practically bouncing on the balls of her feet. "Was she the one who helped Clemmie get into the restricted archives?"

"Was she what?" Luke demanded. "She let Clemmie into the restricted archives?"

"To get *The Ninth Compendium*."

"WHAT?"

Sera blinked. "I'm confused."

"You know who probably isn't?" Clemmie replied. "Verity Walter, that's who. Can't somebody get her on the bloody phone? Like, I don't know, the man who supposedly works for her?"

"You'd think, wouldn't you?" said Luke. "Unfortunately, she's not answering my calls."

Clemmie regarded him speculatively. "Well, if we can't get hold of her, *you* have the potential to be an adequate substitute."

"No," said Luke.

"You thought he was a spy a minute ago," Sera reminded Clemmie.

"That was before I found out he's a sodding historian who works for Verity Walter, and that one of the things he's studied is sodding *languages*, and that he might therefore be one of the few people who knows how to read that sodding spell!"

Movement at the other end of the garden caught Sera's eye. It was Posy, skipping along the edge of a flower bed. For just a few seconds, though, in the sharp morning sunlight, she didn't look like Posy at all. She looked like another little girl, the first of the ghosts, the youngest of all the lost Seras.

The moment passed, as those moments always did, and it was just Posy again. And Clemmie was still talking. "Sera, what if your spell didn't just bring him here because he needed the inn? What if, just this once, your spell also brought you something *you* needed?"

This hadn't occurred to Sera, and there was a sudden, embarrassing lump in her throat at the possibility that magic had not abandoned her after all.

Wearing the expression of a man who wished he'd driven his car in literally any direction but this one, Luke said, in a steely, implacable tone, "Whatever you're thinking, forget about it. I don't think I can possibly overstate just how uninterested I am in getting involved in whatever goings-on are going on."

"What if all you had to do was translate a spell?" Sera asked. "A spell to give me my magic back?"

He stared at her, *into* her, seeing far more than she wanted him to. She couldn't look away. She felt like all the echoes of all those different Seras were watching, holding their breath, waiting to see if maybe this time, unlike every other time, she wouldn't fail them.

"Show me," Luke said, resigned.

"Really?"

He gave her a look. She meekly handed her phone over.

Luke put his glasses on and examined the photographs on her phone, his expression, maddeningly, giving away absolutely nothing. He typed something into her Notes app.

"There." He returned her phone to her. "That's what you'll need to cast the spell. Good luck."

Sera blinked. "You're done? Already? Just like that?"

"I know the language." Luke shrugged.

"I guess that's—well, I mean—I suppose that makes sense—" Sera was deeply distressed to discover she wanted to hug the fuck out of him. She prevented this calamity by tucking her hands under her armpits, where they were instantly swallowed by the fabric of her oversized sweater. "Thank you—I'm really—"

This hopeless floundering was too much for Clemmie. "WHAT DOES IT FUCKING SAY, SERA?"

Slightly wobbly of knee, Sera sat down on the edge of the herb bed again, and Clemmie peered over her shoulder. There were the usual few lines of advice, like the suggestion of the use of a glass teapot and so on, and then the actual ingredients:

> A STRAND OF SUNSET
> A PHOENIX FEATHER
> A THORNY HEART

Sera looked at Clemmie. Clemmie looked at Sera. They both looked at Luke.

"Like I said," said Luke, "good luck."

"I'm going to need something stronger than tea," said Sera.

CHAPTER ELEVEN

*O*h, you're answering your phone now, are you?" Luke demanded.

Verity didn't sound especially contrite. "Your text said you'd translated the restoration spell," she replied, her words punctuated by the chomp of her teeth on her pipe. "Ergo, I reasoned that all had become clear and I no longer needed to dodge your calls."

"All has *not* become clear. You sent me to stay at a cottage that doesn't exist!"

"Now that's unfair, Luke. It *does* exist. I checked the map very carefully before I chose it!"

Luke strove valiantly for patience. "You know what I mean. Why didn't you just tell me the truth?"

"Well, for one thing, you wouldn't have gone to the inn if I had," said Verity unapologetically. "For another, it wouldn't have been sporting."

"*Sporting*," Luke repeated.

With an impatient click of the tongue, Verity said, "Years ago, when Sera Swan first arrived at the Guild, Albert Grey set me the task of studying her spell. The one she cast over that house of hers. He wanted to know how it worked and how she cast it. I was never able to give him an explanation he was satisfied with, but after all that study, I think I can safely say I understand that spell better than anybody else."

"Is there a point in there somewhere?"

"I couldn't send you directly to the inn, could I? What if I'd been wrong about you? The spell on the inn doesn't work on witches who are expecting it, so you'd have been able to breeze right in. And then what? What if you'd told Albert Grey that Sera Swan's trying to get her magic back?"

Luke had no words.

"Besides," Verity swept on, chomping on that ridiculous pipe some more, "I wanted you to choose to help her of your own accord."

Momentarily letting that supposed gesture of generosity slide, Luke said, "It's not like you to go out of your way for someone you barely know. What's this really about?"

"Fifteen years ago, Albert Grey put me in the unpleasant position of having to choose between my work and a young girl's future," Verity snapped. "I'm not saying I made the wrong choice, exactly, but, er, it hasn't sat well with me."

"Then why didn't you come here yourself and—"

"Luke, don't be a twit. Do you think Albert just took my word for it? Deceitful people like Albert Grey assume everybody else is just as deceitful as they are. They don't take people's *word* for things. He had me sign a magical contract swearing I would never communicate the contents of *The Ninth Compendium* to anyone."

"Well, in that case, why—"

"And the other reason I'm going out of my way, as you put it," Verity went on, "is physics."

"What?"

"Physics. Every action has an equal and opposite reaction, et cetera, et cetera. And when it doesn't, when the laws of nature are broken by way of reckless resurrection spells and petty egomaniacs, you end up where we are now. Power like Albert Grey's *must* have an equal to keep it in check."

Luke yanked his phone away from his ear and looked at it in disbelief. "In other words, you're using me, Posy, *and* Sera to knock Albert Grey off his throne and didn't actually bother to ask any of us first."

"Luke, may I refer you back to Sera's spell? Remember how it works? Has it not occurred to you that I did this for you and Posy too?"

With this parting salvo, Verity hung up on him.

"And she has the nerve to say she can't abide drama," Luke said out loud to absolutely nobody.

He returned to the living room, where he'd last seen Posy. She was curled up on one of the sofas, under a blanket, thumb in her mouth. He ruffled her hair. "You okay?"

"Sheep," she replied, pointing to the sheep on the screen of her tablet. "Good night, sheep. Good night, Posy."

"Good night, Posy," Luke agreed. "Lucky you. I'd kill for a nap right now."

She probably wouldn't actually go to sleep, though. It was just her way of telling him she was tired. Between all the running around the garden she'd done that morning (many leaves were acquired, of course) and all the new people she'd met, she'd well and truly worn herself out. She'd probably spend a quiet hour or so with the farmyard animal app and then she'd be full of beans again.

Nicholas, the knight, was on the other sofa, a bag of frozen peas on his head. He gave Luke a shy smile. "Have no fear, good sir, I shall keep an eye on your sister."

"I've been told we're supposed to be keeping an eye on *you*, Nicholas, but thank you."

"I am mortified to be such a nuisance to Lady Sera," Nicholas admitted mournfully. "Her patience in the face of my ignominy has been nothing short of saintly."

"Is there another Sera here I don't know about?"

"If I had my sword," Nicholas declared, "I would challenge you to a duel for saying that."

Luke bit back a smile. "Spoken like a true knight. Want some tea?"

Nicholas's indignation instantly and sheepishly subsided. "Yes, please."

There was nobody in the kitchen, but Luke could see the top of Sera's head as she paced back and forth outside, gesturing like she was talking to somebody, which meant she and the fox were probably still thrashing out the whats and hows of the restoration spell.

The academic in Luke was a tiny, *tiny* bit interested in how a spell like that would manifest itself in Sera's hands, but his desire to stay well clear of whatever shenanigans were afoot outweighed his curiosity. He'd meant what he'd said about not getting involved.

He had an unwelcome suspicion that that was going to be easier said than done, though, which was just one of many reasons he had no intention of staying long. He was grateful for

Sera's unexpected kindness, but that didn't change the fact that this was temporary and, frankly, far from ideal. Apart from the fact that Posy deserved a proper, *permanent* home, the inn was downright incomprehensible, and Luke, to be perfectly honest, was the sort of man who needed comprehensible.

It wasn't just about the magic, either, which was wild and fanciful and didn't work at all the way magic was supposed to. Undead chickens and memories materialising right before one's eyes were only part of the weirdness he'd inadvertently stumbled into; there was, after all, also a knight presently lying on the sofa with a possible concussion, a cursed witch hiding from the Guild, the improbable theft of a priceless book that his own employer had apparently had a hand in, and who knew what else. There seemed to be no rhyme or reason to how things worked here, no line between guest and family, no logic to who did what and when and why.

Footsteps thudded outside and two children cannoned into the kitchen, almost tripping over each other in their haste. The taller of the two grinned at Luke. "Oh! Hi! Are you Luke?"

"Aye. You must be Theo."

"The one and only," said the boy cheekily. He seemed to have a smudge of dirt on his cheek. "This is Alex."

The other child, whose sunny yellow jumper was liberally streaked in mud (had they both fallen off their bicycles and landed in a pigpen on their way here?), gave Luke a bright smile before saying, "Er, Theo?"

"Alex *really* needs a wee," Theo confided in Luke.

"Theo!"

"What? Everyone has a bladder!"

Alex kicked him in the shin and dashed down the hallway

without another word. Theo started to follow but spun back to Luke at the last minute. "Sera told me you have a sister who's a bit younger than me. Posy, right? Alex and I are going to play video games in my room. Do you think Posy would like to play too?"

Luke stared at the boy, inexplicably touched by his generosity. He cleared his throat. "That's a kind thought, but I think she might find it overwhelming right now. Maybe you could ask her once she's had a chance to settle in?"

"Okay," Theo said brightly, and then he, too, was off, cheerfully shouting "Hi, Nicholas! Hi, Posy!" as he clattered past the living room.

"Like a whirlwind, isn't he?" Sera remarked, wiping her grassy feet off on the doormat and rubbing her cold arms as she stepped into the kitchen. "THEO! Were you born in the Colosseum? Shut the door when you come in!"

Luke nodded curiously in the direction the kids had gone. "Does Alex know about you and Theo?"

"About the magic, you mean? You know, I don't know," Sera said thoughtfully. "Theo says he hasn't told them, but Alex *must* have noticed something's a bit different around here by now. Move over for a second, would you?" Luke obliged, stepping sideways, and Sera ducked behind him to rummage in one of the lower cabinets. "Aha! I knew I still had one of these!" She emerged triumphantly, holding a dusty glass teapot aloft. "I can't remember the last time I used a glass teapot to cast a spell. What do you think? Will it do?"

"It won't do much if you haven't got anything to put in it," Luke felt obliged to point out.

"Oh, Luke. Luke, Luke, Luke. Has anyone ever told you that you can be an uptight prig?"

"Not in those exact words, no. Has anyone ever told *you* that you can be a quarrelsome gargoyle?"

"I like that one," Sera said admiringly. "I'll add it to the list."

Luke did not smile, but it was a close thing.

Instead of going back to her fugitive friend outside, Sera lingered, fidgeting with the teapot. Luke was quite certain this didn't bode well for him, and was proven right when, a moment later, she said, "Are you sure you didn't make a mistake when you translated the spell?"

He gave her his iciest look. "I don't make mistakes."

She bit her lip, but not, sadly, in chagrin. She was trying not to laugh. "It's not that I'm not grateful you translated it, because I really am, but those ingredients are so patently absurd that if there's even a *tiny* chance you got a part of it wrong—"

"I didn't." He didn't budge. "And they're not absurd. Complicated, but not absurd."

"Not absurd?" Sera blinked at him in disbelief. "A phoenix feather? A strand of sunset? A thorny heart? You don't think any of that sounds even a *little* absurd? Phoenixes aren't even real!"

"The spell's not necessarily that literal." Luke sighed. "The Guild prefers to teach young witches how to put magic into practice rather than go into the theory, but there are—"

"Inanimates, Animates, Bindings, and Adaptables," she interrupted.

He stared at her, taken aback. "How do you know that?"

"I know you think I spent all that time in the library doing Albert Grey's bidding, but believe it or not, I was there to study."

He didn't have much choice *but* to believe it, considering she knew academic terminology that most witches never learned, and he wasn't sure he liked that she kept surprising him. She'd made it clear the previous night that she hadn't liked his assessment of the girl he'd briefly known, but he'd dismissed that as the inevitable reaction of someone who'd thought quite a lot of herself. Now he found himself wondering just how much he'd got wrong.

Considering her curiously, Luke said, "Then you know that there are different categories of spells. There's a bit of overlap, obviously, but for the most part, they're their own beasts."

"Inanimates are spells cast on inanimate objects, like making a mop wash a floor on its own or alchemising lead to gold," she replied, rattling the words off like he'd issued a personal challenge. "Animates are spells cast on living things, like the resurrection spell I cast on Jasmine, and Bindings are extreme Animates, like Clemmie's curse."

"She should never have messed around with that curse." Luke still had trouble believing Howard's story had been true. "Bindings *literally* bind a person. If you were to cast a revealing spell over her, she'd probably look like she's bound up in hundreds of knotted, tangled threads."

Sera nodded. "I know. I mean, I haven't seen it myself, but I assumed as much. All the books I've ever read about it say that all you have to do to break a curse is undo the bindings."

"Undo *hundreds* of bindings," Luke reminded her. "Most witches would run out of power long before they could finish. That's why she's still stuck."

A hint of uncertainty crossed her face. "Then there's the Adaptables. The least common, least understood sort of spell. Is that what the restoration spell is?"

"I'd say so. There isn't one way to cast an Adaptable spell.

Rigid, literal thinking won't cut it. These sorts of spells are like soft clay in the hands of the witch casting them."

"In other words, an unmitigated nuisance," Sera said irritably.

"On the bright side, you'll be able to cast it without the feather of a bird that doesn't exist."

"That's true." In a flash, enthusiasm replaced her irritation. "So if it doesn't have to be the exact literal thing, maybe the phoenix feather the spell asks for could be a feather that's been set on fire instead? And the strand of sunset could be something like a leaf that's been bathed in the glow of an evening sunset?"

Unmoved by this extravagantly pretty picture, Luke felt obliged to remind her that she was supposed to be casting a spell, not composing an ode.

This didn't dent Sera's enthusiasm in the slightest. Darting for the door, she said, "I'm going to make a list! There are *so* many possibilities! Then I'm going to enchant this teapot, and *then* I'm going to find a feather and set it on fire, and after *that* . . ."

And she was gone.

CHAPTER TWELVE

*L*ater that afternoon, while consulting one of the few magical textbooks that she'd managed to keep hold of after her exile, Sera discovered that the glass teapot had been out of use for so long that it needed to be rinsed with salt water five times before it could be enchanted. *That* took half an hour, after which she had to borrow some of Jasmine's hand cream for her overdried fingers, but then the teapot was finally ready to be infused with the magic it needed to identify and piece together the restoration spell.

Years ago, enchanting a glass teapot would have been the work of a few seconds for her, but now it took almost ten minutes, her magic trickling out of her in dribs and drabs. She ached everywhere, the phantom pain of missing something that had once been there, of closing her eyes and seeing only glimmers of starlight where before there had been galaxies.

At last, the teapot glowed gently. The enchantment was done.

Jasmine, who had immediately provided Sera with a cup of heavily sugared tea to speed up her recovery from the effort of the enchantment, now looked at the glowing teapot with interest. "Why a glass teapot, of all things?"

"Well, you need something transparent so you can see how each ingredient behaves when it's added in," Sera explained. "Glass is also made from sand, and sand's one of the best conductors of magic. And it's a teapot because it's comforting. I mean, that's probably not the *actual* reason witches have used teapots for centuries, but I'd like to think it is. Who doesn't enjoy looking at a teapot?"

"And you're really going to set a feather alight and put it in there?"

"Yep."

Sera was trying really, really hard not to get too excited, because she was nothing if not well-versed in what it felt like to get your hopes up only to have them dashed shortly thereafter. After making sure Clemmie was nowhere to be found and there was no chance of an audience, she took the teapot outside, collected one of a handful of stray crow feathers that were dotted around the garden at any given time, and held a lit match to it.

As soon as the feather caught alight, she dropped it into the teapot.

She counted the seconds, holding her breath. One, two, three—

The teapot spat the feather back out.

Sera stamped on the feather to put the flames out and scowled at the teapot. "No? That doesn't work for you?"

The disappointment was crushing, but she reminded herself that it *had* been her first try and the odds had been exceedingly slim that she'd find the right ingredient on her first go. She'd come up with something else. Maybe a feather from a different bird would work. Maybe the feather had to be the *colour* of fire rather than *set* on fire. She'd figure it out.

Back inside, she found Luke at the front door, signing for a delivery of two boxes packed with old books, manuscripts, and papers.

"What in the . . ."

Luke sighed. "Sorry. They're from Verity. Apparently, when she told me I needed a break, what she actually wanted was for me to start work on a new project immediately."

Professor Walter, frankly, seemed to be both positively terrifying and positively everything Sera wanted to be.

Leaving Luke to his tomes, she spent the rest of the afternoon with a leaf of blank paper torn out of one of Jasmine's old sketchbooks, writing down as many possibilities as she could think of. These ranged from the plausible (*2. leaf at sunset*) to the significantly less plausible (*14. anagrams of the word "phoenix"*) and were liberally annotated by Clemmie's frequent contributions.

By dinnertime, half the ideas on the list had been scratched out for one reason or another, including rejection by teapot (the teapot, it seemed, agreed with Luke that the poetry of a leaf bathed by the glow of a sunset was not what it was looking for), and the rest, like the feather the colour of fire, would have to wait until Sera could actually find them.

With no alternative but to put a pin in it for the moment, she tucked the list safely into a book and went to join the others.

She hadn't been sure if Luke and Posy would eat with them that evening, but there they were. Posy was perched on the edge of her chair, legs swinging, watching everyone else settle into their seats with interest. Jasmine, an expert in making other people feel comfortable, had already started up a conversation with Matilda and was gently including Luke and Posy without putting them on the spot with questions. It was difficult to tell what Luke was thinking, but from the tension in his shoulders, Sera had a feeling he was braced for something to go wrong.

"So it really doesn't hurt?" Theo was asking, coming into the room with Nicholas in his wake. "At all?"

"Well, it does feel a bit tender when I poke it," Nicholas admitted.

"Nicholas," Sera said, despairing, "I can't believe I have to say this, but please do *not* poke the part of your head that got hit when you fell off your horse."

"How else will I know when it's better?"

"That looks fun," Theo said to Posy in a friendly voice, pointing to something on the table beside her. "Is it a fidget spinner?"

"Spinny thing," Posy said cheerfully.

Theo accepted this readily. "Can I have a go with your spinny thing?" She handed it to him and watched delightedly as he spun it on one finger.

"Thank you for dinner," Nicholas said to Jasmine and Matilda with a shy smile. "You didn't have to make mac and cheese just because that's my favourite."

"I think we all deserve our favourite dinner when we've had a bit of a low day." Jasmine smiled.

Judging by the speed with which she emptied her plate, Posy seemed to be as much of a fan of Jasmine's mac and cheese as Nicholas was. As soon as she was done, she rocked restlessly on her chair, smiled across the table at Luke, and said, "Dragon?"

Luke froze. "No, Posy."

She frowned. "Dragon," she said more insistently. Jumping

to her feet, she ran to the door, waiting expectantly for Luke. She giggled. "*Dragon*, Luke."

Everyone looked at Luke. Acute, anguished agony flashed across his face, there and gone in a blink, and he stood up. Looking at Posy, almost choking out the word, he said, "Dragon."

Posy ran. Luke chased her.

Jasmine beamed after them. Sera bit her fist to keep herself from laughing.

"That was *adorable*," Matilda declared.

"Don't let him hear you say that," Sera managed to say.

Two pairs of footsteps raced up the stairs, followed by the sound of Posy's unfettered, squealing laughter, and then, moments later, Posy raced back in, out of breath from the running and the laughing. As soon as Luke reappeared, a few steps behind her, she ran past him, back to the door, and said, "Dragon."

"No, once was enough," Luke said immediately.

Theo leapt up with enthusiasm. "I'll go."

Luke seemed taken aback. "You don't have to do that."

"It's fine, I want to. I just have to pretend to be a dragon and chase her, right? Posy? Can I play?"

"Dragon?" Posy asked, looking at Theo in startled delight.

"Yep, I'm a dragon," said Theo.

Posy let out a shriek of glee and ran. Theo bolted after her.

"She'll let you catch her sooner or later," Luke yelled after them. Turning slowly back to the table, his ears tinged with pink, he said, "Sorry. She shouldn't have run off while everyone else was still eating, but she doesn't always understand—"

"There's no need to be sorry," Jasmine said at once.

"If you're worried about her manners, don't be," Matilda added merrily. "No one here has any. It's grand."

After the kids had come back, out of breath and laughing, and after the last of the cinnamon buns had been polished off, Sera wrangled Theo upstairs to tidy his room, which was both necessary and futile because no matter how tidy his room became under her determined eye, it always looked like someone had vomited up about a hundred socks a mere hour later.

This was normally the time in the evening when, somehow or other, everybody ended up in the living room. The TV would be on and some of them would watch it, Matilda would get a snack, Jasmine would sew at her worktable, Nicholas would polish his armour, Theo would eat half of Matilda's snack and finish his homework while keeping one eye on the TV, Clemmie would slink in and curl up out of sight on top of a bookshelf, someone might suggest doing a crossword, someone else might get a pack of cards out, and Sera would read or doomscroll on her phone or get in on one of the games.

Tonight, she whipped her list back out and set her mind to the restoration spell. Luke came in after Posy had got to sleep, took one look around the room at everybody doing their own thing, looked unspeakably relieved, and came back a moment later with a big dusty book that must have come from one of the boxes Professor Walter had sent him earlier.

At eightish, as usual, Jasmine gave Theo a gentle reminder to shower, brush his teeth, and go to bed. ("And *try* not to stay up too late reading again," Sera added, also as usual.) After that, the room gradually emptied, bit by bit, until it was past ten o'clock and Jasmine, yawning, gave Sera a kiss and retired for the night.

Expecting to be the last one up, Sera was slightly taken aback to see that Luke was still on the opposite end of the sofa.

He'd barely looked up from his book since he'd come in. She tilted her head to read the title on the spine. *Magic, Ethics, and Law* by H. A. Wincombe.

"Did you know H. A. Wincombe also wrote a book about magical folklore?" she asked.

"*The Extraordinary Handbook of Magical Tales,*" Luke said.

After everything, most of Sera's memories of her time with the Guild hid sharp, painful thorns, but even now, thinking about *The Extraordinary Handbook of Magical Tales* filled her with fondness rather than hurt. "I used to have to go to Bradford Bertram-Mogg's winter masquerade every year," she explained, drifting back into her past. "I imagine they'd be quite fun for an adult, but for Francesca and me, it was just a long, tedious night in uncomfortable shoes, so we'd sneak away. She'd go to the kitchens to get extra snacks. I'd go to the family library. The first year, I spotted *The Extraordinary Handbook*. The original bound manuscript."

Luke had looked up. She was struck all over again by how obnoxiously gorgeous he was. His brow furrowed like she'd given him a puzzle he couldn't quite solve. "*That's* how you spent your night?"

"Every year," said Sera. "Bertram-Mogg would never have allowed a book from his precious collection out of his library, so once a year, when I was there, I read *The Extraordinary Handbook*." She fidgeted with her pen, considering him curiously. "You didn't study at the Guild, did you? Before you worked in the library, I mean?"

"No, I stayed home. Studied the books they sent me, sent back my assignments and progress letters, et cetera. More or less what Theo's doing now."

"You didn't miss much," Sera said. "The library's probably the only thing. Of course, my experience wasn't exactly the same as everybody else's, so maybe don't take my word for it. I was there, but I didn't study with the other kids."

"Not ever? What about when you practiced your spellwork?"

She could feel the thorns now. "Albert was the only one I was allowed to practice with. Duels, mostly."

"Duels?" Luke repeated incredulously.

"Not *real* ones, obviously. We'd follow all the rules, ignite the circle of fire, choose recovery times, and cast our spells, but there were no stakes. No one ever got hurt."

There was no conviction in her voice. Why would there be? Someone *had* got hurt. Looking back, what Sera remembered most about those practice duels, even more than the rules and the rituals and the adrenaline rush of spellcasting, was the relentless, crushing weight of her humiliation when she lost. And she always lost. Albert would smile, pat her on the shoulder, and tell her not to worry. *You never had a chance, Sera.* He was older, faster, more practiced, more powerful. *You're good, Sera, but you're not that good.*

"I see," Luke said evenly, and she had a feeling he did.

Clearing her throat, she sought refuge in her list. "So, um, about the restoration spell," she said. "I don't suppose *you* have any ideas?"

"I do not" came the immediate, uncompromising reply. "You know, I seem to remember that when I told you I wanted to have nothing to do with any of this, *you* told *me* the only thing you were asking of me was a translation."

"And I meant it, I really did, but you've turned out to be an invaluable repository of magical knowledge!"

"You have no idea how much I'm wishing I weren't right now," Luke informed her. "Fine. *If* I think of anything, I'll let you know. Can I get back to work now, or do you need something else first? A kidney, maybe? My firstborn?"

"I mean, if you're offering . . ."

He sighed.

CHAPTER THIRTEEN

*L*uke had absolutely no idea how it had happened, but some-how, the following morning, he found himself driving Sera, Nicholas, and Posy to Blackpool to the home of an ornithol-ogist.

"How did you get me to agree to this?" Luke, who was not by any means accustomed to feeling flabbergasted, required an-swers. "I'm convinced that one minute I was drinking my tea and the next I was in the car. You could put me in front of a jury of my peers and I *still* wouldn't be able to explain how it hap-pened."

"I'm surprised too, to be honest," Sera confided from the passenger seat. "I would have bet good money that you'd never have agreed to it. I wouldn't have asked you at all, but my car wouldn't start, and Matilda and Jasmine have bingo on Monday mornings, and Nicholas's car is still at the Fair, so you were the only one left. Maybe I should have waited until Matilda got home, but you know what it's like when you get an idea stuck in your head. You just want to go *do* it."

"I do know," Luke agreed. "Right now, for example, the idea

stuck in *my* head is leaving you in Blackpool to make your own way home."

Sera chortled. "You could have said no."

"If I could have said no, I would have," Luke said with utter certainty. "Nothing you just said adequately explains why I'm here."

"You did tell me that Posy would love the penny arcades along the pier."

It was all coming back to him now. He *had* told her that. It explained quite a bit, but still. "And Nicholas is with us because . . . ?"

"My spirits were low," Nicholas offered from the back, where he'd been playing Rock Paper Scissors with Posy. Inexplicably, he was in his historically inaccurate Fair armour again. "I'm not allowed to go back to work until Wednesday, but Wednesday and Thursday are my days off, so I won't actually be able to go back to work until Friday. Why do I have days off anyway? What sort of knight takes days off? The shame of it is nigh intolerable."

Luke wondered what he'd done to deserve this. "Who's the ornithologist?"

"Retired ornithologist. She used to be one of Jasmine and Matilda's bingo friends before she moved to Blackpool to live with her son. Jasmine says she has an impressive collection of feathers from birds from all over the world." Sera shot a quick look over her shoulder into the back seat before adding, meaningfully, "Some of those feathers will be *red*."

Luke sighed. He really ought not to say anything, but it was too much to ask that he not correct an egregious error. He glanced in the rearview mirror, made sure Nicholas was entirely occupied with Rock Paper Scissors, and said, "I think you may be overlooking one of the things that sets Adaptable spells apart."

He didn't think he'd ever been glared at with such ferocity.

He weighed his survival instincts against his academic integrity before saying the rest. "A red feather from someone you've never even met before is not going to do the trick. The spell's *adaptable*. As in, it adapts to the person casting it. Whatever you put into it has to have some kind of meaning to *you*."

"This has meaning," she said at once. He raised an eyebrow. She looked away, glared out the window, and said, "Okay, it's a stretch, but I'd kick myself if I didn't try everything. Just in case."

He let it go.

They parted ways in Blackpool, with Sera heading into town to find the ornithologist while Luke, Posy, and Nicholas walked to the pier to the penny arcades.

A cold, briny wind blew in from the water and whipped Posy's hair around her, making her giggle. "Silly hair," she said to Luke, who grinned. Maybe it wasn't such a bad thing he'd let Sera rope him into this. He'd never have brought Posy here on a weekend, what with all the people everywhere, but, it being a Monday morning during school hours, there was hardly anybody around, and besides, the sea air *was* rather nice.

If only they'd come here just for the sea air, but alas, as the horrifying musical jingle getting ever closer reminded him, they hadn't.

He steeled himself. The flashing lights and obnoxiously loud music in arcades were his idea of sensory hell, and that was *before* you got into the finer, nightmarish detail of the relentless clatter of coins dropping into machines filled with hideous toys and key chains that hardly anybody ever actually won, but Posy, for reasons he'd never be able to understand, loved it. The lights, the sounds, the act of dropping coins into the machines to make things happen, all of it.

For all the ways Luke and Posy were alike, from their ability to hyperfocus on something they loved for hours to their loathing of crowded places to their uncompromising refusal to wear anything made out of scratchy wool, arcades were one of just as many things that they absolutely did *not* see eye to eye on.

"A DANCE MACHINE!" Nicholas yelled, careening past Luke and Posy, armour clanking.

Resigned, Luke got Posy a bucket of pennies, watched her rush merrily around the room, and wished he'd remembered to bring along a few dozen ibuprofen.

When Sera found them an hour later, Nicholas was a bit woozy (doing a merry jig on a dance machine for an hour while wearing armour and possibly recovering from a concussion was, apparently, not the wisest course of action), Posy had sped through a tenner's worth of pennies and won herself a bag of sweets that was already almost empty, and Luke . . .

Well, Luke had just been to all nine circles of hell and lived to tell the tale, so there was that.

"If it helps," Sera said, sounding both sympathetic and amused, "I have a gloriously red cardinal feather."

"It doesn't help," Luke assured her.

"An early lunch, then? There's a pub on the way home that does the *best* waffles with fried chicken."

That, Luke admitted, probably *would* help.

It did. After a cosy lunch at the White Stag, they piled back in the car, and Posy and Nicholas were fast asleep by the time they returned to the inn. Luke moved Posy inside to the sofa, tucked a blanket around her, and picked up *Magic, Ethics, and Law*, leaving Sera to rouse Nicholas.

Two chapters and a page of notes later, some time after Jasmine and Matilda returned, Sera came into the room to throw more wood on the fire and recast her heat spells. Luke, who'd spent half his life working in a library where people came and went at all hours, barely noticed, but then, on her way out, Sera's footsteps stopped in the doorway.

Maybe it was the hesitation in the sound that got his attention. He looked up.

Her jaw was set. "You were right, by the way. The red feather didn't work."

There was, surprisingly, no satisfaction in being right about that. "I wish I'd been wrong."

"Thanks."

He hesitated, then said, "You'll find what you need sooner or later."

"Thanks," she said again. Light crept back into her eyes, gilding the dark brown with gold, and he had the stray, almost absent thought that her eyes really were lovely.

She left the room. He went back to work.

Over the next few days, between keeping an eye on Posy, helping her draw pictures of chickens and foxes, learning to navigate his way around the maze of a house, and getting through the boxes of reference materials Verity had sent over, Luke kept himself busy.

If he were a different sort of person, perhaps he might have been able to settle into this rhythm. There was a part of him that wanted to, that wanted to believe it was possible for somebody's life to be nothing but this: the work he loved, his sister tearing around a wild, overgrown garden in bare feet with a smudge of jam on her chin, hot cups of strong tea and scones that crumbled in his mouth, and fairy-tale evenings by the fire with a book.

But that, there, was the problem. *Fairy-tale.* Reality was traffic and steeples and old bookshops in Edinburgh. Reality was tedious meetings with Guild bureaucrats over whether the acquisition of a priceless book was *really* worth the funding. Reality was the question mark over Posy's future, and his own, and the cold, secret fear that came late at night and made him wonder if maybe it wasn't *normal*, really, to have nobody in your life you could say all of that to.

This place, this inn, which was every bit as batty as its ridiculous name promised, was not reality as Luke knew it. This was a place of fables and stories and peculiar magic, and such a place, he was certain, *had* no place in the real world.

So Luke did not settle. He waited, calmly, icily, *resigned,* for the fairy tale to end.

Funnily enough, the first disruption to the rhythm of those early days did nothing to dispel Luke's certainty that the Batty Hole Inn was an incomprehensible departure from reality, good sense, and all things regular.

He woke, blinking, groggy, to the sound of *something* going on outside. Posy was fast asleep in the other twin bed, having been awake and remarkably chirpy from the hours of two to six in the morning, but it sounded like everybody else was up and about.

Rubbing the sleep out of his eyes and swapping his sweat-pants for jeans, Luke checked the time on his phone. Half past nine, which was frankly too early for mayhem at even the best of times.

He descended two flights of creaky stairs, passed through the long hallway, and crossed the kitchen to the open back door, by which point the indistinct sounds had become shrieks and hollers of "Catch it!" and "Not that way! *That* way!"

Jasmine stood at the edge of the stone patio, leaning on her cane, tutting gently to herself as Luke drew level with her. The garden looked like a meteor had hit it in the middle of the night. In fact, for a moment, Luke wondered if a meteor *had* hit it—what else could possibly have overturned half the earth, sent large clumps of grass flying in every direction, beheaded a few dozen wildflowers, decimated most of Matilda's vegetables, and even apparently laid waste to Sera's red wellies?—but then, at the heart of the disaster, he saw Matilda and Nicholas.

Trying, and failing, to catch a goat.

"I thought Rule One was *no goats*," Luke remarked.

Jasmine nodded. Luke wondered if her cheerful calm was an ominous indication that these things happened rather too often around here.

"Matilda," Jasmine explained, "was of the view that if she borrowed a goat from the Medieval Fair, and showed Sera just how sweet and adorable it was, Sera would change her mind."

"Just how many goats did she borrow?"

Pressing her lips together like she was trying not to laugh, Jasmine said, "One."

Luke looked at the garden, and then looked at the small goat merrily eluding its would-be captors, and then looked at the garden again. "*One* goat did all this?"

"In just over an hour," Jasmine confirmed.

"Can't see this changing Sera's mind, can you?" Luke said wryly.

"Thank you for that excellent contribution!" Matilda wailed from halfway down the garden. "Now get over here and help us catch this dratted creature! We have *maybe* half an hour to corral this menace, return him to the Fair, and fix this mess before Sera gets back from the supermarket and murders us all!"

"I don't see why she'd murder *me*," Luke pointed out.

"She's not going to murder anybody," Jasmine said in a wounded tone of voice. "She'll be a *little* cross that the garden has been completely destroyed, and who could possibly blame her, but it's not like she's a terrifying dragon who'll gobble everybody up."

"You'd deserve it if she did gobble you up," Nicholas said to Matilda, deeply disapproving. "How *could* you? That you'd even dream of causing Lady Sera the *slightest* anguish—"

"I would never, you sweet, ridiculous, lovestruck puppy!" Matilda shot back. "Not on purpose!"

"Lovestruck?" Nicholas was appalled. "I'm not in love with her! I am a loyal knight! I would no more make advances on my lady than I would cut off a single lock of her glorious hair!"

"Does he say these things *to* Sera?" Luke asked Jasmine with interest.

"He does," said Jasmine.

"Are you sure? He seems to still be alive."

"Don't you start," Jasmine said reproachfully.

Luke relented. "How's she *really* going to feel about this?"

Jasmine gave him a long, searching look before saying, "She'll never say it, but she loves this house. Every creaky stair, every crumbling brick, every bit of dirt under our feet. We all know it. You don't really think Matilda's panicking because she's *afraid* of Sera's wrath, do you?" At Luke's furrowed brow, she explained, "You see, what's going to happen is Sera will come home, and she'll glower, and she'll compete with Matilda to see which of them can be more dramatic, and then she'll put this mess to rights even if it takes weeks, but the whole time, what she'll actually be is quietly, devastatingly upset."

Luke had never heard a word as understated as *upset* hold so much weight, but somehow, in this woman's gentle, dignified voice, and in the honest, tender simplicity of her answer, it felt weightier than almost anything else.

Resigned, Luke heard himself say, "Matilda, maybe you and Nicholas ought to go to the Fair and bring the goat's owner back with you. Trying to catch it yourselves obviously isn't working."

"*Go* there?" Matilda's eyes narrowed suspiciously. "Why? The man must have a phone."

"And risk him saying he can't get away until lunchtime?" Luke replied without missing a beat. "Like you said, we have maybe half an hour before Sera gets home. If you get going right now, you might just be able to get rid of the goat before she sees it. I'll see what I can do about sorting out the mess here."

"I shall be honoured to be of service to you in that endeavour, sir," said Nicholas. "You'll need a strong pair of arms and a devoted, unwavering heart."

"Matilda doesn't know her way around the Fair like you do, dearest," Jasmine said at once. "If we want to be quick, you'd better go with her."

Giving Luke a look of deep gratitude, Jasmine whisked Matilda and Nicholas away, ferrying them herself out to the car to prevent either from doubling back at a most inconvenient moment.

Luke got to work.

First, the goat.

His magic was a library of old books, the rustle of its pages a constant, comforting hum of background noise in his mind. The spines of spellbooks cracked open when he wanted to cast a spell, pages turning until the spell he needed was at his fingertips, and the spell he needed right now was one that would lull an animal to sleep.

It was a tricky spell, particularly for somebody like Luke, who, on top of having a completely ordinary amount of magic, tended not to mess about with spells that affected living things.

Take the goat, for example. The sleepy spell was supposed to conjure lavender and lullabies and other soporific sorts of things, but as the fingers of one of Luke's hands moved in the air, almost like he was playing notes on an invisible piano, the goat wasn't having it. Like a toddler rebelling at the first sign of drowsiness, determined to put bedtime off as long as possible, the goat bucked and baaed and, outraged, tried to chew at the knee of Luke's jeans.

Luke refused to relent, even with one very soggy knee, and bit by bit, the infernal creature was bested.

Once the goat was drooling blissfully on an undamaged patch of grass not far from the disgusted chickens, Luke moved on to his next spell. It was a much easier one, and also a much more tedious one, but frankly, Luke felt like he could do with a bit of tedium right about now. The spell was the one witches usually used when they wanted to summon their coat from across the room or, say, arrest the fall of a child who insisted on jumping off balconies, but on this particular occasion, Luke needed to use it to restore many, *many* clumps of grass and ravaged lumps of earth to their rightful places.

Matilda, Nicholas, and the goat's exasperated owner arrived just as he was finishing up. Matilda grabbed Luke's face in her hands and planted a smacker of a kiss on his forehead, Nicholas goggled at the repaired garden in awe, and the owner of the goat retrieved the goat, muttering, "Don't see what all the fuss was about, everything looks fine to me," as he departed.

After that, the only thing left for Luke to do was to salvage what he could in Matilda's vegetable patch. Jasmine convinced Matilda and Nicholas to go inside for a restorative cup of tea so that Luke could have a few more minutes unobserved. He didn't have quite enough magic to revive beheaded wildflowers or regrow partly digested vegetables, but he took stock of what had survived (one pumpkin, a handful of pepper plants, and three artichokes, all of which probably had Sera's magic to thank for their resilience in the face of the goat's onslaught) and tidied up the rest of the patch.

"It's adorable that anybody thinks *anything* happens in this house that I don't know about," a voice said behind him.

He stood, turning. Sera was studying the garden. Luke had a feeling she could see every seam and stitch of his magic.

She looked intrigued. "Was it a goat?"

He cracked a smile. "Of course it was a goat."

She was quiet for a moment. Then, pushing her windblown hair behind one ear, she turned to look at him. "You fixed it."

"I fixed what I could. You'll need new wellies."

"You didn't have to do that."

"No," Luke agreed.

She smiled, a proper smile, one that reached all the way into her eyes. "Thank you."

It felt essential, somehow, that Luke look away. He nodded at the house. "Are you going to tell them you know?"

"No, I think I'll take that one to my grave."

As she stomped across the overgrown grass back to the house, Luke thought he was beginning to understand. Matilda's despair over the goat she'd so optimistically brought home for a visit. Nicholas's chivalrous outrage. Jasmine saying *quietly, devastatingly upset*. Sera choosing to pretend not to know. It seemed at first glance like ridiculous theatre, unnecessary and a bit silly, but at the heart of it, weren't they just a handful of people trying to be good to one another?

It was the first thing about the inn that made sense to him.

It would probably be the last thing too.

CHAPTER FOURTEEN

Sera had always been good at fortitude. Fortitude was her friend. She had fortituded her way through undependable parents, megalomaniac mentors, scheming foxes, the death of a loved one, the resurrection of said loved one, the loss of her magic, and quite a large number of fiascoes big and small since then.

Unfortunately, she and fortitude seemed to have now parted ways because Sera, glaring fearsomely at an empty glass teapot, was at her wits' end.

Nothing was working.

"You're trying to use magic to restore magic," Clemmie pointed out, thumping her tail for emphasis. "It's a big ask."

"I'm not asking it to be easy. I'm asking it to be possible!"

"Maybe the handsome icicle *did* translate the spell wrong," Clemmie grumbled.

Sera would have paid good money to see Luke's reaction to that description. "He didn't. Like it or not, we're looking for a phoenix feather, a strand of sunset, and a thorny heart. A thorny heart," she repeated darkly. "Honestly. What the actual fuck."

"You seem a bit cross, my love," said Jasmine, poking her head around the doorway. "Has something happened?"

"I'm at my wits' end," Sera informed her. "My wits, as it were, have ended."

Regrettably, as much as Sera would have liked to spend her afternoon swearing at an empty teapot in the hope that the answers (and ingredients) would miraculously present themselves to her, the inn hadn't suddenly and conveniently started taking care of itself, so she put the teapot carefully on a shelf and embarked on an endless list of things that needed to be done.

Fill up the dishwasher. Harvest a few sprigs of lavender and rosemary from the herb beds. Add a second heater to the chicken coop. Check on the bees and collect a full honeycomb from the hive. Extract honey from the comb. Renew the car and home insurance. Call the GP to pester them about Jasmine's next appointment. Put sloe gin and cheddar on the shopping list. Drive over to Theo's school because he'd left his English homework at home. Come back and bake scones. Reply to Malik's text about next week's pub quiz. Recast the heating spells. Sit down and draw pictures with Posy to recover from recasting the heating spells.

On her way to deposit a basket of freshly washed clothes in Theo's room, she noticed a puddle of water gleaming on the old wood floorboards of the corridor. She dipped a toe into it and her sock came away dry.

Great. A magical memo. The inn's way of telling her that the water wasn't real, but it was going to be.

"Roof?" she asked out loud.

The puddle of water, reassured that she'd understood its warning, vanished.

She left the basket on the floor, opened the hatch above her, and ascended into the old attic. Navigating her way around Christmas decorations and childhood toys, she pushed open the dusty skylight and climbed out.

The inn's roof was an uneven, sloping world of chimneys, sun-stained tiles, and birds' nests. She found the hole in the roof straightaway, a spot where a piece of timeworn tile had crumbled to nothing, leaving a crack through which the rain would undoubtedly seep in.

Sera closed her eyes and imagined weaving stardust into all the broken places until nothing was broken anymore. She imagined the night sky wheeling behind her eyelids, steadying her, strengthening her, and shining with millions upon millions of stars.

She opened her eyes, but there was no stardust at her fingertips. Her skin was cold and the stars were few. Her loyal, treasured magic *had* answered, like it always did, but she simply didn't have enough of it to fix her roof.

At times like this, that magical night sky was so utterly out of Sera's reach that it felt like she was drowning.

She'd been whole once. Nothing had hurt. There'd been no leaky roofs, no uncertainties about what she'd make of her life, no ghosts of her lost selves.

Once, she had been glorious. Once, she had bent the universe to her will.

She wasn't that person anymore.

From the peak of the roof, arms wrapped around her knees, Sera looked out over an endless horizon of green hills, knots of woodland, fields dotted with fluffy sheep, winding silver streams, and the tiny storybook shapes of villages and towns nestled in and around the valleys.

The magical night sky was out of reach, but sometimes, for a stolen moment every now and then, the wild green land almost, *almost*, made up for it.

She let that feeling sit for a moment.

For a moment, the world was quiet and still.

For a moment, it was just Sera and the horizon and the few valiant, twinkling stars of magic that had never left.

CHAPTER FIFTEEN

"Psst." It was Clemmie, that unfailing disturber of Sera's peace. Sticking her head out of the open skylight, she said, ominously, "There's trouble afoot."

"Is it your fault?"

"Honestly, I'm shocked that it isn't," Clemmie replied, sounding a little put out that a disaster might have occurred without her consent. "Look, Theo will be back from school any minute. I sped ahead to give you advance warning that he's upset."

"What? Why?" Sera felt a sharp spike in the ever-present worry for Theo that always lived in the back of her mind. "Why do you even know this?"

"I felt a *smidge* of guilt for taking Theo to Northumberland," Clemmie replied, which was quite possibly the most shocking thing Sera had heard all year. "I've been selflessly making up for it by keeping an eye on him when he bikes to and from school."

Sera had mixed feelings. "Following him around is a bit creepy, don't you think?"

"I asked his permission first," Clemmie said indignantly, and actually, *that* might have been the most shocking thing Sera had heard all year.

Moments after Sera got downstairs, Theo came in. His usual smile was absent and his face was stony, like he was trying to hide whatever he was feeling. Instead of his usual hug and insistence that he would *die* if he didn't eat at least eighteen snacks *immediately*, he refused to look Sera in the eye and went upstairs without a word.

She followed him. She stood outside his closed bedroom door and said, "What's going on?"

"I don't want to talk," came the angry reply. "Leave me alone."

Sera was, momentarily, at a loss. This wasn't like him at all. Should she call his parents? Should she handle this on her own?

There were a lot of things she wanted to say, but she went with: "You can have an hour and then I'll be back to make sure you're okay. I'd really like it if you told me what's bothering you, but you don't have to."

She went next door to her own bedroom, where she looked for useful things to do, none of which, somehow, involved putting away the pile of clean clothes that had been sitting in a basket beside her old armchair for over a week.

Twenty minutes later, she heard the unmistakable sound of Theo's door opening and staying open. It was an invitation. Sera accepted it at once.

He was sitting cross-legged on his bed, picking at a hole in his sock. She could tell he'd been crying, which made her want to simultaneously cuddle him and cast a spell that would make whoever had done this to him step on Lego at least twice a day for the rest of their lives.

She settled for half of that. She sat beside him and pulled

him close. It took him a moment or two to speak. "We did family trees in school today."

Sera's heart sank. "Oh."

"There's three of us in my class who don't live with our parents," Theo explained. "We didn't have to say why, but the others decided to. Because they have nothing to hide. Because they have reasons that make sense. Because I'm the only one with parents who are *scared* of me. I know I shouldn't be sad about it, because Alex's mum and dad are *dead* and mine are alive, but . . ."

"Stop that," said Sera. "It's not a competition. Alex gets to have their feelings about the shitty thing that happened to them, and *you* get to have *your* feelings about the shitty thing that happened to *you*. And it *is* shitty, Theo. I'm not going to pretend it isn't. Your parents do love you, but they haven't tried to understand you, and yeah, that sucks. You're allowed to be sad about it. You're allowed to be *angry* about it. If it helps, break something!"

Theo let out a wet sort of laugh, scrubbing a hand across his nose. "I can't break stuff!"

"Why not? Between you, me, and Luke, I'm sure one of us can fix it."

Theo pressed in closer, smelling of that distinctive boy combination of soap, sweat, and birds' nests. She felt each of his breaths go in and out, listened to them grow slower and calmer. After a few minutes, he said, "I *am* angry."

"You have every right to be." She kissed his head. "Look, I know the last time the subject of your parents came up, you didn't want to talk to me about it, but do you maybe want to talk to someone else? A professional, I mean?"

"I don't know." He thought about it. "No, I don't think so. Not yet. Maybe later on?"

"I think the waiting list for children's mental health services is pretty long, so it might be a good idea for me to ask the GP to put your name down now. If you still don't feel ready when a space opens up, we can just cancel and let the next person have your spot."

"That sounds okay to me."

"Okay."

"Have *you* ever talked to someone?" Theo asked curiously.

She nodded. "Years ago. You know that big dent in the door of the cupboard where we keep the broom? I put that there. I kicked the door really hard. Broke two of my toes."

Theo's eyes had gone very round. "Why?"

"My feelings got too big," Sera said simply. It wasn't an easy thing to talk about, but he deserved a real answer. "Years of small things and big things just added up, and one day, it was like I couldn't really feel anything except the big, dark space where everything I was missing was supposed to be. I couldn't deal with it on my own, so eventually, I asked for help."

Theo took this in quietly, and seemed to turn it over and over in his mind a few times before saying, "I've never seen that version of you. Around the house, I mean. Whenever the house shows me memories of you, you're always around my age."

"The house knows it's not supposed to show anyone that particular ghost, not even me."

"How come you always call them ghosts? Aren't they just you?"

Sera shrugged. "They don't feel like me. They feel like ghosts.

Haunting me. Reminding me of all the things I used to be that are long gone now."

Theo nodded, opened his mouth to say something, and yawned instead, like all the feelings that had rushed through him over the day had exhausted him. Sera could very much relate.

She hesitated before asking her next question. "Do you want to go back to live in Reykjavík with your mum and dad? There's no wrong answer here. Whatever you want is fine."

"I miss them sometimes, but I don't want to go back. I like being here." His voice grew very small. "Are you tired of having me around?"

"Absolutely, definitely not," said Sera emphatically.

At that precise moment, Matilda's voice reverberated across the house: "SEHHH-RAAA! THERE ARE TWO PEOPLE WITH A VERY CUTE TODDLER WHO NEED A ROOM FOR TONIGHT! AND I'VE LOST MY LEFT SHOE!"

Theo started to laugh. Sera sighed. "Believe me, Theo, the more family I acquire, the better you look by comparison."

CHAPTER SIXTEEN

*T*he new guests left the following morning, full of honeyed waffles and bacon just the right side of crispy. They'd arrived exhausted and dejected, having only just been evicted from their home and struggling with making the long drive from Cornwall to Aberdeen to stay with family, but a full night's sleep had done them a world of good and they'd left in better spirits.

As Sera stripped the double bed in the room the family had spent the night in, and wrestled the new fitted sheet over the mattress, she became aware of Posy chattering indistinctly to herself in the next room. Luke was probably with her, then, and Sera had been meaning to ask him about his living arrangements.

She poked her head around the open door. Posy was sprawled on the rug, armed with crayons and a piece of paper, a partly built castle of wooden blocks beside her. Across the room, Luke was at the desk, working, with three big books lying open in front of him and a stack of several more beside them.

"So what *is* the new project Professor Walter's got you working on?" Sera asked curiously.

"Right now, stealing magic." Luke propped his forearms on the desk and looked at her over the stack of books. "As in, she wants me to find out if it's possible."

"Dare I ask why she wants to know that?"

"She *says* it's because all knowledge is worth having and no magical scholar worth their salt would leave any path unexplored," Luke said drolly. "What she *means* is she thinks it's only a matter of time before someone like Albert Grey decides the already incredible amount of magic he has isn't enough for him, and she wants to get ahead of it."

"Is it possible to steal magic?" Sera asked, more than a little unnerved at the thought of Albert with even *more* power.

"Steal it? No. I haven't yet been able to find a way." Luke tapped the page of the book in front of him. "Come look."

Sera crossed the room to look over his shoulder. The book was very, very old, with fragile parchment and beautiful illustrations and handwritten text in deep, burnished gold ink. Sera would happily read a good book on the screen of her phone if that was all she had to hand, but there was something about the ink, paper, and dust of an old book that simply couldn't be beaten.

The words on the page were written in the most common of magical dialects, one she *could* read, so it took her only a glance to understand what she was looking at.

"This says you *can* take another witch's magic," she said, appalled.

Luke tapped the page again. "Keep reading."

She did. "Oooooh." Like the resurrection spell, this particular spell was so fraught with peril that it needed an incantation to keep it in shape, but that wasn't the part that had caught her attention. It was the word of caution tacked on.

Take what isn't yours and you shall pay with what is.

"Take another witch's magic and you'll lose yours too." Sera had spent enough time with magical books and their ridiculous, unnecessarily wordy riddles to translate this easily. "I literally cannot think of a single spell Albert is *less* likely to cast."

"Neither can I."

Considering the books on the table, Sera mused, "Don't you think the timing's a little too convenient? Professor Walter catches Theo and Clemmie trying to steal *The Ninth Compendium*, realises I'm looking for the restoration spell, helps them, sends you here, finds out you've translated the spell for me, and then decides straightaway that *this* is the project she simply must have you working on?"

"Oh, it's absolutely too convenient," Luke agreed. "She won't admit to it, but I suspect she's battening down the hatches."

"You think she's worried about what Albert might resort to if I get my magic back?"

"I think Albert Grey is the sort of man who feels threatened by anyone whose power comes close to matching his," said Luke. "And I think Verity likes to be prepared. Happily, I've yet to discover any way for him to acquire more magic."

Sera bit her thumbnail, trying to put a finger on why there was a pit in her stomach. After the years she'd spent as his apprentice, trusting him to do what was best for her, longing for his approval and never getting it, putting herself through the humiliating duels, all of it, it shouldn't bother her that Luke and Professor Walter and who knew how many other people at the Guild detested him. *She* detested him. So why . . . ?

You know why, she thought. *You just don't want to think about it.*

The words came out before she could stop herself. "Can I ask you a question?"

Luke looked up, the tiniest furrow between his brows. Sera leaned against the desk, fingers gripping the smooth, worn wood on either side of her. His eyes dropped to her fingers, to the white of her knuckles. "What's the question?"

"I . . ." Her face grew hot. "The moment I arrived at the Guild, there were all these people telling me how special and extraordinary I was. The same sort of people who tell Albert the same thing. And I . . . I mean, considering what you said the day you came here . . ."

No. She couldn't do it. She couldn't bring herself to ask the question.

Carefully, Luke broke the death grip her fingers had on the edge of the desk. Heat blazed through her skin at every single place his hands touched hers, and, startled, she yanked her hands back to her chest. Dropping his own arms back to the desk, fingers flexing, Luke said, "You want to know what the rest of us *really* thought of you."

"No, not exactly," said Sera. "I've already gathered from the things you said that you didn't think much of me." That he'd thought so little of her bothered her more than it ought to, but *that* was something to put aside for later. "It's more that I want to know if everybody thought I was the same as him."

Because *that* would be unbearable. After all these years, it shouldn't matter to her, it really shouldn't, but it did. The thought that all those people, people like Luke and Professor Walter, people she'd liked and respected, might have thought she was like *Albert* . . .

"You know what?" Sera said quickly, chickening out. "Don't answer that. I don't think I want to know. Really."

"I was—"

"Really," she said again. "Let's just not. Actually, I came in here to ask if you wanted the other room. It seems a bit silly for you and Posy to not have your own space when there's an empty room right next door."

He looked at her for a long moment before going along with her change of subject. "Is there any point? We're not staying long."

"So?"

"What if someone else needs a room?"

"I'll clear out the box room."

He considered it. "How much would a second room cost me?"

"Er, I reckon you could have both rooms for a hundred quid a week."

"That would be daylight robbery."

"I would never," Sera said indignantly.

"*I'd* be robbing *you*," Luke said dryly.

"Oh."

"You should double it *and* ask me to make one breakfast a week, cook one dinner a week, and fix the leaky roof."

Sera was riveted. "Would you muck out the chicken coop too?"

"I draw the line at anything involving the chicken coop," said Luke.

"I did too, once upon a time," Sera said nostalgically. "They were happy days."

Good. They'd got back on normal footing.

(Naturally, she steadfastly ignored the fact that she would undoubtedly spend the rest of her day on reassuringly mundane domestic tasks accompanied by frustrated cogitations about glass teapots, impossible spells, and the significantly increased attractiveness of men who fixed leaky roofs.)

Then, because normal was not a thing that ever lasted long in Batty Hole, apple blossom tea began to rain down on them.

"I thought this only happened on Sundays," Luke said in a slightly accusing tone of voice.

"It would seem the magic's evolved," said Sera grumpily. "It does that."

Tea dripped down her nose and had already drenched his hair, but around them, the rain vanished before it touched any of the books or bedding or surfaces, leaving everything else untouched.

Luke stuck his tongue out. "Tastes nice."

It was such an unexpectedly silly, endearing thing for him to do that her annoyance evaporated. "On the bright side, we'll dry off the moment we leave the room."

He stood suddenly, looking around. "Er, where's Posy?"

And then, from somewhere downstairs, there was an earsplitting scream.

CHAPTER SEVENTEEN

*A*s was usually the way at the inn, though, the scream suggested a much greater degree of drama than was *actually* warranted. Yes, Posy was halfway up the ivy on the back wall of the house, and yes, she was technically *floating* rather than *climbing*, but that wasn't why Matilda screamed.

Matilda screamed because Jasmine, a woman of good sense who had strong views on young children and heights, lurched forward to make sure Posy would have a soft landing if she fell, but Jasmine, who was also not a woman who could lurch without consequences, tumbled headfirst instead.

Matilda, on account of being secretly in love with Jasmine and also not wishing a broken hip on anyone, screamed.

Then Nicholas launched himself heroically into the space between Jasmine and the stone slabs of the patio, Matilda promptly stopped screaming, and by the time Sera and Luke rushed downstairs, everything was fine.

Of course, Posy *was* still floating above them, unperturbed by the kerfuffle, so Sera thought it only fair to offer an explanation.

"I don't see why anyone needs to explain anything," Matilda

said reproachfully. "If I've gone two full years *not seeing* wild-flowers bursting to life in teacups and *not hearing* foxes speak English and *not noticing* implausible skeletal chickens running around the place, I have no idea why anyone thinks a floating child will shake me out of my equilibrium."

Sera hugged her.

Matilda hugged her back. "Don't fret, dearest."

"The fox thing is a bit weird," Nicholas conceded, "but you're wrong about the skeletal chicken, Matilda. That's one of Theo's toys."

Everyone wisely let this slide. "Nicholas, are you saying *you've* heard the fox speak too?" Sera asked.

"Well, see," Nicholas hedged, turning pink, "I tickled her chin one time and she told me to do something I simply couldn't *bear* to repeat."

Luke looked genuinely fascinated. "And you just went with it? You didn't want to ask any questions?"

"It's not a knight's place to question the workings of his lady's household," Nicholas said earnestly.

Sera hugged him too.

Matilda was less impressed with him. "The fox could have been an evil witch in disguise."

"Could have been?" Luke muttered, which was too much for Sera, who needed a full minute to recover from the giggles.

At this point, the only thing to be done was make a pot of tea, stick a tray of gooey chocolate brownies sprinkled with sea salt into the oven, and give Matilda and Nicholas some proper answers. Sera covered all the highlights, from the Guild to the resurrection spell to the restoration spell ("If I could give you my own heart, I would gladly tear it from my chest," Nicholas declared), and Matilda shared all the theories she'd been storing up for two years ("Is the house a TARDIS? Is that why it's so much bigger on the inside?"), and by the time Theo got home from school, everybody knew more or less everything.

The inevitable side effect of this was that both Matilda and Nicholas seemed to think Sera needed to hear *all* their ideas about the restoration spell and its mysterious ingredients, but while absolutely none of their ideas were of any help at all, hearing Nicholas say things like "What about the High Sorcerer who works in the market at the Medieval Fair?" and "He can't be a charlatan, he guessed my card correctly eight separate times!" gave Sera an idea of her own.

She went looking for her coat, which was inevitably buried beneath Theo's because that boy never seemed to hang anything up properly, and was briefly waylaid by the sight of Matilda accosting Luke at the bottom of the stairs.

"Now that this whole magic thing is out in the open, this seems like the perfect time to have a word with you," Matilda was saying. "Because, dearest, I do strive to be tactful—"

"I see," said Luke, who had plainly not yet seen anything to suggest such a thing.

"—and I want to be *very* clear that I'm not blaming you," she'd continued. "You have to work, not to mention you have to simply *exist*, and you can't be with your sister every minute of every day. That's not good for you *or* for her."

"Matilda—" Sera tried to intervene.

"You've been with us a week, and as far as I know, you don't yet have new lodgings in Edinburgh," Matilda went on. "Posy needs an education, however, and structure. I do recognise that that's easier said than done, and I also recognise I can't help with the magic, but I *can* help with everything else. I used to be a dance teacher, you know, and one of the classes I taught for almost twenty years was therapeutic dance for children and young people with high needs. So maybe, while you're here, I could homeschool Posy?"

Luke stared at Matilda, and then at Sera, and then at Matilda again. He looked like a man who couldn't decide whether to be alarmed or grateful. Knowing Matilda as well as she did, Sera felt he ought to be both. Finally, he said, "Matilda, I couldn't ask you to—"

"You didn't. *I'm* asking *you*. Jasmine will help too." Matilda smiled. "Posy's a lovely child, you know. It would be a pleasure to spend more time with her."

"That's—" Luke swallowed, cleared his throat, and tried again. "It wouldn't be for long. We won't outstay our welcome."

Matilda's eyes softened. "Yes, you've said."

"I don't know what to tell you about her reading level, or what her maths is like, because she doesn't learn the way most other kids do or *show* how much she's learned the way they do, but a lot of people have made the mistake of underestimating how bright she is, and she can think her way out of pretty much any—"

"Luke." Matilda stopped him, kindly. "You let me worry about finding out what Posy does or doesn't know. Sera, what are you still doing here? Don't you have better things to do than wait around to see if Luke needs to be rescued? I'm not a *gorgon*, you know!"

Accepting with good grace that she'd been well and truly dismissed, Sera popped into the kitchen to see Jasmine. "I'm going out. I probably won't be home in time for dinner, so don't wait for me."

"Out?" Jasmine, peeling potatoes at the table, perked up. "Are you meeting someone? For a romantic interlude? Is it Luke?"

"No, Jasmine, it is not Luke. It is not anybody at all. Fuck's sake."

"It was just a question," Jasmine said innocently, apparently tickled by Sera's reply. Sera did not believe her. Obviously. Jasmine would never dream of anything so unsubtle and interfering as *matchmaking*, but she nurtured a great and not at all secret fear that she would die (again) and Sera would be alone.

"How come we never talk about *your* romantic interludes?" Sera wanted to know.

Jasmine laughed and bent to scoop Roo-Roo off the floor. As she held him, stroking his beak to give him the attention he felt he had been sorely lacking, there was a quiet and heartbreakingly wistful note in her voice. "I'm afraid I'm past the age for that, my love."

"Not if Matilda has anything to say about it."

"I beg your pardon?"

It truly boggled the brain that Jasmine noticed just about everything that went on around here, but had, somehow, failed to notice Matilda's lovestruck goo-goo eyes. Tactfully, Sera said, "Matilda's what, three years older than you are? She's still determined to find love."

Jasmine smiled tenderly. "Matilda is not me, dearest. She's beautiful and vibrant."

"So are you," Sera said at once. "You *are*. No matter what our family told you."

Roo-Roo propped his head on Jasmine's shoulder. She stroked the top of his bare skull and looked down at him with such unabashed adoration that Sera was reminded, painfully, of Jasmine once telling her that when she'd acquired Roo-Roo as a chick, she'd been forty-eight and he had been the first pet she'd ever had.

As a child with a disability her family had considered ugly, Jasmine had often been alone. She'd longed for a dog but had never been allowed to have one. As far as her family was concerned, pets left messes, and messes, like clubfooted daughters, were unsightly.

The worst part was how unnecessary Jasmine's unhappiness had been. She had been born into an affluent, highly educated family. Jasmine's father and brother had been *surgeons*. They could have helped her. At the very least, they could have gotten her a pair of shoes that actually fit. Instead, she had grown up believing her foot was hideous, that pain was normal, and that that was simply how life *was*. So convinced had she been of her own unlovability that when her parents had died and she had moved into her brother's house, she hadn't blinked twice at being turned into a household drudge. She had believed him when he'd told her she ought to be grateful he was looking after her at all.

The brother in question also happened to be Sera's grandfather. He was still alive, but Sera had never met him and never wanted to.

"You know," Jasmine said now, shifting that look of absolute love from the undead rooster in her arms to Sera across the table, "you were the first person I met who didn't flinch at the sight of my foot. You were so little, and I thought it would frighten you, but you didn't care."

"Dad and I thought us being witches would frighten *you*, but *you* didn't care," Sera returned. "Your foot's not ugly. It's never been ugly. It's held you up all your life, even when it hurt. Maybe it's just me, but I think there's so much strength and beauty in that."

Jasmine reached out to take Sera's hand. Her eyes gleamed with unshed tears. "Why do you find it so easy to be kind to me and so difficult to be kind to yourself?"

"I am kind to myself," Sera said, sharper than she'd intended.

"This quest to get your magic back—"

"Don't."

"I know you think you need your magic—"

"I *do* need it. I was better when I had it. You of all people know that."

"Oh, my love." Jasmine shook her head. "The only thing I know is you are much, much too hard on yourself."

Sera gently pulled her hand away. "I want to get to the Fair before it shuts for the night."

Jasmine blinked. "The *Medieval* Fair?"

"Not my favourite place, I know," said Sera, who had yet to understand the appeal of watching armoured men on horses run at each other with big sticks in hand. "All that stuff Nicholas said about the Fair earlier made me think of their market. What if there's something there that'll work in the spell? The last time I was there, they had so much for sale. Not just random touristy stuff either. There were handmade figurines and old carved decorations and leather and loads of other things. I'll be back soon. There are more scones in the oven."

Roo-Roo nudged her arm with his head. Sera gave him a pat.

She paused at the door on her way out. "You should tell Matilda you think she's beautiful and vibrant. I think she'd really like that."

CHAPTER EIGHTEEN

Sera came home from the Medieval Fair's market with no less than three hearts. As one was a poorly carved decoration covered in splinters ("I was hoping they'd count as thorns," Sera explained tragically), one was a rusted door knocker, and one was a heart-shaped monstrosity with HOME IS WHERE THE HEART IS etched upon it, Luke was not exactly surprised that when Sera dropped them into her enchanted glass teapot, the teapot spat them back out again.

Later that night, when he handed Sera a mug of outrageously sweetened tea on his way upstairs, he said, in an abrupt, forbidding tone that was designed to dissuade any and all further discussion, "You're on the wrong track, and you know it. The cardinal feather? Hearts from the Fair market? These things don't matter to you. They have nothing to do with who you are. You need things that do."

"I know." There was nothing but intense, anguished frustration in her voice. "Believe me, I *know* it's pointless to resort to random tat off the street, but maybe the wrong answers are useful too. Maybe there's a clue to where I ought to be looking . . ."

She lapsed back into thought, chewing on the end of her pen with a fierce seriousness that suggested she was not going to budge one inch off that sofa until she'd had a breakthrough.

Luke, who should have been halfway up the stairs by now, found himself lingering. Waiting.

"I'm thinking of what's outside," Sera finally said, almost to herself. "The crow feather obviously wasn't right for the spell, but it *did* come from that wild, untamed, stupid garden that's been a part of me my whole life. It was also the only thing the teapot kept hold of for a few seconds, like it was actually considering it, so maybe going back to the garden is the right answer. What about the plants? Lots of them have thorns. Do plants have hearts, though?"

"I once translated a spell that asked for a lion's hair," Luke replied thoughtfully, leaning against the doorjamb. "Anyone wanting to cast it *could* try to get hold of the hair of an actual lion, I suppose, but there's also a mushroom called a Lion's Mane—"

Sera let out a short, sharp squeal, sprang to her feet, and ran past him out of the room.

Luke looked longingly at the stairs but, against his better judgment, went after her. She'd already dashed outside and dashed right back, and she met him halfway across the kitchen with something cradled tenderly in her hands.

"It's one of Matilda's artichokes," Sera said in a hushed voice. "I've been keeping them alive. They're thorny." Her eyes shone like entire universes in the lamplight. "And they have hearts."

For no reason at all, Luke felt like there was broken glass in his throat. It took him a second to speak. "Try it in the teapot."

"Could you get it off that shelf for me?"

He put the teapot carefully down on the table. She peeled back the prickly outer leaves of the artichoke, revealing the odd little heart in the middle, and dropped it into the teapot. She was standing so close he could feel her stillness as she held her breath.

One second, two seconds, three . . .

. . . four, five . . .

"It's not spitting it back out," Sera said, exhaling in a rush.

. . . seven, eight, nine . . .

The artichoke vanished in a literal puff of smoke, leaving behind a warm golden mist that swirled contentedly at the bottom of the teapot.

"HA!" Sera squealed. "It worked! IT WORKED!"

As if the house could sense her delight, wildflowers burst out of the dishwasher, the scent of warm scones drifted out of an oven that wasn't even turned on, and soft orbs of light sprang to life along the old wood beams in the ceiling.

"Incomprehensible," Luke muttered.

Practically hugging the teapot to her chest, Sera looked up. "Did you say something?"

He shook his head. "It's late. I should go up."

Up? He should go, full stop. Leave. *Flee*, even. Take his sister, take what was left of his common sense, and go home to Edinburgh.

And then what?

He needed more time to figure out what came next.

One more week, Luke told himself. He'd stay one more week.

He almost regretted that decision when Thursday came around and Matilda had a favour to ask of him. Considering she was now homeschooling Posy, Luke thought the very least he could do was hear her out.

"Between you and me," she declared, "Nicholas needs at least one friend who doesn't have feathers for brains."

"What about Sera?"

"A friend who is neither a woman nor a child," Matilda clarified.

"Matilda, I'm not exactly sure what——"

"You could start with a visit to the pub," Matilda suggested. "I'm told young people like to bond over a pint at the pub. Have you been to the Red Rose yet? It's a *bit* of a walk, but you won't want to drive, will you? Oh, look, there he is! Nicholas!"

Luke gave her an incredulous look. "We're supposed to go now? What about Posy?"

"Isn't she in bed?"

"Yes, but——"

"Jasmine and I aren't going anywhere. We'll keep an eye on her." Matilda beamed at him. "I really can't thank you enough for doing this, Luke. Nicholas's friends from the Fair are twits. Harmless twits, but twits nevertheless. He *needs* you."

And so, just minutes later, Luke found himself cutting through a very large, very dark, and *very* boggy farmer's field with an extremely enthusiastic Nicholas by his side. Luke had conjured a glowing orb that floated ahead of them, giving them just enough light to avoid tripping over a sheep or falling into a hole, and Nicholas was utterly fascinated.

"So." Luke searched for something a man would say to another man when befriending said man. "Er, what did you think of the Liverpool match the other day?"

Nicholas turned his head a full one hundred and eighty degrees to stare at Luke in astonishment. Luke stared back, expressionless, resolutely stoic, until he simply couldn't take it anymore and they both broke simultaneously into laughter.

"Did Matilda tell you I needed a friend?" Nicholas asked, unexpectedly perceptive.

"She might have."

Nicholas grinned. "She told me the same thing about you."

"You know," Luke said, resigned, "I find myself completely unsurprised by that."

The Rose was just the right kind of busy for Luke, which was to say there were enough people to blend in but not so many that his fight-or-flight instincts kicked in. (Well, there was admittedly only so much he could blend in when he was with Nicholas, who was clanking about in armour, but at least most of the pub's patrons seemed to be used to him.)

Luke bought the first round of pints at the bar and was just about to send Nicholas on a scouting mission to find an empty table when an unexpected but friendly hand landed on his shoulder.

"Hiya!" It was Malik, Sera's friend, the farmer who'd come by the inn a few times since Luke had arrived. "It's Luke, isn't it? And Nicholas too! We're just in that corner there if you want to come over. Andy! Another round, please!"

Nicholas was already bounding happily over to the table in the corner, where both Sera and Malik's husband, Elliot, were taking turns at the dartboard, glasses wobbling perilously in their hands. Luke followed, but reluctantly, loath to intrude.

If she minded his presence, though, she didn't show it. "Oh, hi," she said, including both Luke and Nicholas in her smile.

"Nicholas, you're just who I need. *Please* help me beat Elliot at darts!"

"It would be my greatest honour," Nicholas said at once.

"I'm three pints in and still winning, by the way, so it won't be easy," Elliot warned him. "And if you're wondering if a fourth pint is on its way, yes, yes, it is. Don't judge me. This is the one time of the week Malik and I don't have to think about mashed bananas, teething, and the exact consistency of Evie's poo."

"Not judging," Luke assured him. "Admiring your restraint, in fact."

Sera yielded her dart to Nicholas and flopped into a chair at the table. Luke appropriated an empty chair from a different table and slid in across from her.

"I have returned," Malik announced triumphantly, plonking two full pint glasses on the table. "Sera, are you sure you don't want another?"

Sera wiggled her glass at him. "Still working on this one."

Luke couldn't help noticing that her tongue and bottom lip were stained red from the strawberry daiquiri she'd been drinking.

He looked away at once.

"Sera, look!" Nicholas yelled. "I'm winning!"

Sera sprang back up to go see, immediately launching into a spirited debate with Elliot over whether Nicholas's victory really counted as hers ("He's my champion! Of course it counts!") while Nicholas continued to rack up points with the perfect precision of a man who spent most of his time training with pointy weapons.

Malik, meanwhile, watched them for a moment before turning contented, sleepy eyes to Luke. "Sera says you're still looking for somewhere bigger in Edinburgh. Anywhere in particular?"

Luke shrugged. "I'm in Leith right now, but I'll go wherever I have to. The pickings have been pretty slim so far, though."

His phone vibrated in the pocket of his jeans, persistently, and he pulled it out to look at the screen, hoping to see that the person calling him just after nine o'clock on a Thursday night was Verity, or Howard, or even some sort of spam.

Nope. It was his father.

Jaw tightening automatically, Luke stood. "Sorry, I have to answer this."

He strode outside, where it was quiet, and, after allowing his thumb to hover temptingly over the DECLINE button for a fraction of a second, answered his phone.

Sera saw Luke leave the pub. She hesitated for a second before following him.

Outside, in the cold, quiet night, she saw him a few paces ahead with his back to her. "No, she's in bed," he was saying. "No, I really *can't* wake her up so you and Mum can say good night." A pause. "Well, for one thing, that's not fair to her. It's not her fault you didn't get home in time to speak to her before bed. For another, I'm not at the inn." Another pause. "Jesus, no, of course I didn't leave her alone, what's the matter with you?"

There was another, much longer pause. Feeling like she ought not to be listening to this, Sera was about to quietly go back inside when Luke spoke again, sounding weary.

"Fine. We'll see you then."

He hung up. He put his phone and hands in his pockets, stared silently ahead for a minute, and then turned. He stopped, seeing her.

"Sorry." Sera gave him a small, sheepish smile. "I wasn't trying to eavesdrop. I just came out to make sure you were okay."

"I'm fine." His expression softened slightly. "Thanks."

"I'm not sure I believe you, but I'm feeling magnanimous tonight, so I'll let it go."

He smiled a little, which was a pretty big victory as far as Sera was concerned. Stepping out of the path of the cold, biting wind, Luke drew nearer, looking down at her with a curious expression. "Where are your parents?"

"Right now? On a ship somewhere south of Argentina, I think. There's really not much to say about them. They've never been proper parents to me, but we get along fine. We talk on the phone. I see them once or twice a year. I'm used to it."

"You don't mind?"

"No, I don't think I do," Sera said, truthfully. "Jasmine's the one who matters to me."

It was cold, and there was absolutely no reason to linger out here, but she found herself reluctant to move.

"The answer's no," Luke said, abruptly. She blinked at him in confusion. "Your question from the other day. No, we didn't think you were like Grey. Nobody did. Most of us barely knew you, and some of us *did* think you thought you were better than the rest of us, but we could see even then that you weren't like him. You were never cruel. Not once. You could have been, and you'd have gotten away with it, but you never were."

Sera found it difficult to speak. Swallowing, she just nodded.

"That said, you should know I'm probably not the best person to ask that question," Luke went on with a faint, rueful smile. "I did a lot of reading between the lines, but it's not like anybody was actually telling me what they thought of you."

"Why not? Didn't you have friends?"

"I was . . ." He sighed. "I've been told I'm cold."

"Luke, I'm sure that's not—"

"It's fine." He looked away. "It was Verity who first called Albert the Great and Powerful Wizard of Oz, but as soon as the other apprentices overheard her saying it, it caught on. They leaned into it. Poor, silly Gregory Chester became the Scarecrow. And I was the Tin Man."

"The *Tin*—"

"No heart," Luke explained.

Sera's temper blazed. "They *didn't*. Oh, the *audacity*."

"It's fine," Luke said again.

"It's not. But you do know the joke's on them? Because the whole point of the book is the Tin Woodman *thinks* he doesn't have a heart, but the whole time he's actually the one with the *most* heart."

His eyes met hers. There, in the glacier blue, between one blink and the next, she saw something raw and dark and heartbreakingly surprised. She couldn't look away.

"I'm sorry," Luke said at last. "I used to think a lot of things about you that weren't fair. I was wrong."

"No." It wasn't an easy thing to say, but she said it. "No, you weren't. Not totally. I *did* like the attention. I *did* let the praise and the flattery go to my head. Maybe I wasn't like him then, but who knows what I'd have become if I'd stayed? If I hadn't brought Jasmine back, if I hadn't lost my power and been exiled, I don't know, maybe I *would* have become another Albert."

Luke shook his head. "I doubt that. If you were the sort of person who could have become another Albert, you would never have brought Jasmine back in the first place."

"I didn't know what I would lose."

"Someone like Albert could never have cast the spell on the inn."

Sera crossed her arms, cold fingers gripping the fabric of her chunky knitted sweater. "I was angry when I cast it."

"That's the whole point." He took a step closer. "In a moment of rage, *that* was the spell you cast. It wasn't planned. You weren't careful. It just *happened*. And yet in spite of that, it didn't hurt the people who'd made you so angry. Your magic knew exactly who you were. That's why your spell was a shield, not a sword."

She looked up at him, breath catching in her throat, wondering why this moment felt like something much, much bigger than it ought to.

A long, still, suspended moment. She captured it in pieces, saving each one. Her heart, beating out of her chest, exposed. Moonlight. Music from inside the pub. His hand, rising, the whisper of a thumb against her cheek, there and gone so quickly she would have thought she'd imagined it if it weren't for the startled look in his eyes as if it had surprised him as much as it had her.

She retreated, biting her lip, pretending it was just another moment, the most ordinary of moments. "We should . . ."

"Go in?" He cleared his throat. "Right. Yes. We should."

"We should," Sera agreed.

"You said that already."

"I did, yes." Sera was glitching like obsolete technology. "Er, here's the door. Good. I'm going."

Really, the only thing she could say in her favour was that she managed not to trip over the threshold on her way back in.

CHAPTER NINETEEN

*H*alfway through their third week at the inn, Luke and Posy drove back to Edinburgh to visit their parents, which was, frankly, a complete waste of time. He got nowhere with getting them to agree to an actual, permanent plan for Posy ("Let's see where things stand once you've found somewhere for both of you in the city," said their mother, and, when Luke pointed out that *seeing where things stood* was not a plan, she said, "Well, I don't know what you want us to say, Luke! As long as she's still levitating herself into the air willy-nilly, we're stuck, aren't we?"), and left when Posy's repeated exclamations of "Sera's house!" grew more and more distressed the longer she spent away from Batty Hole.

It was this, more than anything, more than their parents' objections and the nightmarish rental market in Edinburgh, that had kept Luke at the inn all this time. That had turned a week into two, then three, then more. Quite simply, Posy *wanted* to be there.

Luke couldn't think of a single other place that Posy had

actually wanted to be. (He didn't count the time she'd refused to get off the carousel at the fairground.)

It was difficult not to conclude that everyone who'd ever been responsible for Posy had failed her. Between their parents, her old school, and the Guild, Posy, like Luke before her, hadn't been able to take so much as a step without someone saying, "Don't touch that, Posy," or "Stop doing that, Posy," or "That's not how one behaves, Posy." It wasn't a coincidence that Posy, who used to retreat into herself and put her headphones on for hours a day, almost never did anymore.

The inn was far from perfect. The soft rugs and crackling fireplaces and sugary baked goods couldn't completely disguise the fact that the house was falling apart, for one thing, and the apple blossom tea that rained in Posy's bedroom every Sunday was decidedly irksome. It was only ever quiet in the wee hours of the night (and then it was almost *too* quiet), the undead rooster was constantly underfoot (and had taken to sleeping at the foot of Luke's bed every now and then, which was by no means a comfortable experience), and the (living) inhabitants of the inn were categorically and unapologetically weird as hell.

But Posy was happy here.

And when Luke stopped to think about it, why wouldn't she be? Where else did Posy get an endless supply of leaves of just the right shape, fresh bread with homemade butter, carrots and cabbages right out of the ground, cinnamon buns aplenty, and warm scones slathered in clotted cream? At the inn, Posy had lessons with Matilda, and while it was certainly an unorthodox sort of education, involving about eighty percent more mushrooms and sixty percent less arithmetic than a typical school, both Posy and Matilda seemed to be enjoying themselves thoroughly. At the inn, when Posy jumped on the sofa, she was firmly but gently asked not to, and then the following day, there was a trampoline in the garden. ("Theo's been asking for one for ages," Sera said, which, judging by the surprised look on Theo's face, was news to him.) At the inn, Posy was obliged to brush her teeth, even when she made a fuss about it, but she was also given eighteen different kinds of toothbrushes to try until she found one that she liked. ("It's no trouble at all," Jasmine insisted.) At the inn, Posy was praised and appreciated for putting things in their proper places and never, ever shouted at for putting them in what might, perhaps, not actually *be* their proper places.

And above all, at the inn, Posy had Theo.

Posy had adored Theo since the day he'd played the dragon game with her. She was willing to share her beloved trampoline with both Theo and Alex, and she had a definite soft spot for Sera, who had been the provider of chocolate cake on that first bewildering night, but there was absolutely no doubt that it was Theo who had replaced Luke as her favourite person in the whole world. When he came home late from school for one reason or another, Posy would stand at the back gate and say "Theo?" with the air of a tragic waif abandoned on wintry Dickensian streets. It was the purest love Luke had ever seen.

"Don't go yet," Theo would say every week, and every week, Luke would say, as gently as he could, "We're not going yet, but we can't stay."

"Why not?"

"This isn't our home," Luke would reply.

"What if it could be?" Matilda would chime in.

Ah, Matilda. She gave Luke not one moment's peace. He had no idea how she'd done it, but in the space of just a few weeks, Matilda had managed to, well, *manage* him.

Luke's usual weapon of choice was an arctic politeness that expressed implacable, unbudging refusal, but Matilda had discovered his fatal weakness: he couldn't bring himself to use that arctic politeness on someone as sweet and gentle and fundamentally *kind* as Jasmine. And so, on the occasions Matilda failed, she swiftly and shamelessly deployed Jasmine, who, with an apologetic smile and complete sincerity, would say, "It's impossible to get Sera to do anything, you know, even if it's for her own good, so I think Matilda's decided she stands a better chance with you," and Luke would find it very difficult to argue with her.

One time, torn between amusement and exasperation, Luke said, "You two are a lot more dangerous than anyone realises, aren't you?"

Preening like he'd just given her a compliment, Matilda smiled at Jasmine. "We do make quite the team, don't we?"

Jasmine blushed a deep, charming crimson and, slightly flustered, retreated to her worktable to mend a pair of curtains.

When she had left the room, Matilda, gazing down the hallway in the direction Jasmine had gone, said, "I should tell her how I feel, shouldn't I? Sera says I need to give her time, but really, at our age, how much time do we have?"

"Can't be much," Luke agreed, which was just the sort of clipped, ruthlessly direct reply that usually put people off telling him anything more about their private lives.

It didn't work on Matilda. "Sera won't permit anybody to hurt Jasmine."

"I don't doubt that."

"Wonderful, isn't she?"

"Jasmine? Absolutely."

"That goes without saying, but we both know it wasn't Jasmine I was referring to."

Luke gave her a hard, icy look.

Her twinkling, mischievous eyes softened. "You think I ought to mind my own beeswax, but how can I? *Someone* has to look out for you."

He rejected that immediately. "I'm not your problem, Matilda."

"I'm making you my problem, dearest. You and I are more alike than you think, you know. Nobody ever looked out for me either. This is the first place I've ever felt sheltered. This is the first place I've ever had space to be exactly what I am. It could be that for you, too, but I suspect you're determined not to let it. *I*, however," she went on, "am much harder to keep at a distance, so I *will* stick my nose in, and I *will* interfere, and I *will* look out for you."

Luke didn't say anything. He couldn't.

After *that*, it seemed a *little* churlish to object to her utter certainty that if he would simply let her make all his decisions for him, he would soon ascend to a realm of joy no human being had ever had the privilege of experiencing before.

November sped by, the colours deepening into the warm, lazy, saturated tones that marked the end of autumn. The rolling hills yellowed into soft olive shades, and in the woods at the top of the hill, dark and spiky evergreens mingled with the toasted golds, burnt oranges, russets, and deep poppy reds of the oaks, birches, and poplars. In the garden, hazy golden sunlight dappled the wild grass. Late-blooming wildflowers added pops of white, lilac, and scarlet. Clemmie, with her orange and red fur, got even better at vanishing when it suited her.

As for Sera's glass teapot and restoration spell, Luke was doing his very best not to take any interest in it, but it was impossible not to notice that nothing had changed since the artichoke. There'd been no discovery of a phoenix feather and no epiphany about a strand of sunset, and anybody with eyes could see that as time went on, Sera, who had been so eager and so full of ideas when Luke had first translated the spell, was losing heart.

"We're getting nowhere," Clemmie groused, kicking petulantly at a handful of pebbles on the stone patio. The weather had turned, bringing bitter December winds to the wild garden. "I'm going to be stuck like this forever."

Luke, who had had the temerity to venture outside to make sure the kids were still alive and accounted for (yes and yes), and had been immediately accosted with this information, was unimpressed. "Sorry, I forgot this was all about you."

"*I'm* the one without opposable thumbs."

"If you mention opposable thumbs one more time—"

"It's not *my* fault nothing we've tried has worked!"

Sera, who was sitting in the old, battered rocking chair that lived outside next to the herb beds, knees close to her chest, her expression far away, said nothing. Luke wasn't even sure she'd heard them.

You've gone away, my love. It was what Jasmine would say, quietly, whenever she happened to see that expression on Sera's face. Luke didn't know where *away* was, but he couldn't help thinking Jasmine had been saying it a lot lately.

Sera stood abruptly. "I have to go recast the heat spells."

Before he could stop himself, Luke said, "I'll do it."

"It's fine, it's my job."

Exactly. So why was he saying it again? "I'll do it."

"Oh. Okay." She blinked at him, coming back from wherever she had gone. "Thank you."

So Luke cast the heat spells (half of which had to be worked with an undead rooster on his shoulder), put the kettle on, and went back to his books.

Like it was a normal part of his day.

In fact, a lot of things had started to feel normal. He'd even started to look forward to some of them.

Like the evenings. Firelight, hot tea, buttery toast, and a cranky innkeeper. Luke and Sera were, inevitably, the last ones awake each night, the last to leave the living room, and Luke couldn't help but notice that he was going up later and later. He wasn't even sure why. Sometimes the TV was on in the background, and sometimes they talked about something that had happened that day or about the kids or about a random obscure fact from magical history, but mostly, they just did their own thing on opposite ends of the sofa, not even touching, her feet just inches from his leg, his forearm propped very nearly on her ankle.

And yet, for some reason, it felt like that was exactly where they were supposed to be. Like this was a thing that had, somehow, become important. Like his lonely and her lonely fit perfectly into the empty spaces at the other's side, saying nothing, asking nothing, just keeping each other company.

The incomprehensible, it turned out, was becoming comprehensible. Whether it was Sera, who'd forgotten how to fly and longed for the sky, or Jasmine, who hadn't been loved and now loved everybody else twice as hard, or Nicholas, who had walked away from a life of luxury in Mayfair because he couldn't bear to be a part of a family that had built its wealth on the blood and bones of others, these people were becoming clearer and realer, all of them. Their fairy-tale peculiarities side by side with the quiet, ordinary things they dreamed of. Their unwavering hope for the future hand in hand with the desolation of their pasts.

That, Luke could understand. History was how he made sense of the world, after all, and what was history if not a collection of stories to make the incomprehensible comprehensible?

The downside of this understanding, of course, was the discovery that *he* was the odd one out. This was a place stitched together by resistance, by acts of defiance by people who could not or would not go gently down the path the world had decided was inevitable, but Luke had never resisted. He had never defied. If resistance had an opposite, surely that opposite was resignation, and if there was one thing Luke had always done *very* well, it was resigning himself to the inevitable.

He didn't belong here, any more than he'd ever belonged anywhere else, but for the first time in thirty-four years, oh, how he wished he did.

CHAPTER TWENTY

*N*o," said Sera.

Theo unleashed the full force of his pleading puppy eyes on her. "Pleeeeeease?"

"I can't do it," Sera said, refusing to allow that look to melt her heart. "I refuse. I've taken you there three times already, Theo. Three. Times. Alex, your grandma can take you both."

"She says she's done it three times too," Alex said with a grin. "She says it's your turn."

"No," said Sera at once.

Theo spun around to look at Luke, who didn't even wait for the question before saying, "Not a chance."

Theo protested this injustice immediately. "You haven't *ever* been there. Not even once!"

"And I intend to keep it that way," Luke insisted.

Alex giggled. "I don't think we're winning this one, Theo."

"Why don't you ask Malik?" Sera asked impishly.

On cue, Malik strolled into the living room, a sleeping baby propped against his shoulder. "Ask me what?"

"Can you please, please, *please* take Alex and me to Nicholas's tourney at the Medieval Fair this Sunday?" Theo asked at once.

Malik, ever amiable, said, "Yeah, why not?"

"Yay!" Theo whooped. "You're the *best*, Malik! Thank you!"

Having thus achieved this most ardent of goals, Theo and Alex dashed happily out of the room.

"Ta," Malik said dryly to Sera, who grinned back at him. "Joke's on you, though, because apparently this means I'm the *best*. Luke, do you want me to take Posy too?"

"God, no, she'd hate it," said Luke. "Thanks, though. I'll take her to the coast for the afternoon instead. She'll get to splash about in the obscenely cold sea and eat her weight in salty chips, so she'll be happy."

"I owe you," Sera said to Malik, and she meant it with her whole heart. If Nicholas were to ask, she would perjure her soul without hesitation, but the truth was she found jousting mind-bogglingly tedious. There were only so many times she could watch two people riding full tilt at each other with wooden sticks in hand before she started to wish *she* were one of the wooden sticks so that she might be swiftly demolished and put out of her misery.

Theo and Alex, on the other hand, being youthful and therefore not yet jaded by the cruel passing of time, loved it.

"Has anyone ever told you you're a grouchy old codger trapped in the body of a young woman?" Malik asked when she repeated this observation.

"How do you feel about cabbages and peppers planted side by side, Malik? Do they, perhaps, make *you* a bit grouchy?"

"Don't you bloody get me started on that," Malik said affably. "God, I need a cuppa. No, actually, I need a triple espresso. Here."

And, displaying highly questionable paternal instincts, Malik deposited baby Evie in Sera's arms and walked off to the kitchen to procure himself a hefty dose of caffeine. Sera was aghast. "Really?" she shouted after him. "Me? When everyone knows I'm about as nurturing as a dustpan?"

"If by everyone, you mean just you, then you're absolutely right," Luke agreed equably.

"What's that supposed to mean?"

"It means you're the only one who thinks it" came the withering reply. "Everyone else knows that you are, in fact, a nurturer. You're scowling at me while simultaneously snuggling that baby."

"I am not!" Sera could not quite resist rubbing her cheek against Evie's downy brown hair, but that was for the sensory enjoyment and most certainly *not* because she was doing any nurturing.

Luke shut the book he'd been reading. Firelight flickered in his eyes. "You smother Theo in kisses. You've stuck with Clemmie. You keep Matilda's plants alive because you know she loves them. And," he added, with an unexpected, wicked grin, "I've seen the photographs."

Sera froze. "*What* photographs?"

"The ones on Jasmine's phone. Of the zombie chicken last winter. Wearing a sweater you took off one of your old dolls. Because you were afraid he might get cold."

"And just think," said Sera, "I could have spared myself this mortification *and* kept my magic if I'd just let Jasmine go meet her maker all those years ago."

"I heard that!" Jasmine called sunnily from her bedroom next door.

"You were supposed to!"

Evie stirred awake, regarded Sera for a few fraught seconds, considered bursting into tears, and then, apparently deciding Sera was an acceptable substitute for her father, went promptly back to sleep.

Luke's phone vibrated with a text. He glanced at it and, abruptly, the warmth in his face was gone. Without a word, he left the room.

It took Sera a good three minutes to wriggle off the sofa without jostling Evie. She returned the baby to Malik and went outside. All three kids were kicking a ball around under the oak tree by the side of the house, and Matilda was gardening on her beloved patch, but Luke and Jasmine were standing at the edge of the patio, looking expectantly down the length of the garden.

Jasmine turned to Sera. "Posy and Luke's mother is dropping in for a visit, but, well—"

"She can't find us," said Luke.

"Her satnav's not working?"

"Her satnav's fine," Luke said in a clipped voice. "She says she's driven up and down that road over there half a dozen times now, but she can't find the inn."

Sera couldn't help feeling like she was being accused of something. She crossed her arms protectively over her chest. "I don't decide who the magic lets in, and I don't decide who it keeps away. It obviously doesn't want her here."

"Sera, this is not Nicholas's father," Jasmine said gently. "When the magic kept *him* away that time, it had good reason. More to the point, Nicholas didn't want him here."

"Do you want her here?" Sera asked Luke. "Does Posy?"

Luke's jaw clenched. "She *is* our mother." Sera couldn't help noticing that wasn't an answer. "If she wants to see Posy, if she wants to see where Posy's living, she gets to."

"Posy's happy here. What if your mother decides she doesn't like what she sees and wants to take Posy back to Edinburgh with her?"

"*I'm* going to do that sooner or later."

Why did he keep saying that? Yes, it was true, but why did he feel like he had to keep *telling* them? And why did it hurt every time he did?

Sera suppressed that thought and said, "If *you* take Posy back, you'll be doing it because it's what's best for her. Your mother, on the other hand—"

"—gets to do it anyway," Luke said shortly. "Whatever you think of her, whatever *I* think of her, she's still Posy's mother."

"Apparently only when it's convenient for her!" Sera said sharply. She looked down, scuffing her socked foot against the stone slab beneath her. "I'm not being difficult, Luke. I just don't know what you want from me. I'm not what's keeping her away."

"It's your spell. You could ask it to let her in."

Every single part of Sera hated that idea. Pushing back against her own spell? She trusted her magic. It had earned that trust, over and over again. Pushing back against a choice it had made felt wrong.

"My love," Jasmine said softly, crossing the patio to take

Sera's hands in hers, "I know you think you're responsible for everybody here—"

"I *am* responsible," Sera replied at once. "I didn't plan it, or ask for it, but *I'm* the gargoyle of this particular castle. It's *my* job to keep everybody in it safe."

"But you don't have to do it alone," Jasmine insisted. "You *don't*, Sera. I'm here. We're *all* here. Maybe it is a mistake to let Posy's mother in. Maybe it isn't. Either way, this is not all on you."

Sera gave in. The night sky in her mind wheeled, the stars glimmering with a question, and she answered it. The magic pushed back, gently, doubtful, but she repeated her request. *Make an exception. Let her in.* The magic relented.

A minute later, a car came to a halt outside the garden gate. Sera went back inside.

It had been easier than she'd expected, asking the magic to make an exception, but it had left her feeling unsteady and exposed, probably much like Nicholas felt if someone asked him to take off one particular piece of his armour.

"Come on," Malik said, taking one look at her, "we're going out."

"Where to?"

"Nowhere. We'll just drive."

So that was what they did. Up the narrow, twisting roads lined with crumbling stone walls, down into the green valleys, past bare, leafless trees. With music on and a baby asleep in an infant seat in the back. Talking about nothing in particular.

Theirs was the sort of old, familiar friendship where talking about nothing in particular was the kindest, most comforting thing they could do for each other. The other things, the big things, were understood but went unsaid because sometimes saying things out loud made them hurt that much more. It was why Sera had never told Malik in so many words about the magic and the clipped wings and the terrible sadness that snuck up on her with no rhyme or reason, but he had seen wildflowers blooming in teacups and he had seen glimmers of translucent Seras out of the corner of his eye and he had held her hand when she'd cried about big things and small things. It was why Malik had never said in so many words that he was rootless, banished like his parents and grandparents before him from his ancestral homeland, but she had sat beside him all through the night his mother had died and she had seen the rusted key he wore around his neck and she had stared, time and time again, at the old cartoon framed above his fireplace of Handala, a little boy who never grew any older and never would, either, not until he got to go home again.

They didn't talk about the IMMIGRANTS OUT! poster they'd once seen at the Red Lion, their favourite local pub until that exact moment, but it wasn't a coincidence they'd started going to the Red *Rose* after that. They didn't talk about the way it messed with their heads to belong to this country, at least on paper, and still know from experience that that white flag with a saint's red cross on it was something to be afraid of.

Theirs was a friendship built on the unspoken, shared understanding that you can love the home you've made with the whole of your heart and still know the land it's built on will never claim you.

Theirs was a friendship that did not talk about the things that cut deepest, but it understood that those things were there, and respected them, and gave them space.

So Malik didn't ask Sera what was bothering her that afternoon, and even if he had, Sera couldn't have told him because she wasn't sure she even knew. So they drove and talked about nothing in particular. Until it was dark, and dinnertime would soon be upon them, and they had to go home and get shit done.

The first thing Sera saw when Malik dropped her off at the inn was Posy, collecting pebbles outside the front door, and a knot in Sera's chest loosened. She hadn't realised until that moment just how afraid she'd been that she'd come home and Posy, sweet, headstrong, joyful Posy, would be gone.

"Oh, Posy," she said. "You're still here."

Posy smiled up at her. "Sera's house. Posy's house."

Sera smiled back. "I couldn't have put it better myself."

They went inside together. Sera, still feeling a bit shaky and exposed, didn't ask any questions about what had happened when Luke's mother had been here. She helped Jasmine and Nicholas make dinner, but skipped eating it and went upstairs instead. She put her oldest and softest pyjamas on, got into bed, and fell asleep at once.

Predictably, forgoing dinner and going to bed at half past six meant she woke just after midnight with a peckishness that wouldn't be ignored. As the chocolate stash in her bedroom was woefully depleted and she probably ought to eat something that wasn't pure sugar anyway, she made her way down the creaking stairs and down the dark hallway.

She froze.

There was a ghost in the kitchen.

It was ridiculous, really, to feel like she'd been betrayed by a *house*, but betrayal was exactly what she felt. She'd thought she and the inn had an understanding that she would put up with all the other ghosts as long as it never showed her *this* one.

Yet there she was, glimmering faintly at the edges, ever so slightly translucent. Not a child, or a girl, but Sera from just a few years ago. Deeply sad, savagely angry, and more than a little wild.

Sera tried not to think about those months when things felt like they were at their worst, before medication, before she'd asked for help. She *hated* that version of her. Hated the fights she'd have with Jasmine, the speed with which she'd lose her temper, the long days of not being able to get out of bed, the dark and terrifying things she'd think about doing. Hated, more than anything, the way it felt like she simply had no control over anything, not even herself. It was one of the sharpest, most crooked things on her memory lane, and she tried not to get too close to it.

And still, there she stood, that *other* Sera, in the middle of the kitchen, perfectly framed by the open doorway. Trembling, wrists pressed to her ears, mouth open in a silent scream of impotent rage and grief, until keeping all that bottled up simply didn't work anymore and, *bang*, she kicked the nearest thing. Hard enough to dent the cabinet door. Hard enough to break two of her toes.

Sera watched, rooted to the spot, as the ghost staggered back, first shocked, then crumpling in pain. She slid to the floor, back against the wall, and started to cry, head buried in her arms, arms clutched around her knees, the foot with the broken toes sticking out and away.

That moment was what had finally convinced her that she needed help, but it had come later. Right then, watching herself,

Sera wasn't thinking of the later. All she was thinking about was how much she'd hated herself in that moment, hated what she'd become, hated Jasmine for dying, hated Clemmie for the resurrection spell, hated the Guild for abandoning her, hated the country for rejecting her, and hated herself all over again for hating all those other things. She'd felt nothing but rage and desolation and ugliness.

Her heart raced, panicked, fluttery, taking her right back to that moment—

And then—

Footsteps. Quiet. Careful. Not Sera, frozen in the dark hallway. Not the ghost, breaking into pieces on the floor. Someone else.

Luke stepped into the frame. Had he been in the kitchen the whole time? Had he *seen*—?

He had. He had seen the whole ugly spectacle.

So why—

Instead of recoiling, instead of walking away, Luke stepped closer. The other Sera didn't react. Of course she didn't. She didn't know he was there. She wasn't real, not anymore. He knew that too. He had seen enough of these strange, translucent fragments of memories to know that they were just echoes, pieces of history that the house kept safe, unaffected by the present.

So why was Luke still there?

He didn't say a word. He just sat down on the floor, shoulder to shoulder with a ghost, keeping her company.

In the hallway, Sera knew it didn't, *couldn't*, change the memory, because that night had already happened and Luke hadn't been there, but what it could do, what it *did* do, was a simple magical act of transmutation. She saw the memory through his eyes. And what she saw, for the first time, was not ugliness at all but pain so enormous and consuming that it had felt like dying.

I'm sorry, she said silently to her past self. *I'm sorry I hated you. I'm sorry I wasn't kinder.* All the shame that had been tangled up in the memory was annihilated, leaving only compassion and regret in its place.

Her hand lifted to the opposite shoulder, to the exact spot where the ghost's shoulder touched Luke's. She shouldn't have been able to feel anything, of course, yet she could swear she did. As if that touch, that moment, had crossed the boundaries of time and space, travelled miles of night sky and stardust, and become infinite.

CHAPTER TWENTY-ONE

*S*era retreated to the stairs to wait the memory out. Luke found her there a few minutes later. He stopped in the darkened hallway, studying her, then stepped closer, raised a hand—

—and prodded her cheek.

She laughed, smacking his hand away. "I'm real."

Luke smiled. "Can't blame me for checking."

"No, I suppose I can't."

He leaned against the opposite wall, hands in his pockets. "I missed you earlier."

Her heart thumped unsteadily. "Why?"

"Turns out I've grown accustomed to spending the hours of nine to midnight on the same sofa as you."

Had he been drinking? Was he high on magic mushrooms? "Have you been drinking?" Sera asked. "Are you high on magic mushrooms?"

"No. Well, no to the mushrooms. Yes to the drinking. Ish. Does Matilda's apple cider count?"

"Considering that woman makes her apple cider strong enough to intoxicate a rhino, yes, it definitely counts." Sera had never seen Luke after anything more than a couple of pints at the pub, so this was most intriguing. "So you missed me?"

Luke rolled his eyes. "I'm not saying it again, Sera."

"Well, I didn't miss you. On account of having been asleep during that time." She frowned, thinking about it. "But I think I would have if I'd been awake."

His mouth twitched. "Thank you."

"I'm here now," she pointed out somewhat unnecessarily.

"It's after midnight."

"You don't look like you've turned into a pumpkin yet. Come on, I'm hungry." She clambered off the stairs and went to the kitchen. No ghosts in sight.

Luke followed her and watched with a dubious expression as she pulled a tin of condensed milk, a packet of rich tea biscuits, a bottle of dark rum, and three peaches out of the cupboards. "And *that's* going to make you less hungry?"

"You'll see. Can you get that tin open for me?" She arranged biscuits over the bottom of a large ceramic dish, breaking off pieces to make them fit. She sliced the peaches and layered them over the biscuits, then added a second layer of biscuits on top. "I know what you're thinking. You're thinking there's not enough fruit and far too many biscuits. But you're wrong. This is the perfect biscuit-to-peach ratio."

Absently licking sticky fruit juice off her thumb, she looked up to see Luke watching her, eyes dark, a muscle ticking in his jaw. Her heart fluttered wildly, like a bird in a cage, and she couldn't resist licking her thumb again.

Luke's voice was like gravel. "I'm pretty sure you got it all."

"You don't look at me like that very often. I'm making the most of it."

That made him laugh. "God, you're a menace."

"I do my best."

Sera stirred a splash of rum into the condensed milk, drowned the sliced peaches and broken biscuits in it, and found some double cream in the fridge to pour over the top.

"And now," she said triumphantly, holding out a spoon, "we get to eat it."

Luke took the spoon in the manner of a man resigned to the hangman's noose, but like everybody else who had ever had the good fortune of catching Sera when she was in a rum, biscuit, and peach sort of mood, he was instantly won over.

They made decent headway through the bowl of boozy, sugary deliciousness before Sera finally worked up the nerve to say, "Thank you. For what you did earlier. For staying with her."

"Her? You mean you?"

"That's not me anymore."

Luke studied her from across the table, a furrow between his brows, absently turning his spoon over and over in his fingers. "What happened that night?"

Sera fidgeted with her own spoon, just to give her something to look at that wasn't him. "Clemmie and I had a row. A proper, raging, screaming fight. The inn was empty. No guests. Jasmine was at a weekend-long dressmaking workshop at the Medieval Fair. It was just Clemmie and me, and my head wasn't in a good place, and she just wouldn't *stop*. Why hadn't I got my magic back yet, why wasn't I trying harder, was I sure that there were still holes in the night sky, did I really expect us both to spend the rest of our lives stuck here with about a thimbleful of magic between us—" She broke off, sighed. "Like I said, my head wasn't in a good place. It hadn't been for a while. I told her to leave me alone and to stop acting like I owed her something, and she said I did owe her, actually, because she could have kept quiet about the resurrection spell and she didn't, and we shouted at each other some more, and eventually I said that if I ever *did* get my magic back, the *last* thing I'd do was break her curse. That didn't go over well, obviously, and she said she'd go find someone else to help her and she'd only stayed here as long as she had because I was alone and pitiful and she'd felt sorry for me, so I told her that yes, she *should* go, and she shouldn't ever come back . . ."

Luke listened to this without interrupting, and when she finished at last, he said, gently, "Did she go?"

Sera nodded. "I thought she'd just stormed off, like she often does after a squabble, and that she'd be back any minute. Then it got dark, and it got late, and she didn't come back. There was this sort of shiver in the house, in the magic, and I *knew* she'd really gone. And everything she'd said about how pitiful I was, everything I'd already been thinking, it just grew and grew and, well, you saw the rest."

"And you were alone," Luke said quietly.

Sera looked up at him then, attempting a wobbly smile. "Yes. That's why what you did, when you stayed with her . . ." She swallowed. "It feels like she's not alone anymore."

Silence crackled between them, the seconds stretching into minutes, and Sera couldn't look away.

"I . . ." Luke started, and stopped.

When she couldn't bear the silence any longer, she said, "Clemmie was gone three days, but she came back. Obviously."

His eyes searched hers. "And you?"

"I changed," said Sera.

"Did you? I mean, yes, you changed, but the way you talk about it . . ." He shook his head like two and two weren't adding up to four. "You talk about it like all those other Seras aren't you at all, but how do you know that? How are you so sure you've left them behind?"

"I didn't," Sera said at once, sharply, sharper than she'd meant to. "*They* left *me* behind."

The sharp, jagged edge of her voice echoed through the kitchen, and when it was gone, when the words had come out, it was like every blade of grass, every breath of wind, every old, creaky beam in the inn had gone completely quiet.

She'd never said that before. She'd never even thought it, not really, not in those words, but it was true.

They left me behind.

"Sera," Luke said, rough and quiet.

Her feathers prickled at once, sharp and spiky, and maybe he could see that because he stopped. She shook her head. "I don't . . . I . . ." It took her a minute to find the words. "When I was seven or eight, everything was possible. Then I became Albert Grey's apprentice and I gained this huge, dizzying, limitless world at the Guild, but I also lost something. He took little pieces of me, to keep me small, to keep me smaller than him. Then Jasmine died and I lost something else. My magic. My future. That belief we cling to as children that death's something that happens to other people, not to us. And that's what it's been like ever since. Like little pieces of me keep chipping away, bit by bit, and each time something goes, that version of me dies. Sometimes it's big things that do it. Sometimes it's small, stupid things. A dead great-aunt. A leaky roof. Exile. Ugly posters at the pub. Lost magic. A fight with a friend. It's like the world gets just a little less magical each time, and I get a little smaller. And every time I close my eyes, there's a huge, dark emptiness where the stars are supposed to be."

She was saying too much, but maybe she'd put too much rum in with the biscuits because she couldn't seem to stop. There was a lump in her throat, but no matter how many times she swallowed, it wouldn't go away.

"My name is Sera *Swan*," she said. "My magic is a *galaxy*. I belong in the sky, but I stopped being able to fly. And maybe that would have been okay if I could have become a creature of the earth instead, but this world, down here, it doesn't want me. The posters in the pub remind me of that. The Guild reminds me of that. It feels like I'm drowning. Which is a funny thing for a swan to say, but it's true. The earth doesn't want me and the water could drown me, so I don't belong anywhere anymore, and the ghosts remind me of that more than anything else. I talk about them like they're not me because they're not, because they left me behind, one after another, and each time, they've left me smaller and *heavier*, and heavy . . ." Her voice cracked. "Heavy things can't fly."

Luke stared at her, stricken. "You really don't see, do you?"

Her feathers were still prickly, still ready to cut anything that got too close, but she searched his intent arctic eyes, remembering that just an hour ago he'd made her see an old, terrible memory in a completely different way, and she wondered if maybe, just maybe, he could do it again. "What do *you* see?"

He gave a short, quiet laugh. "I don't think you understand

just how many times over the past few weeks I've wished I were more like you."

"Why would you—" Sera caught herself, bit the rest of the words back. He'd listened to her, after all. Yes, it sounded downright ridiculous to her that someone like *him*, who was incredibly intelligent and fiercely protective of his small, spirited sister and unexpectedly kind and extremely capable when goats ran amok, would want to be more like *her*, but the least she could do was listen too.

"I don't want to speak for Posy, or make assumptions about what she's thinking," Luke said, running his fingers over the old, worn grooves in the wood of the table, "but it always seems to me that she doesn't care about what other people think of her. She hasn't yet let the way other people have treated her change her. She's so completely, extraordinarily sure of who she is and just lets herself *be* that person. I mean, is it annoying when she wakes up between the hours of three and five in the morning and wants to tell me the name of every single animal in that farm app she loves so much? Yes, yes, it is. Do I sometimes find myself just a *little* unenthusiastic about pretending to be a dragon and chasing her up the stairs for the five hundredth time in a row? Yes, yes, I do."

Sera smiled in spite of everything. "But?"

"But I'll take it," said Luke. "I'll take it because it means she's still *her*. It means she's not disappearing inside herself, she's not putting miles of empty, frozen space between the real Posy and other people, she's not going *quiet*."

The penny dropped. "Like you did?"

He shrugged. "I was loud and excited and too much of

everything as a child, but I learned very quickly that it was much easier and that my parents liked me much better when I wasn't so *me*. So I did as I was told, and I was careful about what I said and what I did and how I behaved, and eventually, I didn't even have to try very hard anymore. I put so much cold, empty space around myself that the Tin Man thing wasn't exactly unexpected."

Sera scowled. "I thought we'd agreed the other apprentices were colossal fuckwits who had no idea what they were talking about and who probably ought to have actually read *The Wizard of Oz* before trying to be clever." She shook her head. "You made yourself into what you needed to be to survive, Luke. There's nothing wrong with that."

"I don't want Posy to have to survive."

"No, of course not," Sera agreed, emphatically. "Like you said, though, she isn't just surviving. She's happy. She's herself."

Luke laughed without much humour. "No thanks to me. I spent nine years of her life doing the same thing I did for almost twenty years before that. Giving in instead of fighting. Retreating instead of standing my ground. Resigning myself to the inevitable instead of resisting."

Sera was incredulous. "Is *that* what you think? Luke, hasn't it occurred to you that maybe the reason Posy hasn't yet changed is you? You didn't have anybody when you were her age, but she's always had you. Hasn't it occurred to you that maybe *you're* the reason she's still herself?"

He shook his head. She had a sudden, peculiar, upside-down sort of feeling and she wanted to laugh because if he, who could see right through *her*, had not seen this about himself, how much had she, who could see *him* as clearly as if he were glass, not seen about herself?

"*You're* the one who took her to the Guild because you wanted something better for her," she said. "*You're* the one who brought her here because the Guild wasn't right for her. *You're* the one who's still here even after your mother's visit today."

Luke's jaw tightened. "That went about how I expected it to go."

"Meaning?"

"I think her exact words were *a place like this is going to make Posy even wilder and unrulier.* I said that was fine by me."

"Posy is not unruly," Sera said crossly.

"I know that."

"I know you know that. That's my point. What happened after that?"

"We argued. I won."

"Is that so?" said Sera. "You won? In other words, you stood your ground?"

"I did that because of *you,*" Luke growled, standing abruptly. He looked down at her, furious, and she couldn't help thinking he looked like he wanted to either shake some sense into her or kiss the sense right out of her. "That's *my* point. You fight. You fight everything. Everything you just told me, about the night sky and the lost magic and the drowning, is a story you tell because you think it's about how small you've become, but what *I* heard was a story about how you're anything *but* small. You fight. You were fighting *today,* out there, for Posy, when you told us you were the gargoyle of this castle and you had to look out for us. *That's* why I stood my ground."

She would turn those words over and over later, like they were the most unexpected of treasures shining in the dark, memorising them, taking them apart, learning them from every angle, wearing them smooth with the pads of her thumbs. She would hold the words close, feeling her way around the unfamiliar edges of them, and later, much later, she would think that she didn't *totally* agree with him, and that he was giving her too much credit, *but*, and this was the important part, she would notice she didn't feel quite so small anymore.

But that would come later, and was future Sera's epiphany to have, because right then, at that very moment, present Sera was a little tipsy, and it was *very* important that she stand up too, and stomp around the table, and flatten one palm against his chest, right over his hammering heart.

And smile, and say, "That doesn't feel like tin to me."

His eyes widened, ink darkening the icy blue with a hunger that matched hers. He reached for her hand, like he wasn't even thinking about it, like it was a reflex that came as naturally as breathing, and held it in place on his chest.

And anything could have happened next, anything at all, but what *did* happen was the back door opened, and Nicholas stumbled in after what must have been a rowdy night out, whispered a drunken "Shhhh!" as if *they* were the ones clattering about in historically inaccurate armour, and tottered out of the room again.

Sera was tempted to be annoyed, but then it occurred to her that she was emotionally overwrought, not especially sober, and was wearing old, holey pyjamas that gave her all the sex appeal of a moose on Benadryl, so maybe Nicholas's interruption was for the best after all.

CHAPTER TWENTY-TWO

*T*hat Sunday, Theo came home from the Medieval Fair in high spirits, pink-nosed from the cold and hopped up on too much sugar (Malik's revenge, no doubt). He arrived just minutes after Luke and Posy, who'd spent the afternoon by the sea, and wasted no time in whipping out his phone to show them *all* the pictures he'd taken.

"That's Nicholas before the first round, and that's him after he won that round, and that's the girl who won the second round, and that's Alex and me with Nicholas's horse—"

"Nicholas," said Posy, pointing. "Theo. Alex. Horse."

"Good job, Posy," Theo said enthusiastically. "And this one's a picture of the huge slice of carrot cake Malik got me, and ooh, look, this is the Black Knight. He's the *villain*."

"Black Knight," Posy echoed.

"Alex thinks he's swoony," Theo told Sera and Luke, rolling his eyes with youthful disgust.

"He's wearing a spiky black helmet and full armour," Sera pointed out. "How does Alex know what he looks like?"

"They said that's what makes him swoony. He could be

anyone. He's not anyone, though," Theo added, addressing this last bit solely to Luke in the manner of one imparting vitally important information. "His real name is Greg. Sera knows him in the biblical sense."

"Theo!"

"What? That's what Clemmie told me."

Luke arched an eyebrow at Sera. "In the biblical sense? Him?"

Sera shrugged. "He kept most of the costume on."

Luke looked at Sera. Sera looked at Luke.

Theo looked at both of them. "Why are you being weird?"

"SEHHH-RAAAA!"

Matilda's timing had never been so perfect. Sera bolted.

As soon as Sera had dealt with Matilda's crisis (the persistent attentions of a crow that Sera had once had the audacity to leave a leftover cinnamon bun out for, which meant it now returned to the inn on an almost weekly basis, bringing sticky gummy bears and bubble-gum-flavoured lip balm and other gifts that suggested it thought Sera was thirteen years old), Matilda whisked her to the chicken run, where Jasmine was feeding the chickens, and said, "So?"

"No," said Sera at once. "No goats."

"I wasn't going to ask for a goat!" Matilda said indignantly. "I want an explanation! Jasmine! Tell her we want an explanation!"

Jasmine's eyes twinkled. "Matilda is suffering from a rather serious case of unsatisfied curiosity, my love."

"What about?" Sera asked.

"The sexual tension, that's what!"

"Where?" Sera asked with interest. "Has Nicholas met someone? Oh! Did you finally tell—"

"No!" Matilda said at once.

"What?" asked Jasmine.

"Nothing," said Sera and Matilda at exactly the same time. Jasmine looked confused. Turning back to Matilda, Sera said, "Who exactly are we talking about?"

Matilda looked like she dearly wanted to take one of her wellies off and throw it at Sera. "Who. Do. You. Think?"

Oh. "Me? And Luke? No, that's not a thing." Sera looked from one deeply loving and deeply unconvinced face to the other, gave in, and admitted, "Fine, there may have been a moment."

"I KNEW IT!" Matilda cried. "I mean, no, I didn't know there was a *moment*, per se, but there's positively a *crackle* in the air when the two of you are in the same room!"

Sera opened her mouth to object, thought about Theo looking at her and Luke just a minute ago and asking them why they were being weird, and closed her mouth again.

Matilda was still going. "Something's changed in the last few days. Something happened. Hence the *crackle*."

Jasmine shushed her. Hanging the bag of chicken feed off the end of her cane, she leaned on it with both arms and said, in her usual calming, gentle, steadying way, "Tell us about this moment."

"It was a couple of nights ago. Nothing happened."

"Did you want it to?" Jasmine asked.

Sera wondered if she could blame the sharp, bracing wind for the way her cheeks were going pink. "Yes. I don't know if he did, though. I thought he did at the time, but in hindsight, I might have been imagining something that wasn't there, and in any case, I'm pretty sure his senses had been addled by Matilda's apple cider."

"You have *got* to be joking." This contribution came from

Clemmie, who had materialised on top of the chicken coop and was looking down at them in disgust. "Sera, I was under the impression that you and I were sensible adults who had our priorities straight. *You* want your magic back. *I* want to not be a fox. Where, pray, does sexual tension fit in?" Before Sera could come up with a suitable reply to this, Clemmie turned to Jasmine and Matilda and said, "I can't believe she thinks his senses were addled by cider."

"I don't think she's seen the way he looks at her," Matilda mused.

Jasmine, ever loyal, objected. "We can't blame her for that, dearest. He only does it when she's not looking."

"She doesn't have fox ears either," Clemmie admitted somewhat grudgingly. "She doesn't hear the way his heartbeat stutters when he looks at her."

"How did this turn into the three of you gossiping about me like I'm not even here?" Sera demanded, seeking refuge in overly exaggerated grumpiness to hide the fact that her heart was doing all sorts of fluttery, flippy, thoroughly obnoxious things in her chest. (It didn't help matters that Clemmie could probably hear *that* too.)

"Nobody panic," Jasmine said suddenly, obviously not panicking in the slightest, "but I think we ought to start talking about something else. Right away."

"Oh, *no*, that's not true at all," Matilda insisted, rising to the occasion at once. "Pigs are actually *very* clean! And who can resist their tiny, snouty noses?" Apparently foreseeing that Sera would have no qualms about sharing that she could very easily resist all noses, snouty or not, Matilda went all in on the drama and added, "Look at me, Sera. Look at my ancient, fading bones. How can you deny me what could be my very last wish in this cold, cruel world?"

"Even for you that's a bit much, don't you think?" Sera said under her breath, trying not to laugh.

Matilda promptly began to wail into an enormous, flowery, and remarkably convenient hanky that she whipped out of the front pocket of her dungarees. Sera, who had seen mushrooms, daisies, cinnamon buns, satsumas, birdseed, an umbrella, a whole cabbage, and at least two grasshoppers come out of that exact pocket on one occasion or another, couldn't help thinking Mary Poppins's bag could learn a trick or two from Matilda's dungarees.

From somewhere behind Sera, Luke's dry voice said, "What set her off this time?"

"I think I said hi," said Sera.

Matilda's noisy wails were interrupted by a short, wheezy laugh, but if Luke noticed, he didn't let on. He jerked his head off to the side and said, "Can I interrupt?"

"Please interrupt," said Sera, clambering over the fence of the run and following him away from the sounds of fussing chickens and fussing Matildas. "What's up?"

He held up a wrinkled piece of paper. "I found this." It was Sera's list of ideas for the restoration spell, almost the entirety of which had been ruthlessly scratched out. Luke tapped something about halfway down the page. "Why's this scratched out?"

It took Sera a second to make out the words in the darkening twilight. "Essence of sunlight? Oh, I was excited about that for roughly five minutes, but Clemmie said it wouldn't work."

Luke shook his head. "Clemmie's wrong. It's a good idea."

Clemmie, who had no trouble hearing him from the top of the chicken coop, yelled, "Anybody with a halfway decent magical education knows essence of sunlight is too volatile for spellcasting!"

"Not if it's been tempered with black sand," Luke replied.

Clemmie froze. "That's not a thing."

"It's definitely a thing," said Luke, and, with what must have been heroic restraint, didn't even add that in future, Sera might want to run her ideas past someone whose magical knowledge *wasn't* almost twenty years out of date. "Look, I'm not saying this is going to work. I'm just saying it's possible. There's every chance your teapot will just spit the essence of sunlight right back out, but we won't know until we try."

"We?" A tiny smile tugged at the corners of Sera's mouth. "You were pretty adamant that you weren't going to get involved."

He gave her a faint answering smile. "And here I am anyway."

Oh, fuck this.

She hugged him.

The top of her head collided with his jaw, her chin banged into his shoulder, and she ended up practically hanging off his neck, but for the few seconds it lasted, it still, somehow, felt warmer and more comforting and more *right* than anything had in a long, long time.

Stepping back and moving on hastily, she said, "How good are our chances? You keep saying that whatever goes into the spell has to matter to me . . ."

"I think this counts. Do you remember getting your magic tested?"

Sera would never forget it. On her first day at the Guild, she'd been whisked off to a restricted alcove of the library where, surrounded by dusty books and old records and strange, glittering bottles of ingredients, she'd met old, haughty Bradford Bertram-Mogg, who'd looked down his nose at her before pointing one bony finger at a granite pedestal.

The pedestal was black, polished smooth, and its surface perfectly round and perfectly flat. Pursing his lips like she was putting him to a great deal of unnecessary trouble, Bertram-Mogg had plucked a small, round bottle off one of the shelves. Sera had had no idea what was inside, but she could see that it gleamed so brightly that she almost couldn't stand to look directly at it.

"That's essence of sunlight," Chancellor Bennet had explained, clapping his hands with childlike excitement. "We use it to find out how much magic a witch possesses."

"Who did you say her father was?" Bertram-Mogg had asked Chancellor Bennet. "Where is he from? Why can't *his* country take her?"

"For one thing, Bradford, she lives *here*, and for another, if you'd seen what *I* just saw when I visited her home, you wouldn't want anyone else taking her."

Impatient, Albert had intervened. "Get on with it."

With a grumble, Bertram-Mogg had carefully uncorked the little bottle and had let exactly one drop of the essence of sunlight fall to the surface of the pedestal. Instead of spreading like water, it held its shape like mercury and waited, a small, vibrating bead of burning gold light.

"Touch it," Bertram-Mogg had instructed, extending the tip of his index finger to demonstrate.

"Will it hurt?"

He'd tutted. "No."

"What's supposed to happen?"

"It will be absorbed into the tip of your finger and, if you are indeed a witch, it will light up under your skin and show us how much power you have. Don't expect much." He sniffed. "A single glowing finger is all some witches get. Even those of us from the best and brightest families are lucky to get a full arm." *And you,* he might as well have added, *are certainly not one of us.*

With Chancellor Bennet hopping from one foot to the other beside her like an overexcited sparrow, and Albert watching from the corner with narrow eyes, Sera reached for the bright, quivering drop of light with a nervous finger.

It didn't hurt, Bradford Bertram-Mogg had been right about that, but she got more than a glowing finger.

The light had spread under her skin, warm and a little tingly, shooting up her arm, shining so brightly you should see it through her clothes, flooding outward into every limb, every hair, every cell, until her body couldn't contain all the light anymore and the three men had backed away in shock, shielding their eyes.

For one extraordinary moment, Sera *was* the sun.

"I'll never forget the look on their faces," she said to Luke. "They couldn't look down their noses at me anymore. They couldn't believe a nobody like me could possibly be that powerful, but that one drop of sunlight told them they were wrong."

"To be a fly on that wall," Luke said with a grin. "It seems to me that we could make a pretty good argument that essence of sunlight is special to you, don't you think?"

"Oh, I do very much think," Sera agreed at once.

Clemmie, who had jumped off the coop and stalked over to

them, puffed up her russet fur in annoyance. "Well, that's all well and good, Mr. I Know All There Is to Know about Magic, but I've yet to hear how we're supposed to get our hands on any essence of sunlight. Are *you* going to go back to the Guild and get it?"

"No," Luke admitted, reluctantly. "The Guild doesn't do the tests at the castle anymore. Four or five years ago, after Bradford Bertram-Mogg kicked up a fuss about having to leave his country house every single time someone needed to be tested, Chancellor Bennet let him move the location of the tests. His house is just about the only place we'll find essence of sunlight, and no, Clemmie, before you ask, Bradford Bertram-Mogg is not going to give me any."

"What about your employer?"

"He doesn't like Verity either."

"Marvellous," said Clemmie in a sour voice. "Great. Spectacular. So what was the point of this, then?"

But Sera was too excited to let this stand. She refused. She had not gotten her hopes up for nothing.

"So you're saying the only way we get the essence of sunlight from Bradford Bertram-Mogg's country house is by taking it," she said slowly, ignoring the prick of the thorns as she searched her memories of her years with the Guild. "We'd only need a drop, wouldn't we? He'd never notice it was gone."

"We could need a drop, a bottle, or an entire blooming *vat* of it, Sera, and it wouldn't make a bit of difference," Clemmie grumbled. "It's the *taking it* part that's the problem. The Bertram-Mogg manor is a big, ugly behemoth where, at any given time, you'll find about a dozen Bertrams, Moggs, and Bertram-Moggs in residence *and*, I might add, a few dozen of their staff. Unlike the Guild's castle, where any witch is welcome—"

"Hardly," said Sera.

"—they're not going to just let anyone in," Clemmie went on, undeterred. "*I* might be able to sneak in unnoticed, but fat lot of good that'll do when I haven't got—"

"Don't you dare say it," said Luke.

"*Opposable thumbs*," Clemmie snapped.

A possibility tickled the back of Sera's mind. It was slightly terrifying, and undoubtedly reckless, but—

"It's the sixth," she said.

Luke and Clemmie stared at her.

Okay, that *had* been a little vague. "The date. It's the sixth of December."

"So?" Clemmie sounded well and truly ready to wash her hands of the whole affair.

"*So*," said Sera, meeting Luke's intent, steady gaze, "does Bradford Bertram-Mogg still host his winter masquerade in the second week of December?"

"No," Luke said at once, icy, implacable, and more than a little incredulous.

"He doesn't?"

"Yes, he does. No, we're not doing what you're thinking right now."

"Why not? Professor Walter used to be invited every year, so now that *you're* up there with her as one of the Guild's best magical historians, *you* must be invited too." He didn't deny it. It was all Sera could do to keep herself from squealing with glee. "You could go! You could take me as your date! This is *it*, Luke. This is how we get in and get the essence of sunlight!"

"How *we* get in?" Luke growled. "*You* can't be seen anywhere near that house. You're in exile."

"It's a *masquerade*," Sera pointed out. "Everyone will be masked, and it's been fifteen years since any of them have seen me, so even if Howard Hawtrey or Bradford Bertram-Mogg or someone else who knows you recognises you, they won't have any idea who I am."

"No," Luke said again. "Even *if* I thought this was a good idea, I would absolutely *not* be taking you."

"No," Sera said right back, fiercely. "You'd be risking everything you have. You're the one they'd recognise. You're the one who would get in who knows what kind of shit for trying to steal something from one of the wealthiest and most prominent families of the Guild. So no, you have to take me. I'm the one who wants this. I'm the one who doesn't have a place there anymore. Besides," she added, playing an ace she was pretty sure he couldn't beat, "how many times have you been to that house?"

A muscle jumped in his jaw. "I haven't."

"I have. I went to every winter masquerade when I was at the Guild. I know that house. I know where to find what we need."

Luke stared at her for a long time, his arctic eyes dark and furious, but she could see he was thinking about it, that he knew how much it meant to her and how impossible it would be to change her mind. After a minute, resigned, he said, "Albert will be there. He's too powerful. If we try sneaking off to steal something right under his nose, it could set off every magical alarm bell he's got. Besides, if anyone is going to recognise you after all this time, it's him."

She nodded. "We won't be able to stop him going. It's the biggest night of the year. He won't be able to resist the opportunity to show off." She thought about it some more. "What if we could make him leave for a little while?"

"Oh, really?" Clemmie demanded. "And how, exactly, are you going to do that?"

"*I'm* not," Sera replied. "*You* are."

"I hate you," said Clemmie.

Sera smiled. "And here I thought you'd spent almost twenty years longing for an excuse to break into Albert Grey's house, spit in his favourite cognac, and knock over his obscenely expensive and dangerously fragile marble statue of himself."

And Clemmie, the fox, showed all her teeth.

CHAPTER TWENTY-THREE

*T*he last time Sera had put on an actual *gown*, she'd been just shy of her fifteenth birthday and had been going to the last winter masquerade she'd attended, so it was decidedly unsettling to look in the mirror and see herself dressed up like that again.

She rather liked the way she looked, though. Jasmine had outdone herself. With just five days in which to come up with something that would fit in at the Bertram-Mogg country house, she'd bought an emerald gown from the Medieval Fair, taken it apart, restitched it to Sera's exact measurements with layers of green silk and tiny glass beads, and crafted a gorgeous mask to match. The result was a flowy, corseted work of art that made Sera feel like she'd been transformed into a beautiful, powerful, and morally ambiguous sorceress.

Clemmie, watching from the windowsill, heaved a nostalgic sigh. "I used to look fantastic in a corset."

"What did *you* wear corsets for?"

"My everyday style could best be described as Renaissance opulence," Clemmie replied. "It suited my body. I had

Rubenesque proportions. I was roundly, wholesomely lovely. Big, long-lashed eyes. An innocent rosebud pout."

"Innocent," Sera scoffed.

Clemmie was indignant. "How dare you? I was precious. A true girl next door."

"Only if that door belonged to Beelzebub."

Frowning into the mirror, Sera realised her swan necklace was a problem. The neckline of her dress was too low to hide it, and having a literal *swan* on display seemed a bit much when the whole point was to go incognito, but it also felt wrong to go out tonight without her talisman. Hmm. What if she turned it around and let the pendant hang down the *back* of her neck? Her long hair would hide it. Problem solved.

It was almost time to go. Sera picked up her phone, her keys, and her masquerade mask and stashed them carefully in the dress's many ingenious pockets. Jasmine had also fashioned a matching cloak out of a bolt of sumptuous velvet fabric, it being December after all, and Sera tied this tightly at her shoulders, covering up the entirety of the dress.

"The last fifteen years have been quite the adventure, haven't they?" Clemmie said suddenly, looking up at Sera, her fur haloed in silver by the moonlight behind her.

"You're saying that like the adventure's over."

"Don't we want it to be?" Clemmie looked out the window like she was already a long way away. "Isn't that the whole point? Finally? Don't we *want* to get out of the snow globes we've trapped ourselves in?"

Yes, Sera wanted to say, but she couldn't help thinking that you could only get out of a snow globe by shattering the glass, and shattered glass always hurt.

Absently, Clemmie went on. "It's been a long time since I last went to Grey Manor. Do you remember that big fight we had? When I was gone for three days? I went to my grandfather's house. He was so happy to see me. He wanted to go straight to Grey Manor and demand that Albert break my curse. We got as far as the doorstep. I lost my nerve and ran away."

Sera blinked at Clemmie in the mirror. "Back up a second. You told me your family wanted nothing to do with you after the curse."

"They don't. My grandfather's the only exception."

"And he thought he could march up to Albert Grey's front door and *demand* things of him?"

"He was used to people doing what he asked of them." Clemmie gave a laugh that was all teeth and claws. "He *was* the Chancellor."

Sera spun around. "The Chancellor? Chancellor *Bennet*? Is your grandfather? *You're* a Bennet?"

"Is that really so surprising? I told you Albert and I were classmates. Do you think just anybody gets to rub shoulders with a Grey?"

"But a Bennet! You're pretty much Guild royalty!"

"Am I?" Clemmie snapped bitterly. "Ask your historian about the Bennet family tree. He'll tell you I'm not on it. My family was so ashamed of the scandal that they've all but erased me from our history." She jumped off the windowsill, stalking to the door. "You're wondering why I didn't tell you years ago, but it's pretty obvious, isn't it? I never told you my real name because I'm not even sure I get to keep it. I never told you about my family because I don't have one. Good luck tonight."

"Clemmie, stop," Sera said. "Enough. This is me, remember? It doesn't matter what your name is. *I'm* your family."

Clemmie stared at Sera, still bristling, eyes wide and dark. Then, predictably, she let out an exasperated growl. "I never expected to love you, you know. Jasmine. Theo. None of you. I don't like it. I don't appreciate the way it's snuck up on me. When *I* sneak up on people, they call me a villain, but I'm supposed to believe it's acceptable when *love* does it?"

"Love does have a way of creeping up on you," Sera admitted.

Clemmie nodded. "Like black mould."

"And it's just as hard to get rid of. Sorry."

"I'll live."

"Be careful tonight, Clemmie."

"You too," said Clemmie, and she was gone with a swish of her tail.

Sera took a deep breath, smoothed the front of her cloak, checked herself one last time in the mirror, and left.

Jasmine, Matilda, and Nicholas had taken the children to Malik and Elliot's for dinner, which had been planned weeks ago and which Sera and Luke had had to apologetically get out of at the last minute, so the inn was unusually quiet.

Coming down the stairs and passing through the familiar, softly lit rooms, Sera found herself thinking about snow globes again, and it struck her that no matter how much she missed her magic, no matter how deeply she ached for it, this inn, with all its creaks and groans and inconveniences, was no snow globe. It was her home, where she knew the story of every dent and scar, where the notches on that doorframe over there told the tale of Jasmine measuring Sera's height every year until she was thirteen, and the scorch marks on Sera's bedroom wall spun a fable about a little girl casting her first spell. Here, the handmade curtains on the windows had laughter stitched into the seams, the cracks between the floorboards were filled with old magic and Nivea cream, and the wild, unmanageable garden was the scene of a hundred teatimes and starlit dreams.

The inn breathed magic, *her* magic, and maybe it was the fact that she was on the brink of getting the next part of the restoration spell, but Sera hadn't felt this close to that magic in a very long time.

The front door opened and Luke stepped in, car keys in hand. "There you are. Nice cloak."

"I thought I'd left holes in the sky," she heard herself say. "Exit wounds that kept bleeding stardust. I used up my magic when I brought Jasmine back, and I was never going to get it all back without something big like the restoration spell, but I should have got a *little*. That's how it's supposed to work. Magic replenishes itself."

"You thought yours couldn't," Luke said.

"I thought that every time it tried, it bled out again. Because of the exit wounds. What if that's not it, though? What if . . ." She looked up at the soft, golden starlight glimmering faintly in the corners. "What if those little bits of stardust that keep coming back, that keep regenerating, aren't actually disappearing at all? What if they're still here?"

Luke watched her intently. "Go on."

"I think it's the spell. *My* spell. The one that protects us, the one that makes the inn shine in the dark so that anyone who needs it can find it."

"I guessed as much the day my mother came to visit," Luke admitted. "The inn never made sense to me. I know magic. I know spells. They're finite. Once they're cast, they're cast.

They're not ours anymore. And yet yours was. You were able to change the spell to let her in. You shouldn't have been able to do that, but you did, because it's still yours. You're the one keeping it alive. It's like stoking a fire. It's the same spell you cast twenty years ago, the same fire, but you've never let it go out. That's where that little bit of stardust is going."

"Why didn't you tell me?"

"You already knew."

He was right. She had known. She just hadn't seen. From the very moment she'd cast the spell over the inn, she must have been keeping it alive, giving it that little bit of stardust to keep it going, but she'd had so much of it then that she'd never noticed. Who notices a few stars scattering into the aether when there are millions more? Then, the first time she *had* noticed, she'd resurrected Jasmine, and there was just a smattering of stars left in her night sky, so she'd finally seen the few that were going away.

She'd thought of them as exit wounds bleeding stardust, but she'd just needed to look at it a little differently.

"I could have stopped," Sera said softly. "I could have let the spell die out. Taken back that little bit of extra magic I kept giving away."

"You could have, but you were never going to," Luke said. "You cast the spell that made the inn what it is. You cast the spell that brought Jasmine back to life. *Those* things are you. You've always given your magic away when it matters most, and I think there are very few things in the world that matter more to you than the home you and Jasmine made for each other, so no, you were never going to let the spell die out."

Stupid, crumbling, ridiculous Batty Hole.

He was right again. There were very few things in the world that mattered more.

Sera traced the old, knotted surface of a wooden beam beside her, smiling a little, and gave herself another minute to listen to the familiar, comforting heartbeat of the magic all around her.

Luke leaned against the open front door, waiting patiently, hands in his pockets, and as she looked at him properly for the first time, it occurred to her that if Luke in jeans was obnoxiously attractive, Luke in a black jacket and tie ought to be illegal. For one thing, the black made his eyes even bluer, the mere existence of the tie immediately conjured images of her fingers undoing it, and she *really* ought not to get started on the way the jacket fit over his shoulders and how the stark white shirt underneath did nothing to hide the planes of his torso—

He looked at her in confusion. "What?"

She refused to blush. "You, er, you look nice. No, that's a lie. You look a lot better than nice."

"So do you." His voice was rougher than usual.

And he hadn't even seen the dress yet.

Right. It was *definitely* time to go.

Unlike the clunky metal bucket Sera drove around in, Luke's car actually did the things cars were supposed to, so they'd barely pulled out of the driveway before the heating was on, the seats were toasty, and Sera's breath no longer fogged white in front of her.

She was beginning to really feel the enormity of what she was about to do. She'd let herself get swept up in excitement and hope, in ideas and planning and making sure Clemmie knew what she needed to do, and it had all happened so fast that she'd been able to avoid thinking about how it would feel to go back, however briefly, to the world that had expelled her.

She bit the end of her thumbnail and looked out of the window, counting the minutes.

"Sera." Luke reached for her hand, tugging it away from her mouth before she completely massacred her fingers. "It's going to be okay."

She looked at him, her eyes tracing the lines of his profile, the angle of his jaw, the sharp, icy blue of his eyes, and she felt such a fierce, painful yearning that it took her breath away.

He met her gaze for a quick moment, and she had to look away.

And counted the minutes some more.

"There's chocolate in the back," Luke said.

She smiled then. "You know me well."

She reached behind her, feeling for the pocket on the back of her seat where Luke usually stashed Posy's tablet on longer drives so she could reach it, but her hand hit something in the dark footwell instead.

There was a yelp. "Ow!"

Sera shrieked. Luke yanked the car onto the verge and slammed on the brakes. "What the *fuck*."

A head of grey corkscrew curls popped up between their seats. "Now before you get too cross with me," Matilda said, uncurling from the footwell like a demon summoned from the lowest depths of Tartarus, "I didn't plan to send us right off the road. You weren't supposed to find me until we got there."

Sera, trying and failing to calm her thundering heart, was outraged. "You could have been an axe murderer!"

"I'm not an axe murderer," Matilda said soothingly. "For one thing, I don't have an axe."

"The fact that you addressed the axe part and not the murderer part is really not very comforting."

Luke twisted around in his seat and levelled an arctic stare at Matilda, who, Sera noticed with increasing dread, appeared to be wearing a very nice frock. "What the hell are you doing here?"

"Luke, she's not wearing dungarees," Sera whispered.

Luke sighed. "Christ on a wee bicycle, she thinks she's coming with us."

"Exactly!" Matilda said happily, settling herself comfortably in the back seat. "I was lying in bed last night, you know, tossing and turning and thinking about it, and every bone in my body revolted at the thought of squandering the only opportunity I might ever have to attend an *actual* magical ball. An. Actual. Magical. Ball. Where did you say that chocolate was, by the way? Are there any other snacks? I simply can't miss supper at my age."

"Then you should really have gone to Malik and Elliot's for dinner, shouldn't you?" Sera retorted.

"I'm taking you home," Luke said sternly.

Matilda objected at once. "You can't do that! We're over an hour away from the inn! Isn't Clemmie supposed to kick up a ruckus at Albert Whatshisname's house at ten o'clock on the dot? Doesn't that mean the two of you have to be at the Bibbly-Bogg house when that happens? You won't have time if you take me home first!"

"Bertram-Mogg," said Sera.

"That's what I said. Bibbly-Bogg."

"It's gone eight already," Luke said quietly to Sera, glancing at the clock on the dash.

They shared a long, exasperated, and increasingly resigned look. Sera nodded. Sighing again, Luke looked over his shoulder and said, even more sternly, "You do what we tell you. You don't tell anybody your real name. And *don't* drink anything gold, purple, or blue."

Matilda practically did a jig of glee. "Why not? Will it trap me in Hades forever?"

"We should be so lucky," said Sera, and Matilda flicked her lovingly on the ear.

Luke started the car and pulled back into the road.

There were a few minutes of silence and then, unexpectedly, Luke started laughing.

Sera and Matilda stared at him.

Practically wheezing, Luke said, "Bibbly-Bogg," and then Sera, too, was laughing until she could hardly breathe.

CHAPTER TWENTY-FOUR

Luke's friend Howard met them in the grand, lamplit driveway of the Bertram-Mogg house (or, as Sera would now forever think of it, the Bibbly-Bogg house), resplendent in a glittery cloak and deep blue tuxedo that strained over his belly.

His mask, which matched his cloak, was little more than a sliver of fabric over his eyes and did nothing to hide his identity. Luke's was bigger, in velvety black, with an embellishment on either end that distracted from his distinctive blond hair and looked a bit like horns. Sera, who had put her own mask on before getting out of the car, was very glad hers covered her eyes, most of her nose, *and* both her cheekbones. Yes, it was highly unlikely that anyone would recognise her as the skinny teenager with the permanent high ponytail that she'd been fifteen years before, but she wasn't taking any chances.

"It is enchanting to meet you, my dear," Howard said affably.

Sera's old training kicked back in like a reflex. "And you, Minister Hawtrey."

"Call me Howard, please. If you're Luke's date, I insist we become fast friends." Howard beamed at her with an open sincerity that made it rather difficult not to smile back. She was beginning to see why Luke liked him. He gave Luke a hearty wallop on the shoulder. "Good to see you, old chap! And after all those times you insisted you'd never show your face at a Guild event!"

"Still not showing my face," Luke said dryly.

Howard roared with laughter. "I've missed you, Luke. Where have you been? How's Posy? And who is this?"

"I," said Matilda momentously, extending her hand like she'd read one too many historical romances, "am Fortuna."

Incredibly, Howard took her hand and gallantly kissed it. "A name as beautiful as you are."

Matilda giggled. "Oh, I like you. I shall be your date for the evening."

Howard looked delighted. "Nothing would make me happier, but, er, who *are* you?"

"Why, I'm Luke's beloved grandmother, of course," Matilda said without missing a beat. "I know I'm not strictly on the guest list, per se, but you wouldn't turn old Nana away, would you?"

"I wouldn't dream of it," said Howard, offering her his arm and sweeping her up the steps of the entryway.

"Oh, aye, makes total sense," Luke said wryly, watching them go. "I'm so white I'm practically translucent, but sure, *she's* my grandmother."

Sera choked on a giggle. *"Fortuna."*

"God help us."

Howard and Matilda had paused at the top of the steps, waiting for them, but as the reality of the moment hit her again, Sera discovered she couldn't move.

It had been nearly sixteen years since she had last been here, but it was like the Bertram-Mogg country house had been frozen in time. The shining white steps, the velvet drapes in all the windows, the floating orbs of light, and the towering hedges were exactly as she remembered them. Acres of immaculate grounds stretched out around them, soaked in the purples and blues of the night, landscaped and manicured to within an inch of their lives, and Sera was tempted to laugh slightly hysterically at the contrast between this pristine, opulent place and her wild, tumbledown inn.

Ahead of them, guests were entering the manor in twos and threes. Most were unrecognisable behind their masks, but some were only too familiar, like that pair of Grey cousins over there or that Bennet boy in the lilac suit. In the shimmering, hazy lights, she could almost see their younger selves, sneering at her, admiring her, envying her, feigning friendship just to get closer to her power.

Her heart raced, and she was drowning, and past and present were so tangled up in her mind that for a moment she was afraid she'd forget which was which.

Then Luke took her hand, and she held tight, and the jigsaw of their fingers fitting together felt like a lifeline pulling her out of the water.

"I'm okay," she said, shaking away the cobwebs of the memories. Piercing, worried eyes searched hers from behind his mask. She didn't look away. She wanted him to know she meant it. "It's a lot, but I'm okay now. Really."

He nodded. "Okay."

"Come on, ducks," Matilda called from the top of the steps.

Luke didn't let go of Sera's hand.

At the door, an honest-to-God *footman* stood waiting to take their coats and cloaks. Sera, still a little unsteady with nerves and not *quite* brave enough yet to show off her gown, pretended she was cold and kept her cloak on.

Inside the house, the vast lavish rooms heaved with glittering guests. They were dancing, playing cards, whispering to one another in the alcoves, even competing to see who could cast the most impressive spell. And drinking, of course. *Lots* of drinking.

"Remember," Luke said to Matilda, when Howard was distracted talking to someone in a blackbird mask, "nothing gold, purple, or blue."

"What about silver?" Matilda asked, eyeing a passing tray of flutes filled with sparkling silver liquid.

"Silver's fine."

Sera had been searching the crowd, every sense on high alert for a glimpse of Albert, but she whipped her head around at once and said, "Nooooo. No silver. Sorry," she added to Luke, "I forgot about the silver. You've never been here before, so you couldn't have known about it." As another tray passed by, wielded by an unobtrusive server, she pointed. "*Pink* is fine, though. That's just strawberry and lemonade with optional vodka."

"Optional," Matilda scoffed, plucking a pair of flutes off the tray and keeping both. "So what's in the silver one?"

"Witch wine."

Luke raised an eyebrow. "So *that's* the fabled witch wine? Famously enchanted in a secret brewery at the foot of Ben Nevis and aged for exactly twenty-two years and twenty-one days? Renowned lowerer of inhibitions and provoker of orgies?"

"What?" Matilda demanded. "And I'm not allowed to have any? Rude!"

"The stories are greatly exaggerated," Sera said in a pained voice, trying to rid herself of an unwelcome vision of Bradford Bertram-Mogg engaged in an orgy. "As for you, drinks with magic in them have unpredictable side effects on people who aren't witches, so no, you can't have any."

"According to Verity, her sister turned green after a single sip," Luke added. "And I don't mean green like she looked a bit seasick. I mean Wicked Witch of the West green. It took a *year* to fade."

"Pink it is, then," said Matilda, round-eyed.

As soon as Howard had extracted himself from his friend in the blackbird mask, Matilda whisked him off to dance. Sera and Luke lingered at the edge of the room, among a handful of card tables. Sera glanced at the time on the antique clock on the wall. Nine thirty-eight. If Clemmie stuck to the plan and wreaked havoc at ten like she was supposed to, they had about twenty minutes or so before they'd need to get to Bradford Bertram-Mogg's large and impressive private library.

It was hot in the room, and Sera tugged at the ties of her cloak, regretting keeping it on. Maybe it was time to get rid of it.

Her eyes snagged on a table of youngish women playing enchanted pontoon. Was that Francesca? No, not with that posture. She relaxed a little. Francesca was the one other person who might recognise Sera. Yes, she'd helped her after Theo and Clemmie had taken *The Ninth Compendium of Uncommon Spells*, but she was also Chancellor of the Guild, and she'd been pretty clear that Sera could not allow Albert to find out what she was up to, so there was no telling how she'd react if she found Sera here.

Where *was* Albert anyway? Sera knew he would be here, so as much as she dreaded seeing him, it was almost worse *not* knowing exactly where he was.

And then she felt it, a sudden sharp, painful prickling along every inch of her skin, like her magic, like the universe, like every ghost of every past Sera, was warning her.

A second later, there was a ripple across the room, as if other people had reacted to the thing Sera had already sensed, and Luke's icy, narrowed eyes landed on something over the top of Sera's head, somewhere behind her. They were standing so close together that she felt the sudden tension in his body.

"He's here, isn't he?"

He nodded. "All the way across the room. He's not looking this way."

Slowly, carefully, Sera turned.

He was older, of course, with more lines around his eyes and his hair the steely colour of the lightning his magic manifested as, but she'd have known him anywhere. The immaculately tailored clothes, the hawkish features that might have been handsome if he'd ever smiled with real warmth, the proud tilt of his head, and of course the power. An invisible magical force you couldn't ignore, crackling around him.

Sera, who had once had power like that, knew that it didn't have to be so obvious. It didn't have to snarl at your side like a chained, muzzled beast. He *chose* to do that. She had once been awed by his power, had admired it, but all these years later all she could see was how lazily he wore his magic, how little respect he gave it, and how easily and unapologetically he used it to make everybody around him submit.

He was holding court, surrounded by a handful of eager, fluttering guests. Then Bradford Bertram-Mogg pushed his way to the front to fawn, and as Sera watched Albert nod at whatever he was saying, with an expression that perfectly combined indulgence and impatience, she remembered all the times he'd looked at *her* with that expression and remembered how it had made her feel like she was lucky to have his attention, and she ought to be grateful, and she *certainly* oughtn't to waste his time.

Past and present collided again and Sera was ten, uncertain and eager to please and hoping she'd found a father figure at last; and she was thirteen, aware by then that she'd never please her unpleasant mentor and basking in the admiration of everybody else instead; and she was fifteen, realising at last that this man she'd admired and trusted had been trying to make her small the whole time she'd known him.

"All hail the Great and Powerful Wizard of Oz," Luke said quietly in her ear, and Sera laughed, and the past fell away.

She looked up at him. "Thank you for this. For everything."

"You don't have to thank me. What you and the inn have done for Posy, for me, it's . . ." He shook his head. "I could do a lot more and we'd never be even."

"Is that why you're here?"

He laughed. It sounded like sandpaper. "You know that's not why I'm here."

She opened her mouth (to say what, she didn't know), but then the musicians stuttered to a stop and the dancers stumbled and the room went suddenly, terribly quiet.

Albert was in the middle of the room with another, younger man, in an empty space a dozen dancers had scuttled out of. Now that the music and conversation had stopped, every word out of Albert's mouth rang clear and cold as a bell.

"It does seem a bit rude, Martin," Albert was saying, examining his fingernails idly, but Sera knew that quiet, coaxing voice too well, and every muscle in her body went rigid with dread. "I was here for ten minutes and you still hadn't bothered to come up to say hello."

"I didn't—I hadn't seen you—" Martin faltered. "I was—I was dancing—I just thought—another dance—"

Albert nodded understandingly. "You were dancing. Of *course*. Well, by all means, Martin, dance."

And Martin's feet began to move. Sera watched him look down at them in horror, because he certainly wasn't making them move, and then the musicians began to play again, their eyes wide, their limbs stiff and stilted, as if *they* weren't making them move either. It was horrible. Martin was literally dancing at the end of Albert's strings.

"Albert—" Martin gasped, as his feet flailed faster and faster and faster, "Albert, please—"

Beside her, Sera could feel Luke's fury, burning as fiercely as hers, but they couldn't move, either of them, because they couldn't draw attention to themselves, and even if they did, what could they do? What could *she* do? She wasn't the girl she'd been fifteen years ago. She was all but powerless.

"Albert," Sera heard Howard say, laughing nervously, and she knew he meant well but she wanted to yell at him to shut up, shut *up*, because he was standing right next to Matilda, and

Matilda wouldn't stand a chance if Albert's ire got anywhere near her. "Albert, old chap, don't you think that's enough now?"

Albert ignored him. Poor Martin was almost in tears.

Then, just like that, Albert snapped his fingers and it stopped. Martin dropped, a puppet whose strings had been cut.

Albert patted him on the shoulder. "Not to worry. I forgive you."

He strolled back to his gaggle of courtiers without a backward glance. Martin dashed out of the room. Slowly, uneasily, awkwardly, the music and the dancers and the card games started up again.

Under his breath, Luke murmured, "Every action has an equal and opposite reaction."

Sera looked at him, confused.

"Verity said it. It's why she helped Theo and Clemmie take the spellbook. Without an equal to keep him in check, Albert Grey isn't just a smug bastard lording it over everybody else."

"No," Sera agreed. "He's more than that. He's a monster."

On the wall, the clock struck ten.

CHAPTER TWENTY-FIVE

M atilda wove her way over to Sera and Luke, her fourth pink flute in hand. She'd been shaken by what she'd seen, but she'd obviously recovered with her usual aplomb. She nodded at the clock. "Any minute now. Good luck, ducks. I'll keep Howard busy."

"What if he notices we're missing?"

"That one's easy," Matilda said brightly. "I'll just tell him your simmering passion got the better of you."

Luke choked on his drink. "Our what?"

Beaming, Matilda gave them each a kiss on the cheek and trotted away.

"Sometimes I don't know if I'll murder her or Clemmie first," Sera remarked conversationally. "Guess which way I'm leaning right now."

Five minutes past ten. Six minutes past ten. Seven. Eight.

Then someone was rushing into the room, making a beeline for Albert, and whispering urgently in his ear. Without a word, Albert stalked out of the room, and maybe it was Sera's imagination, but she felt like the entire house let out a relieved breath as soon as he was gone.

It was time.

They had to be quick. Clemmie's hijinks would hopefully keep Albert distracted for the rest of the night, but there was always the possibility, however unlikely, that he'd decide to come back to the party. Grey Manor was only five minutes away.

"You shouldn't come with me," Sera said to Luke. She'd tried saying it before and had been entirely ignored, but she had to try one last time. "If I'm spotted, at least you won't be involved—"

"Let me be very clear," Luke interrupted her. "I'm not letting you out of my sight."

Against all odds, Sera grinned. "You know, I never thought the stern, sexy academic thing would work on me, but it really does."

Luke stared at her in incredulous silence.

She bit her lip to hide her smile. "We'd better get going."

Sera doubted much of this colossus had changed in the last hundred years, let alone in the last fifteen, so she knew (or at least *hoped* she knew) which of the house's many rooms would be empty and which would not, which hallways the servers would take between the kitchens and the party, and, most importantly, how to get to Bradford Bertram-Mogg's private library without being seen.

Her memory served her well. Mostly. There were an awful lot of people in the hallways, which slowed them down considerably, and then there was a canoodling couple blocking one of the doorways, and then, *just* when they thought they were in the clear, one of the Bertram-Mogg cousins almost caught them in a darkened corridor—

Luke grabbed Sera and yanked her behind the heavy drapes

beside the window and neither of them dared to breathe until the girl had sauntered past.

As soon as she was gone, Sera bolted across the corridor, pulling him with her, and then they were finally safely ensconced in the empty library.

Sera locked the door for good measure, overcome by a fit of relieved giggles. "Well, that was fun."

"It was, in every possible way, the literal opposite of fun," Luke said emphatically.

"Uptight prig," she teased.

His eyes twinkled. "Quarrelsome gargoyle."

After that little adventure, their masks felt like lead instead of velvet, and it was *far* too hot for a cloak. They left their masks on a chair and Sera worked on the knot she'd tied at her throat. Luke, meanwhile, went over to a shelf of antique curiosities. Sera shrugged off her cloak.

"This is four thousand years old," Luke said in disbelief, glancing back at her. "It's the only one of its kind and it's just sitting here, in this—"

He stopped. Froze. And just looked at her.

Sera knew she ought to be thinking about the essence of sunlight right now, and she knew that there was only so long they could stay here before Howard would ask too many questions or Albert would return to the masquerade, but every one of those sensible thoughts had gone clean out of her head. She couldn't look away.

His voice grated out an order. "Tell me to stay where I am."

"Do you *want* to stay where you are?"

"You know I don't."

She bit her lower lip. "Then come here."

He stood very still for a fraction of a moment, and then it was like a tether snapped. He crossed the space between them in two steps. One hand braced against the solid wood of the old door behind her, right beside her ear, while the other went to her waist, pressing her into the door, his fingers burning hot through her dress. His eyes were flames of the fiercest, iciest cerulean.

She had forgotten that the hottest part of a fire burns blue.

She smiled at him. "Is this what it takes to beguile the stoic, icy historian? A corset?"

"It helps." He smiled back. "That's not the real answer, though. It's you. *You're* what it takes."

Sera leaned up on her toes, slid one hand up the back of his neck, and tugged his mouth to hers.

She came alive. The kiss was hungry and furious. Their legs tangled and his thumb stroked the edge of her hip. He tasted like lemonade and white rum and the sky. Stars burst against the dark of her closed eyelids.

When he broke the kiss, Sera made a plaintive, protesting sound. Luke dropped his forehead against hers, breathing hard. She bit lightly down on his lower lip. He groaned and kissed her again.

"Just so you know," Luke said, his voice low and rough, "I'm not fucking you against the wall of the Bibbly-Bogg library."

She laughed. "There you go, being all sensible."

"If you move about half an inch to the left, you'll feel just how *not* sensible I am right now."

"Don't tell me that," Sera complained, consumed by regret. "This is hard enough already."

Luke dropped his head, shoulders shaking with laughter. "Not the best choice of words."

Sera wasn't exactly sure how it was possible to be blazing with intense desire *and* almost crying with hysterical laughter at the exact same time, yet here she was, and it was a good minute or two before either of them was able to recover.

Smiling ruefully, she kissed him one last time and said, "I suppose we do have a job to do."

Luke reluctantly let her go. "We do."

"Right." Sera took a deep breath, squared her shoulders, and faced the library. The last time she'd been here, she'd tucked herself into that corner over there to read *The Extraordinary Handbook of Magical Tales*, but there was no time to look for favourite books tonight. "Where do we think that horrible man keeps the essence of sunlight?"

Considering how large the library was, and how cluttered with old treasures, priceless manuscripts, and looted antiquities that had no business being here in the first place, they found the essence of sunlight remarkably quickly. In a rear nook, behind a large, imposing desk from which Bradford Bertram-Mogg no doubt enjoyed looking down his nose at intimidated young witches waiting to be tested, was a glass cabinet filled with his stash of spellcasting ingredients. The essence of sunlight was on the third shelf from the top, seven small, round, dusty bottles of it tucked away among enchanted mushrooms and copper coins.

Sera picked up one of the bottles, a sudden ache in her chest. There was still one more ingredient to go, but she was so much closer now . . .

Luke pulled a small glass vial out of his pocket. It looked empty at first glance, but when you looked closer, you could see the black sand sitting at the bottom.

"You do it," Sera said, looking down at her slightly unsteady hands. "I'm too anxious."

She carefully uncorked the bottle and handed it to Luke, then uncorked the vial too because his hands were full. He tipped the bottle over the mouth of the vial, his hands sure and steady, his brows knitted with concentration. Three blazing, blindingly gold droplets trickled into the vial, one after another, and then it was done.

Luke returned the bottle to the cabinet and Sera clutched the vial in one hand, feeling the reassuring warmth of the essence of sunlight radiate through the glass.

"We did it," she said, slightly stunned.

Luke nodded, looking equally surprised. "We did it."

She laughed. "I think now's a good time to get ourselves out of here, don't you?"

And that, of course, was when it all went to hell in a handbasket.

The door rattled, like someone had tried to open it and discovered it was locked. An instant later, the bolt Sera had been so careful to latch shattered and the door was flung open.

Sera spun around, instinctively clutching the vial protectively to her chest, and found herself face-to-face with Albert Grey.

"Ah, Sera." He gave her his favourite smile, the one without any warmth in it whatsoever. "Long time no see. You look well. Ish. Bit pale. Almost like you weren't expecting me."

Words. Sera needed to say some. She couldn't. She couldn't speak.

How had he gotten back here so quickly? Whatever Clemmie had wrought at Grey Manor ought to have kept him away at *least* a while longer.

Albert strolled closer, hands linked casually behind his back. "To be honest, Sera, I expected this to happen sooner or later. I *hoped* you'd never find a way to get your magic back, but I knew there was always a chance you'd get your hands on the restoration spell. I knew silly things like the *rules* or our *laws* wouldn't stop you. After all, they haven't before, have they?"

The words came back in a flash of fury. "You're one to talk. I'm pretty sure what you did to Martin out there isn't exactly playing by the rules."

"Your mistake," Albert said, ignoring that inconvenient fact, "was trusting any part of this ridiculous plan to Clementine. What did you think would happen when I returned to Grey Manor, found my priceless statue in pieces and my handcrafted walnut desk on fire, and saw a *fox* dashing away into the woods? Did you think I wouldn't realise straightaway that you were involved?"

Damn it, Clemmie. He wasn't supposed to see you.

There was an angry crack of lightning across the ceiling. Sera tried not to flinch. She would not let him make her flinch.

Albert gave her an elegant shrug. "Why, I wondered, would Sera and Clementine do something so incredibly stupid after all this time? And on tonight of all nights? So of course I came straight back here. And look what I found."

He waved a hand and Matilda drifted through the open door, hovering a few inches off the ground. Sera's heart plummeted. Matilda's eyes moved, alarmed and outraged and practically spitting needles in Albert's direction, but the rest of her was stiff and frozen, like he had bound her in invisible ropes.

"This is my fault, not hers," Sera said at once. "She didn't know why I brought her here."

"Nobody doubts it's your fault, Sera," Albert tutted. "And

there's no need to fear for the little old lady. I'll happily release her. You, on the other hand, have broken our laws *again*. Exile's no longer an appropriate punishment for you." His eyes narrowed in on the vial she was clutching to her chest like it was a lifeline. "I'll take that, thank you."

To her horror, Sera felt the vial wobble in her hands and then slip out of her grasp, yanked by the unseen force of Albert's magic. She squeezed her fist tighter, desperately, but the vial was still slipping—

—and then it stopped.

Albert raised an eyebrow, then regarded Luke like he had noticed him for the first time. "Really? How long do you think that will stop me?"

Luke shrugged. In her panic, Sera hadn't even noticed that Luke had cast a spell, but there it was. A shield, shimmering faintly between her and Albert, blocking his power.

"Aren't you one of Verity Walter's historians?" Albert asked curiously. "Larry? Lawrence? Something like that. Not that it matters. Do you think you'll ever work in the Guild's libraries again after this?"

Luke didn't answer. He'd spent thirty-four years learning that icy, implacable calm, learning how to take away the satisfaction of someone seeing him react, but Sera knew him, and she also knew what it was like to go up against Albert Grey's magic, so she knew exactly what it was costing him to protect her. Her throat closed up.

And I'm not even pushing very hard, Albert's voice said in her head.

She jolted. She'd forgotten he could do that. She'd forgotten it was one of the very few things he'd ever taught her, long ago, and that she'd used the spell to send Francesca silly secret messages from all the way across the castle.

I could push harder, Sera. He's already in pain, but I could push so hard I break him. It's up to you.

"Luke, stop," Sera said quietly, swallowing hard. "It's done. He's won."

Luke looked at her, eyes searching hers, wondering what changed in the last thirty seconds. "What did he say to you?"

"Just let it go. Please."

"Sera . . ."

She shook her head. Pleaded with her eyes. He stared at her for one more moment, then, defeated, let the shield fall. He staggered a little.

Sera faced Albert, *hating* him, and opened her clenched fist.

Albert twitched a lazy finger, and the essence of sunlight flew from her hand to his.

"The strand of sunset, I suppose?" He shook the vial lightly, examining the bright drops inside. "Tenuous, but I imagine it could have worked. I'm curious, though. Where did you think you were going to get a phoenix feather?"

Sera was spared the necessity of having to answer (or, rather, the necessity of revealing she didn't *have* an answer) by the clatter of footsteps outside the library. The next moment, Howard burst in, anxious and out of breath, with Francesca in his wake.

"Father!" Francesca froze in the doorway, taking the scene in with something like horror.

Howard wheezed. "I thought—I thought I'd better . . . fetch the Chancellor."

"Good," Albert said genially. "You're just in time, Francesca. Would you like to do the honours of deciding what consequences would be most appropriate for this latest of our Sera's infractions?"

Howard's eyes almost popped out of their sockets as he saw Sera without her mask for the first time. "Sera? Sera *Swan?* Oh." He looked at Sera, and at Matilda, who was still frozen and definitely still fuming, and finally at Luke. He cleared his throat. "I say, er, Albert, don't you think that there may be some sort of misunderstanding? Perhaps Miss Swan could, er, go back to Lancashire and we could forget this ever happened?"

It was downright heroic, really, that Howard Hawtrey, who had every reason to side with one of his own, was even *trying* to stick up for her for Luke's sake, but Sera knew it would do no good.

Sera looked at Francesca. Francesca looked back. She hadn't yet said a word.

Finally, with only the smallest tremor in her voice, she said, "Father, let it go. Sera didn't get what she came for. It's over."

Albert looked at her in disbelief. "What has gotten into you?"

"I'm the Chancellor of the Guild and I've decided on the appropriate consequences for this infraction," Francesca replied, her voice a little louder. "She's going home. It's over."

For a long, tense moment, Albert simply stared at her. She refused to meet his eyes.

Slowly, Albert turned back to Sera. He was seething, but he was also Albert Grey and he *had* gotten the most important thing he'd wanted after all, so he said, "Very well. You understand, of course, that you'll never get your hands on essence of sunlight again. I'll make sure of it."

Then Albert dropped the vial of sunlight to the floor and crushed it beneath his heel.

CHAPTER TWENTY-SIX

"hen he *stood* on it," Matilda finished, naturally injecting as much drama into her reenactment of the scene as possible. "He'd already taken it from her, and it wasn't like Sera could get it back, but he still took the time to make her watch him destroy it."

"I fucking hate him," said Nicholas.

"Fucking hate him," Posy echoed brightly.

"Nicholas," Jasmine protested.

By the time Sera, Luke, and their stowaway had returned to the inn the previous night, a bit shaken but no worse for wear, the rest of the household had been in bed. Sera, who'd imagined coming home with the essence of sunlight, seeing it turn into gold smoke in the glass teapot, and then finishing what she and Luke had started in the library, hadn't been able to cope with such a promising night having such an unpromising end. She'd stayed up just long enough to make sure a very quiet, sullen Clemmie had gotten home safe and sound (she had) before cocooning herself in bed. Then, after a restless night of tossing, turning, tears, and rage, she had tottered down to breakfast and found everyone waiting for her.

They'd all been warned in advance that things hadn't exactly gone according to plan, of course, but Theo in particular wanted to know the whole story. He'd made it through exactly five minutes of breakfast, during which he, Posy, and Clemmie had competed to see who could eat the most bacon, before asking for *all* the details. Matilda, of course, had been more than happy to oblige.

"No one's explained how he knew what you'd done, though," Theo objected now. "He said he saw Clemmie sneaking away from his house, right?"

"It wasn't my fault!" Clemmie shouted down from the top of her favourite cabinet.

"Er, okay," Theo said, sounding like he thought it was perhaps a *little* Clemmie's fault for letting herself be spotted. "He saw you, figured out Sera was up to something, came back to the party, found Matilda, and guessed that the uninvited unmagical stranger must be part of whatever was going on. Then what? How'd he know to check the library? Matilda didn't say anything, so how'd he guess what Sera had gone there to get?"

"Magical spidey sense?" Matilda suggested.

"His power's something else," Luke agreed somewhat bitterly.

"I fucking hate him," Nicholas said again.

With a faint, tired smile, Sera said, "I really do appreciate that you're all so angry on my behalf, but I did just put half of us in real danger for nothing, Luke's never going to be allowed to go back to the Guild again, and I'm probably not getting my magic back, so maybe we could talk about something else?"

"You didn't *put* anyone in danger," Matilda objected at once. "Luke chose to be there. I chose to be there. Clemmie chose to be there. You didn't *make* any of us do that."

"And you know how this spell works by now," Luke added. "You know there isn't just one right answer. We might not be able to get hold of any essence of sunlight ever again, but we'll find something else that'll work as the strand of sunset."

"Sunset," said Posy.

"Exactly," Luke repeated, ruffling her hair. His eyes met Sera's across the table. "I don't care what Albert said, Sera. I love the work I do, but I promise you, Verity will find a way to get me to do that work even if I'm not allowed to return to the castle. Besides, when you get your magic back, and you *will*, you'll knock Albert Grey off his throne and break Clemmie's curse, and he won't be able to keep any of us away anymore."

"That was inspiring," Matilda said admiringly. "If I wasn't gay and your grandma, I'd be very attracted to you right about now."

Luke tipped his mug of tea at her. "Thanks."

Nicholas looked from Matilda to Luke to Matilda, thoroughly confuddled. "You're his grandma?"

"In a manner of speaking."

"What am I, then?" Nicholas asked with interest.

"Endlessly entertaining," Matilda said fondly.

"Who isn't in this place?" Nicholas pointed out, not entirely incorrectly.

Posy nibbled thoughtfully on a slice of toast, a red crayon in her other hand. "Sunset."

"Where's Clemmie?" Theo asked. "Wasn't she here a minute ago?"

"Maybe she's tidying your room," Matilda suggested.

Jasmine laughed. "The day Clemmie tidies anything is the day my name is no longer Jasmine Ponnappa."

This was one revelation too many for Nicholas. "Wait, what? Your name *isn't* Jasmine Swan?"

"No, dearest, that's just Sera's name."

Sera, acutely pained, said, "We really don't need to hear the whole story."

Which was, of course, the worst possible thing she could have said, because Theo choked out a laugh that he hastily turned into a cough and Matilda's eyes lit up with immediate glee. "Oh, I think we do indeed need to hear the whole story. Jasmine? Would you like to tell us what all the fuss is about?"

"There is no fuss," Jasmine insisted, entirely dignified. "My nephew's name is Sarath. Sera's mother's name is Svana. It's an Icelandic word for swan. That's all."

"All?" Matilda repeated incredulously. Even Nicholas looked appalled. "They named her after themselves! Twice! My poor, poor girl," she said to Sera, who laughed in spite of herself, "I'm so sorry, I shall never bring it up again, cross my heart."

"So why wasn't it Sara with an *A*?" Nicholas wanted to know.

"Go on, Jasmine," Sera said pointedly. "Tell them. Why *wasn't* it Sara with an *A*?"

Jasmine sighed. "They thought an *E* would make it more interesting."

"Well, Sera is perfect no matter what her name is," Nicholas insisted gallantly.

"You know what *is* interesting?" Matilda remarked, her bright, birdlike eyes scanning the length of the table. "None of us share a surname. Not one of us."

That couldn't be right, could it? Sera looked around the room, silently ticking names off as she went.

Theo was just as unconvinced. "What about Luke and Posy?"

"Different names," said Luke.

"Luke has their mother's name," said Matilda, who over the weeks of homeschooling had done enough paperwork on Posy's behalf to know this. "Posy has their father's. Funny, isn't it?" Her twinkling gaze fixed on Sera. "Families share a name, apparently, yet here we are."

"I get the impression you're making a point," Sera said.

"I'm just saying we're here for you," Matilda said. "No matter what happens with your magic. Whether you get it back or not. We're here. You know that, don't you?"

Sera smiled, her heart aching with love. "I do know."

And because of that love, she went looking for Clemmie. It took some time to find her, mostly because Clemmie, who was trying *not* to be found, was in the woodshed at the bottom of the garden, perched on a crate of firewood.

"What?" Clemmie said sulkily.

"I don't blame you for last night, Clemmie. It's not your fault."

"I know it's not my fault!" Clemmie snapped.

"Then why are you hiding?"

"I'm not," Clemmie replied, her voice losing its edge. "I'm just getting comfortable in my snow globe, seeing as I'm probably not getting out of it this lifetime." Hopping off the crate of firewood, she looked up at Sera and said, quietly, "I just need to be alone for a bit."

"Maybe you could be alone inside where it's warm?"

"I have *fur*," Clemmie muttered, but she slipped past Sera's legs and slinked back to the house.

Sera stayed in the doorway of the woodshed, leaning on the old, cobwebby frame, trying to regain even a sliver of the hope she'd felt the previous night.

It was the coldest day they'd had yet, and the sky was a stark, blinding white. Green hills and dark, woody thickets crisscrossed the horizon. The wind whipped through the trees, carrying a hint of satsumas and woodsmoke, and in the background, the chickens clucked disapprovingly at Roo-Roo, who had wandered into their run to pester them.

"I don't understand."

That was Jasmine's voice, but it was Jasmine's voice as Sera had never heard it, unsteady and uncertain. She poked her head around the side of the woodshed, worried, and froze when she saw Jasmine and Matilda standing in the shelter of a satsuma tree.

Instinctively, she knew this was a conversation she ought not to interrupt, and she ducked back a bit so that she was out of sight.

Unlike Jasmine, Matilda sounded completely calm. "What's not to understand? I've fallen quite madly in love with you."

Sera stifled a squeak. She'd finally said it!

"But . . ." Jasmine faltered. "But . . ."

Matilda waited patiently.

"I just don't see how you could possibly have fallen in love with *me*," Jasmine tried to explain.

Matilda's dark eyes flashed with anger and Sera wanted to hug her for it. "That, sweetest of hearts," said Matilda, "is because you had the misfortune of being born into a family who did not show you all the many, *many* reasons it's easy to love you. I would even argue it's impossible *not* to love you. There is a quiet strength and gentle kindness in you that I find quite irresistible. Your face doesn't hurt either."

Jasmine blushed. "My face isn't the thing people tend to notice about me."

"Very true. Your gentleness is the first thing, *then* your face." Matilda's eyes had gone soft and were bright with humour. "But if you mean your clubfoot, I can only speak for myself, and *I* find your foot every bit as lovely as the rest of you."

Jasmine dashed at the corners of her eyes with one hand like she was wiping tears away. "I've known you for two years, Matilda. You're my dearest friend. I never imagined you might . . ."

"I know," Matilda said ruefully. "That's you all over. Meanwhile, everybody else knows exactly how I feel about you because I'm just *that* obvious. I've been trying to be patient. You never talk about past loves, and I don't know if you've ever fallen in love with a woman, so I didn't want to push you . . ." Pausing, Matilda looked out over the horizon before saying, with a faint smile, "Last night decided me. For a few horrible moments, when I was frozen in place, watching helplessly as that man talked about punishing Sera, I had no idea if I'd get home to you, and all I could think was how much I wished I'd said something. How stupid I'd been to waste the time we'd had. And I promised myself I'd never waste another minute."

"Aren't we too old to fall in love?" Jasmine wondered, still sounding uncertain but also, to Sera's delight, downright *giddy*.

Matilda laughed. "You were over forty when your life really started. You of all people know that we're never too old for anything." She smoothed a single, windblown lock of Jasmine's hair back, an expression of utter joy on her face. "You know I used to teach dance. I've always loved it, the teaching *and* the dancing, but it wasn't quite enough. *This* is the life I wanted. This life of contentment and unexpected excitement, of little everyday joys, where I don't just get to *be* myself but also get to be *embraced* as myself. It's miraculous."

"We have built a miraculous life," Jasmine agreed softly.

"Imagine, then, how impossibly lucky I feel that not only have I found the life I always dreamed of, but I've found you too."

There was an expression on Jasmine's face that Sera had never seen before, an enormousness of feeling that seemed to come all the way from the inside, as if the darkest shadows of her past had finally been chased out by the light.

Matilda's smile faded. She took Jasmine's cane from her, gently, propped it against the tree, and took both of Jasmine's hands in hers. "Jasmine, I'm going to say something to you now, and then I promise I'll never mention it again if that's what you'd prefer. What I'd like more than anything, if you would like it too, is to spend the rest of the time I have in this world with you."

"I think . . ." Jasmine said softly, weighing each word as if it was precious, "I think I would like that."

"Do you love me?"

"I do." There was no uncertainty in Jasmine's voice anymore. "I've loved you for some time. I just didn't know I loved you like *this*."

Matilda's face glowed. She cupped Jasmine's face in her hands, bent her forehead to hers, and kissed her.

Biting her lip to suppress another squeal, Sera edged back

into the woodshed because she'd already seen more than she ought to have, really, and this was *their* moment.

So she waited, only a *little* impatiently, until they decided to take their moment indoors, where it was firelit and toasty and nobody would catch their deaths of pneumonia, and only then, when she was certain they were gone, did she come out of the woodshed.

As she went back to the house, she felt it again.

Hope.

Inside, in the living room, Posy looked rather cross.

"Sunset," she said insistently, holding up a piece of paper she'd drawn a picture on.

"I know, Posy," Luke said, sounding like this may have been the fourth or fifth time he'd said it. "It's a sunset. It's a good sunset. All the reds and yellows and oranges are perfect. Do you want to add a bit of blue or purple in too?"

Posy gave him a baffled look, then turned to Sera. "Sunset?"

"It's pretty," Sera said admiringly. Posy's crayon sunset was more of a blob with some sticky-outy bits, it was true, but Luke was right about the colours.

This was not the answer Posy had been hoping for. She stomped her foot in frustration.

"I don't understand, Posy," Sera said apologetically. "Do you need help with the sunset?"

"Is that a tail?" Clemmie asked from where she was stretched out by the fireplace, one eye squinting at the piece of paper in Posy's hands. "Why does her sunset have a tail?"

"Oh, I'm sorry, Van Gogh, is the nine-year-old's artistic ability not *quite* up to your lofty standards?" Sera demanded.

Theo walked into the room. "Has anyone seen my—"

"Theo," Posy interrupted, thrusting the picture at him. In the voice of someone who has lost all faith in the good sense of adults, she said, "Theo, sunset."

Theo took the picture, took one look at it, and yelled, "AHHH! Posy! You're brilliant! OF COURSE! It's so obvious! Sunset!"

"Sunset," Posy agreed smugly.

Theo grinned at Sera and Luke. "Posy and I'd better get extra cinnamon buns for this."

He strode across the room, pounced on a startled Clemmie, and yanked a hair out of her tail.

"Oi!" Clemmie was outraged. "I was already having a bad day, thank you very much!"

"Look!" Triumphantly, Theo held up the gleaming, reddish-orangey hair. "It's a strand of sunset!"

CHAPTER TWENTY-SEVEN

*T*he short version: Clemmie's hair worked.

The longer version: the glass teapot glowed bright, and there was a lot of squealing, and Theo and Posy got enormous hugs *and* extra cinnamon buns, and the undead rooster flapped excitedly from one pair of arms to the next, and Nicholas cried actual happy tears, and Matilda threw open the kitchen door and shouted down the garden at the top of her lungs, "FUCK-ING TAKE *THAT*, ALBERT GREY!"

"Well," said Clemmie, a little too smug for someone who hadn't actually done anything, "I always knew I'd end up saving the day."

And in a quiet moment, Jasmine tucked her arm in Sera's, Sera leaned her head on Jasmine's shoulder, and her great-aunt said, "I will love you with or without your magic, Sera. You will always be enough for me just as you are."

"I know," Sera said softly.

Jasmine smiled. "Still, I'm happy for you."

Sera smiled back. "I'm happy for you too."

Winter arrived in earnest that night, the first snow settling gently over the inn. Sera, who'd had enough excitement in the last twenty-four hours to last a lifetime, had retrieved her old list of ideas for the spell, determined to find her third and final ingredient, and had barely glanced at it before she'd promptly fallen asleep on the sofa.

She woke to Luke's hand on her hair. "Hi." He jerked his head at the window. "Come look."

Sera was a tad grumpy about this at first, and was determined to remain tucked under one of Jasmine's handmade blankets with nothing but her nose poking out of it, but then she blinked sleepily at the window and saw the snow, and her heart leapt.

Oh, give it a week and she'd be sick of scraping ice off her car and getting slush in her wellies, but for now, it was lovely. That first snowfall was always dreamlike and storybook perfect: the sky gone silver day or night, the fluffy layer of sparkling white covering the hills and valleys, the frost dusting the trees and chimneys and roof tiles, the crystalline flakes clinging to the glass of the windows.

Here, at last, was the season of hot chocolate topped generously with whipped cream and mulled wine laced with cloves and satsuma slices. The season of curling up on the sofa under the weighted electric blanket, with a piece of perfectly sugared shortbread in one hand and a cup of boozy coffee in the other, while the fairy lights twinkled soft and gold across the mantelpiece and along the curtain rods.

Some people simply weren't winter people. Sera, on the other hand, was the most winter person to ever winter. No matter how tedious it was to keep the firewood topped up and keep casting the heat spells, no matter how annoying the inconsistent hot water and temperamental boiler, *this* was her time. Give her a white, starlit winter's night (and the pipe dream of a completed to-do list) and she'd happily hibernate until springtime.

Yawning, she wriggled out from under the blanket and followed Luke to the window. She caught her breath. *"Oh."*

Out in the garden, Jasmine and Matilda were dancing. They had their dressing gowns on over their nightwear, which Sera couldn't help feeling was entirely inadequate protection from the cold, but they didn't seem to care. They had their arms around each other. Matilda was helping Jasmine stay on her feet, and they swayed gently to a song Sera couldn't hear, their eyes closed and heads together. Snow dusted the tops of their heads like spun sugar.

It was one of the most beautiful things Sera had ever seen.

Then Luke choked on a laugh. "Look."

The undead rooster was in the snow too, just a few feet away from Jasmine and Matilda, kicking gentle flurries into the air. Copying their exact movements. *Dancing.*

"Roo-Roo's always loved the snow," she said, suddenly and ridiculously choked up. "That's why I put that stupid sweater on him last year. He was always flailing around in it."

Luke was quiet for a long time before saying, "You've built a beautiful world, Sera Swan."

Had she? It hadn't always felt that way, it was true, but Sera wondered if maybe it was beginning to.

She still longed for the stars and the sky, because they were a part of her and nothing would ever replace them, but there was, nevertheless, something rather lovely about the weird, wonderful, *ordinary* everydayness of living. Flowers in teacups and the pages of books turning themselves and ghosts lingering at the edges, waiting, wanting something from her that she could never name. The familiar, comforting routines of casting heat spells, hitting old pipes with a hammer to make them behave, tripping over the undead rooster, baking loaves of crusty bread, drinking sugary tea and boozy coffee.

And then Luke said, "I'm going to miss this," and everything stilled.

Sera stepped away from the window, almost unconsciously putting some distance between them. "Miss this when? Because normally, when you talk about going back to Edinburgh, you use a different voice and you don't say things like *I'm going to miss this*."

He turned around to face her and said, in a perfectly, painstakingly level voice, "Verity called me a few days ago. She has a friend who's moving to Edinburgh at the beginning of the year. She works with young witches. Teaches the ones who chose not to go to school at the Guild but who need more help than just studying the books at home. Verity says she's nothing like the Guild instructors and governesses, and she's willing to work with Posy, so it's probably the best thing for her."

"I see." It was all she could bring herself to say. Her chest hurt.

She'd known this was coming. Luke had said it again and again. He'd been very clear that, sooner or later, he and Posy would go. She'd always known their future was in Edinburgh, not here, and she had no right to feel blindsided just because they'd stayed for all these weeks and it was becoming impossible to imagine the inn without them and she'd made the mistake of forgetting that it was only temporary.

"You said Verity told you a few days ago. Why didn't you say anything before?"

"We've done nothing but make plans for the winter masquerade for almost a week. It didn't seem like a good time to bring it up. But . . ." He closed his eyes like he was in pain, then opened them again. "I shouldn't have done what I did in the library without telling you first. I wasn't thinking. I saw you and I *stopped* thinking. It wasn't fair. I'm sorry."

"Don't be. I wasn't thinking either." She tucked her arms around herself. "The thing is, if I *had* been thinking, I probably wouldn't have done it. I wanted to. I still do. I just don't think I *can*. You're leaving. Maybe not for a few weeks yet, but you *are* going. And maybe if you were somebody else, I'd say okay, well, it doesn't have to be a serious thing, let's just fuck each other's brains out until you have to go, but you're *you*. I don't think I could *not* do serious with you."

Luke's throat worked. "I'm not going to just walk away. I wouldn't do that to Posy and Theo. I wouldn't do that to any of us. We'll visit. You'll visit."

"We will," Sera agreed. "For a little while, anyway. And it might work for the kids and for Jasmine and for Matilda, but I don't think either of us wants that to be the way *we* do this. If we were together, would *you* want to drive over three hours just to spend a day with me every now and then?"

"No," Luke admitted. "No, if we were together, I don't think I'd be able to stand not seeing you all the time, but I'd try to stand it. It couldn't be worse than not being with you at all."

Her resolve almost broke. She blinked back tears. "It wouldn't work."

"You don't know that."

"Luke, when you leave, you'll *leave*. You're *already* leaving. You've had one foot out the door since the day you got here."

Her voice wobbled. "I get it. I do. It's what you do. You always expect to leave, so you're always waiting for it. Ready for it. Even now, right this minute, you're already halfway gone."

He stared at her, stricken. She hated that she'd put that look on his face, but she hadn't said it to hurt him. She'd said it because it was true and she'd forgotten it.

She took a shaky breath, pulled herself together, and said, gently, "I hope this works out for Posy. You're thinking about what's best for her, and you should be, of course you should be, but maybe don't forget to think about what's right for *you* too. If going back to Edinburgh is what's right for both of you, if it's what you really want, you should do it."

Then, before she could fall apart, before she could give in and be selfish and ask him to stay for her, before she could risk feeling the way it would feel when he refused, she walked away.

CHAPTER TWENTY-EIGHT

*L*uke and Posy spent Christmas in Edinburgh with their parents. The winter markets and carousels and Yule logs kept Posy busy, while the sizeable research project Verity had handed him right before the holidays ("A real scholar doesn't take holidays," she'd said) left Luke without even the time for a spare thought.

Which, to be perfectly honest, suited him just fine. Spare thoughts were to be avoided at all costs.

He and Posy met Zahra, Verity's friend, and Posy seemed to like her, while Luke, meanwhile, found absolutely nothing to object to (was he *looking* for things to object to? Maybe). Then, like the universe was conspiring against him (or maybe it was *with* him? He wasn't sure how he was supposed to feel about it), a little house came up for rent that had two bedrooms and a small garden, was just fifteen minutes from Zahra's flat, and would be available from the beginning of February. There really wasn't much more Luke could ask for than that, so he visited it, found it to be perfectly nice, and said he'd take it, ignoring the way saying so made him feel like he had turned hollow.

Like he had become nothing more than tin.

After Christmas came Hogmanay, with all the usual flutes of champagne and cheese boards and Auld Lang Synes, and then the week was over, and Luke and Posy headed back to the inn.

It was a cold, foggy evening, and as Luke drove up to the house, it emerged from the mist like the quintessential home of a witch. He could imagine that the warmly lit windows were made of spun sugar, the craggy chimneys of marzipan, the bricks of chocolate and gingerbread. An enchanted refuge in the middle of nowhere, a light in the dark. Not, thankfully, the kind of place where the witch in question would stick you in the oven (though there was no denying Sera was obviously tempted to do just that to Clemmie, the rooster, or both at least twice a week), but rather the sort of place where you might find shelter. Hot tea. A sticky cinnamon bun straight out of the oven.

The freedom to be you.

Hope.

Home.

It *hurt*.

Posy was out of the car as soon as it stopped, racing for the front door, leaving it wide open ("Were you born in the Colosseum?" Luke imagined Sera yelling). Warm light and joyful hellos spilled out from inside, as well as the distinctive clatter of Nicholas's armour, and Luke was about to go in too when he was distracted by the sound of other voices from round the side of the house.

He followed the sound to the tall, rustling oak tree, where he found Sera and Theo.

"Well, this is a pickle," Sera was saying from somewhere out of sight, sounding even more annoyed with the world than usual.

Luke saw Theo standing at the foot of the tree, head tipped all the way up, looking like he was trying very hard not to laugh. "I think you should let me go fetch Nicholas."

"Don't think I won't put you in the post and mail you to the moon, Theodór," Sera growled, which sent Theo into a fit of giggles. "We will not be sharing this little adventure with anyone."

"But it's not like it was *your* fault. It was *my* spell that went wrong."

"The answer's still no."

Snow crunched under Luke's feet. Theo turned. His face lit up. "Luke, you're back!"

"Oh, this is all I need," Sera muttered from somewhere above them.

Luke came up beside Theo, who immediately tucked himself into Luke's side to keep warm. Following his gaze up into the tree, Luke cocked his head, intrigued, at the sight of Sera sitting on a large branch a good ten feet off the ground, legs swinging, a rip down one thigh of her tights, one arm wrapped around the trunk of the tree.

"I'll throw my shoe at you if you laugh," Sera said direly.

Luke did not laugh, but it was a close thing. "How the hell did you get up there?"

"Sera's been teaching me how to cast the levitation spell Posy's always using," Theo confided sheepishly. "I was supposed to make myself levitate, obviously, but I, um, levitated Sera instead."

"Into a tree," said Luke.

"Clearly," Sera bit out.

He ruthlessly suppressed a grin. "Do you want me to levitate you out of it?"

"I'd prefer not to levitate ever again."

"Can you jump?"

"Too far."

"Not if I catch you."

Sera scowled. "No, thank you. Could you please just bring me the ladder from the woodshed?"

"It'll take me five minutes to bring the ladder over and five seconds to catch you," Luke pointed out. "Get it over with, Sera. Jump."

Sera considered this for a moment, saw the sense in it, and sighed. She wriggled to the edge of the branch, glanced down once more, winced at the height, squeezed her eyes shut, and jumped.

He caught her, letting her slide down the front of his body until her feet hit the ground. Easy.

Easy, that is, if Luke hadn't been able to feel every curve and dip of her body. If her skin hadn't radiated heat, if she hadn't bitten her lower lip, if there hadn't been a frantic pulse in her throat that he wanted to kiss. If his heart hadn't kicked so violently in his chest that he couldn't believe she hadn't felt it.

"See?" His voice sounded raspy and unlike him. "All done."

A tremor ran through her. He stepped back, hands flexing at his sides to keep himself in check.

"Right. All done. Thank you." Her eyes, large as a doe's, looked hunted. She was about to flee. "Nicholas is doing dinner today, so I'd better go check it won't kill us all . . ."

Then she was gone. Luke let out an uneven breath. For a few moments, when she'd been in the tree, he'd forgotten that they'd barely spoken for the last few weeks, since the night of the first snow, since he'd told her about Zahra and she'd told him he'd had one foot out the door since the very beginning.

"Did you meet Posy's new teacher?" Theo asked, startling him. He turned. Theo was still standing under the tree, arms tucked around himself. "Are you going to move back to Edinburgh soon?"

Luke nodded.

Theo's lip wobbled for a fraction of a second before he clenched his jaw, tight, like he was trying very hard to be brave.

"Hey." Luke swallowed. "Come here."

Theo didn't need asking twice. He flung his arms around him, tight around Luke's chest, and his voice was muffled as he said, "I'll miss you, I'll miss Posy, but it's okay. If you have to go, you have to go."

And very quietly, like it was a secret he was afraid to say any louder anywhere else, Luke said, "I'd stay if I could."

You've had one foot out the door since the day you got here.

It haunted him.

He buried himself in his work, but even the old books and long hours of research couldn't make him forget that everywhere he looked was another reminder of a life that seemed to glimmer just out of reach.

He'd look out the window and see Matilda reading to Posy, or teaching her the names of plants, or showing her how to string together longer sentences by tapping buttons in an app.

He'd come down the stairs, long after he thought everyone else would be finished with breakfast, and find that Jasmine was waiting with tea and a stack of pancakes and that kind, gentle smile that never asked anything of him.

He'd go up to the roof to fix another leak and spot Nicholas below, cleaning his armour and patiently explaining to Theo and Posy how each piece fit together.

He'd see Sera everywhere, all the time, even in his fitful dreams. Sera playing with baby Evie while Malik dozed on the sofa beside them; Sera straining honeycombs through cheesecloth, her tongue poking out the corner of her mouth in concentration; Sera putting a hand on the old bricks and beams of the house like they were having a conversation; Sera arguing with Clemmie; Sera refusing to look him in the eye; and Sera in his head, in countless dreams and memories and fantasies, her mouth on his and her skin under his fingers.

His longing to touch her, to make her laugh, to provoke her into one of her grumpy, overly dramatic speeches, *any* of it, was very nearly unbearable.

About a week into the new year, Howard rang, wondering if Luke fancied a drink. As Luke was no longer permitted on Guild property, Howard was strictly not supposed to be seeing him in the first place, and Lancashire was a bit far for Howard to drive just for a drink, they met halfway, in a gastropub in Durham.

"How's Posy?" Howard asked.

"Asleep, apparently," Luke said, slinging his coat over the back of his chair. He'd checked in with the inn when he'd parked, and Matilda had assured him that Posy had gone to bed without a fuss and was already fast asleep. It was nice (and maybe also a little bit galling) that she no longer seemed to need him for things like that. "You don't have to do this, you know. You already stuck your neck out for us at the masquerade when you went and got the Chancellor. If she hadn't turned up when she did . . ."

"Don't be daft," Howard said. "Albert Grey's temper tantrum isn't going to keep me from seeing anybody I want to see.

Besides"—he poured himself a hefty cup of tea, shuddering—"it's rather nice getting out of Northumberland for a bit. Albert's been in a frosty sort of mood since the masquerade. And I mean that literally. The temperature at the castle's a lot lower than it should be."

"But you're okay?"

"Pshaw, I'm fine. I do my best to avoid him." Howard took a sip of his tea and let out a blissful sigh. "Now that's good stuff. I saw Professor Walter yesterday. She says you'll be back in Edinburgh soon."

Luke nodded, tensing. *You've had one foot out the door since the day you got here.*

"Good city, Edinburgh. Best battered Mars bars I've ever had. That famous hill, what's it called? I got *very* drunk there, oh, almost twenty years ago, and had an extraordinary night with a woman named Lucy . . ."

Even now, right this minute, you're already halfway gone.

". . . do wonder every now and then what became of her. Not to toot my own horn, but I *think* she enjoyed herself. I wonder if she ever wonders what became of me . . ."

You've had one foot out the door since the day you got here.

"Ahem." Howard cleared his throat pointedly. "You're obviously no longer here with me, old bean. What's eating you?"

Luke blinked back to the present. "Sorry. It's been a long week."

Howard called for another pot of tea. "Does this abstraction have anything to do with Sera Swan?"

"What's Verity told you?"

"She didn't have to tell me anything," said Howard cheerfully, rolling his eyes in a most un-Howard-like manner. "I saw you with her, if you'll recall, even if I didn't actually know who she was until the very end. If you could have seen the way you looked at each other! And you! I've never seen you like that, Luke. You were open. Warm. *Happy.* Why *are* you going back to Edinburgh anyway? For Posy?"

"Zahra can help her with her magic."

"I can't quite believe I'm about to say this, but, er, have you considered that magic isn't everything?" Howard had even lowered his voice like he was afraid magic would hear him. "If Posy learns to hide her magic from nonmagical people, that's all well and good, hurrah and everything, but is that what's right for her *or* for you if it means giving up the one place you've both been happy?" When Luke just stared at him, struggling to come up with a reply, Howard prompted him. "You've been planning on going back to Edinburgh for months, long before you found out about this Zahra person, so it's plainly not just about her. So?"

There was a time, not very long ago, when Luke would have retreated into icy, forbidding politeness and shut the conversation down. Instead, with his hands clenched tightly around his steaming mug, he found himself trying to explain the last few weeks.

"Er, hang on a tick." Howard interrupted the explanation, looking utterly confused. "You say you told this boy that you'd stay if you could? Well, why can't you?"

"Posy's magic?"

"Yes, yes, you've said, but setting that aside for the moment, why can't you stay?"

"I . . ." Confronted with the question, asked so bluntly, Luke was startled to find he didn't know how to answer it. "I . . ."

You always expect to leave, so you're always waiting for it.

". . . I'm getting ahead of it."

"Ahead of what?"

Luke shrugged. "Outstaying my welcome."

"Ah." The creases in Howard's brow vanished. "I see. You're doing that thing you do."

It's what you do. You always expect to leave, so you're always waiting for it.

"Look, your parents did a number on you, old bean, and I'm not going to pretend the Guild has been particularly welcoming either," Howard said, shuffling a little awkwardly like it was uncomfortable for him to acknowledge that the Guild he knew was not necessarily the same one that people like Luke and Sera knew. "You haven't, er, had the easiest time fitting in anywhere you've been. That doesn't mean it's going to happen again. You don't have to exit, stage right, before you've even been asked to go."

You've had one foot out the door since the day you got here.

Luke had never felt like his parents' house was home, and he'd certainly never felt like the Guild was home, but he'd thought he'd learned to live with that. He'd thought he'd accepted that his choices were to be icy or to be alone.

Then he'd seen the same thing happen to Posy. He'd seen their parents and her schools and the Guild governesses treat *her* like she was an annoyance, a burden, *unwelcome*, and it had been so familiar, so uniquely painful, that he'd refused to see it unravel the same way. Refused, for Posy's sake, but he'd never actually let his *own* history go.

"She was right," Luke said quietly, stunned. "She tried to tell me, but I didn't hear it."

You've had one foot out the door since the day you got here.

It was true. He had. He *had* been halfway gone already. *It's what you do.* Every time he started to let his guard down, every time his mask cracked, he expected to have to go. It was what he'd learned. He, Luke, the *real* Luke, was not acceptable. Posy, the *real* Posy, was not acceptable. Sooner or later, they were too much, or not enough, and they had to go. So he'd been expecting it. Waiting for it. He'd gotten ahead of it at the inn, over and over, insisting time and time again that he wasn't staying long, that they'd leave soon, and he'd thought he'd been protecting them both, but it hadn't occurred to him that what he'd really been doing each time was hurting the people he'd insisted he was leaving.

"She was right," Luke said again. "*You're* right."

"There really *is* a first time for everything," Howard said, settling contentedly back into his chair.

There was a reason the house in Edinburgh had turned him back into tin. It didn't matter how nice it was, or how much he loved the city, or what their parents wanted. It wasn't home. Home was somewhere else.

Maybe it was time to believe in other people again. Maybe it was time to take a chance on them.

Maybe there *would* come a day when he'd outstay his welcome. Maybe there *would* come a time when he wouldn't be wanted anymore.

Maybe that day would never come.

Luke would never know if he didn't stay.

He stood abruptly. "Howard, you're a very good friend and I promise I'll see you soon, but right now, right this minute, I'm going home."

CHAPTER TWENTY-NINE

*I*t had been the sort of day that Sera couldn't wait to see the back of. The north chimney had fallen prey to the winds and tumbled right off the roof, Theo had gone to bed in a grump because he hadn't been able to beat a level on his video game, and to top it all off, she was now outside the front of the inn, in the bitterly cold night, trying to determine whether the stranger lurking suspiciously next to Nicholas's car was an axe murderer.

It was possible Sera spent a little too much time worrying about axe murderers.

The stranger turned at the crunch of Sera's footsteps in the snow. "Sera?"

"Nicholas?" She let out a relieved, exasperated breath. "Why are you lurking about in the dark?"

Nicholas stepped away from his car, into the light spilling from the inn windows, his breath fogging white in front of him. She blinked. And blinked again. *Was* it Nicholas? His hair had been combed neatly and ruthlessly back from his forehead, making him look older, and there was a dullness in his eyes that she'd never seen before. He wasn't wearing leather, armour plating, or gauntlets, either, but had put on dark blue jeans, scuffed white trainers, and a grey jumper with the white collar and buttoned cuffs of a shirt peeking out from underneath.

The bizarre doppelganger of Nicholas fidgeted with the cuffs of his shirt, obviously ill at ease. "I was just on my way out."

"Where to?"

"Er." He shifted. "I'm supposed to be meeting my father for a drink in Manchester."

Sera did not know how to process this information. She had never met Nicholas's father, but from everything she knew about him, the best way she could think to describe him was that he was Albert Grey with even more inherited wealth, an even bloodier family history, and no magic. Nicholas didn't talk about him, but Sera knew that his father had been persistent in trying to bring his son and heir back into the fold.

About a month after Nicholas had arrived, his father had appeared uninvited in the lane at the bottom of the inn, driving back and forth like Luke's mother had, getting increasingly frustrated with the fact that he simply couldn't find it. Sera's spell had kept him away, but they could see him, and she would never forget the way Nicholas had huddled in the kitchen, gauntleted arms over his face, shuddering in the throes of a panic attack at the mere possibility of his father setting foot in the only place he'd ever been free of him.

"Do you *want* to see him?" Sera asked now.

"No."

"Then you don't have to."

"I think I do," Nicholas said, fidgeting with his cuffs again. "Not for him. For me. I ran away."

"You're twenty-three. You're not a child. You didn't run away. You left."

"No." Nicholas smiled weakly. "I ran away. Like a coward. I couldn't live in their world anymore. I didn't want to have anything to do with them, but instead of saying so, instead of telling them why I was walking away and that I was never going back, I just ran away."

"You got out the only way you knew how. That's okay."

"Thanks. That's a nice thing to say." He looked at the ground, cheekbones pinking slightly. Then, fists clenching at his sides, he said, "He's going to keep coming. I need to put an end to it. I need to say what I should have said when I left. It's time."

"If that's what you feel like you need to do, okay," Sera said slowly. "Why are you going like this, though? Why aren't you wearing your usual clothes?"

He looked away. "It's a costume. It's ridiculous."

"Has someone said that?"

He shrugged.

"Does it make you happy?"

"Yeah."

"And is it doing anyone any harm?"

"No?"

"Then who the fuck cares what anyone else thinks?" said Sera. "If *I* told *you* that someone thought *I* was ridiculous, you'd demand to know who so you could run them through with your very shiny, pointy sword."

"*Did* someone say you were ridiculous?" Nicholas demanded at once, temper igniting.

Sera smiled. "Nicholas. Why aren't you this fired up on your own behalf?"

"Because a knight is supposed to be kind and brave and loyal." He stared at her earnestly. "A knight is supposed to protect other people, not themself. A knight shouldn't make themself bigger by stepping all over everyone else."

"A knight can't protect other people if he doesn't protect himself too," Sera said gently.

"But . . ."

"You're happy when you're in your leather and your gauntlets because that's what feels like the real you, right? The you that you want to be?" He nodded. She squeezed his hand. "So *be* that you. Don't let your father take that away from you."

"My armour *is* in my car, so I could put it on when I get there . . ." Nicholas thought about it for a minute. He rocked back and forth on the balls of his feet.

Watching him, overcome by an unexpected, protective ferocity, Sera said, "Do you want me to come to Manchester with you?"

"Almost as much as I want to not go," Nicholas admitted with a short rueful laugh. His puppylike green eyes shone down at her, brighter than they had been a minute ago. "But it's not about what I want. I need to do this by myself."

"Then why don't you take this with you?" Reaching up to the clasp around her neck, Sera took her necklace off.

Nicholas looked horrified. "What? No! That's yours!"

"Keep it just for tonight," she said. It was the first time she'd taken the necklace off in fifteen years, but it didn't feel wrong to take it off for this. It felt perfectly, absolutely right. "Wear it, or put it in your pocket, or whatever. Just so you have it whenever you need a reminder that you're stronger than you think and that you did a very brave thing when you walked away from everything you knew."

Nicholas let her drop the necklace into his palm. He stared at it in silent awe. (Honestly, it was *far* more awe than the silly necklace deserved, but Sera of all people knew how much a symbol could matter.)

"Look after her," she said. "That swan's tough, but she *can* break."

"I didn't know it was a swan," Nicholas said in surprise, which was such a Nicholas thing to say that Sera laughed. "I always thought it was a firebird."

Sera froze. "What?"

"You know, the one from the fairy tale? The firebird? I reckon it's because whenever I see you wearing it, the light catches on it and the crystal looks like it's red and gold."

Sera's voice shook. "I've never—I didn't—I've never looked at it that way."

"Well, no, I guess you wouldn't." Nicholas shrugged. "You've been wearing it since you got it. You've only ever seen it one way."

He gave her a sweet, lovely smile and loped off to his car, and then, before Sera had fully realised what she'd done, before she could open her mouth to call him back, he had driven off into the dark, taking her necklace with him.

Firebird.

Her knees wobbled, giving way, and she dropped to the thick, packed snow, framed by the triangle of light spilling out of the open front door.

Firebird.

She couldn't see the ghosts, but she could feel them, all of them, close, and they were holding their breath, waiting for her to *finally* understand.

"You didn't leave me at all, did you?" Her voice broke. "I

thought you were haunting me, reminding me of what I'd lost, but that's not it, is it? You were trying to show me you never left. You were trying to tell me you've been here all along."

She hadn't lost them. She'd kept them with her. Because each time something had tried to break her, she hadn't become smaller. She hadn't become something less.

She'd become something *more*.

Firebird.

"Phoenix," she whispered.

A creature of the sky and the stars, burning, dying, once, twice, a hundred times, only to come back, stubborn and persistent, to rise out of the ashes, to be resurrected, to *live*.

Firebird, phoenix, a stitched-up Frankenstein creature made out of every Sera she had ever been, and still here.

Still. Here.

It took Sera a long time to realise she was crying.

They were not dainty tears trickling prettily down her cheeks. They were great, big, ugly, gulping sobs. They came from somewhere deep inside, punching past her throat, as if a dam that had held back the tide for years had finally burst.

A car pulled into the driveway. A door opened, there was a startled pause, and footsteps crunched quickly across the snow. Then Luke was beside her, and as she sobbed and sobbed, lifting her face to look up at his, he gripped one of her knees.

His face was stricken. "What . . ."

Her shoulders heaved and she tried to speak, but all she could say was "Nothing's wrong, everyone's fine, I'm just . . ." and then she couldn't say or do anything else except cry.

Luke tightened his grip on her knee, and she dropped her head against his chest. He was solid, immovable, *here*. He stroked her hair, sifting through the shiny dark strands with ink-stained fingers. She gripped fistfuls of his shirt in her hands as she sobbed into it, quite unable to do anything except let the tempest pass.

There was a rumble of thunder, the skies opened, and rain cascaded down to the earth. They were drenched in seconds. The timing was *so* inopportune and yet *so* very typical that Sera found her sobs turning, inevitably, into choked, sputtery laughter.

"I think I liked it better when it was tea." Luke sighed.

She swallowed back the slightly hysterical laughter and looked up at him, blinking past the rain. "I'm the phoenix."

Understanding sparked in his eyes at once. "You are."

"And I just sent Nicholas away with my necklace!"

As this seemed to be an entirely unrelated segue, it needed some explaining. Luke was quick to reassure her. "He'll bring it back."

"I know. I just can't believe . . ." Her throat closed up again. "Phoenixes and swans and ghosts. There were all these things about me I never really understood, but then Nicholas said he'd thought my necklace was a firebird and suddenly it just *fit*. I just needed to see things a bit differently."

"There's a lot of that going around," Luke said quietly. He pushed her wet hair off her face, his fingers lingering on her skin, and said, "I don't know if this is a good time to say this, but I'm going to say it anyway. I don't want to leave."

Her heart leapt. She stared into his eyes and caught a glimpse of a quiet, terrible fear, and she realised she'd made a lot more mistakes than she'd thought. "I'm so sorry. I was so afraid of how much it would hurt if I asked you to stay and you said no that I never asked. I should have, Luke. I should have told you how much we want you here. Please stay. *Stay*."

He let out a shaky breath. "As long as you'll have me."

She flung her arms around his neck, not completely sure if she was crying or laughing or both. He pressed his mouth to hers, which ended that confusion because now she was no longer crying *or* laughing but just kissing him back. The rain was cold, but his mouth was warm, and she would have quite liked to stay there forever.

Then Luke said, "Can I take you upstairs?" and she decided that actually no, she *didn't* want to stay here forever, and she stumbled to her feet, as unsteady as a fawn.

They made it as far as the threshold of Sera's warm, cosy room before she yanked at his wet shirt, pulling it off over his head, and started wriggling out of her leggings. Really, she reasoned, it was only good sense. They were far better off out of their wet clothes.

Luke closed her door with a click, making sure to strand Roo-Roo on the *other* side. He cupped her jaw between both hands, tangled fingers in her hair, and kissed her. She flattened her palms against his bare skin, feeling the warm, hard planes of his chest, listening to his sharp intake of breath, listening to the thunder of his heartbeat, and kissed him until it occurred to her that as long as they were kissing, she couldn't get her jumper off, and that was *not* acceptable.

She tore her mouth away and grabbed the hem of her jumper. His eyes burned into hers, inky dark, and he stopped her, took the jumper from her, and peeled it off, bit by bit, his throat working as he ran his hands up her ribs.

She reached for his belt buckle. He paused. "Wait. I don't have any—"

"I do." She yanked open the drawer of her nightstand, looking for the condoms she knew were in there somewhere. She almost expected not to find them, her luck being what it was, but happily, the universe decided to be kind to her.

He gave her a wry look. "Is this from that time you got to know the Black Knight in the biblical sense?"

"You sound a teensy bit jealous, Luke," she teased.

"I am jealous." He backed her against the wall beside her nightstand. "Not as glad as I am that you have them, though."

The familiar wall of her bedroom pressed against her back. Her thin, faded, and wet white T-shirt, the only thing left between him and her bare skin, did nothing to hide anything underneath. Luke stared at her for a long time, pupils wide and black, desire driving out all thought and reason.

"Luke, stop looking and get back here," she complained.

He obeyed, crossing the space between them, and, mouth half a breath from hers, said, "If you knew the things I want to do to you."

Heat blazed across her skin everywhere their bodies touched, driving out the last of the cold. "Show me. Show me all of it." She pulled his mouth back to hers.

He slid a knee between her legs, leaning into her until she was more or less straddling his thigh, and she could feel how hard he was, and she didn't think she'd ever wanted anything as much as she wanted more of this. She kissed him harder, teeth scraping against his lip, thrilling at the sound of his groan.

"Tell me to slow down," Luke said unevenly.

Sera rocked against his thigh, needing the friction, needing more, needing everything. "Do *not* slow down."

He swore into her mouth, low and ragged like he was in pain

from wanting her, and *God*, she could relate. He broke the kiss, yanked off her T-shirt, and kissed her throat, her collarbone, her breasts, all teeth and tongue and heat. She dropped her head back, eyes fluttering shut, and it felt like the world was gone and there was only her and him and the frantic sound of their breathing.

They tumbled onto the bed and she got his belt buckle off at last. "I know I asked you to show me all the things you wanted to do to me, but that's going to have to wait," she said. He raised his head to look at her, questioning. "I need you inside me."

"Now?" His voice wasn't much more than a rasp.

"Now."

He let out a shuddering, relieved breath. She pressed her mouth to his again, hands and legs tangling, kicking off the last of their clothing. Then, as he braced himself over her and she hooked her bare legs around him, her eyes met his and they stopped, for just a moment, to look at each other. To see.

Because they *did* see, at long last. Each other, yes, but also, by that act of looking, they saw their own selves too. He, the Tin Man who recognised his own heart at last, and she, not a shadow or a ghost of what she once was but *alchemy*, a phoenix who had gone up in flames again and again and yet, each time, had outlasted the fire.

Then Luke was inside her, at long last, and Sera stopped thinking altogether.

Much later, Sera was yawning and on the edge of sleep when there was a clink of metal outside her door, followed by a soft knock.

She got up, put on one of the oversized T-shirts she usually wore to sleep in, and opened the door. Nicholas stood in the hallway, sheepish, her necklace in one hand.

"Did I wake you? I would have waited until the morning, but I thought you'd probably want this back sooner rather than later . . ." Nicholas trailed off as his eyes moved past her, landed on Luke in her bed, came back to her, noticed that she was a bit rumpled and glowy and wearing very little, and, finally, went hilariously, impossibly wide. He immediately clapped his hand over them. "OH MY GOD! MY EYES!"

"Nicholas, everything's covered," Sera insisted, ignoring the choked sound of Luke trying not to laugh behind her. "It's safe to look."

"Er, I don't think I should. I'm sure there are rules against knights seeing, er—"

She interrupted hastily. "How did it go with your father?"

"What? Oh. It was fine. Well, no, it wasn't. I was terrified. I almost turned the car right around and came back, but I didn't. I went in and I did it. I saw him. I said everything I needed to say, and I feel *so* much better now."

She smiled at him. "I'm really proud of you."

Nicholas peeked between his fingers, looked at Sera, looked at Luke, and looked at Sera again. For just a moment, the knight was gone and a shy, silly, boyish grin broke across his face. "I'm really, really glad you two did, er, this. Can I be the one to tell Matilda?"

"Have at it," said Sera.

Once he'd clattered off to bed, Sera shut the door again and looked down at the necklace in her hand, surprised by how difficult it was to accept that she had to let it go. Luke watched her without speaking, letting her have the moment she needed.

She slid the crystal swan off the chain. The glass teapot was on the windowsill, glowing with the swirling golden mist that the artichoke heart and the strand of Clemmie's hair had left behind.

She held the pendant in her hand for a moment longer, missing it already.

Then, her heart fluttering in her throat, she lifted the lid of the teapot and dropped the pendant in.

The swan vanished.

The spell was complete.

CHAPTER THIRTY

*F*ifteen years adrift and untethered, cast out of the sky, un-
wanted by the earth, finding a way to survive anyway. Fifteen years of yearning, of dying little deaths, of climbing
wobbly-legged out of the ashes and building the most unexpected of lives. Fifteen years in the company of ghosts and great-
aunts, foxes and farmers, hobbits and knights and children
bursting with light.

All of that, and it ended with a glass teapot.

There was a tremor in the air. A breeze of salt and earth and
starlight. It blew outward from the teapot and the witch holding
it in her hands, knocking books to the floor, rattling the shutters,
ruffling the feathers of sleeping chickens in their coop, and tou-
sling the hair of a man who looked like he'd fallen out of a myth.

Then, like that breeze had gone to collect magic from all over
the universe, it blew back in a thousand times stronger, wild and
untameable, returning to the witch like she'd called it home.

The old inn went quiet and still.

Sera closed her eyes.

And found entire galaxies of stars waiting for her.

CHAPTER THIRTY-ONE

*E*veryone knows that when something good happens, something you've dreamed of for a long, long time, you're filled with this wonderful, dizzying, joyful conviction that there's nothing in the world beyond your reach. Everyone *also* knows that as lovely as that feeling is, it's best not to let it run away with you entirely, because next thing you know, you've tried to do too much and you're wilting on your sofa with two ibuprofen and the sort of headache that makes you feel like there's a herd of elephants stampeding across your skull.

Sera, being part of everyone, knew this, but did that matter? No, it did not. She was wholly, absolutely, one hundred percent going to let the feeling run away with her entirely.

The thunderstorm was gone by morning and a gentle flurry of snow settled over Batty Hole again. Sera, possessed by a heady combination of joyous, manic energy and terror that the restoration spell hadn't worked after all (not to mention a *very* nice post-orgasmic high), hurtled up to the roof of the inn.

Mist rolled over the white hills, drifting through the spikes and brambles of the dark green forests and curling like smoke against the windows of the inn. Soft flakes of snow landed on her bare cheeks as she clambered onto the old tiles and looked across the slopes and chimneys and nests of the shabby, patched-up roof that had sheltered them so valiantly for years.

She saw all the cracks and splinters and holes. She saw the broken chimney and the missing tiles and the empty birds' nests. She knew exactly what needed to be done. She pictured the spell in the dark behind her closed, star-filled eyelids, excited and afraid, remembering only too well the day up on the roof just a few weeks ago when she'd tried and failed to cast this very spell.

This time, she called and her magic answered. Instantly. Effortlessly. It *sang*.

"Hello again," she whispered with a tearful laugh, like she'd found an old friend she'd thought she'd lost.

It was laughably, absurdly, *outrageously* easy. It took seconds. The broken chimney flew up from the ground below, re-forming itself in the exact spot where it was supposed to be, stronger and sturdier than it had been before. The empty birds' nests blew away into twigs and feathers on the wind, the cracks in the tiles sealed over, the holes and rifts where the rain came in were mended, and all the rusted joists and bowed beams and old wood were made new once more.

"Haaaa!" Sera laughed giddily, shouting into the winter day. "I'll fix the boiler, and mend all the window frames, and straighten out the creaky steps, and enchant the fires so they never run out, and—"

"And when *exactly*," Clemmie interrupted, poking her head out of the loft hatch, fur bristling in annoyance, "do you plan to fit in the breaking of my curse?"

"Now, if you like," Sera said sunnily. "I mean, it's been fifteen years since I last cast a big spell, Clemmie, and I *thought* you'd prefer it if I first got some practice in with spells that don't actually affect a living person, but maybe I'm wrong? Maybe you'd *like* to be turned into a frog? Lose all your hair? Meet an untimely end? Because those, after all, are all things that could happen if I make a mistake!"

"That's a good point," Clemmie acknowledged grudgingly. "As you were, then."

So off Sera went to fix all the things that needed to be fixed, and patch up all the things that *didn't* yet need fixing but probably would if she didn't get ahead of it, and shine up a whole lot of other things (even if some of those other things were chairs, and people were sitting in them, and didn't necessarily enjoy having the cushion beneath their bottom magically fluffed up while they were simply trying to drink a cup of tea).

She was a whirlwind, cannoning from one part of the house to the next. She magicked new parts into her car, gave herself heated seats, and then turned it a bright, joyful lollipop red. She made the dishwasher twice as efficient. She did everybody's laundry with a snap of her fingers. She took the faded, peeling wallpaper and restored it so that it looked new. She conjured up a chocolate fountain for Theo and Posy, then conjured up an outdoor shower so that they didn't track melted chocolate into the house. She added new panelling to the hallways, decided she didn't like it, and put in a different kind instead. She enchanted Jasmine's room to make it twice its previous size so that Matilda could move in without having to leave her many, *many* belongings upstairs. She repainted all the rooms ("A tangerine kitchen is a step too far, my love," Jasmine said, looking slightly shell-shocked, and Sera, admitting that it was a bit much, agreed to simply give all the rooms a new coat of their *old* paint. For now).

"Should we expect any other big changes in the immediate future?" Luke asked her wryly, scrutinising her like he was expecting her to crash any day now. "A blacksmith's forge in the woodshed? A biscuit bakery just for the crows? Witch wine brewing in the loft?"

"No, but I like all those ideas."

And, well, she ended up exactly where you'd expect, which is to say that by the end of the week, Sera was wilting on the sofa with two ibuprofen and the sort of headache that made her feel like there was a herd of elephants stampeding across her skull.

"Fine," she said, blinking up from a pile of pillows at Luke and Jasmine, neither of whom was above saying they'd told her so. "I should have taken it a bit slower. But look! Look how *pretty* everything is!"

"Prettier than you are right now, certainly," Matilda offered. "You've got the bug-eyed, jittery look of a meerkat that's eaten an entire bag of sugar."

"That's because that's more or less exactly what she is," Luke said severely, his voice much sterner than the hand stroking her hair. "Only it's not sugar, it's magic, and it's not a bag, it's a fucking *truck*. You need time to adjust to it."

He was right, which made her scowl.

"Hey." He kissed the top of her head. "You have time. You have all the time in the world. Your magic's not going anywhere."

So she slowed down and let herself simply enjoy the wheeling, golden galaxies of stars behind her eyes and the fierce, beating heart in the places she'd been empty. It was like sitting quietly and contentedly in the company of a dear friend. It had been a long, twisty road, but she and her magic had never given up on each other.

Before long, she was more settled and the headaches were gone and she felt ready, at last, to tackle something big.

The day of Clemmie's cursebreaking dawned cold, white, and distinctly blizzardy, which might have been enough to put her off such an arduous undertaking if it didn't seem unfair to make Clemmie wait any longer.

Clemmie reinforced this point. "Don't you dare back out on me now," she said, watching Sera with an intensity that might have unnerved someone made of feebler stuff.

"How about you go away and let me pee without an audience?" Sera said irritably.

Sera went downstairs to eat her weight in Jasmine's blueberry and chocolate pancakes. By the time she came back, having left everybody else downstairs so that they wouldn't have an audience, Clemmie had scratched nervous grooves in the floorboards. Sera, who took pride in being able to contain multitudes, was easily able to be annoyed and sympathetic at the same time.

She got to work on the curse. Undoing a spell that *literally* bound a person was tricky. It was spellcasting in reverse, an unmaking instead of a making, so the first thing she needed to do was see the original spell Clemmie had cast all those years ago.

She wiggled a finger, revealing the spell, and winced. Clemmie was surrounded by hundreds of gleaming magical knots, the threads of her curse looping this way, tangling that way, leaving her thoroughly (and, frankly, impressively) bound. The easiest thing to do would be to simply cut through the spell, breaking a curse by breaking the threads, but no witch would dare take the easy way out like that. You'd have no idea what such a violent breaking would do to the person who'd been bound.

Sera was going to have to untangle the curse. Unpick the spell, knot by knot, until Clemmie was unbound.

"Get comfy," Sera said, bracing herself for a long day. "We're going to be here a while."

The whole thing probably looked absurd to anyone who didn't know what they were really seeing: the fox perched tensely in an armchair, trying to move as little as possible, grumbling under her breath, and the woman sitting cross-legged on the edge of her bed a few feet away, brow furrowed in concentration, hands weaving in the air, picking at invisible knot after invisible knot.

It was tedious, intricate work, but it was enormously satisfying to watch each dreamlike thread of the spell dissolve as she unknotted it and pulled it away from the others. As the curse loosened, Clemmie shifted nervously like she could feel something changing, and Sera had to warn her more than once to stay put.

It took her most of the morning, but then Sera was finally down to the last knot. She undid it and the spell extinguished into nothing.

There was a blinding flash of light. Sera shielded her eyes with her hand automatically, turning her face away until she could be sure the light had faded.

"Sera?" Clemmie's voice *sounded* almost the same. Sera lowered her hand.

The fox was gone. In its place stood a naked white woman in her fifties. She had lines at the corners of her hazel eyes, a freckled nose, rounded limbs, long waves of black hair with grey roots, and a face that was downright cherubic.

Not a flea in sight either.

Sera picked up a blanket and placed it gently around Clemmie's round shoulders. Slightly startled, she noticed that Clemmie was taller than her now.

"Clemmie? Are you okay?"

Clemmie blinked at the question. She looked down at her own hands, holding the blanket around herself, and promptly burst into tears.

CHAPTER THIRTY-TWO

*S*era walked into the living room and did her usual double take at the sight of Clemmie on the sofa, watching TV, stretched out and taking up as much room as humanly possible. *Humanly* being the key word there. It had been four days since Sera had broken Clemmie's curse, but the sight of her still took everyone by surprise.

Upon regaining her human body, Clemmie had moved into Matilda's old room and had refused to come out until she was bathed, was appropriately clothed, and had stopped walking on all fours out of habit. This had involved Sera having to borrow clothes from the Medieval Fair until Professor Walter, roped into coming to the rescue by Luke, could sneak them the paper-work Clemmie needed to reactivate her old bank account. Once that had been sorted out, Clemmie had sallied forth from her room with the air of a corseted conquering hero.

Now, the corseted conquering hero in question twisted around on the sofa to watch Sera check that Theo had finished his homework.

"He's a *witch*," Clemmie pointed out, as if none of them had known this already. "What does he need to know grammar for?"

Theo laughed. Sera didn't. "If I wanted your advice, I'd ask for it."

"Well, if you insist on sending him to that woefully conventional school," Clemmie went on, "I ought to at least give him a proper magical education as well. Posy too."

Now Sera laughed. "Clemmie, I would entrust them to literally anyone but you."

"There's no need to act like I'm a career criminal. My unlawful activities have been limited to a single curse and one act of thievery."

"Didn't you also set fire to Albert Grey's study when you broke into his house?" Theo asked with a grin.

"A single curse, one act of thievery, and an entirely justified incident involving arson," Clemmie amended. "It doesn't sound so bad when you put it like that, does it?"

Having established that he had indeed finished his homework, Sera packed Theo off to Alex's house before Clemmie could put any ideas in his head.

Luke came in, phone in hand, jaw set. "It's for you."

Sera took the phone from him, puzzled, and found a pair of unlikely faces looking back at her from the screen. "Professor Walter," she said, blinking, ". . . and Francesca." It had only been a few days since she'd talked to Francesca, to let her know the restoration spell had worked, so she hadn't been expecting to speak to her again this soon.

"It's time," Verity said without so much as a hello.

"Father's in Nairobi at the Congress of International

Witches," Francesca explained. Her face was a little paler than usual, but her mouth was set. "He'll be away for another three days. Professor Walter and I think this is the best opportunity we have to . . ." Her voice faltered.

"To oust Albert from the Cabinet and eliminate his influence over the other Ministers," Verity finished.

Across the room, Clemmie sat bolt upright.

"It won't stop him being *Albert*, of course," Verity went on in her gruff voice, chewing on the end of a pipe. "On the other hand, nothing will. This, at least, will give the Chancellor and the Cabinet a chance to oversee the Guild without his interference. As you know, as long as he's in the Cabinet, with more than half the Ministers too afraid to disagree with him *and* a veto to boot, he will always get his way."

"Aha," Clemmie said in a smug undertone. "And so it begins. They need you."

"We need you," Francesca said quietly at almost exactly the same time. "He can't be voted out of the Cabinet so long as that binding magical contract he made them sign is in place. You're the only one with the power to break it."

"If you're agreeable, we'd like you to come up tomorrow, meet with the Cabinet, and break the contract," Verity added.

Francesca tugged on the perfectly ironed cuffs of her blazer, obviously struggling with plotting against her father behind his back, but her eyes were earnest when she looked up. "Whatever you decide, Sera, you should know you're no longer in exile."

Sera hadn't said a word so far, but now she said, "And Luke?"

"Luke's exile has been rescinded as well," Verity said at once. "I already discussed that with the Chancellor."

Clemmie cleared her throat pointedly.

"What about Clemmie?" Sera asked.

Francesca opened her mouth to say something, but Verity got there first. "To be perfectly frank, Sera, the answer's yes to whatever it is you want. Just get here. Do you want to bring Clementine with you? Fine. Do you want to bring the pope? That's fine too. *We're* the ones who need *you*."

This was a little overwhelming. "I think I'll manage without the pope" was all Sera felt able to say.

She looked at Luke over the top of the phone. His face was entirely expressionless, a far cry from the man she'd woken next to this morning, his blond hair falling boyishly over his forehead, his face open in sleep, his (*not* tin) heart beating against her.

"Hang on a second," she said to the screen. She muted the call, put the phone down, and took a step closer to Luke. "You don't like this."

He didn't deny it. "Not much, no."

"You were the one who said Albert needed an equal to keep him in check. Isn't this what you wanted?"

Luke sighed. "He won't be happy. If you do this, it'll put a target on your back. That's the part I'm not keen on."

She put a hand to his face, running her thumb over the line of his jaw. "I have my magic back. He doesn't frighten me anymore."

He turned his face into her hand and kissed her palm. "Then I guess we're going to the Guild."

"And by *we*, he means me too," Clemmie said at once.

Sera picked up the phone, unmuted the call, and said, "We'll see you tomorrow."

She wasn't sure how she felt about it. In a way, it was everything she'd wanted all those years ago, the fantasy she'd clung to when she'd first lost her power: the Guild acknowledging her worth, revoking her exile, more or less begging her to come back. A child's fantasy, undoubtedly, but she wasn't above feeling a certain satisfaction at hearing the words *we're the ones who need you.*

It was true, too, that Albert wasn't the threat to her that he'd been just a few weeks ago. So why did she feel uneasy? Just a little. In the back of her mind. Like she'd forgotten something.

The next day, she, Luke, and Clemmie drove up to Northumberland, crossing the snowy, craggy breadth of the north of England. They skirted the Bennet ancestral home, bypassed the Bertram-Mogg country house, came within a stone's throw of Grey Manor, and finally wound their way up the long, twisting drive of the Guild's estate.

For the first time in fifteen years, Sera stood in the old courtyard beside the statues of Meg of Meldon, Michael Scot, and Mother Shipton, and looked up at the grand, imposing spires and towers of the British Guild of Sorcery. It was a pompous, unwelcoming, and slightly ridiculous world, but it was also the only world young witches had, and it had *so* much potential. It could be so much better.

"Morning, Meg," said Clemmie, patting the base of the statue. If she was having the same sort of emotional upheaval that Sera was, she was doing a very good job of hiding it.

"In Reykjavík, the Wise Women have a bust of the witch goddess Freyja in their gardens," Sera commented.

"In Canada, they have a statue of a bear," said Clemmie.

Sera was dubious. "You're making that up!"

"I am not! You've obviously never come across the legend of the Witch-Bear of the Rockies." Clemmie tossed her black waves of hair (which were now enchanted to hide any grey) and jerked her head at the doors. "Shall we?"

Luke didn't say anything. He just waited patiently for Sera to decide she was ready.

She nodded. "Let's go."

The castle's huge, lavish entrance hall was thankfully empty when they entered. It was the middle of a weekday, and they were expected, which meant the Cabinet Ministers would be awaiting them upstairs while the young witches would be in their classes and any other adults on the premises would be instructing them, working, or visiting the library.

Portraits of illustrious witches from generations past stared disapprovingly at Sera from the walls as she climbed a long, sweeping flight of stairs, and she marvelled at how alike they all looked: white, aristocratic, and bored.

"This one's a Bennet," she said to Clemmie.

Clemmie snorted, looking up at the portrait of a sour woman with a powdered wig. "Dear old Agnes. An ill-tempered bag of bones, if her diaries are anything to go by. She was my great-great-great-great-grandmother. I think. I've probably got the number of greats wrong."

Footsteps clattered down a hallway just off the landing above, then stopped abruptly. A man looked down at them incredulously. "Clementine? Is that you?"

"Stephen! Darling!" Clemmie's voice became a catlike purr, which disturbed Sera greatly. "We used to bang, as you young people like to say," she whispered in Sera's ear, before sidling off in the astonished man's direction and raising her voice again. "Well? This is your cue to declare *why, Clementine, you haven't aged a day . . .*"

"Well," said Luke, a tremor of laughter in his voice, "at least that's got rid of *her* for the moment."

Upstairs, Francesca and Verity were waiting for them outside the Cabinet meeting room. They'd been pacing the corridor, like they hadn't dared to believe Sera would actually turn up. Verity had an unlit pipe sticking out of the corner of her mouth and, even more inexplicably, was wearing riding boots. Francesca was in her best pantsuit, her hair arranged in an elegant, efficient knot, every inch a Chancellor demanding to be taken seriously.

"There's a hole in your jumper," Francesca said, slightly despairing. "Right there, under your arm."

"It's my comfiest jumper, thank you very much," Sera said, plucking at the soft, rust-red fabric. When she'd looked into her chest of drawers this morning, trying to decide what to wear, she'd refused, utterly *refused*, to dress up for the Guild.

Sera had been to the Cabinet meeting room a handful of times before, in her role as Albert's apprentice (or, rather, as the provider of tea), and had found the room to be more or less exactly as she'd expected it: big stone fireplace, shaggy rugs, expensive wood table, wingback armchairs, a lot of tweed, a drinks cabinet stocked with rare vintages, and the persistent smell of cigars.

It hadn't changed. Francesca strode into the room first and took one of the two empty chairs left, the one at the head of the table, leaving the other one for Sera. You could have heard a pin drop as Sera sat down. She scanned the faces of the Ministers around the table, ten men and one woman, all white, all English, most over the age of fifty, their expressions ranging from a bashful smile (Howard) to uncertainty (Martin, the man who'd been forced to dance at the masquerade) to downright hostility (Bradford Bertram-Mogg. Of course).

Luke and Verity came in too, fortunately, refusing to leave

her to the wolves. They stood by the door, where she could see them.

"Right," Francesca said in her cut-glass voice. "We know why we're here, so let's not waste everybody's time. This is Sera. You will all remember her, of course, though I think a couple of you were elected to your positions since her exile. She's here to break an enchanted contract that the Cabinet, the ruling members of the Guild, signed almost thirty years ago, awarding Albert Grey, the twelfth Minister and currently absent, several privileges." She took a deep breath, steadying herself, and added, "Once the contract's broken, we will vote on the matter of expelling Albert Grey from his position on the Cabinet."

Stirring in his chair, Bradford Bertram-Mogg, who honestly looked *less* animated than Sera's zombie chicken, said, "I really must object—"

"You have objected, Minister Bertram-Mogg," Francesca interrupted. "Repeatedly. Tediously. You'll get an opportunity to object again when it's time to vote."

"Ahem." Howard, sitting two chairs to Sera's left, coughed politely and extended a scroll. "The contract."

Sera took the scroll, its paper creased but robust, and unfolded it. She read down the page. It was all there, penned neatly in Albert's handwriting, everything about his permanent position on the Cabinet, his right of first refusal over nominations for the position of Chancellor, his right to expel any *other* Minister without reason, his veto, and more. At the bottom of the paper were the date, Albert's signature, the eleven other signatures of the Cabinet Ministers who'd been serving at the same time (over half of whom were still here in this room today), and, most importantly, Albert's enchanted seal.

"Has anyone tried to break the seal before?" Sera asked curiously, running a finger experimentally over the crimson wax imprinted with the Grey crest.

"Professor Walter and I have both tried," Francesca replied, leaving unsaid that Verity had undoubtedly also used the opportunity to get as many other willing witches as possible to try breaking the seal too. "We've found that my father's magic is too powerful for any of us to take apart."

Sera looked at the contract for a long time, her thoughts turning over and over.

"Is something the matter?" someone asked.

She looked up. "If I do this, I'd like you to do something in return."

Halfway down the table, red-cheeked Lionel Bennet (Clemmie's uncle, Sera realised) let out a contemptuous bark of laughter. "I told you." He looked triumphantly around the room. "I told you that we'd be no better off with her than with Albert Grey. At least *he's* the devil we know."

"Oh, fuck you, Bennet," Luke said in his most arctic voice.

The Ministers looked scandalised. Lionel Bennet swivelled around to glower at Luke and opened his mouth to reply, but Sera got there first. She was actually rather glad Lionel Bennet hadn't been able to help himself. It was a relief to stop having to play nice.

"You'll notice *I'm* not asking you to sign any enchanted contracts, you unmitigated jackass," she said, ignoring the gasps that followed (and was that a snicker? Howard, probably). "What I'm asking this Cabinet for is a promise. For you to do the right fucking thing. Because you exiled me for fifteen years, and now that I'm useful again, you want me back, so you know what? No.

No, you don't get favours from me for nothing. Now do you want me to break this seal or not?"

Lionel Bennet stood up. "I won't stand for this—"

"Sit down, Minister Bennet," Francesca said firmly. "I'd like to hear what Sera's asking of us."

Sera didn't need to be asked twice. "I want things to be different. I want the Guild to change." She scowled around the table, lingering on Lionel Bennet, on Bradford Bertram-Mogg. "I know many of you are *very* comfortable with the way things are right now, but you're kidding yourselves if you think Albert became what he is all by himself. You let him. You helped him. The Guild's obsession with the *right* families and the *right* bloodlines and the *right* sort of people is so outdated that you should be embarrassed. It needs to change. You *know* it needs to change. *You* know." She stared hard at Francesca, at Howard, at Martin, all of whom could barely meet her eyes. "You sit up here pretending to decide what's best for everybody, but you're really just deciding what's best for you and your families. You've let everybody else down, *all* those young witches who deserve better, and you know it."

Bradford Bertram-Mogg, predictably, found this unacceptable. "Well! Well, I never! You have some nerve, young lady!"

"And *you* need to repatriate all the looted artefacts you have in your private library," Sera shot back. She spun around to Lionel Bennet. "*You* need to put Clemmie back in your fucking family tree, because you don't just get to *erase* people when they do stupid things. And *you* . . ."

She'd turned to the man on her right, but he was only in his twenties and looked frankly terrified of her.

"Well, I don't know who you are," she admitted, "and you

obviously haven't been here long, so it doesn't seem fair to shout at you." A little calmer, she addressed the rest of the table: "Look, the point is, this thing you've got going here, where the same ten families seem to make their way into the Cabinet every single time? It needs to stop. It shouldn't matter who our families are. It shouldn't matter what our names are, or what our skin colours are, or who our grandmothers were. By making those things so important for so long, you've let *generations* of witches down. You let me down. You let Luke down. You let Posy down. She's fucking *nine*." Howard dropped his eyes. "You need to do better. Promise me *that* and I'll break this contract."

"*I* never wanted to break the contract in the first place—"

"Minister Bertram-Mogg, if you don't shut up, I will gag you," Francesca snapped.

"Chancellor, you cannot expect me to tolerate this *interloper* coming in and trying to tell me what I ought to do with *my* artefacts!"

"Interloper," Sera repeated quietly, and had the satisfaction of seeing almost every face around the table redden guiltily. "I think that's done a pretty good job of making my point for me, don't you?"

She sat back, contract on the table, waiting. There was a long, awkward silence.

"She's right," Howard mumbled.

"She is," Francesca said. She looked Sera in the eye. "I'll make you that promise. I can't promise that the *real* changes, the big ones, will happen today or tomorrow or even next year, but I swear, Sera, the Guild *will* be better."

There were quiet noises of agreement from around the table.

It wasn't like she'd left them much choice, and she couldn't hold any of them to their word without turning into another Albert, but it was something. It was a start.

She picked up the contract.

Sera searched the seal, looking for the seams of the enchantment Albert had cast over it, and found a *very* strong spell. It was what she'd expected, but that didn't mean she was happy about it. In the grand scheme of dethroning Albert Grey, this was her first test, and she had no idea if she would pass it. What if, after that whole angry speech, after everything, she discovered her power *couldn't* match his after all?

She pushed at the spell on the seal. It held. She pushed harder. It didn't budge.

Okay. Fine. Firm yet gentle wasn't going to do it.

Sera called for the stars, and they answered, kicking up a storm of rage and stardust and magic, and

SNAP

The seal broke clean in two.

So did the table.

There was a long, startled silence.

"It was terribly ugly," Howard finally offered with a shrug. "Good riddance."

Tearing her wide eyes from the broken table, Francesca recovered her composure and said, "Er, thank you, Sera. Shall we move on to the vote?" She put her hands down as if to rest them on the table, realised that wasn't going to be possible, and quickly said, "I propose we expel Albert Grey from this Cabinet and revoke his privileges. Show of hands from all the ayes?"

Six people raised their hands at once, Howard and Martin among them, and then four others joined them a moment later, including Lionel Bennet. Bradford Bertram-Mogg, predictably, was the only one to refuse. He glared sullenly around the table.

"I think that means the proposal passes," Francesca said, letting out a slow breath. "I'll break the news to my father when he returns from Nairobi." Traditionally, a Cabinet meeting couldn't end until the Chancellor stood up, so she stood. "Thank you all for your time."

The room emptied very quickly. Howard trotted happily over to talk to Luke and Verity. Sagging back in her chair, Sera picked a loose thread off her jumper and let her stiff shoulders relax for the first time since she'd walked into the room. Francesca came over.

"Thank you," she said.

"Thank you too," Sera replied. She stood, wiggling her stiff shoulders.

Francesca crossed her arms over her chest. "*Did* you bring Clementine with you?"

"Like she'd have given me a choice. She's around here some-where."

Nervously biting her lip, and looking much more like the younger Francesca that Sera remembered, Francesca said, "Sera, there's something you ought to know. The night of the winter masquerade, Father didn't go looking for you in the library by accident. He knew you'd gone there. He knew you'd be trying to steal the essence of sunlight. He knew everything."

Sera was confused. "How? The library, okay, that's an edu-cated guess, but how could he have known about the essence of sunlight before he saw me holding it?"

Francesca just looked at her. It was the pity in her face that gave it away.

Sera spun on the ball of her foot and stormed out of the

room, past Luke, Verity, and Howard, the blood whooshing in her ears. Down the hallway, around the corner, down the sweeping flight of stairs, until she was on the front steps of the castle and there was Clemmie, alone, waving off her old friend as his car trundled out of the courtyard.

"You're done already?" Clemmie demanded. "And I missed it? Sera! You could have waited for me!"

Sera didn't hear a word. "Albert didn't see you running off into the woods that night, did he? You talked to him. You *told* him."

There was a part of Sera that had hoped there would be another explanation, that whatever Albert had told Francesca had been a lie, but as she watched Clemmie's eyes widen and her face lose all colour, that hope died a brutal death.

"*Clemmie*," Sera protested, her voice catching.

"I was still in the house when he came back," Clemmie said in a rush. "He stopped me leaving. He told me he'd break my curse himself if I told him what you were up to. So I . . ." A bitter laugh slipped between her teeth. "Obviously, he didn't do it. Sera, don't look at me like that! I'm sorry! I *know* I shouldn't have done it, and I *know* I shouldn't have believed him, but you of all people should understand why. I couldn't take it anymore. I *had* to get out of the snow globe."

Sera had been right. You couldn't break a snow globe without shattering the glass, and Clemmie had, and the shattered glass *hurt*.

"It worked out in the end!" Clemmie insisted. "We got what we wanted!"

"I'm going home, Clemmie," was all Sera could bring herself to say. "Without you. After all, you got what you wanted. You don't need me anymore."

CHAPTER THIRTY-THREE

What do you think they're having that confab about?" Matilda demanded.

Jasmine gave her a fond look. "Something to do with magic, I presume," she said, putting the last of the dishes into the dishwasher and shutting the door. Outside, a fat, full moon twinkled over the snowy hills.

"Don't you want to know more than that?"

"I've come to terms with the fact that I neither understand nor especially wish to understand the niceties of sorcery," Jasmine said serenely. "You are the sort of person who likes to know *everything*, my love. I am not."

Deeply dissatisfied with this, Matilda glared out the window, her head cocked to one side like she was hoping the new angle would somehow grant her the power to hear what Sera and Luke, who were halfway down the garden, were saying.

Sera and Luke had returned from the Guild's castle two days ago. Nobody had failed to notice that Clemmie had not come back with them, but the quick, warning shake of Luke's head was enough to stop everybody from asking any questions. In Jasmine's view, questions were overrated anyway, so she'd simply plied them with hot chocolate and buttery pancakes.

After that, the inn had more or less settled into its usual rhythm, but all too briefly.

Jasmine, typically the earliest riser in the house, had woken this morning to a wrongness she couldn't put her finger on. It was like someone in the next room had tuned a radio to a high, keening frequency that was almost undetectable to her ears. She had eased herself out of bed, making sure to tuck the covers back around Matilda, and had limped out to the kitchen to put the kettle on.

Someone had beaten her to it. The room was empty, but the kettle had been gyrating on its cradle, already on the boil. Jasmine had looked to the open back door, where Sera stood on the step, almost invisible in the predawn mist. Her feet had been bare, her coat absent, and her dark hair rippling in a breeze that was not wholly natural, but she didn't seem to notice the cold.

She had turned her head as Jasmine had approached. "You can hear it too, can't you?"

"Just about," Jasmine had replied, more concerned with the practicalities. "My love, what in the *world* are you doing out here without your coat or even a pair of socks—"

"It's the house," Sera had interrupted, nodding at the inn.

"I have no doubt it is, dearest, but pneumonia is no laughing matter."

"It's a warning," Sera had added, like she hadn't heard a word Jasmine had said.

Jasmine was not by any means a fanciful sort of woman, but

in that moment, she could have sworn that the mist that was tangled through Sera's hair and twined around her limbs was turning into long, spiky feathers.

"Darling, what are you afraid of?"

"I'm not afraid," Sera had said, turning back to face the dawn. "I'm ready."

There were people who might have reacted to such a pronouncement with alarm, but Jasmine was not one of them. Briskly, she had said, "I have no doubt that you have a sensible course of action in mind, my love, but consider for a moment that you might find yourself even *more* ready if you were to put a pair of shoes on."

Later, Sera and Luke had abruptly announced that Theo and Posy would be going to stay with Malik, Elliot, and baby Evie overnight, and it was this, the haste with which the children were sent away for an evening of movies, popcorn, and far too much sugar, that had had Matilda in a tizzy of unsatisfied curiosity ever since.

"Do you know what your great-niece said to me earlier?" Matilda demanded now, still staring fixedly at the two standing outside in the cold. "She said, and I quote, *there's a storm coming.* Let me tell you, that was the first time in my entire life that I have been bereft of speech. Have we or have we not established that *I'm* supposed to be the dramatic one?"

Anxiety disrupted the composure Jasmine had been steadfastly maintaining (no, *clinging* to) all day. She, who had known Sera since her toddlerhood, knew full well that when Sera was confronted with feelings too big or too unwelcome, she hid them (and from them) with an exaggerated air of grouchiness and theatrical hyperbole.

"Sera's afraid of something," Jasmine admitted. Matilda turned to look at her. "She says she isn't, but . . ."

"Afraid *of* something?" Matilda's voice was thoughtful. "Or afraid *for* something?"

That was when Jasmine noticed movement at the bottom of the garden by the gate. She stiffened.

Sera and Luke had noticed it too, but neither of them seemed surprised.

"Matilda," Jasmine said quietly, watching Albert Grey striding up the garden. "Could you fetch Nicholas, please? And maybe ask him to bring his sword?"

Matilda had spotted their unwelcome visitor as well. "Him! What's he doing here? Isn't Sera's spell supposed to keep people like him away?"

"As I understand it, it doesn't work on witches who know it's there."

"NICHOLAS!" Matilda bellowed, and then, taking no chances, bustled off with all haste to physically retrieve him.

Jasmine went to the threshold, hand clenched over her cane. As she stared down the length of the garden, dappled by starlight glancing off the snow and lamplight from the house, she thought for just a second that she'd been mistaken. She had only ever met Albert Grey twice before, but she remembered both of those entirely unenjoyable occasions only too well, and the man from her memory had been dismissive, haughty, and completely in command of himself.

This Albert Grey was not that man. Electricity seemed to crackle dangerously around him, but it was, somehow, less frightening than the seething, palpable rage in his face.

It's a warning. That was what Sera had said this morning.

The magic woven into the very bones of their home had been warning her. That warning had put Luke on edge all day. It was the reason Theo had been subdued and Posy had kept her headphones on. They'd felt the wrongness Jasmine had felt, only worse, but it was only Sera, the most powerful of them, the one who had woven that magic into the house in the first place, who had understood. *There's a storm coming.*

Here it was.

Albert slowed as he drew closer. The crackling, hateful intensity of his stare didn't waver from Sera. It was like nobody else existed. "How *dare* you."

"I don't like to say I told you so, Albert, but I did tell you so," Sera replied. "Right here, fifteen years ago, I told you you'd rue that day. And here you are. Rueing."

Even from where she was standing, Jasmine couldn't mistake the sound of Luke's resigned sigh, and truly, she felt it like it was her own. A person less versed in Sera's ways might have hoped she would employ even a single survival instinct at this point and not provoke Albert any further, but Jasmine and Luke knew better than to cherish any such hopes.

Albert's power crackled so violently that the snow under his feet turned into steam. "Do you really think your failings as an apprentice justify engineering a vote to expel me from the Cabinet? That they justify turning my own daughter against me?"

"If you had ever spared a thought for anything other than yourself, none of this would have come as a surprise to you," Sera said in exasperation. "All I did was break your contract. *I* had nothing to do with the outcome of the Cabinet's vote. *I* didn't turn Francesca against you. You did that all by yourself."

"They wouldn't have dared to expel me if it hadn't been for you!"

"Do you even hear yourself? They wouldn't have *dared* to expel you? Meaning what? You thought you'd cowed them into submission?" Sera threw her hands up. "Does that give you a little hint, perhaps, about why they wanted rid of you?"

Albert's temper got the better of him. Without warning, there was an unnatural *crack* and a shaft of lightning speared into the snow at Sera's feet. Jasmine let out an involuntary cry.

"Stop it," Sera snapped. "You don't get to play these games anymore, Albert. You don't get to scare me like you used to. Empires *always* fall, one way or another, and yours is *finally* done."

Abruptly, Albert started laughing. "Oh, Sera. So fierce, so angry. So determined to hide that you *are* scared. You never learn, do you? You make it so *easy*. There are so many exposed places between those prickly feathers of yours." His eyes skimmed pointedly over the inn, over Luke, over Jasmine. "You have power, but you're still just one person. How many of those soft, exposed places can you really protect at once?"

"Let me at him!" Matilda shouted in outrage, popping up beside Jasmine and startling her. "I have a sizeable pumpkin that would make an excellent projectile!"

Then Nicholas was charging past Jasmine and Matilda, sword in hand. "Halt, fiend!"

Albert gave him a contemptuous look, flicked a lazy hand, and turned Nicholas to stone.

CHAPTER THIRTY-FOUR

*B*itterly, Sera realised *this* was what she'd forgotten. *She* might have nothing to fear from Albert, but what about everybody else? Albert knew her too well. Like he'd said, he knew exactly where to find the soft, exposed places between her prickly feathers. He'd used her loyalty to Clemmie to trick her fifteen years ago, he'd used her love for Luke to make her hand over the essence of sunlight just weeks ago, and even then, even after that, she'd gone and broken that contract behind his back because she'd forgotten that *she* wasn't the one he would hurt. Luke had been afraid she'd put a target on her back, but it wasn't *her* back at all. It was her home, her family, everybody she loved.

She stared in horror at Nicholas, frozen in place, turned entirely to stone.

"Tick tock," Albert said cruelly. "Ask me *really* nicely and I'll release him. I don't think he can breathe in there, you know. Stone and all."

Sera swiped a hand at Nicholas, putting every bit of her fury and stardust into it, and the stone encasing him shattered. He started running again, like he hadn't noticed anything had happened to him, and Luke grabbed him around the shoulders.

"No," Luke said quietly, gripping Nicholas tightly by the arms. "Nicholas. Listen to me. Stop."

"How can I?" Nicholas asked, bewildered. "I have to defend my home. I have to defend *Sera*."

"Not this time," Sera said softly, putting herself between Albert and Nicholas. "Go back inside. Please."

His eyes gleamed with unshed tears. "But . . ."

"I need you to do this for me." She kissed him on the cheek. "I love you." She looked at Luke, still holding Nicholas back, and said it again. "I love you. You know that, don't you? I do. I love you. I love you all. It's going to be okay."

Luke froze. He opened his mouth—

Albert lost patience.

Sera felt the lightning snap past her, singeing a hole in her sleeve. She batted it away, just *inches* before it hit Luke straight in the chest, and turned furiously.

Albert struck again, and again, angry bolts of lightning blazing from his hands, and Sera could barely stop them in time, was terrified that one would slip past her. She opened her mouth to beg him to stop, to ask him what he wanted from her, to tell him she'd do whatever it was if it meant he'd leave everybody else alone, but then, suddenly, someone lunged out of the shadows with a familiar, gleeful laugh.

"Clemmie?" Sera said in disbelief.

How long she'd been lurking in the dark like the fox she'd once been was anyone's guess, but Clemmie tackled Albert around the middle, catching him completely off guard, knocking them both into the snow.

"Clementine," Albert snarled, spitting snow. "Don't be stupid. You're one of us. You can't choose them."

"I am choosing them," Clemmie snarled back. "I am. I *am*."

Luke sprang before Albert could recover, pinning him down, and Clemmie started to screech the words of a spell to *keep* him down.

There was a silent explosion in the air, a *boom* that rattled Sera's teeth, and Luke and Clemmie were both flung back. Albert stood, seething, knocking snow off his clothes, lightning crackling so violently in his eyes that you couldn't see anything else.

Roo-Roo zoomed down the garden with a merry "Bok!" and cannoned into Albert's legs. Looking down, Albert, who could have easily ignored the little rooster skeleton, kicked spitefully at it instead.

Roo-Roo flew through the air and crashed into the stone slabs of the patio. Jasmine covered her mouth, stifling a cry.

"Oh!" Matilda cried. "Of all the *unforgivable* things!"

And Clemmie, who must have pounced on and chased and dismantled Roo-Roo a hundred times, seemed to feel the same way. Her face contorting with outrage, she clambered unsteadily to her feet, tottered across the space between her and Albert, pulled back her fist, and punched him in the nose.

Albert let out a roar.

Slashing her hand through the air again, Sera put a shield between Albert and Clemmie, too powerful for either of them to break through. Jasmine, meanwhile, scooped Roo-Roo's pieces up and tenderly put him back together.

"*Enough.*" Sera's voice trembled.

There was a terrible ache in her heart, a fierce and dreadful understanding that no matter what happened, no matter how tonight ended, Albert would always be a threat to everything she loved. It had been naïve of them, all of them, to think she could keep him in *check*. Look what he'd done already. No, there was only one way out of this, and it broke her heart.

Everything she had ever done had brought her here, to this moment, to *this* choice, and it broke her heart, but it was also *right*.

Aloud, she said, "There's a way for you and me to put an end to this right now."

Albert cocked his head with interest. "Are you suggesting a duel?"

"Oh, good," said Nicholas. "A duel's more my speed."

"I don't think this would be that sort of duel, dear," Matilda said, patting his hand.

Keeping her eyes squarely on Albert, Sera said, "Yes. A duel. Just like we used to, only this time, of course, it's not for practice. Winner takes all."

"Define *all*," Albert said.

"Pride, for one thing," said Sera. "We get to find out once and for all which of us is more powerful. Oh, I know, I know, you think it's you because I'm a girl and I have no family of note, blah blah blah, but still. You don't *know*. This way, you'll know. Also," she went on, thinking quickly, "I think it's become clear there's only room for one of us at the Guild, so the winner gets to stay. The loser leaves the country for good and never, ever bothers the winner again."

"What?" Matilda exclaimed from the top of the garden. "You can't leave the country!"

"Oi! What makes you think she'll lose?" Nicholas demanded, instantly offended on Sera's behalf.

"Hush, both of you," Jasmine said anxiously.

Clemmie, for once, had nothing to say.

Luke, staggering up from the snow where he'd been thrown, a nasty cut above one eyebrow, stared at her, hard, his jaw working like he was fighting the urge to protest.

Albert looked thoughtful. "Who goes first?"

"First one to cast gets to start." Sera had spent a lot of time trying to forget the duels of her childhood, but even so, she was fairly sure she was remembering the rules right.

Not that the rules really mattered. All that really mattered was getting Albert to agree.

"Recovery time?" Albert asked.

"Thirty seconds."

"Victory terms?"

"If the other one's thirty seconds of recovery ends without a counterspell," said Sera, "or the other one yields."

"Are you sure you want to do this?" Albert asked. "You've never won a single duel against me."

"I haven't won one *yet*," said Sera.

He narrowed his eyes. "Fine. I accept."

A large ring of snow around them burst into white flames that burned, harmlessly, at knee height, keeping everyone else out and keeping them in the duelling ground until it was over. Luke glared at Sera from over the flames. He knew she was up to something, something that would probably cost her, and he was furious with her for doing it.

The beauty of a magical duel was that neither opponent could break the terms of the duel while it was going on, but the downside of a magical duel was that once it was over, there was nothing to stop either of them from breaking their word about leaving the country and leaving the other one alone.

Sera knew that. She wasn't going to make the same mistake Clemmie had. She wasn't going to trust Albert Grey to keep his promises. She knew that whatever the outcome of the duel, Albert had absolutely no intention of going anywhere. (To be fair, *she* had absolutely no intention of leaving *her* home either, so she couldn't exactly get too self-righteous about that part.)

She didn't care about what happened after the duel ended. She just needed the actual *duel*.

She needed him to not be able to stop her when she cast the only spell that mattered.

The wind, rippling through her hair, died. The snow settled. The world went quiet.

Albert struck first.

A mottled snake slithered across the snow, hissing, and lunged so fast Sera barely had time to blink. She gasped in pain, her ankle buckled, and she dropped to her hands and knees.

Heal it, heal it, she thought frantically, clamping a hand over the puncture wound, from which dark, poisonous veins and terrible pain began to spread. With one hand, she healed, and with the other, she dissolved the snake into smoke.

Twenty-seven seconds. She'd need to be faster.

It was her turn. She whirled snow into Albert's eyes, and he recoiled, clawing at his eyes as the snow burned, but he recovered quickly. His next spell was a Minotaur conjured out of smoke that charged at her, horns first, but she dodged it, transformed it, and set a murder of crows on him.

He scattered them into a rain of black feathers and flung a

vicious lightning bolt at her. It struck her in the shoulder, scorching her jumper and piercing her skin, and she yanked it out and, once again, rushed to heal herself.

This time, though, she didn't have to worry about a snake. This time, she could look at Luke, across the flames, and she could use a silent, secret spell.

I need an incantation.

He jerked back, startled, at the sound of her voice in his head.

I'm sorry. I should have asked permission first, but there wasn't time.

His brow knitted, asking a silent question. *Which incantation? Which spell?*

She told him.

His eyes widened. He shook his head.

Twenty-two seconds. Twenty-three. Her shoulder had almost healed.

I only saw the spell once. I can't remember the incantation. She staggered to her feet. *Luke, please. You know this is the only way.*

Twenty-five seconds. Twenty-six.

Luke's mouth moved silently, shaping the syllables of the words she needed.

And then, at the end, four more words:

I love you too.

She smiled.

Twenty-nine seconds.

She opened her mouth and cast her spell.

A spell she'd seen in a book one time. A spell for stealing magic with a vicious sting in its tail.

Take what isn't yours and you shall pay with what is.

The spell struck fast and fierce, sending first Albert and then Sera to their knees.

"Don't you *dare*," Albert snarled. "You can't. You *can't*."

He lunged, as if he would strangle her into silence, but an invisible wall stopped him before he could touch her. It was *her* turn, after all. Bound by the circle of white flames and tied to the terms of the duel until it was over, Albert could do absolutely nothing.

"What's she doing?" Jasmine cried. "What's happening? Sera! Are you hurt? Sera!"

"She's taking away his magic," Luke said quietly. "All of it. And it's going to cost her all of hers."

"Make . . . her . . . STOP!" Albert roared.

It hurt, *everywhere*, but Sera didn't stop. This was the only way to stop Albert for good. This was the only way to protect these people she loved so much.

If this was the last magic she would ever cast, at least it would mean something. At least it would be extraordinary.

Snow swirled around her, carrying a hint of Nivea cream and woodsmoke and hot, buttery scones straight out of the oven. It was a reminder of who she was. Firebird. Phoenix. Witch. And terribly, agonisingly, magnificently *human*.

She was the gargoyle of this castle, the caretaker of this inn where light reached even the darkest corners.

Every choice she had made since she'd cast the resurrection spell had been about bringing magic back into her life. She had looked for magic for fifteen years, had blamed every bad thing that had happened to her on the *loss* of magic, and now here she stood, having found the thing she'd fought so long and hard for, and she was trading it away.

Or was she? Magic for family. Magic for home. Wasn't she really just trading one kind of magic for another?

Sera waited for those glorious, valiant stars to answer her one last time. They gathered and gathered, coming to her from every fragment of her bones, brushing warmth against her skin, whispering a farewell as her magic, all of it, surged to her fingers and into this last and greatest of spells.

The last of the stars bled out of Sera's fingers.

And Albert Grey's terrible, destructive lightning went out for good.

CHAPTER THIRTY-FIVE

*S*era didn't get out of bed for a week.

In fairness, she spent the first two days of that week unconscious. So did Albert. When she woke at last, he was back at Grey Manor, powerless and disgraced, and she was in her bed at Batty Hole, powerless and pretty much a Guild hero.

She had no interest in being a Guild hero. She had no interest in anything, really. When she closed her eyes, all she could see was the dark of a starless sky. It was heartbreaking. It was *hard*.

She was a mess.

What this feeling was, she wasn't sure. It didn't feel as wild and dark and dangerous as the depression that had come so often a few years ago, and she was *fairly* certain this time wouldn't involve any broken toes, but whatever this was hurt just as much in a whole other way.

Maybe this was grief.

She slept a lot and cried quite a bit. Jasmine barely left her side in the day, rocking quietly in the chair beside the bed, and

Luke stayed with her all night, holding her when she cried, but she didn't say much, not even to them. What was there to say?

She slept some more.

Gradually, bit by bit, she began to feel like the dark behind her closed eyelids wasn't quite as desolate and lonely as she'd thought. Even in the dark, after all, she could hear the noisy, chaotic inn. Theo's chatter, the *boing boing* of the trampoline outside, the clank and clatter of Nicholas's armour, Matilda and Malik bickering over companion planting, Jasmine's cane, Posy putting farmyard animals to bed on her tablet, conversations, laughter, rousing Viking battle songs, and the comforting rustle of pages turning, always, all the time, as Luke worked or read or just stayed beside her.

On the fifth day, Matilda entered the room and threw back the curtains to let the light flood in. Sera winced.

"Hmm," said Matilda. She put something on the nightstand. Sera saw that there were a handful of carrots poking out of the chest pocket of her dungarees. "You look like you need a gentle talking-to."

"What I need," said Sera, "is to wallow. Let me wallow."

Matilda nodded in an understanding way that usually meant she was about to do the exact opposite of the thing she was nodding at.

Sera sighed. "Jasmine thinks you ought to let me wallow. She said so just yesterday. I could hear her."

Matilda did not seem impressed by this argument. "The fact that I am quite wildly in love with her does not preclude me from recognising she can be wrong."

Sera scowled. "Matilda, I barely have the energy to brush my teeth right now, let alone argue with you. I just want to—"

"Wallow," Matilda finished for her. "Yes, you said. You *have* wallowed."

"I want to wallow some more."

"Wallow all you like," said Matilda. "And while you do that, why not have a tiny listen to what I have to say?"

Sera considered this proposition. "I accept your terms. I'll need tea. To facilitate the wallowing."

"Very sensible, dear," Matilda said, promptly retrieving a steaming cup from the nightstand. She'd come prepared. "Now, what you did the other night was difficult and important and incredibly brave of you, so I don't want you to think I'm not sympathetic to that. I am. I do, however, feel that you cannot heal properly without fresh air. A shower wouldn't go amiss either. Without wishing to be hurtful, Sera, you smell like a sewer."

"I'm not hurt," Sera assured her. "I am, in fact, proud of my seweriness."

"Duckling." Matilda's face grew serious. "Tell me how to help."

Sera smiled faintly. "I'm just a bit sad and a bit tired. I don't know how long the sad will last, but I promise I'll get up when I'm not tired anymore."

"Hmm," Matilda said again. "Tired, you say? In the bones or in the brain?"

"Both, I think."

"And given how you're always running around this inn doing this and that, might I hazard a guess that this is the first proper rest you've had in years?"

"Er, I suppose so?"

"Well, why didn't you say that in the first place?" Matilda

demanded. "Wallowing is up for debate, but rest is *essential*. You rest as much as you need. Never mind me."

And with a brisk, triumphant air, Matilda picked up the empty teacup and trotted away.

The next day, Luke came in with a peculiar expression on his face. Settling into what was now very much his side of the bed, he gave her a searching look as if to decide how much she could handle, kissed the top of her head, and said, "There's good news and there's bad news."

"I want no news," Sera said at once.

"The Cabinet has reshuffled."

Sera frowned. "Isn't that what the Prime Minister's always doing in London?"

"Well, the new Chancellor's decided to do some reshuffling in Northumberland too. Howard's the only one from the old Cabinet to make it into the new one. Verity's in it too." Luke cracked a smile. "I wouldn't start celebrating a new and improved Guild just yet, but it *is* a start."

"Er, you're going to have to rewind, Luke. What do you mean, the *new* Chancellor?"

Luke's mouth twitched. "That's the bad news. In a manner of speaking. Francesca resigned. Happily, I gather. She says she never wanted to be Chancellor in the first place. She's taken a position in the new Cabinet instead. And, er, over the last few days, there was a snap election for a new Chancellor and, well . . ."

Sera suddenly saw where this was going. "*Luke*. Don't fucking say it."

"Clemmie," said Luke, sounding both highly entertained and highly appalled, "won."

"Clemmie. *Clemmie.* Is the new Chancellor."

Luke sighed. "I keep checking the sky for flying pigs, but no luck yet."

Sera collapsed into helpless laughter.

Clemmie. Chancellor of the Guild.

After a while, she said, "I haven't forgiven her yet. Not completely."

"I know."

"But she chose us. In the end. When it counted. She chose us."

"She chose you."

Abruptly exhausted, which was happening a lot at the moment, Sera tucked herself into Luke's side and lapsed back into silence. He stroked her hair.

"I spoke to Zahra," Luke said after a minute. "Verity's friend, the one who was going to tutor Posy in magic. She's agreed to work with Posy *and* Theo a few times a month. I'll take them to Edinburgh every other Saturday, they'll see Zahra, and I'll bring them back in the evening."

"That's good. It's a lot of time in the car, but it does mean they'll get *some* proper magical instruction. It's more than you or I ever had."

Luke looked down at her, catching her halfway through a yawn, and kissed the top of her head. "Go back to sleep. I'll see you later."

"Will you stay for a bit?"

"I'm not going anywhere."

She snuggled into his side and closed her eyes.

She missed the stars.

After a full week of wallowing (and/or rest), Theo bounded

into the room and asked her, with great expectation, if she was all better now.

"I feel like I could sleep for another week."

"I guess you can if you really, really want to," Theo said with an air of tragic martyrdom. "I've just missed you, that's all. Everyone has."

Sera couldn't quite bring herself to refuse him, so she said she'd get up after she'd had another few hours of sleep. She didn't know if she felt ready to face the world again, but maybe no one ever knew if they were ready for something until they tried.

She closed her eyes, but there was nothing to see. No galaxies of light. No starbursts. No stars at all.

It felt a little like dying.

Wait.

Wait.

There *was* something. A single flicker of light. A twinkle.

A solitary star.

She would never be able to cast another spell, but that single, lonely star was still there because, if you know where to look for it, there is always a little magic in the heart of a person who loves it. So that star would stay for Sera, always, flickering in the dark, letting her know she had not been abandoned.

Like the old Seras, who hadn't abandoned her either. They'd stayed with her all this time to tell a story, every time she forgot it, about flying and defying and what an incredible, joyful act of resistance it was to simply exist.

You're still here, they said, those echoes of all the Seras that ever were. *You went up in flames, but you're still here. You'll go up in flames again, but that's okay, you know what to do now. You've done it already.*

The dying wasn't what mattered. Unfurling your scorched feathers from the ashes and getting up again. Growing. *Staying.* That was the part that *really* mattered.

So Sera slept. Woke. Unfurled.

And got up again.

CHAPTER THIRTY-SIX

*I*t was remarkable, really, how quickly life went back to normal. Which was to say there were levitating children, evenings by the fire, homemade toast with honey, Nicholas pledging undying loyalty at least once a day, Sera tripping over the undead rooster at least *twice* a day, and, oh, the list went on.

But there was still one unanswered question bothering her, and, at the kitchen table one afternoon, with a teacup full of daisies in her hands, she asked it.

"What's going to happen to the inn?"

Jasmine paused in the middle of her sewing on the other side of the table. Luke looked up from his laptop, looked down at the teacup of wildflowers in her hands, and understood at once. "The magic?"

Sera nodded. "If my spell on the inn only lasted as long as it did because I was keeping it going the whole time, is it going to disappear now that I can't?"

"I expect so," Luke said quietly.

"So the teacup flowers and the apple blossom tea in Posy's room and everything else . . ."

He nodded. "It won't happen today or tomorrow, but yeah, over time, without you stoking the fire, the spell will fade away."

"Oh. Right. Of course. Makes sense." She'd known this already, really, but there was a small part of her that had hoped *some* of the magic would stay. "It'll be weird. It's been so long. I don't really remember what the house was like without it."

"It won't matter, my love," Jasmine said reassuringly. "With or without your magic, Matilda and I will make sure the inn is always here for anyone who needs it."

This last bit was news to Sera. "Matilda and you? What about me?"

"This will always be your home, pet, but you never really wanted to *run* the inn," Jasmine pointed out. "Now, with Matilda here for good, you no longer have to."

Sera thought about that. Thought about the fact that, for the first time in a long, long time, she no longer felt like she owed something to the inn she'd spelled, the great-aunt she'd resurrected, and the wonderful, irregular people she'd invited in out of the cold. *You don't have to do it alone,* Jasmine had tried to tell her once. *This is not all on you.*

For the first time in a long, long time, she felt like she could do what she wanted, and believe it or not, what she wanted was the inn.

"I'm not ready to give the inn up." Sera smiled. "But I might step back a bit. You know. Sleep in more. Watch more TV. Try something new. Spend a bit more time with todays and a bit less time with yesterdays and tomorrows."

Jasmine smiled back. "That sounds perfect."

Soon, it was the day of Clemmie's oathtaking rite, a more or less unnecessary but nevertheless traditional bit of pompous nonsense that was supposed to mark the start of her time as Chancellor of the Guild. They all went up to Northumberland for it.

The rite itself was dreary, a bit of spellcasting followed by a series of oaths about service and duty that were to be read out loud from a dusty book followed by the appearance of a hideous purple cloak (Clemmie, who had obviously gone to great lengths with her outfit of beaded corsetry and Renaissance opulence, looked acutely anguished at having to ruin the effect with anything so ghastly as the cloak), but it was worth putting up with the whole tedious affair because there was a positively *lavish* feast afterward.

(Including a tiny and entirely predictable hiccup when Nicholas found himself in possession of a flute of witch wine, drank it in spite of express instructions not to, and turned a lurid shade of green, but as he was surrounded by a hundred or so witches who could undo the effect in time, he would not, thankfully, have to spend the next year or so looking like the Wicked Witch of the West.)

"Clementine Bennet, Chancellor of the British Guild of Sorcery," Luke said in a wry undertone to Sera. "God help us all."

Clemmie, who wasn't far away, scowled. "What was that?"

"Mind your own business, Clemmie."

"Times like this," said the new, not very dignified Chancellor, "I *really* miss my fox ears."

"Are you still planning to come round for lunch next Saturday?" Sera asked her.

"Am I still invited?" Clemmie replied.

"Grudgingly," said Sera, but she smiled as she said it.

"Then I'll be there," said Clemmie, smiling back.

After the feast, Luke and Verity had to swap notes on their latest project, and Francesca had invited Sera to come meet her young twins, so Nicholas drove Jasmine, Matilda, and the kids home in his car while Luke and Sera stayed a while longer.

"So what's next for you?" Francesca asked over tea. The twins had polished off their cake in seconds and were now rummaging in the biggest box of Lego that Sera had ever seen.

"There's always plenty going on at the inn, but other than that, I'm not sure yet," Sera replied. "I feel like my whole life's just been reset. I'm taking a minute to let that sink in."

Francesca stretched a hand across the little table. "Sera, your magic may be gone, but I hope you know you'll always have a place here."

Touched, Sera thanked her.

"Don't thank me." Francesca shook her head. "Honestly, I just want my friend back."

Sera squeezed her hand. "Me too."

Then, mere moments after Sera left Francesca, Howard commandeered her in the hallway and dragged her off to his office to see an old manuscript he'd gotten from Bradford Bertram-Mogg "for an absolute *steal*. After the books and treasures he's had to repatriate, he was just grateful to get *anything* for this one at all!"

"No way!" Sera positively squealed at the sight of the beautiful, familiar manuscript. "You snagged *The Extraordinary Handbook of Magical Tales* from him! I used to love this so much when I was younger!"

"Yes, Luke told me," Howard said, smiling bashfully. "Take it. It's a gift."

"Oh, *no*, I can't take it from you!"

"You misunderstand me, my dear." Howard laughed. "I got it from old Bertram-Mogg *for* you."

Sera hugged him. "Howard, I could *kiss* you."

Holding the precious, carefully wrapped manuscript to her chest, Sera went to the library to find Luke. She roamed the familiar stacks, drifting between shelves of old books, tracing the spines.

On the second level, tucked between a mullioned window and a stairway, she spotted two young witches huddled over a book. They couldn't have been more than thirteen years old, dressed in their Guild uniform of grey jumpers, grey skirts, and red ties, and there was a giggly, barely suppressed excitement in their hushed voices that reminded her of another time and another Sera.

She watched them for a moment. There was something bittersweet about seeing the next generation of witches take her place.

Bittersweet, but not bitter.

When she thought about it, the truth was that what she had now was worth so much more than what she'd had before. The magic of her past had been a gift, but the magic of her present had been earned.

"There you are." Luke had found her first. "What've you got there?"

"Luke, you're never going to guess what Howard gave me! Actually, you probably already know about it because he said you told him how much I used to love *The Extraordinary Handbook of Magical Tales*. Look! Isn't it incredible? I told him I could have kissed him."

"Yeah, kissing Howard is very, very out of the question, love."

"He's not into women?"

"He's not into women his friends are more than a little territorial about."

She laughed. "Territorial?"

"My lizard brain's taken over," Luke said apologetically. "It's looking at you right now and thinking *mine*. I'm sure it'll calm the fuck down sooner or later."

"Later, I hope." She shifted the manuscript tenderly to one arm, stood on her toes, and pressed her mouth to his.

The laughter vanished from his eyes. He kissed her back, harder. "Later it is." His voice was all gravel. He gripped the back of her neck, running his thumb over her jawline. "Want to go home?"

"More than anything."

When they arrived back at the inn, where the old roof tiles and chimneys were dusted with powdery white like a gingerbread cottage, new snow lay softly across the hills, dells, and woods. Across the entire garden, from the oak tree all the way down to the coop, the sparkling white blanket was interrupted by wildflowers.

They ought to have been impossible, but there they were, peeping out of the snow in the unlikeliest colours. Ice blues and posy pinks, fox reds and steely silvers, and of course, again and again, the bright, fiery gold of phoenix feathers. Thousands of tiny blossoms defying the frost.

Surviving.

Thriving.

Like that one solitary star Sera saw every time she closed her eyes, they were a reminder that she would never be abandoned by the magic she had loved so much. Not the magic of hygge spells and enchanted cabbages, no, but the magic of a lit window on a dark night, the magic of the wild green land, the magic of birds' nest boy hair and trampolines and hot tea and glacier eyes lit with laughter, the magic of living, living, living.

That was the magic that made the wildflowers bloom.

ACKNOWLEDGEMENTS

Writing a book is typically a quest you start all on your lonesome, but like any good quest, you pick up a lot of trusty allies along the way. And that's never been truer for me than it was with this book. *A Witch's Guide to Magical Innkeeping* has been years in the making, and there were a lot of times I wasn't sure I'd get myself to the finish line. The fact that I did is down to the patience, enthusiasm, and unwavering support of my trusty allies.

Steve, the truest and trustiest of all. Words aren't enough.

Mum and Dad, for everything.

Penny Moore, the fiercest and best of agents. You've changed my life.

Jess Wade, the most patient and passionate of editors. Somehow, you put up with me.

The rest of the wonderful team at Berkley and Penguin Random House: Stephanie Felty, Jessica Mangicaro, Gabbie Pachon, Ariana Abad, Jessica McDonnell, Marlyn Veenstra, Kristin del Rosario, Katie Anderson, Tawanna Sullivan, Lisa Perrin, Amy J. Schneider, and so many others. From publicity to design to subrights to the assistants, you all work such magic behind the scenes, and I'm so grateful.

I've been fortunate enough to have a fantastic publishing team on the other side of the pond too. Molly Powell and Kate Keehan, you've been a joy to work with over the last few years. Enormous thanks to the rest of the Hodderscape and Hachette team too: Sophie Judge, Marina Dominguez-Salgado, Lydia Blagden, Claire Offord, Irene Neyman, Laura Bartholomew, Juliette Winter, Carrie Hutchison, Sarah Clay, and Jess Dryburgh. (Side note, but has anybody else noticed how many people named Jessica work in publishing?!)

To the friends and family who've seen me through all the ups and downs, you know who you are. I owe you a drink. Or ten.

And finally, as always, thank *you*. Thank you for reading these books. Thank you for your wonderful messages and for your endless enthusiasm. You're a huge part of how I got here, and I couldn't have written this book without you.

A
WITCH'S GUIDE
to
MAGICAL
INNKEEPING

SANGU MANDANNA

READERS GUIDE

---

1. The inn is a focal point in the novel. What specific need does it meet for each character? Do you think it feels like a character in its own right?

2. Sera is likened to a phoenix. How does she grow and transform over the course of the story?

3. Luke's peers called him the Tin Man when he was younger, a *Wizard of Oz* reference that's stuck with him ever since. Why do you think he continues to identify with this character?

4. Even though Sera and Luke don't seem compatible at first, they fall for each other. Why do you think their personal differences become strengths in a relationship? What similarities do they have?

5. Sera equated her value to her degree of magical ability, and Jasmine devalued herself because of her limb

difference, which are both elements that are out of their control. What did their respective journeys teach them about their own inherent value?

6. Sera's magic manifests as a starry night sky. How do you think *your* magic would appear?

7. Who was your favourite secondary character in the novel, and why?

8. Clemmie reveals Sera's plans to Albert because she hopes he'll break her curse. What would you do if you were in her place?

9. Francesca helped get Sera kicked out of the Guild when they were children. Do you think Francesca's helping Sera in the end makes up for her past behaviour? Why or why not?

10. If you had access to the Guild's library, what is the first spell you would look up?

Author photograph © Ella Hunter

Sangu Mandanna is the author of *A Witch's Guide to Magical Innkeeping*, *The Very Secret Society of Irregular Witches*, *Kiki Kallira Breaks a Kingdom*, and several other novels about magic, monsters, and myths. She lives in Norwich, a city in the east of England, with her husband and three kids.

CONNECT ONLINE

SanguMandanna.com
🔲 SanguMandanna

Ready to find
your next great read?

Let us help.

Visit prh.com/nextread

Penguin
Random
House